PRAISE FOR THE NOVELS OF BEST SELLING AUTHOR ALYSSA RICHARDS

"THE HAUNTING OF ALCOTT MANOR is a great read...an escapist read, full of secrets and surprises that caught me out completely!" —*Jeannie Zelos Book Reviews*

"Man oh man! Alyssa Richards has seriously outdone herself with THE FINE ART OF DECEPTION trilogy. It encompasses love, passion, deception, heartache, reality and alternate reality. Just stunning from start to finish. This trilogy is awesome. If you're looking for a paranormal romance that's focused around psychics and time travel, definitely grab this trilogy. It's simply amazing!" — *Nay's Pink Bookshelf*

"...undoubtedly Alyssa Richards has just become one of my new favourite authors for this year." —*Living in Our Own Story Blog*

"This is well written with complex characters who reveal more of themselves as the story progresses. It is a great mystery with paranormal elements that make it enthrallingly different and captivating." —*Splashes into Books*

A MURDER AT ALCOTT MANOR is very definitely a thrill-a-minute tale of evil trying to keep a stranglehold on the living. This is a perfect book for readers who enjoy non-stop action and suspense with a dash of sexy. —Fresh Fiction Review

"An intriguing read that kept my interest until the last page. Very enjoyable and definitely recommended." —*Archaeolibrarian, I dig good books!*

"This book was loaded with mystery and suspense. The plot was well executed and kept me on the edge of my seat. The sizzling passionate scenes between Addie and Blake were red hot." —*Smut Book Junkie Book Reviews*

"I was very drawn to the characters. Richards did an excellent job weaving you into their world whether it was the good guy or the bad guy you just wanted to know what they were thinking, doing and their next move. I definitely recommend." —*The Reading Pile"*

THE HAUNTING OF ALCOTT MANOR

Book One

ALYSSA RICHARDS

Ebook ISBN — 978-0-9792265-9-5
Library of Congress Control Number: 2017944806
Editing by Book Alchemy, LLC
Formatting by Formatting Fairies
Proofreading by Theresa M. Cole

Sign up for Alyssa's newsletter at to receive special offers and news about her latest releases.

You can follow her on:
Twitter
Facebook
Instagram

Contact Alyssa at:
alyssa@paranormalromancebooks.com

CHAPTER 1

It was the wind that stopped her.

Not the force of it, but the message it carried on its course. Cold air tumbled over warm currents, whipping around her legs and across her chest. It swirled about her body like a lover who simultaneously promised what was next and took control to make it come about.

Seventies rock blasted in her ears and she slowed her run. Her feet stopped their rhythmic pounding on the packed sand of Stinson Beach.

Her beach.

She tried to catch her breath and searched the deep lapis waves that rode toward her. It was cold air that blew over the warm, a pattern her mother said meant that upheaval rode on the appearance of calm.

"No," Gemma said between gasps for air. Her voice was low. Determined. Firm. "Not again."

She pulled the earbuds from her ears, stared at the waves that rolled over the depths of the ocean, and the wind settled as though backing down from her challenge. It switched to a sun-warmed draft that caressed her face and neck.

Something tingled inside of her from it, like the effects of a possessive kiss. An awakening, a calling. The result of an event already put into motion.

She tried to cast aside her mother's Native American wisdom, especially because it had proven itself right more often than she liked.

"Stay away." Her voice held no mercy and no patience. She fit the earbuds into her ears again and cranked up the volume.

The gray shingles and glass of her house were in her sight now. She ran toward it with all the speed she had left, along with the sinking feeling that this wind pattern was signaling yet something else she couldn't outrun.

CHAPTER 2

Gemma flipped on the gas stove to heat the kettle for tea. She wanted to shake off the warning that rode on the early ocean wind, and a plunge into her morning routine was the way to do it. There had been enough abrupt and recent change in her life. Permanent change that could not be undone. Change that had been predicted by the wind patterns then, too.

She paused in front of the eight-foot Victorian coatrack in the foyer, a ghosted memory of her mother formed in the center mirror—her mother's long dark hair smoothed and tucked behind her shoulders, as always.

This antique from her childhood home had captured lots of precious memories over its lifetime—that's all this was. Like when her mother brushed Gemma's red hair into two bristly pigtails that burst to the sides when she was five, and when her mother hemmed her party dresses as a teenager. And when she passed on her favorite advice. "There's someone for everyone," her mother would say mid-embrace. "You just have to trust your instincts to find him."

She forced herself to relax her grip on the ache in her chest and the coat in her hands.

On with routine.

She gathered a large can of cat food, a can opener, and two small, white bowls in her arms. Her hip bounced the screen door open, she stepped onto the back deck that faced the ocean, and the door shut behind her with a satisfying slam.

It would have been more design-perfect for her to stick with the sliding glass door that had been there when she moved in. Though this was the same type of screen door slam she and her brothers had grown up with in their parents' lovingly restored Queen Anne Victorian.

Gemma's door didn't yet have a good squeak to it, but she hoped, with time, it would come. She had long dreamed of the day when this screen door could whine and slam, then three sets of small, sandy feet would trample through the house like a herd, leaving giggles in their wake.

The collection of bowls and metal clattered against the glass-topped bistro table. She scooped the fish and gave the spoon an exaggerated tap against the porcelain edge to call the two strays she cared for.

Her eyes scanned the beach, expecting to see her two furry neighborhood friends galloping from behind a bush or another yard, their tails twitching behind them.

"Fred! Ethel!" She clicked her tongue against the roof of her mouth and placed two small white bowls full of chopped fish-scented meat on the floorboards of her back deck. Finally, two cats, both light gray with darker stripes, meowed and trotted around the seagrass that lined her property.

"You're late," Gemma said with warmth and love for her stray friends.

Both sandy-pawed felines stopped in front of their feast and stared at her. Actually, it may have been closer to a glare.

"Well, clearly, I was early." The left side of her smile tipped in a smirk. Her phone vibrated and she ignored it.

"Gemma!" Cameron, her neighbor with the angular glasses and slightly oversized veneers waved and headed her way. After too many invitations, she'd finally gone out with him, but, no. He was just—no. Too needy.

"Call." She pointed to her phone. "Have to take this."

She stepped inside and glanced at the caller ID: *Platinum Life Magazine*. Her heart danced a triple beat to the tune of hope. *Platinum Life Magazine* was a national publication that was widely considered the arbiter of taste on every area of design, from interiors to fashion. They covered the globe with their opinions and they were calling *her*.

She made a wide press-perfect smile before she answered the call—in part to bolster her confidence in case they were calling to offer her a subscription, but also to lend her voice a friendly, agreeable tone. "Gemma Stewart." Clear and succinct. Professional and approachable. *Well done.*

"Hello, Ms. Stewart, this is Dawn with *Platinum Life Magazine*."

"Yes, hello."

"I hope I'm not calling too early; I didn't want to take the chance that I might miss you." Her voice was curt. Sharp. Clearly on a mission.

Gemma relaxed her PR smile. If the other woman didn't give soft and fluffy edges to her words, Gemma was relieved she didn't have to, either. "No, this is fine."

"Excellent. We're doing our resort issue four months from now, and we decided on a last-minute addition entitled 'Top Ten West Coast Resorts.' I was narrowing down the candidates and was impressed to find that the top three resorts on our list were designed by your firm."

Gemma was impressed, too. It had been a long, hard climb to this place in her career.

"We would like to add a one-on-one interview with you to the issue."

She hoped her quick inhale didn't sound like a gasp on the other end of the phone. "I'd be honored." A wow-I-did-it feeling lit in her chest and burned as bright as the early morning sun.

"Perfect." Dawn said it with all the conviction of a deal closed. "Now. I'd also like to include a sidebar on the page highlighting a custom top ten from you. Maybe you could talk about the top ten design tips for creating an oasis at home? Or the top ten relaxing features to include in your vacation home? We can refine it later. Just come up with a top ten list, and we'll work with it."

"Sounds great." She kept her voice calm, but her heart fluttered such that she had to walk around the room. She inhaled deeply, well aware that this was a dream-come-true moment.

"I'd like to do a photo shoot of you at one of these signature properties you've done, really show off your amazing talent. Could we shoot the one in San Francisco?"

"Sure, I can make that work. How soon?"

"We're on a tight deadline—can you do Monday? That would give you and the hotel the weekend to stage for the photo shoot."

A bullet of adrenaline shot through her heart and ricocheted down her arms. The weekend was not nearly enough time to take care of current work *and* get everything staged. "Plenty of time," she heard herself say.

They traded email addresses and said their goodbyes. Gemma flipped her phone onto the driftwood dining table and did an air high five. "Yesss!"

This would be a new level of success for her business. *Platinum Life* was a career-making publication. She paced the kitchen floor, pumping her fists now and then.

The new all-too-quiet of her empty house was so loud it almost echoed. She glanced out the window. Fred and Ethel had moved on with their day, their empty bowls waiting for her on the porch. Preston was gone. It was too early to call friends.

She sighed at her ocean view amidst her moment of silent victory and decided she'd phone her assistant Charlotte in about an hour to get the shoot organized. They could toast with a glass of champagne at the staging. Other than that, there wouldn't be any available time for celebrating. Too much work to do.

The teakettle scream-whistled. She reached for her phone and noticed that it had slid next to a puffy envelope that she'd brought in from the mailbox the night before. Johnston and Lewis was printed in the upper left-hand corner. These would be the final divorce papers, the ones she hadn't wanted to look at last night.

She lifted the kettle from the flame. "Okay, Mom. You're right about one thing. I have to trust my instincts." The memory of Preston's betrayal ignited a special strain of fury, and her voice sounded strangled. "Right now, my instincts are telling me this divorce is the right decision."

She ripped open the envelope and double-checked a couple of items on the document. Though he had asked, she was not going to pay him alimony. He had plenty of family money; he could run back to Daddy if he needed a check. And he would. She knew he would.

She had a keen sense of justice, which demanded that he'd never see another dime from her.

Damn it.

There it was. His attorney said they would take that clause out. They hadn't. She rifled through the drawer in the island for a pen and crossed through that line item several times. In the margin, she wrote in all caps: NO ALIMONY.

Maybe this was what the had wind pointed to, the finality of her divorce. She signed her name on the line. "There. Done. Free." The chokehold on her voice relaxed.

With a personal policy against doing work barefoot—it made her feel too informal—she slipped on her most-loved black boots, the ones with the silver chains hung around the ankles. She grabbed her favorite tea and mug and poured hot water over the pungent herbs while she searched out the window. Now that she'd signed the papers, the wind patterns ought to have relaxed.

Her sight stumbled on a tan suit that she'd tossed over the back of an upholstered chair. Her freshly christened ex-husband had called and told her he'd forgotten the suit in the closet and asked her to send it to him. It was custom-made, he'd explained.

Hot tea in hand, she picked up the suit and headed to the outdoor alcove. She tossed it on top of the wood in the outdoor fireplace and lit it with a long-neck lighter. Then she settled into the niche that was protected from the wind by three sides of her house. She crossed her ankles such that her boots were now the center point of her view of the ocean. Now and then, she glanced at the fireplace, the last remnant of her wasband disintegrated in a satisfying burn.

She should have gone for more old-fashioned qualities of love like loyalty, honesty, and kindness. She ought to have avoided someone who had drop-dead, all-too-perfect quali-ties. Those opened doors to temptations that few knew how to resist.

She tapped the play image of the first voicemail message and immediately, her call waiting buzzed through. *Dad.* She walked to the gravel garden she'd designed at the southwest corner of her lot.

"Hi, Pop."

She dragged her boot over the dark gray pebbles that

formed a mock river and flowed into the alcove. She knew he would be happy to hear her news about the magazine feature. "How are you?"

"Not bad. Gotta minute? I have an opportunity I want to discuss with you." His voice sounded mostly upbeat, but a certain amount of emotional weariness weighed his enthusiasm. When she heard the fatigue, something caught in a tender place in her heart, and she decided to hold off on telling him her news.

Never one to beat around the bush, her dad launched right into his idea—a project he and her mother had been working on for a year before her death, one that he and Gemma could finish together.

"Alcott Manor?" Old memories sprang to life and squeezed her voice thin. "I don't know, Dad. Didn't Mom say that the original owner killed his wife there?"

Her father cleared his throat. "Well, the jury of public opinion is that he killed his wife. The husband always claimed that she killed herself. The first half of the opinion poll is what has made it so hard for the owners to raise enough funding to finalize the renovation. But they've done it, and they want the job completed."

She walked into the alcove again and silently counted her steps to the couch—a self-calming behavior she hadn't done in a long time. When she caught herself doing it, she stopped.

The cool ocean breezes washed over her face, and she sniffed the restorative salty air deep into her lungs. Her father went on with more details, so she put the call on speakerphone and inhaled the mind-centering herbs of her tea. This was not a job she would take.

"Your mother, the team, and I have taken the property a long way in the past year. The job has had a lot of setbacks, though, and I need for you to clear the land so we can finish out the project on time. I need you to work your special expertise. We need our house whisperer."

House whisperer. That wasn't a title she would put on her business card or company brochure. Her mother had taught her how to heal the energetic imprints that history abandoned in its wake. Negative events or repeated behavioral patterns left marks behind. Like a shadow or a ghost, a flavor of what used to be. Those imprints influenced people and their futures. Removing them from land and houses resulted in greater harmony and prosperity for the owners. Left untouched, they wreaked havoc.

She redirected the conversation. "Your buddy from West Point still helping to oversee things?"

"Yeah. Tom's good people. He runs the Charleston Historic District Commission now, so he's been a great help in pushing things through."

"Who owns the property?"

"It's family-owned. They elected one representative to serve their interests and to oversee the renovations."

"Who?" Her fingers were poised on the screen of her iPad to look up names.

"Ah, his name is Henry Alcott. He's a wealthy expat who has lived in London for the past decade. Interestingly, he's a direct descendent of the original Benjamin Alcott who built the house. Tom insists that everyone call him Mr. Alcott. Anyway, he's contributed most of the money for the restoration."

She tapped Alcott Manor into the browser on her phone. Up popped very few images of the house and its original owner. The black-and-white photos revealed a magnificent Greek revival estate home. It dwarfed the tiny figures in front of it, people whom Gemma figured were the original family owners. Even without color in the picture, the white paint gleamed, and the house seemed to own the family that stood in front of it. The surrounding trees boasted pride at the privilege to surround a home of such extraordinary elegance.

In another photo, Benjamin Alcott, a U.S. Senator from South Carolina, was a character to behold, and from tip to toe, his appearance played the part. His longish white hair was neatly combed. His wide handlebar mustache fit perfectly with his highly-starched cravat and the asymmetric horizontal bow that accented his conservative black suit.

She could just envision him sitting on the wooden church pew with his subdued, order-obeying wife and children lined up next to her.

"Doesn't look like a wife murderer."

"They never do," her dad said.

She tapped "Henry Alcott London" into the search bar with one finger, and several articles about hotel acquisitions came up. "So, I'm guessing that this Henry Alcott is single, and that's the real reason why you want me on this particular job."

Her father coughed and cleared his throat. "I wouldn't have any idea," he said with caught-red-handed alarm in his voice.

"I think you probably have a lot of ideas. Especially if this guy is single and has amassed enough money to rehab his ancestor's estate." She clicked on the articles, which didn't reveal any significant details about Henry, while she single-handedly batted away her father's matchmaking efforts.

"He may be single; I don't really know. But I do know you've overseen too many projects at once, and it may be time—"

"Projects that have set my career." She wasn't in the mood to be match-made, now or probably ever. She wouldn't be talked into doing this job.

"I think we ought to work together on this one." His tone swelled with fatherly concern. "It wouldn't hurt for you to slow down for a minute, enjoy life, allow us to spend some time together."

She sighed and her will softened. Her dad's deep and gravelly voice was a comfort to her. Now that her mother was gone, he was the single steady—albeit infrequent—force in her crazy, busy life.

"Is 'slow down and enjoy life' code for 'get married'? Because we've been over this. If there were someone special in the cards for me, I would know by now. I'm happy, Pop. I'm at my best when I'm working and independent. And I'm not stepping foot in a house with a tragic history like that."

Her dad argued his point, and she questioned whether he really needed her talents or if he just wanted her company on the job. She sat on the edge of the wraparound koi pond she had designed for the house before she moved in. The previous owners had divorced and sold the house as a part of their settlement.

It was important to transform the energy from prior owners *before* you moved into any home. Otherwise, their problems could become your problems.

She and Preston were already headed toward divorce before she'd moved in. She didn't want to settle into a batch of energetic ingredients for another one. These particular fish and their gently moving water represented good fortune and prosperity. Though it didn't much matter. She wasn't interested in trying for another relationship.

"There's someone for everyone, Gem." His voice deepened into the gravity of hard-earned wisdom.

Gemma put her fingers into the cool water and counted the fish that nibbled at them. She used to believe that. With all her heart, she did. When she was young, she saw the kind of love her parents shared, and she took for granted that she would have it one day, too.

It had never happened, though.

"Just because you and Mom had forty-five great years together doesn't mean everyone gets that in life." She pushed the disappointment over Preston's broken promises down to one of the dark corners of her heart, where it usually lived. Where she couldn't see it.

"Call me a romantic, Gemma Rose, but I think it means exactly that. What I'm saying is that we need to go after this job because it would be fun for us to work together on a project this size, and healthy for you to be in one place for a while. And who knows? If you weren't switching coasts every few days, you might meet someone."

She heard the squeak of her dad's office chair, and she knew he sipped his coffee while he tilted back as far as the old black leather chair would let him. She could almost smell the dark roast.

"I know you. You're ready to sink your teeth into a project where you could really use your creativity. An 1800s Greek revival—this could open new doors for our family business. If we do this one well, we'll have our pick of any historical renovation project in the country."

"This job's not for me, Pop. I don't do haunted." Her voice was firm, despite the shiver that traveled along her torso.

"The past is the past. Nothing like that would ever happen again—that was just a freak situation. Plus, I'd be there with you. Doing this job together would be like old times. I'd bet we could even find some antique furniture in the home that we could restore. Remember when we used to do that, just you and me? You always enjoyed that. What do you say?"

He sounded uncharacteristically eager, and she decided he was lonely. He had his buddy, Tom, though. She knew they had a close friendship, so he wouldn't be alone on the job. And though she wouldn't work with him day-to-day on the property, she'd plan a visit to spend time with him. He would benefit from a real connection with someone who shared his last name, with someone who understood exactly how much had been lost when her mom died.

"No, I'm sorry. I can't. I have very firm boundaries where even a hint of haunted is concerned. I know you understand. You have Tom and a good team. I'll help you find someone local to the area to clear the energy on the land if you need that, and I'll come out for a visit. On a related note, it might be about to get really busy for me. I got a call this morning from a national magazine. They want to do a feature, and the business coming in from that will be..." She waited for the congratulations and the "Aw, honey I'm so proud," but he didn't respond.

The quiet became heavy between them. "Pop? Are you okay?"

She heard his chair squeak to an upright position.

"The truth is, I need your help."

She stood and walked to the front of the alcove. "Tell me what you need." She knew he had long been more dependent on her mother than he realized. Her recent death was a big adjustment for him. She'd talk with him in detail about the visit she was planning. That would give him something to look forward to.

He sighed for the second time and she tightened her grip on the phone.

"We didn't want to tell you this because we thought we could work it out on our own. The authorities said there was a good chance that after they liquidated his assets, there would be enough for everyone to get at least half of their money back."

"Pop. What authorities? What money?" She tried to force herself to sound calm, but the words rushed from her mouth in a race for answers.

There was a third and even heavier sigh. "Your mother and I invested in a hedge fund through our stockbroker a few years ago. The returns they showed us were impressive, and, as it turns out, too good to be true. We were counting on those returns to finish out our retirement."

She felt her knees turn to liquid. Her parents had worked tirelessly for forty years in their own business for those savings.

"He took everything."

"Oh." Panic gathered in her chest, rose upward, and hit her head in waves.

"The authorities thought they might get us about half of what we placed with him. It's all tied up in the courts now, and it's a lot bigger case than they originally anticipated. No one really knows when or how it will work out."

She paced over the white and gray gravel garden she'd designed and rubbed her forehead. "Do you have…anything left?"

"I have the proceeds from your mother's life insurance policy. I'll have to keep working, though. For a long while."

Worries swirled around her like sharks. Her father was not young. He had a heart condition, which had to have been put to the test with the stress of her mother's unexpected death, and now this. "I know you didn't plan on working much longer at your age, at least not for income. I would also imagine you needed those personal funds as capital in the business. To fund cash flow and front payroll? Particularly with this Charleston project that you want to finish."

"Yes," he said.

She'd never known him to ask for help. The humiliation must be killing him.

"Pop, I'll give you whatever you need—"

"No, Gem. That's not why I'm calling."

"It's no trouble. I would enjoy giving back after everything you've done for me over the years."

"I would never take your money." Her father's tone was sharp and final. "If you can spare the time for it, though, I would accept your help with this job. There's a hard stop in place just a few months from now. We've had a difficult time getting projects wrapped up."

A fierce updraft from the ocean blew across the sand, and she zipped her shirt over her chest. She wondered if she could help her father with this property and say yes to the business that the *Platinum Life* article would generate.

She thought of her parents' company, how many people worked there, and how they would lose their jobs if the business folded. She didn't have enough funds to pay for her expenses, her retirement, his retirement, and fund his business for this job.

She could afford to send him a check every week for his living expenses. And he would take a check from her if that's the option she gave him. But she also knew that would kill him. He was a proud man. He would never have told her about his mix-up in this Ponzi scheme if he hadn't been forced to ask for her help.

Yes, if he had to close the business and live off her income, he'd be dead within a year. He'd have nothing to live for, no one to share his life with, and nothing to look forward to.

Gemma rubbed at the tension that pulsed through the back of her neck.

"I don't want to interfere in your life. You may not have time to do this." His tone softened to a near mumble. "I think you mentioned something about a magazine article a minute ago."

"Oh, don't worry about that." A cold wind blew at her face while warm currents twisted around her legs. She closed her eyes and braced against it. *This* was obviously what the wind foretold.

"You know your mother and I have been working on the property for a while."

Gemma chose not to bring up the fact that her mother had died on the property. Yes, it had been the result of natural causes—a heart attack—but with the probable murder committed by the original owner, she didn't discount the effects of those imprints on the property. "No...strange experiences?"

"Well, there's always something a little strange here and there in an older home. We handled it. You can always handle it when you have to, right?"

Bricks of quiet built between them once again.

"I don't want to put you in a bad position. I can try to work this out a different way."

Of her parents' three kids, she was the youngest and the most responsible one. She took care of what needed to be done. It's what she did. Maybe this time she could take care of her father's business and her own. "No, Pop, it's good. I can make it work. How about if I come out to the property, do my research, and clear the imprints? Then I'll need to come back. I'm expecting a significant uptick in business here over the next few months. I need to be here for that."

She made a note to ask Charlotte to send Dawn some of the publicity shots of her in the San Francisco hotel. She wouldn't have time to do the shoot now. Which was okay, she rationalized. This was a family emergency and the photo Charlotte would send was good. Dawn would understand. Hopefully.

"Then you'll come back out? It's a big house with a lot to do in a short amount of time."

"I'll clear whatever you need me to, so your team can get the work done. But I can't do the restoration work." Her memories created a chill from the inside out as they always did. She tried to push them away. "I just— I can't."

There was yet another long sigh on the other end. "All right. I understand. I'll try to find some extra management-level people and make that work. Though they won't replace you. You're the best."

She wrestled a surge of guilt, then made a mental note to schedule time for additional trips to South Carolina. The magazine feature would bring in lots of new business. She would just schedule longer deadlines on projects to make time to help her dad.

"You okay, Gem?"

"Yeah. It's—it's just that the wind is blowing some crazy patterns out here today."

He clicked his tongue against the roof of his mouth. "Aha. Your mother's wisdom. She was usually right about these things. 'All truth can be found in nature,' she always said."

His chair squeaked several times, and Gemma knew he was rocking. "Maybe you're about to meet someone. Or maybe this job will open new doors for your business. That's what I'm hoping anyway. You could really leverage the work you used to do with those skills of yours."

"I don't—never mind." She knew she wouldn't work historical renovations again. "I signed the divorce papers this morning. Maybe that was it." She didn't think that was it. Some sort of change—she didn't think it was positive—was stalking her, and she wasn't sure which direction to turn in to get away from it. If she started running, she just might hit it head on.

"Well...I know that was hard."

"Had to be done."

"Only good things ahead, Gemma-bean. I can feel it. I've got to run, but we're staying at The Elliott House, a little bed and breakfast in Charleston. I'll meet you there on Sunday night. We'll head to the manor together on Monday morning."

They said their goodbyes. Gemma stared at the white water that crashed onto the sand, ignoring the Pacific Ocean winds that whipped in circles around the seagrass. Her dad had just skipped over all the specifics he would normally cover for a new job: the detailed history of the home, what projects needed completion, if the main client contact was easy or difficult to work with, deadlines...

Especially deadlines. With restoration jobs they were usually somewhat flexible, since you never knew what you were going to encounter once you dug beneath the surface. But he had said *hard deadline*.

There was probably a story there. One he didn't share. Which was all too like him. Her mother called it his "tip of the iceberg strategy." He would only share a tiny bit of the story until he had your buy in. Only after the fact would you realize what you'd gotten yourself into.

What concerned her most with this strategy of his was the haunted detail. She had been firm that she would not work on a haunted project. He'd agreed. But he'd never denied that the property was haunted.

CHAPTER 3

Gemma couldn't open her mouth wide enough to get her lips around the giant biscuit. She tried several different angles but only succeeded in dripping butter down her chin when she mastered a half bite.

Preferring a slightly larger restaurant than the small dining area that the B&B offered, she had gone to The Iron Skillet down the street. She'd texted her father, as well as her cousin Janey, who worked with the family business, as to her whereabouts. They would meet her there shortly.

"We call 'em cat head biscuits. Big as a cat's head." The older waitress's dark braid curled around her protruding collarbone, and Gemma immediately wondered how she stayed so thin while working in a restaurant that served such rich food. Her white name tag was engraved in black with the name Tammy, and she nearly dropped a white plate of giant pancakes in front of her.

Gemma eyed the height and width of the biscuit before returning it to her side plate. It was, oddly, about the size of a cat's head. "What do you call the pancakes?"

"We just call them pancakes. Here, sugar, don't be so

brave about it." She picked up a knife and cut Gemma's biscuit in half. "I know you're not local. What brings you here?"

She stumbled for something to say. The woman had just cut her food for her. "Ah, my dad's company is restoring Alcott Manor." Several men who were seated at the bar shifted their attention in her direction.

"Ohhh." The waitress put her hands in her lace-tipped front patch pockets and pressed her lips together as though she were forbidden to speak any further on the topic.

"You're familiar with the home?"

She hunched forward as if to whisper, the flavor of tobacco heavy on her breath. "Everyone is. And I could guess which side you're on."

"Which side?" Gemma lowered her own voice to match the waitress's secretive tone, but she had no idea what was so hush-hush.

"You're obviously on the side to restore. The family is divided—half for it, half against it. Started when that girl was killed in the house. Now it's a battle between the owners. Everybody in town has picked a side." She squinted her eyes as if she weren't sure that Gemma really didn't know.

"Why are we whispering?"

"Because if the ghost did kill those people, I don't want him to hear me talking about him. I don't need that kind of attention. Also, that man halfway down the bar there is Asher Cardill. He's a member of the Alcott family, and he's on the side that doesn't want it restored. I don't want his kind of attention, neither."

She cleared her throat and straightened her back. "My name's Tammy," she said at a more normal volume. "Let me know if I can get you some more hot tea." She placed the handwritten check on the table and touched it lightly before she walked away.

She thanked Tammy with a smile and snuck a glance at the middle-aged man at the bar she had mentioned. Sure enough, he stared over his white coffee cup at her. Side part, thinning brown hair, dark eyes with a touch of hardness to them.

She tried not to stare at his outfit—a baby blue button-down, tan pants, and a pink belt. She didn't think she had seen anyone other than a little girl wear a pink belt lately. Of course, ninety-eight percent of her closet was black, so if preppy was back and she'd missed a new fashion trend, she wouldn't know it.

She opened her laptop and managed a bite of that now half biscuit while she googled, "Alcott Manor family battle and girl's death." The buttery, layered cake melted unexpectedly on her tongue and she closed her eyes for a moment. Obviously, cat head biscuit was Southern for French pastry.

Up popped a list of articles, and she clicked on the top one from a local newspaper: *Tragedy at Alcott Manor Starts Legal Battle Among Owners.*

The photo of a teenaged girl was posted just beneath the bold headline. With her blue eyes and straight blond hair held back with a three-inch, sky blue grosgrain headband, she resembled an older version of Alice-in-Wonderland. She was the quintessential southern beauty queen with a smooth-as-a-peach complexion. Gemma's heart melted in empathy over a young life cut tragically short.

Sixteen-year-old Brittney Allen was found dead at Alcott Manor on the anniversary of Anna Alcott's death. The manor had been locked up and, as usual, it was in the throes of a failed restoration attempt. Brittney's two girlfriends said they broke into the manor to see if the house was as haunted as its reputation suggested it was. The girls say they were separated from Brittney when they heard her scream, then watched her fall from the second story as though she had been pushed. She was declared dead at the scene.

The Alcott descendants, whose family corporation retains sole ownership of the home, have since divided their support for the restoration efforts. While half of the family supports the continued restoration, the other half of the owners believe the house is cursed and that a restoration is not possible. They support tearing the manor down and selling the land to developers, and they have filed a lawsuit. A resolution is expected soon from the court.

So far, every attempt to restore Alcott Manor has failed. Restoration specialists claim that work performed on the property is quickly damaged or undone, making a complete restoration impossible. Whether these efforts are the result of vandalism or the supposed undead spirit of Benjamin Alcott is an issue of local debate.

Taylor Reconstruction was the last company to work on the manor. CEO Oliver Taylor had this to say about his attempt to restore the home, "I don't believe in ghosts. Never have. But I honestly don't know how to describe some of the things we saw and heard in that house. There's something dark going on in there. I don't say that lightly because I don't scare easy. Frankly, I'm just glad to be done with it, even though I damn near lost everything on that one. Every last improvement we put into that place was destroyed. By who, I just don't know."

The manor has long been reputed as one of the most haunted homes in the southeast.

She skimmed the rest of the article and rubbed at the pain that built in the back of her head. The hidden underside of her father's "tip of the iceberg" was starting to reveal itself.

She typed "Alcott Manor haunted" into the search bar and clicked on the first article that came up: *Most Haunted Places of the South.*

Alcott Manor was number two on the list, right behind an abandoned mental asylum based in Tennessee. She covered the front of her neck with her hand—to protect, to guard, to soothe.

Anna Alcott was shot and killed at Alcott Manor in 1883. Her husband, Senator Benjamin Alcott, was convicted and hung for her murder. He maintained his innocence until the very end, claiming that his wife had committed suicide and that she had left a note. However, no such suicide note was ever found.

To this day, it is rumored that Benjamin Alcott roams the house, searching for the suicide note that he claimed his wife left. Desperate to prove his innocence, he sabotages any efforts to restore the home for fear that the construction might destroy the evidence he thinks exists.

Two people have died in the home over the past year, during yet another restoration attempt. Coincidence? We don't think so either. The first was a teenaged girl who broke into the manor with her friends to investigate locals' claims that gunshots and screams can be heard coming from the property on the anniversary of Anna Alcott's death The other death was an expert who restored the frescoes on the ceilings of the music room and library and was killed while performing his work.

Dread fell through her like a rush of water from the top of a fall, the sensation nearly took all her will with it. She'd say she couldn't believe that her dad had kept this information from her—but she could believe it. It was just his style.

She fought the flash—a memory of the wind patterns that popped into her head. The first one happened just before her mother's death. The last one just before she arrived here. Both were tied to this godforsaken house.

The wind pattern only means change. It doesn't necessarily mean anything bad is coming. She admonished her thoughts to get back in line.

She lifted her head from the screen to the sight of two people rounding the corner, one waving at her. Both smiling.

"Morning, Gemma Rose!" Her father's hair was a solid gray now, parted on the side and cut short. A fresh haircut. A good sign, she thought. One that said he was taking care of himself. His fair skin was reddened across his nose and cheeks, probably from the Southern sun.

Janey, her cousin and the bookkeeper-slash-general-coordinator-of-everything for her dad's company, was in perfect step at his side. It was another detail that gave her comfort. In these still-early weeks after Mom's death, he didn't need a lot of time alone. Her thick brown ponytail swished behind her and she flashed her impish grin.

Gemma hugged them both and answered the usual questions about her flight, whether she slept well the night before, and was she ready to head on to the manor?

"Yes, I'm ready." She closed her laptop, dug into her front pocket for cash to pay the bill, and lowered her voice to a stern whisper. "Now I did promise I'd clear the land for you, and I will. But I want to be super clear about my limits here. I'm not going in that house."

Her father's eyebrows shot up at the same time his mouth opened, as though he was going to play innocent. But when she raised a scolding eyebrow at him, his mouth closed and he obviously thought better of it.

Janey's eyes shifted left toward her uncle. "I told you she'd find out about the house and that you'd be in trouble."

Gemma waved to Tammy on her way out the front door.

"Fair enough," her dad said. "I'll take whatever help you'll give."

She made her way down the front steps and followed her dad toward his car. Warm air coiled around her legs while the fingers of a cool breeze caressed her face. Dread boomed soundlessly inside of her at its touch, like a growl, like a moan, like a long and painful warning cry she could not ignore.

CHAPTER 4

J aney handed Gemma a small fountain cola from the back seat. "You know everything down here is a Coke. Nothing is soda. When you ask for a Coke, they want to know what kind of Coke you want—regular Coke, lemon lime, or orange. Anyway, I know you just had breakfast, but I thought you might want something to drink."

"Thanks, Jane." Gemma made a smile she knew her cousin would accept, sipped the drink, and tried to decide which questions to ask, which ones to let go.

"I know what you're thinking." Her dad gave her a quick glance before looking back to the road, his knuckles white on the wheel.

"What am I thinking, Pop?"

"Now that you know more about the eccentricities of the job, you're wondering why we would work on such a case."

Eccentricities. "No, after our last phone conversation, I know why."

"We didn't really have a choice," Janey said. "It's the only restoration project out there that solves all the problems."

"I assumed as much."

They'd driven well out of the city center now. Her father's car moved along at the posted speed limit, though she felt the pace was too slow. The two-lane road was deserted, excepting its overstuffed side margins of possessive kudzu vines. It was a world or two away from the busy sophistication of her west coast life.

She'd visited this area once before when her family vacationed on one of the barrier islands. The beach was known as the Bloody Coast because of an English and Indian battle that had left the shores red with blood. She'd spent the entire vacation sick with fever.

"Bad imprints," her mother finally decided.

"I'm guessing the hard deadline you mentioned has something to do with the court's involvement?"

Her dad paused, a brief flash of anxiousness tightening his features just slightly and only for a moment. "They shouldn't have been onsite in a construction zone. Her death was probably an accident. Or some think she may have been murdered by—"

"A ghost?"

"Well, yes, of course. Because that makes for good lore and fodder. No, I was going to say a homeless person. A couple were seen on the property that week. They could have found a way in.

"There was some talk of selling among some of the owners before this incident. But after the girl died, lawyers were hired, battle lines were drawn, and the judge imposed a deadline to settle the argument. The judge's punch list of restoration items has to be completed two months from now, or he's going to side with the prosecution and force the owners to sell."

"Is it a reasonable list?"

"Nothing extraordinary. Just enough that a certain amount of restoration progress has to be evident. So, two months from now, Judge Wertheimer will take a tour of the property, along with Tom, who represents the Historic District Commission, an inspector, and two family owners, one from each camp. When the judge is satisfied that his list items have been met, that will put concerns to rest, and we can finish the second half of the restoration."

"And you're in danger of missing the deadline."

"Only because our work—" Her father cleared his throat again.

"Is being destroyed." She finished his sentence and thought of the articles she'd read that morning, and how no restoration had ever been completed. "These are the setbacks you mentioned, and why you want me to clear the negative imprints from the land."

He stared at her as he never had, with his eyes pleading. This monument of a man in her life, who, up until recently, had never really asked her for anything. "If we miss our deadline, we'll be lucky if we break even. We need the full job to make enough money so that we're in the clear personally. So, yes. I need you to clear the land, and I'm hoping that will do enough good that we can finish our work here."

There was a desperately stern, fatherly edge to the way he said it. As if he were saying, "You cannot date that boy," or "You need to study tonight instead of going to that party." But vulnerability tweaked his voice thin, and she worked hard to keep the floodgates of emotion closed and hidden deep in her heart.

She couldn't help him more than she had already promised. She'd clear the land. That was it. Anything more and she knew she would live to regret it.

"This is Alcott Manor?" She squinted from the sun that bore through the front windshield of her father's rented gray sedan. Only a glimpse of Alcott Manor was visible in the distance among the majestic water oaks and ancient magnolias. She and her father leaned to the side to see it as their car idled on the quiet road.

"Yep, this is her. Built in 1832. Sixty-five acres in all. We've taken her a long way over the last year." He put the car in park, and everyone stepped out.

A seductive swirl of wind and emotion spiraled around and through her. Warm currents spun possessively about her lower body while cool ocean breezes tossed her red hair like a playful spirit.

"Don't," she whispered into the midst of a force that felt bigger and more in control than she was.

A white van with the words Private Workforce Security on the outside and a picture of binoculars turned slowly onto the main road in front of the manor. "I'm having some additional security added." Her father pointed to the van. "More hidden cameras and a security guard."

"Smart," Janey said.

Alcott Manor sat halfway between the road and the ocean on a wide expanse of short-trimmed green. "Was there anything original left of the house that you could salvage?"

"Quite a bit, actually. Wait until you see the inside, it's magnificent. There are frescoes on several of the domed ceilings."

"I won't be seeing the inside, Pop," she sing-songed in a quiet reminder-like-voice. She didn't like the way he spoke about the house. Properties could become an obsession, especially when you were trying to restore them. It wasn't unusual to develop a relationship with a home when you were trying to bring back its original glory. But she didn't want him to have a close relationship with this house.

"What's that, sweetheart?"

"You heard me, Pop." She reached the grassy edge of the property and strolled next to the black iron fence. She focused hard on the structure and thought for a moment about the original owner. Whether Benjamin Alcott had been the murderer or not, his wife had died tragically on the property. Gemma would have to figure out where that happened so she could clean up the effects of that event. Then she would head back to her life on the west coast.

She felt the house return her attention, and a chill produced goose bumps along her skin. At first, she felt an attraction, a warmth that drew her close and seemed to know her. Without a guarded thought, she leaned into it, explored it.

That was quickly followed by a grabby and hoggish sensation, like a demanding mistress who held too tight to her lover, and Gemma jerked back quickly.

Must be the effect of Benjamin. Possessive, arrogant ass.

She stepped away. One foot forward, then another. Quietly, she counted her steps on her way to the car.

"Is someone in there?" she asked.

"Tom might be, I guess. Plenty of workers." Her dad ducked his head beneath the sun visor and tried to see the property through the blinding rays of sunshine. "Why, did you see someone?"

"No, I just got a creepy feeling. Like I was being watched or something." Gemma shivered again and buckled her seatbelt. "Ran right through me." She wanted to tell him that she didn't like this house, that she didn't have a good feeling about it. But he couldn't back away from this project. So, she would just stuff her concerns and clear the land for him. That was the best way she could help him. She wondered for a moment if her mother had done something similar—just wedged her concerns to some out-of-sight place and went to work because they needed this job.

Two cars passed in front and she took note of them.

"Are you okay, Gemma?" he asked.

"Yeah, I'm fine."

"Because you just counted the cars."

"No, I didn't."

"I saw your mouth move, honey. You said, 'one, two.' You haven't done that since..." Glenn shook his head. "I shouldn't have asked you to do this. I just thought all of that was over and done with. In the past."

"It was. It is. I'm fine." She touched his arm. "I'm okay. I promise. Now, I'm here to help you. So, let's get on with it." She gave his arm a squeeze. "Do you know where the wife was killed?"

"Look at that rose garden on the side. Do you see a funny glow around it?" Janey asked.

"Where?" Her dad frowned in the direction she pointed, and Gemma made a mental note to get him to the eye doctor. It might be time for a checkup.

She also observed the new lines that had appeared on his face almost overnight. He'd aged about ten years since her mother died.

"Over there, to the right and toward the back. It's filled with red roses, and they're huge."

"Oh, look at that, the roses are blooming now. There's a woman in a wide straw hat to the side of the house, over there clipping the flowers," he said. "Your mother did love that rose garden."

Gemma pushed the home button on her phone: 10:45 a.m. "Oh, Pop, it's almost time for the meeting. Tom ought to be here soon. Let's pull the car to the front of the property and call him. I don't want to be late."

"All right, Gemma-bean, don't you worry. We'll work this out. Just like old times."

HE LOOKED out of the second story window at the three

people who had walked around the far corner of the property. The driver he recognized as Glenn Stewart with Stewart Historic Renovations. Glenn and his wife had worked tirelessly on his family's home for the past year, even in the face of the manor's resident ghost and other paranormal problems. He owed them a great deal for their perseverance.

He also recognized Janey, Glenn's right hand. The redhead was new to him. Her hair was a deep red, more auburn, with a few lighter streaks from the sun, he guessed. That color was unusual in this town, where most women were blonde. She wore her hair loose around her shoulders and the wind played with it, teasing at it like a cat playing with yarn.

She made a point to stand straight, tall, and bold, as though she faced a challenger when she turned to the manor directly. Her chin tipped up and her shoulders were forced down and back. For a moment, he thought she had looked straight at him while he stood there in the second story bay window. There was a connection between them, an unexpected spark. He'd felt it pulse through him.

The great lawn stretched between them like a physical extension of the house, and he wondered if the manor was connecting them. Maybe it was allying them in an unexpected partnership, teaming them together to attack an ambitious goal.

He'd seen the house act as a conduit in that way before. It drew people in, almost as though they had been handpicked to come into the home. Sometimes they never left.

The group climbed into their car, and he watched while it idled. Slowly, the car rolled forward. Unintentionally, it seemed. Without purpose. They'd be at the house soon, discussing renovations and shortened timelines. He gripped the windowsill—the renovation *had* to work out this time. The house was on its last life. If they failed at this renovation, he would lose the house that had been in his family for generations. He couldn't let that happen.

From his elevated perspective, he saw what they didn't—the red pickup truck that sped toward the intersection. Their gray sedan that continued to roll. Unknowingly, he guessed. They must have been looking at the manor. "No..." His hand curled into a fist and banged on the glass. "No! *Stop!*"

The red truck ignored the stop sign and hit the gray car on the driver's side between the front and back seats. There was no horn, only the sickening shatter of glass and the crunching of steel.

Then...quiet.

CHAPTER 5

Tom Watson stood silently next to Glenn Stewart's hospital bed while he slept. Tom's short, straw-colored hair curved outward at the top with too much fullness and the length was too short, just as Gemma had always known it to be. In fact, most of her father's West Point and Army buddies had hairstyles that were too short.

Tom and her father had served in the military together, and their friendship was more like a brotherhood. They would have done anything for each other, and had. It was because of Tom that her father had even known about the Alcott Manor restoration opportunity.

She didn't know how much her dad had told Tom about his financial problems, so she didn't mention anything about that to him. But she had thanked him for letting her dad know about the job.

"The stuff they give him for the pain is a little heavy for him. So, he sleeps a lot. But I'll let him know that you came by." She felt silly standing next to someone she hardly knew while wearing only her hospital gown and white, waffle-print robe. She hadn't checked her hair lately, but she was pretty sure she was a fright to behold. She tried to fluff the back of it where it had been flattened from the pillow, but all she felt was a matted mess.

The door to Glenn Stewart's hospital room swung open, and a nurse backed into the room. "Time for your medicines, Mister Stewart," she sang. Her maroon pants clung too tightly to every curve and spread of her figure.

Her black, short-sleeved top was covered in koi and Gemma wondered distractedly why the manufacturer used this deep shade of red for the fish when a brighter red or orange would have been more accurate. Then again, the outfit would have to coordinate, and no one wanted to see anyone's lower half covered in bright orange. "Black would have worked. But I guess black and orange aren't exactly comforting colors for a hospital," she mumbled. "White's passé. Maroon it is."

"Pardon? Oh! I didn't realize you had company, Mister Stewart. How nice." The nurse smiled and nodded in a polite greeting. "I'm Layla Alcott, and I'm his nurse until this evening."

Gemma squinted at Layla's name tag. She elbowed Tom and pointed at it. "Her last name. Alcott." She kept her voice softer than a whisper and hoped Layla couldn't hear her. She also hoped Layla was on the *restore* side of the family argument and not the *sell* side.

He rubbed his arm where she'd jabbed him.

"I'm just going to change this IV bag for his medicines." Layla took the half glasses that hung around her neck and rested them on the near-end of her nose. Gemma figured Layla to be in her late twenties, maybe early thirties, too young for librarian glasses.

Layla pushed a series of buttons and the IV machine beeped and squealed. "Come on, now." She pushed one button repeatedly until the squealing stopped.

"Everything okay?" Tom asked.

"Oh. Technology and I don't have the best relationship. I swear, it sees me coming and it acts up just to irritate me. I always win in the end, though, don't I, Mister Stewart?" She patted Glenn on the chest, and her rounded pink cheeks rose with an angelic smile.

Gemma's heart softened at Layla's kind touch to her father. "Your last name..."

"Are you by chance related to the family that owns Alcott Manor?" Tom spoke over her.

Layla squeezed the IV bag several times. "I sure am. A direct descendent of the Alcott originals. Not that I ever saw any of Benjamin Alcott's riches." She winked and her eyes twinkled. "Though I wish I had. Workin' to pay the bills is about all I do these days. My husband's business isn't doing well. Anyway, I do have some ownership in the estate that was passed down to me from my grandparents. We're trying to restore it again—at least, our half of our family is. Which is good, because if we can get it fixed up and get some revenue from it—you know, tours and such—I would probably see some of that. That would really help."

Gemma stepped away. She didn't want to tell Layla, but she wasn't sure how they were going to get the manor restored now.

Layla flicked a syringe with her finger three times and inserted it in the IV tube. "My girls like to look at the house from the beach, but we don't go inside. I just feel too uncomfortable about it. Too many people have died there. We need to burn some sage or something to, you know, get rid of all that negative energy.

"Now, my husband..." Layla rolled her eyes. "He just can't get enough of the history of that place.

"He goes over there any chance he gets. He's not for the restoration, though. We don't really talk about it. And he's not an Alcott. He's a Cardill. Which is also an old Charleston family, but I kept my maiden name when we married. I just couldn't bear to part with it."

"I'm part of the team that is restoring the property," Tom said.

"Well." Layla put her hand to her chest. "Are you?"

"Yes, ma'am." Tom ran his hand through his hair, and it got puffier on the top. "It's an important piece of our history, and I think it can be saved."

"Is he—a part of your group?" Layla rested her hand on Glenn's chest again.

"Yes, ma'am," Tom said.

"He's my father."

Layla clicked her tongue against the roof of her mouth. "Shame. That house... I'm serious. Someone needs to clear the energy there."

"He's going to be okay?" Tom asked.

"Complete recoveries happen every day, even when you least expect it. I've seen it so many times." Layla dropped the empty syringes into the red sharps box. "Now, once he recovers, he's not going to go back to work for a while. I can tell you that. You'll have to do the house without him. After he leaves here, he'll need to continue his recovery at home with in-home nursing care." She typed on her computer keyboard.

"I'm praying for him. Now I'll pray for y'all, too. Your team might just be able to work miracles over there. We sure could use them." Her voice was even and cheery, not fake or syrupy, and it rode smoothly on a paved road of hope and encouragement.

Gemma thought about what a special gift Layla had to embody such positivity in the midst of so much tragedy and suffering.

"We will." She breathed deeply with the peace she knew she borrowed from Layla's optimism.

"Thank you, Layla. We'll take all the prayers you've got," Tom said.

Layla smiled and finger waved while she backed out of the door with her cart full of equipment.

Tom took Glenn by the hand and squeezed it. "It's just unbelievable. First your wife dies, and now this accident. This property is cursed."

His tenderness brought tears to Gemma's eyes. "We're all going to be fine, Tom. Listen..." She bit her lip before she said it and paused, just to be certain—even though there wasn't really another choice for her, not given the sort of person she was, the sort of daughter she was.

Nerves poured over her stomach like a bucket of freshly melted ice, and she waited for the chill to pass. "Why don't I move ahead with this project? You and I could work together. I'll need your help. Our family has a lot riding on it. Somebody has got to see this through for them."

Tom nodded through his own tears, his expression struggling to remain stoic. He was worried. Very worried. Of course, so was she, but she wasn't going to admit it. Not out loud. And not to Tom.

"Okay, that's good. I appreciate that." She patted him on the shoulder. "You know, I was raised in the restoration business. I could hammer a nail into a piece of wood without splitting it before I could ride a bike." She added a laugh to make Tom feel more comfortable, but her voice sounded shaky and scared. She cut the laugh short and cleared her throat.

"We've been friends for a lifetime." Tom still held her father's hand.

"He's going to be okay." Gemma could tell that seeing her dad like this made Tom feel his own mortality too much. Her dad did look pale, lying there in that hospital gown. But she knew he was going to be a new man once he recovered from this. She could feel it in her gut. If there was one thing she'd inherited from her mother, it was a good gut.

She cleared her throat again and shifted into her entrepreneurial mode. It was time to accept responsibility for what had to be done.

"I need two things from you right now. First, I want you to double the number of workers and the hours that they've been working. We're short on time, long on work, and I'm not missing this deadline."

Tom sniffed and wiped a tear with his fingertips.

"That means you have one crew working six a.m. to six p.m., and the second crew works from six p.m. to six a.m. All exterior work gets done during the day. I don't want to hear about anyone falling off the roof at three in the morning because they couldn't see where they were going.

"Second—and I realize this sounds strange—I want you to find someone who can get rid of ghosts. A shaman, a medium, someone along that vein. Preferably someone who doesn't have an affinity for the spotlight. Have them come out to the house and ask them to get rid of whoever is haunting the place. Okay?"

His eyes were glued to Glenn, though he nodded with a sigh. "Okay. We'll get this damn house wrapped up on time."

"Good," she said. "And let Henry Alcott know that I'll be there tomorrow."

With luck, they would pull this off. Yes. That's it. With luck.

THE NEXT DAY...

"Well, what are you going to do if you don't work this job?" Gemma asked her dad while they pushed him on a gurney through the bustling hospital. She dodged harried visitors who were distracted with their own concerns. "Once you've recovered, you can't just sit around. You're too young for that."

"When I'm finally cut loose, I'm going to head home to rest for a while. I need some time." He patted her hand, which she had placed on his shoulder.

"Are you sure you don't want to recover in Charleston? It's warmer here, and the Alcott project would give you something to focus on."

The automatic door opened, and Gemma walked alongside her father into the crisp, early spring air. Car horns blew in the distance.

She knew he needed more time to feel like himself again; car accidents were life changing events. She just didn't want him so far away—he was all she had left. He'd been right when he told her they should just settle into one project, spend some time together, and enjoy life for a while. You never knew what tomorrow would bring.

"Where's your bag?" She looked around.

"Janey took all my stuff." He faced his daughter. "Gem, I'm sure you could do with a rest yourself."

"I don't do nothing all that well, Pop." She scrunched her face to let her dad know her displeasure. "Besides, I'll enjoy this. Maybe you could come down after we've met the judge's deadline and help outline the next half of the project? I don't want you to spend too much time by yourself."

Her dad squeezed her hand. "I'll have family around, and I won't be alone. And I'll be checking in on my precious Gem."

She kissed him goodbye and waved to the transport until it left the last of her sight. The scent of orange blossoms carried on the breeze, and she felt a tug from somewhere deep within her gut. It was like the call from a jealous lover who wanted her back. She recognized the insistent command. It was the manor. She'd heard its signal twice before now.

The winds slipped around her, silky and gentle as a lover's tempting caress, and she stiffened her resolve.

The upheaval that rode on the appearance of calm.

Something or someone in the manor wanted her there; she could feel it. That someone was either the new beginning her father wanted for her or the darker spirit of Benjamin Alcott that she feared waited for her.

CHAPTER 6

Gemma wheeled her black suitcase down the rest of the tree-canopied dirt drive. Bits of dry dust from the path kicked up in the breeze, and she tasted the bland on her lips. Due to the delays of the accident and the arrival of the PGA golf tour in town, she'd lost her room at The Elliott House Bed and Breakfast. Every hotel in town was booked. She would have to stay at the manor for a couple of weeks, at least until the tour left and people cleared out.

One, two, three, four, five...

She mentally counted her steps toward Alcott Manor and tried to connect with it.

To her, houses were like people. They had a history, a personality, a public and a private side. They had positive attributes that needed emphasizing, negative aspects that needed minimizing, and even wounds that needed healing. When she restored a house, she had to address all those areas. That meant she would have to learn everything there was to know about Alcott Manor, inside and out, and she wasn't looking forward to it.

Six, seven, eight.

THE HAUNTING OF ALCOTT MANOR

She focused her steps into more of a determined march toward the manor, and tiny bits of shell crunched beneath her black boots.

Nine, ten, eleven, twelve.

The sun was setting behind her, and its rays cast a golden warmth on this majestic piece of architecture. What should have been a photo-perfect sight didn't strike Gemma that way. Properties undergoing restoration work as this one was typically carried the energy of new life, rebirth, and excitement. Alcott Manor didn't. Troubled memories were lodged to the brim in the fibers of this home, and they detracted from its beauty.

The same white van she'd seen on the day she'd approached the manor with her father was parked out front. Private Eyes was imprinted on the side, just above a pair of binoculars and the scripted line Confidential Workplace Security.

"Good. They're still following Pop's instruction."

She ran her hand along a pillar on the porch and sensed a dark, downward pull toward the ground. This house was deeply and fully anchored to the land. Not by good things, but by tragedy.

She'd seen it a long time ago on older restoration projects that she'd worked on with her mother. A house that had weathered a significant difficulty became defined by its energetic imprints. The house was stuck at that point in time, so to speak, such that any future events were flavored by the negative ones. Bad luck, some people said. Negative energetic imprint, Gemma said.

With Alcott Manor, her theory was that when Anna Alcott died on this property, her death set off a chain of events that cursed the land and would destroy people's lives for over a hundred years.

It was likely that there were many deeply negative experiences that had rooted themselves here, and the effects of Anna's death upon the land might not be the only problem. No job was so simplistic as to have only one issue.

Stuck energy didn't take too long to find. Her clearing work was most effective when she knew the history of the home, as well as the most intimate details of the people who had lived there. Healing specific events was far more powerful than just working on generally stagnant areas.

She knew if she could heal the land and the tragic memories that were held within it, there would be a domino effect for anyone affiliated with Alcott Manor.

First and foremost, the home would be fully restored, and the Alcott family members who owned the property would be able to keep their ancestral home. Benjamin, the ghost who probably still lived in the house, might finally be able to cross over. Her father and his company would get paid, their debts would be satisfied, and he could retire. He could then sell his company, which would allow his employees, many of whom were either family or like family, to keep their jobs. Most importantly, her dad's pride and honor would be intact.

She scanned the area to make sure no one was watching, then placed one palm firmly on the curve of one of the pillars. It was her way of reading the manor's energetic meter. She felt a slow vibration then heard a low moan, the kind of deep suffering that rose from the depths of a man's soul. She jerked her hand away. The moan subsided.

"My God." This dark energy ran deeper than she'd suspected. She held her hand just to the outside of the pillar. With her eyes slightly open, she hummed a low chant, the pattern of it just like her mother had learned from her ancestors. It was designed to call up the negativity trapped in an object, and with concentration and intent, it did.

She envisioned a violet flame next to her, one she would use to destroy the darkness. As if it were ready to leave, a swell of black energy rose to her palm. She let it fill her hand until it finally broke free. Nonchalantly, she tossed it into the flame and a burning scent filled the air.

She gazed up at the manor and pressed her teeth together. There was a tiny bit of free in the house now. A handful of light that was a signal to the manor and its spectral inhabitants that transformation was coming and good things were on the way.

She shifted into restoration mode now and made a few notes while she strolled along the wide front porch: *Get four white, armed rocking chairs (what old Southern home would be complete without them?), two square planters (consider large blooms, maybe blue, lots of green, trailing ivy), place wind chimes in alcoves before judge's visit for subtle aesthetics and to imprint/encourage more positive reactions in the area.*

She knew it would have been faster if she could have typed all her notes electronically on her tablet, but the muscles of her hand much preferred the feel of script against paper as opposed to the tapping of icons.

It was the end of the day and a few workers walked toward the dirt drive by way of the side of the house. She caught sight of one man who stood at the edge. The ocean breeze blew his thin, brown hair away from his face. It was Asher. The man she'd seen at The Iron Skillet that morning. What the hell was he—

"Ah!" Her foot gave way to an unexpected hole and she fell to her knee.

She hissed inward through her teeth and pressed her stinging palms against her jeans. She carefully removed her leg from the hole and examined the boards that were new and freshly painted. The edges of the wood were splintered as though someone had used a crowbar or hammer to break into it. She clicked her ballpoint pen and made a note inside her portfolio: *Repair front porch.*

Old hinges from the double front door groaned, and she stepped around to see who'd opened it. A young man in his early thirties stared at her with greenish-brown eyes so unique she found herself wondering their exact color. Cinnamon, she wanted to say. But with a heavy dash of seafoam-green that kept them from being too dark.

His countenance was thick and well-guarded. His lips were full and smooth, and with an uncharacteristic appetite, she wanted to run her fingertips against them, to feel the life and warmth that ran beneath.

There was no greeting, just an intense stare that questioned the reason for her presence. She cleared her throat to return herself to her more typical stance of professionalism. "I'm Gemma Stewart." Tom must have forgotten to tell him she was coming today.

"Are you...Henry Alcott? I think you know my father, who worked onsite for the past year." She put her hand out and pressed her lips together in her most professional smile. It was the smile that pulled a little tight but showed a lot of effort and willingness to get along. People usually responded well to that smile.

His stare intensified for a moment so long that she thought maybe he wasn't her father's client. He sighed in apparent and deliberate consideration of her. "I am," he finally said, with a long, rounded *I*. His genteel Southern dialect was seductive, its slowness matching the lazy cadence of their surroundings. He extended his hand to meet her own. "Henry Alcott."

To her surprise, his wasn't the overly aggressive handshake that many successful men offered. It was firm and slow and gave her the impression that he hadn't been expecting her, as though he were somehow trying to figure her out.

"I hope Tom let you know that I was on my way."

He eyed their still-joined hands. A distant light sparked in his eyes, and one corner of his mouth tipped up in the slightest of grins. As if it were fresh and new, as if he didn't smile that often, and as if something about her or the way they touched had inspired it.

She silently cursed his too-good looks: *Perfection*. Also known as *fool's bait*. The central part of her heart slipped itself into a knot in an effort to resist feeling the temptation at hand.

"Tom? With the Historic District Commission? Was he able to let you know I was coming today?"

"Tom's out today. But you must be with Stewart Historical Renovation."

"Yes. Sorry. I—yes. Glenn Stewart is my father, and I'm helping him out for a few months."

Henry Alcott stood a towering six-feet-four and was far younger than she'd expected. And since he had invested several million on this historic renovation, she had an older image in mind. Older and pudgier. Maybe even pasty from all those hours spent inside of an office earning money.

Here he stood, on his mostly finished front porch, a near shoulder-length tumble of black, wavy hair, a self-possessed, brooding expression, and a thin, inch-long scar beneath his right eye. He was a rough and steady picture of fitness and health with a tool belt slung low around his hips. The sleeves of his loose white shirt were rolled to the elbow and revealed strong, tanned forearms smudged with dark brown dirt and touches of white paint.

Her suspicions were now confirmed as to why her father wanted her to meet Henry Alcott. He was handsome, wealthy, evidently successful, and in a word—perfect. Everything a father would want for his daughter. If this was what the wind was trying to sell her into, she wasn't buying.

"You're doing a little work on the house yourself?" She pointed to the tool belt and shifted her weight. Nerves over his unexpected attractiveness made her body feel gangly and not quite her own. She struggled with where to put her free hand, trying it across her waist, then hanging straight. She finally decided on her hip.

"As much as I can."

She distracted herself with the history that sheltered its owner. "My father tells me that some of the bigger issues we tackled a year or so ago have been wrapped up. We have a tight deadline, so my goal will be to get the remaining work done early. We don't want to worry about meeting the judge's inspection deadline, so I've asked Tom to double the workforce. Maybe put a night shift in place. As long as we can push straight through our list without interruptions, we should be fine."

"Except those are something of a problem around here." His hypnotic stare flustered the professional boundary she'd brought with her, and she felt her typically pale cheeks flush warm.

"Yes, I've heard about them. The interruptions. Could this be a minor example?" She pointed to the hole in the porch without turning her head.

He turned slowly, his gaze the last to follow. His sigh was exasperated, slow and heavy. He kneeled and peered inside the hole. "Clear view to the underworld of my front porch. Whatever that got them."

"You know who did this?"

"Possibly."

"Prowlers or someone more...paranormal?"

"Prowlers, I believe." Henry's face was steady and unbothered by the suggestion of a paranormal source of destruction. But a chill fell over his tone, and the light she'd noticed just a moment ago was now gone. Damage to property or a project could do that.

She looked around for the man from the cafe who had been standing to the side of the house, but no one was there.

"I would guess they threaded a small camera below to see if they could find anything."

"Why would prowlers look under your front porch?"

He dusted his hands on his thighs. "The manor is rumored to have all sorts of treasures hidden within its walls, Ms. Stewart. From Anna Alcott's missing suicide note to valuable pieces of her jewelry to property deeds to Benjamin Alcott himself. If you plan to work on this restoration, I hope you know what you're getting into." His tone reflected a mix of irritation, bitter impatience, and perhaps a loss of faith.

She simultaneously shivered at the thought of Benjamin Alcott being on the other side of that front door and bristled at Henry's hostile tone. "Any truth to those rumors?"

Factual. Keep it factual. Objective. I am not going to be scared away from this job. Or pushed away, either, for that matter.

Henry welcomed her inside the manor with a gentlemanly wave of his arm, though his face remained unemotional. "This home has a unique history. I would caution you to think twice before engaging in any work here."

When she crossed the threshold, a subtle force tugged at the center of her being and welcomed her into the home. It was the same sensation she'd felt yesterday at the hospital and last week on the beach. The house seemed to be the origin of it.

She quickly felt a part of the manor, as though she'd just been accepted into the family. She took it as a good sign that bode well for the healing work she needed to do. Maybe it was also a sign that she was where she needed to be—some guidance, perhaps. Maybe this change would be a positive, as her dad had suggested.

She rubbed the back of her neck and noticed that her body wasn't buying into her own words of comfort. But that really didn't matter. This was where she had to be. For now, anyway.

"I'm aware of this home's history, Mr. Alcott, as well as its eccentricities. None of that is a concern. I'm here to finish a job for my father's company. It's very important that I meet this deadline. As I think it would be for you, as well."

Henry Alcott's mouth parted in apparent consideration—or maybe it was surprise—in light of her firm response. When he finally spoke, he said, "Well, I doubt you are aware of *all* the home's 'eccentricities', as you put it. And I must say, I question how much of the restoration you can complete in the time we have left. Your car accident placed our restoration dreams firmly in the past." His stare was cold enough that it left a chill on her skin, but his words lit a flame of fury in her gut.

Jackass. It's all about you, isn't it? Never mind the fact that we almost lost our lives. Self-obsessed clients were one of the many reasons why she had lost interest in historical renovations.

"I don't know nearly as much about this home as I need to know for my work. I'm hoping you'll educate me on all the facets of its personality and history. In terms of what we can get done, I've had plenty of experience running large restoration jobs like this." She placed both hands out in front as if she could ward off the curse of an objection. "I know you've had setbacks, and the accident didn't help any of us. But I'm not running the job alone. Tom will still be onsite to help. We're going to get this done."

She flashed her most professional smile, once again, as a show of respect. Only this time, she felt the fury from her gut filter through her stare. This may be his house, but he was not going to get in the way of the job she had to do.

Henry didn't offer a response and his solemn expression didn't give any clues as to how he felt about her taking her father's place. She knew she was his last hope to save his ancestral home. And she knew that if Benjamin was indeed in this house that the proverbial deck was stacked against them. Henry needed her. And she needed him, too. She had to know what he knew about the house and its history so she could get her clearing work done.

The house was filled with the distant and intermittent harshness of banging hammers and whirring electric saws. Muscled men in yellow safety vests, jeans, and light brown work boots lumbered through the far end of the foyer. The circus of activity, along with bright work lights and a flood of natural sunlight, calmed her. She had grown up around restorations, and she felt quite at home around them.

Even in a sketchy situation like Alcott Manor, there could be protection in numbers. With enough people around twenty-four-seven, she might be able to get through this after all.

Besides, she thought optimistically, on a job several years ago where she helped her mother clear some land, her mother told Gemma she had walked right through a ghost. She never even noticed. So, if there was a ghost in this house, maybe she wouldn't notice this time, either.

"I'll be completely honest with you, Ms. Stewart. I don't have much faith left that this restoration can be completed, by you or anyone else. But especially not by you."

Jackass. Jackass. Unbelievable Jackass!

"Really, Mr. Alcott?" She gave him a broader version of the professional smile she'd flashed him twice already, and she hoped this one irritated him. This was her political smile—her say-what-you-will-you-won't-get-to-me smile. "And why is that?"

"Aside from the fact that we hardly have any time left before the deadline hits and you've lost two-thirds of your management team? I have my reasons."

"I'm going to assume that those reasons have to do with

your past disappointments and not because I'm a female and working this project without our silver-haired patriarch. I have a contractual and familial obligation to be here and to complete this work. Doing so will be a lot more effective with your help. But if I have to complete this work without your support—you should know that I will."

She nodded at the end of her last sentence to hopefully land on a note of finality. *That* needed to be the end of *that*.

Jackass.

She turned toward the focal point of the black and white marbled entrance hall, which was a large, gold, six-paneled chandelier. Its bright light shone against faux-marbled walls.

Faux. Who in the hell puts faux in a house that was on the National Register?

Two security cameras were nearly hidden in the corners.

"Ms. Stewart. I would ask you one last time to reconsider your intent to restore this home. You can't possibly be aware—"

"I've done my research. I know about the paranormal nature of the home's identity. I'm also aware that you—we—have had a lot of setbacks. I'm prepared to help with that and to meet this deadline. Come hell or high water." She didn't discuss how she would help. It wasn't necessary for him to be aware of her gifts or how she planned to use them. She spoke with such strength that she almost had herself convinced that she wouldn't be bothered by anything that went bump in the night.

"We have had more than our fair share of setbacks. And hell and high water, as well. None of that will stop just because you're here."

She studied the walls and the faux treatment, and while her back was toward Henry, she rolled her eyes at his arrogance. He was too much like Preston—too much money, too good looking, and it all added up to a deficit in character.

When she spun around, she noticed a black curl that had fallen to the side of his forehead. She wanted to punch him for his crap attitude and then lick that place on his neck, right next to the length of another curl.

She cleared her throat. "I'm up to the challenge. I'm going to assume you are, as well."

Henry tipped his chin up just a little and looked over her face, as if he measured her strength, as if he considered her comments. And maybe, in that slight softening of his stare, as if he appreciated her appearance. Finally, he nodded. "All right. If you really are, then I am, as well."

Gemma tapped the wall with her finger and tried to ignore how her body acted. Or reacted. She didn't need another gorgeous jerk in her life. Even if she were willing to eat from this beautiful, poisonous Alcott tree, she couldn't. This man was her father's client, and he was smack in the eye of a no-touch territory.

"Good. You don't have to like me, Mr. Alcott. But I do know how to move this job forward. All we have to do is get through the next few weeks together to meet this deadline. After that, my father will be back to run the show, I'll go back to my own business, and you'll never have to lay eyes on me again."

"There will be a condition to my support—"

Gemma was already across the room and scratching at the faux with her fingernail, her teeth set firm. She closed her eyes against a wave of frustration.

No. No conditions.

She would do this her way, not his way. He had no clue how to fix the problems of this house.

She moved on. He would have to catch the hint. "Whose call was the faux marble treatment? I can't imagine that the original plans for the house called for *faux*."

"Ah, Tom hired a rather young woman named Paisley to

help with some design and management issues while you were delayed. I believe the faux may have been her call." His tone was drizzled with bitterness, and she knew she caught the hint.

"Paisley? As in—the print?" She made another note in her portfolio and shook her head.

"Yes, exactly. She's not very tactful, but she seems to have some talent for tying together the many loose ends of a large project."

"Mmm."

"From what I've seen so far, anyway."

She examined the faux treatment. She definitely didn't agree with this choice, but if the gal had some good project management skills, maybe she could make use of that. Gemma needed time to figure out where the heaviest imprints were, then she had to go about her process of healing them. In a house this big, that would take time. Maybe she could rely on Paisley to take a few things over.

Henry leaned slightly to the side and glanced out the window. "There she is now, actually."

She peeked out the window just in time to see a large moving truck back into an unloading position at the front door. The truck's reverse signal cried in cadenced beeps while a very skinny twenty-something girl with long, crow feather black hair directed the movers.

"The upstairs is completely finished, so they're moving the original Alcott bedroom furniture back into the house."

Gemma thought she caught a sparkle of something like Christmas morning excitement in Henry's eyes. Perhaps he was encouraged now by seeing the potential of final success. "Was it in storage?"

"The Charleston Museum of History had it on display for the past fifty years or so. The house wasn't restored enough to protect antiques like these." He nodded to the truck.

"Tom and Paisley thought the authentic staging would make a good impression on the judge."

"I agree with that. Shall we go outside to see the furniture?"

Henry's head rocked in a half nod, and his lips parted slightly. "Ah, no. I have something else to discuss with you. We'll see the furniture once it's in place."

His tone was serious and in control. He was a man with an agenda. Sadly, some part of her liked the feeling of being marched to this principal's office—jerk that he had shown himself to be thus far.

Yes, she was up to the challenge.

Gad. What sort of sick star was she born under that he was who she was attracted to? She turned and wheeled her black bag off to the side so she could ignore the way his tanned chest peeked through the top opening in his shirt. "Something happened to the original marble, I guess?" She tapped the wall when she passed by.

No conditions, Mister Alcott.

"Someone knocked a large hole into the center of it with an instrument of some kind. I don't think it was repairable within our current deadline."

She scowled at the wall. She still would rather have had the authentic marble. "Faux doesn't belong in a renovation project like this one. Flat paint or wallpaper would have been the better design choice. This is too distracting." She made another note. "Since this isn't a huge space, I'm going to have the painters add a couple of coats of golden yellow here."

His glance combed over the foyer, and she didn't wait to hear if he agreed with her. He was going to have to take a backseat. If he could have done this without her, he would have already.

"What do you do when you aren't helping your father in his business?"

"I have my own business. I work with hotels and spas and individual clients to create relaxing and healing environments. Like retreats. My dad mentioned he was having some new security installed—are these cameras new?" She brought the conversation back to business. She had a deadline to meet.

"These have been there for a while." Henry pointed to the rectangular cameras in the eaves. "The gentleman installing the additional security is out back at the moment. On the porch, I believe."

"Okay, great. Pop has always had a good sense about these things, and I don't want to drop the ball on any of his ideas. He was hiring a security guard, too."

Henry nodded toward the kitchen. "His name is Everett Hines. He started the other day."

"Perfect."

"He actually worked here on the property when another restoration firm tried to finish the house. He's full of stories."

Gemma ignored the reference to a firm that wasn't successful with the house, and she took a last look at Paisley, just in time to see two movers bump an antique secretary against the doorway of the truck. Paisley's hands flew to her head.

The jury was definitely out on how well Paisley could manage things—she did look awfully young. And she ought to have hired movers who had experience with antiques. Gemma hoped Henry didn't see what happened to the desk.

"I guess you've recovered from the accident?"

"Just had a bump to the head. Devoted seatbelt wearer." She raised her hand as if this admission were a sworn testament. She was trying a little humor to try to lighten the tension. They were going to have to work together on this job, and she'd rather he chill a little. "Janey and my father are still recuperating. We're all very lucky, really. Could have been so much worse."

But her efforts didn't work. He didn't laugh or even smile. He only kicked a few loose pieces of plaster aside. They approached one of the bookshelves that reached toward the high ceilings of the library. "I'm not sure how it could have been worse."

Disgust rose within her at his comment. *They could have died. Don't you think that could have been worse? Yes, it is all about your house. We've now confirmed that beyond a doubt.* She glanced at the fresco on the ceiling and quickly realized where they were. The artist who restored that painting died in this very room. She hadn't had time to ask her father, but she assumed the artist was one of his team members.

The bullish confidence she'd conjured before she entered the manor faded in this empty room. Anxiety painted the inside of her chest as broadly as the colors on the ceiling. She knew about the heinous things that ghosts could do to a person. They weren't all harmless footsteps or bodiless voices in the dark as folklore would have you believe.

She drew in a deep inhale that hitched at the peak. It was time to get on with the research she needed to do so she could clear the land. She needed to know where Anna was killed so she could start her work at *that* location first.

Henry strolled with his arms clasped behind his back. "I'm not sure how much your father told you about the manor. But we do have a resident ghost. That would be our esteemed Benjamin Alcott, one of the original owners of the manor. He's one of the manor's *eccentricities*, as you called them." His voice lowered, and a hint of concern colored the edges when he spoke about the ghost.

She visually measured the distance between the ceiling where the artist had painted the fresco and the hardwood floor where he'd fallen. "Yes, I'm aware of Benjamin. Do you think he's dangerous?" The words walked out of her mouth in a slow procession, each of them heavily weighted with her worst fear.

He stepped in front of her confrontationally, and she wondered if he was about to present his...*condition*.

"Over the years, some people have died here. General consensus is that he was the one who killed them."

She swallowed hard, lifted one of the several antique books that were scattered on the floor, and placed it gently on the bookcase.

"You can move them if you like. But tomorrow morning, they'll be all over the floor again."

She lifted another book and held it mid-air. "Because...Benjamin?"

When he took the book from her, their thumbs grazed against one another. It was a simple and subtle touch, insignificant under any other circumstance, but something electric stirred between them with this connection.

His gaze locked with hers for a moment longer than necessary, until he nodded with the slow certainty of experience. "We believe so."

She tried to ignore the warmth that flushed in her cheeks, and she made a mental note to stack the books on the floor the night before the judge arrived. "The same books?"

Henry cleared his throat and stepped away. "Different books. He seems to search for something, and he just moves anything aside that might be in his way. Sometimes the damage he leaves behind is a minor mess, like these books." He picked up several volumes and returned them to the lowest shelf. "Other times, he rips open walls. The wreckage has been so significant that he's scared away every renovation company so far, nearly putting some of them out of business. Except for yours, of course. I'm sure yours will be different." Sarcasm coated his last few words.

It will be different. Watch and see, Mister Alcott.

She knew he wasn't saying this to help her understand the house and its history. He was trying to scare her off. Push her away. He'd lost faith that his ancestral home could be saved.

She would turn this discussion in a direction to suit her research needs. "You think there's truth to the story that he's trying to find proof of his innocence?"

Henry ran his fingertips against the frayed bindings of a row of books. "From what I've seen over the years? I'd have to say yes."

It was unusual to see someone as accomplished as Henry say that he believed in ghosts. People didn't usually believe in the paranormal unless they'd had an experience that gave them reason to. A slow chill crawled along her arms. "Have you seen him?"

Henry leaned against the edge of the bookcase, tall and strong, and she saw a flash of something on his face she hadn't expected. Something completely incongruous to the strength of his confidence. Fear. Was he trying to get her to leave the manor for some reason other than he'd lost faith in a successful restoration?

"I've seen his handiwork."

"Recent...handiwork?"

"Pretty recent."

She realized she must have appeared pale or concerned or something, because he asked, "Are you bothered by ghosts, Ms. Stewart?"

"Ah, no." Her laugh sounded more nervous than she'd intended. She gave her head a little shake and tossed her hair, both to look casual and to fend off questions. "No."

"Well, that's good." From his expression, she could tell he didn't believe her.

She didn't believe herself, either. There was nothing left to do in the library except to shake the creepy crawly feeling from her skin. Too much talk of ghosts and murder left her with that out-of-control feeling that the past could repeat. She glanced at the fresco on the ceiling again and fought the shiver that worked its way along her skin.

"You're certain that you won't be bothered by Benjamin?"

She wasn't going to tell him the truth. Clients didn't want to play therapist; they wanted their work done, and they were usually happy to let you jump through all sorts of sacrificial hoops to that end. Besides, it didn't matter what bothered her. She had a job to do.

She turned around to answer him and found him closer than she'd expected.

"Oh!" She put her hand out and could have touched his chest he was so close. "I'm fine. I don't see ghosts. I never have. If I were to come across Benjamin, I'd probably never know it. So, I'm really not concerned about that. My worry is that he might further wreck our restoration efforts, and we have such a tight deadline. We don't have the bandwidth to redo much of anything."

A subtle spiced scent rose off his skin, and she breathed it in, against her better judgment.

Criminy.

He was a *client*. *Her father's* client, no less.

Do not smell the clients.

"Do you know much about the story of Benjamin Alcott?" He asked the question more like he was issuing a warning. As in, "Did you know that sharks hunt in these waters where you're swimming?"

She glanced at her black boots—dust and dirt from the front drive covered the tips and edges of them. "Some. I was hoping to learn more about him and his house from you." It dawned on her that much of the hammering and sawing she'd heard when she first entered the house had gone quiet. She strained to hear noise from the workers. She had wanted them on task around the clock as she had suggested to Tom

THE HAUNTING OF ALCOTT MANOR

—not just a double shift during the day. A busy home was a less haunted home.

"Then I'll share a little bit of it with you." His tone was condescending as he led them down the hallway. "Anna was shot and killed one night during a party that celebrated Benjamin's nomination to run for President of the United States. He claimed that Anna had killed herself and that there had been a suicide note. But several people saw Benjamin holding the gun and standing over his wife's dead body. No one ever found the note, either, so he was hung for her murder.

"Since then, his spirit has often been seen here, angry and searching. Every morning, for over a century, there has been evidence of his nighttime efforts. Initially, there were simple stories of furniture moved or drawers left open. Doors that were usually locked were found ajar. As time passed, the family found holes in the walls and other such damage.

"When the restorations began, the damage got significantly worse. For the record, your restoration won't go any differently than the others. He won't want you here. You'll not be—effective."

Jackass.

She hung on to the s at the end of that word. *Jackasssssss.*

Someone wanted her here. If it wasn't Benjamin, it was the house—the spirit of it, maybe. In a possessive way, she knew. She just didn't know why. "Mr. Alcott, I have a plan—"

"Which brings me to my condition." His voice became quite loud and overbearing.

She squared off with him and crossed her arms in front of herself. And though she had to look up to him to do so, she did look him directly in the eye. "Fine. I'll hear your condition, but I can't promise that I'll agree to it."

He closed the distance between them. One deliberate

step and then another. She caught sight of her chest rising and falling more quickly. He affected her, she knew.

She was surprised to see the soft, focused look in his eyes when he leaned toward her. She knew this expression. She'd first seen it in college when Bobby Ellsworth saw her across the room at his fraternity Halloween party. It was the kind of look a man had when he was attracted, maybe even entranced with you.

"If you want to make sure that Benjamin won't get in our way, then you'll have to find proof that he didn't kill his wife. Finding that suicide note is the only way that the restoration will go off without a hitch this time."

She cocked her head to the side. "I'm sorry, *what*?"

"I need you to find Anna's suicide letter."

She couldn't believe what he was saying. "How is finding this suicide note even a valid possibility? After all this time? I mean, he might have actually killed her. Maybe there never was a note."

A darkness shadowed Henry's face before he answered. It was only there for the breadth of a moment, and she doubted he even knew it had slipped his composed demeanor. She forced a swallow down her tight throat and braced herself. Bad news was coming.

"Ms. Stewart, if you don't find the letter, Benjamin will ruin your chances of completing this renovation on time. I've seen it too many times."

She nodded and felt her mouth open, but no words passed over her lips. Now she understood why her father had avoided going into detail about Henry. He knew how she would have felt about this kind of crazy request.

If there ever was a suicide note, it would have already been found by now. No. She simply needed to get her crew to work and to finish this job.

A diplomatic response would work best. "Okay. I'll make sure all the workers know to keep their eyes open for this note. If anyone finds it, I'll have them deliver it to you immediately.

"Other than that, I can't offer a guarantee that I or anyone else can find this proof that may have been hidden in this house for a hundred and thirty years. I will make darn sure we get this renovation job done, and I'm going to handle it differently than the other firms have. I've got this. You'll just have to trust me on that."

He scoffed. "No offense. But after so many attempts at restoration, I'm clean out of trust. Your agreement to find the letter is the condition you'll have to meet if you want my support on this job."

The air sparked between them with the electric mix of frustration and attraction.

Damn it! If she could have left, she would have. On the spot. She would even have slammed the door behind her in a childishly satisfying way. This had to be the most ridiculous request she'd ever heard of. With hardly enough time to complete the restoration, the last thing she needed to do was to head down a waste-of-time rabbit trail that could ruin everything.

"It seems to me that if there was a suicide note tucked away in this house somewhere, it would have been found before now." She explained this in a common-sensical, almost grandmotherly way, and she hoped she didn't sound condescending. "What I mean is—"

"I know what you mean, and I understand. Believe me. This property has been through ninety-five restoration attempts. *Everyone* thinks they can push it forward. *No one has.* I've been through this process too many times, with too many people to know that it won't work unless we can move Benjamin out of the way." He extended his right hand to her. "I think we ought to call it quits. I'll speak with Tom."

She looked at his open hand and quickly ran through all

the business she had waiting in the wings at home. She tossed in a random figure for the amount of new business that would come in as a result of the national magazine feature.

She could pay off part of her father's business debt, then, when he was fully recovered, she could bring him out west. He could help her with her jobs. He would learn to love it. Or maybe she would just write another check for ongoing therapy for the both of them.

"This is my problem. You don't need to take this on." He pressed his open hand toward her as if to bid her *adieu*. Stoic. Resolved.

She sighed with the realization that she didn't have another card to play, and her chest ached with dread on the exhale.

Then she had an idea.

"If finding the letter is what's required to be successful with this job, then finding the suicide note is what we'll do."

"You're certain?" His voice had an x-ray quality to it, as though he searched her insides to make sure she wasn't lying.

But she lied anyway. "I am." She met his eyes with an assuring smile, one that hid her lack of genuineness. She shook his hand. Though she had no intention of letting this job get offtrack.

CHAPTER 7

Henry paced back and forth in front of the fireplace, which was tall enough that he could have walked into it without stooping. He recited the details of every restoration job he could remember, locations where workers had already searched for the suicide note, and features of the house that Benjamin had destroyed.

She thought only some of the information useful since she didn't plan to conduct a search. Like the majority of the people who were familiar with Alcott lore, she didn't believe that the suicide note had ever existed. What she had learned from her mother was that a ghost's personality in death was similar to his personality in life. Given the unexplained deaths that had occurred in this house, Benjamin the ghost, indeed, appeared to be a murderer.

Searching for a made-up suicide note wouldn't move him on, and she knew she would have to start with her healing work. Tonight. With an ounce of luck, Benjamin would be gone before morning. She'd start by clearing the land where he'd killed Anna. In a situation like this, where there had been an extreme and tragic event, she was most effective when she could work on the exact spot where it happened. First chance she had, she would ask Henry where that place was.

Right now, she had to give him a few more minutes of her attentive listening to make it look as though she would search for Anna's note.

The last of the day's sun warmed her arm and the side of her face and neck. The contrast between the gentleness of the sun's affection and the head-to-toe black she wore like armor unexpectedly softened her guard. The cause could also have been Henry's impassioned retelling of the manor's restoration history.

His voice was deep and rich as though it had been steeped in authority. She found herself rocking along with the rise and fall of his voice, swimming along its timbre until she realized he was mesmerizing her.

Snap out of it.

This was the most important job of her father's life. So that made it the most important job of her life. There was no time to be googly-eyed and hypnotized. Especially around this guy. If he thought for a minute that she found any part of him attractive, he'd humiliate her for it. She'd lose her credibility with him. Ass that he was, she needed to keep her wits about her. So far, every conversation with him was a battle.

Except for this one. Not that this was a conversation. It was a speech. He and his ego had full reign. She figured he liked it that way. Probably got along best with people when they stayed quiet.

Inane requests for century-old proof of innocence and client status aside, he was appealing, she had to admit. Rugged and handsome.

Attraction buzzed through her, something she hadn't felt for a while. She'd come to think of all romantic relationships as unnecessary risks. They felt ominous and dangerous, always worked out badly for her, and often caused irreparable damage. Same as driving at high speeds on neighborhood streets, experimental hair color, or ghosts, for that matter.

Even though most of their communication had been sparring, there was a rhythm between them that twirled to a soundless waltz. They shared a dance, one that dipped and spun and made her swoon. One that woke her up and made her feel more alive than she'd felt in years.

"Benjamin attacks when he feels someone's work might interfere with his search. He tends to leave surface-type design work alone, but deeper restoration work upsets him, and he'll undo workers' efforts by the next day. So, whatever this *plan* that you have in mind, you'll have to take that into account," he said. Condescension dripped all over the word *plan*.

And, of course, he could also be—a jackass.

"You'll also have to consider that the anniversary of Anna Alcott's death occurs on the same day as the judge's deadline. We'll need to have everything completely wrapped up that day."

She remembered from the articles that bad things—the girl and the artist who died, for starters—fell into full swing on that night.

"Right." She made a note. "Has anyone brought in a paranormal professional to see if they could get Benjamin to move on?"

"Professional." A sarcastic smile flickered with his chuckle, and he rested his hands on the waistband of his dark pants. "Quite a show, that was. The last one came in the day before you arrived. Come with me; I'll show you something that happened right after they left."

He escorted her through the wide hallways and described the psychic who came through the house. His distractingly ideal presentation made the manor shine despite the low light of the evening.

Once in the dining room, her gaze was immediately pulled to the beautifully finished coffered ceiling.

"This is the last room your father finished with his team."

The majestic size of the dining room was made nearly claustrophobic by one wall of stained glass windows. The deep reds, greens, and blues kept the last of the day's light on the outside of the house and closeted the room in a thick church-like stillness.

She stepped around the deep mantel and saw what Henry was referring to—a five-foot hole in the opposite wall that was as wide as it was tall. She sighed heavily and took in the view of the ocean that should only have been visible from the next room. "They really weren't very effective, were they?"

"Not really, no."

"Benjamin? Or vandals?"

"I think Benjamin."

"How would you know?" She desperately wanted to poke a hole in his ghost theory, even if she was wrong. She could feel her denial flexing its well-defined muscles. Disassociating, distancing—an automatic coping behavior in times of stress, so she'd been told.

"There are some typical characteristics of his work. Recently finished rooms where deep restoration work has been performed always attract his attention."

"Well." She craned to see inside the wall and found wires dangling inside the opening. "The judge won't like this when he makes his inspection. Easiest solution is to just knock out this wall entirely. This isn't a weight-bearing wall, and that morning light would go a long way to lifting the energy in this room. It's so claustrophobic in here I can barely breathe. You'd invite some beautiful views of the ocean, which is a welcoming feature in dining rooms."

She noticed Henry held an expression she'd often seen on the face of most men she'd dated, as well as a few clients. The one that said she had been too blunt.

Maybe she ought to have asked Henry his opinion first, or just tried to shave off the sharper edges of her words. Wherever those sharp edges were, she was never sure. Though what was the point of holding back when you knew the answer? Wasn't that what she was hired to do? Give answers?

She sighed and hoped to dear God that he wasn't one of those clients whose ego needed to be stroked or propped up. This would go badly if he were. She simply didn't have that skill.

He nodded once. "I'll give it some thought."

She took it as reluctant agreement and decided she would tell Tom tomorrow to take care of it.

Henry motioned toward the doorway and bowed slightly. Their footsteps played in counterbalance to one another on the wood floors.

"Let's get you settled into one of the furnished guest rooms. I think the one down the hall from my room is ready. Then I'll have dinner arranged on the back porch for us."

"Oh." Gemma stopped short. She hadn't thought of Henry staying in the house, as well.

"Unless you have other plans, of course."

"No. No plans." She found a gracious smile to offer, even though an evening with her clearing work would have been the safer option.

CHAPTER 8

Some part of that red hair must be genuine Irish, Henry thought while he watched her wrestle her bag up the stairs. She'd refused his help with her luggage and with finding her guest room, saying that she could handle both herself.

His attraction to her had been immediate, staggering, and a complete surprise to him. Since his wife's death, he'd distanced himself from romantic relationships altogether and occupied his time with work. A choice that suited his life, since there simply wasn't anyone who interested him. But now, Gemma's fiery presence reminded him what he had known in his heart when he was just a young man. That there was someone out there who was meant just for him.

He'd encouraged Gemma to leave, for reasons—not the least of which—were Benjamin. There were other dangers in the house that she didn't know about. Ghastly secrets that if he told her about them outright, she wouldn't believe him. He knew there was no point in sharing this information. Not today. Actually, he wasn't sure that it would ever make a difference since she was so determined to finish this restora-

THE HAUNTING OF ALCOTT MANOR

tion, despite the fruitlessness of it all. He'd even told her of the threat of Benjamin's destruction, a threat he knew the menacing ghost would follow through on, no matter who tried to restore the manor.

There was the possibility that the house would reveal its secrets all on its own. If that were the case, he would try everything in his power to protect her, but he knew he might not succeed.

He would give her a brief chance to make progress with the restoration. If she didn't, he would have to make sure that she left the property forever.

CHAPTER 9

After much discussion, she talked Henry into letting her find her own way to her guest room upstairs. Though he was reluctant, she was emphatic. "Been making my way through this world without help for a long time. I hardly need assistance finding a guest room." She'd said it with a closed-lipped smile at the end—professionally friendly, but serious.

In response, he had checked his watch as though they were on a schedule and finally acquiesced—which was good because what she really wanted was some distance from Henry.

It was unfortunate for her that he wasn't subtly attractive, something she could distract herself from. His appeal was more of a stunning quality. And stun her, he did. With those damn wavy locks and smoldering eyes that made her want to own some part of him. In fact, the whole presentation made her feel as though she'd been waiting her entire life just for him.

She'd watched too many Disney movies as a child.

He also had that sort of presence she couldn't escape. Some people had such a hushed way about their energy you could be in the same car with them and forget they were even there. Others might be less quiet, but you could tune them out or strengthen your focus and at least have *some* emotional distance from them.

Henry had that sort of aura that took inhabitance of you. It was impossible to get away from him. Even when you were.

She hoisted her black bag up the well-worn path that the maids and other servants would have used over the years to service the family bedrooms. She could imagine the staff from 1880 bustling around in white aprons and bonnets, wearing sensible—though probably uncomfortable—shoes. She could nearly hear the clatter of coal buckets when they brushed by her to light the fireplaces in the bedrooms for the evening.

When she was finally on the second story landing, she ran her fingers over the textured wall coverings that papered the dimly lit hallway in green and gray. She felt a subtle expansion and contraction—a slow, rhythmic inhale and exhale of the structure that owned the space she was in. The house responded to her like a cat who arched its back under her touch. She curled her hand away from the wall and pressed it to her chest. She shook it off. Houses didn't do that. This one didn't, either. "You're overtired, Gemma Rose."

She opened the first door on the right, as Henry had directed her, and was relieved to find that her guest room overlooked the ocean, just as she had requested.

When she was a child, her parents took her to the beach for several weeks to recover. From then on, she learned that waterfront views could make everything more bearable in life.

The door clicked when she closed it behind her, then she exhaled long and steady. Surely this brief time and distance from Henry would allow her the space she needed to get back on center.

He was off limits. He was someone who had way too

much control over her father's future and livelihood. She needed to stop allowing his better qualities to creep into her focus. He was just a man.

No, not a man. A client. Just a client. Well, an important client. The most important client.

Jesus.

Besides, she was not a lustful person. She had no interest in meaningless, short-term relationships. She was a professional—with a business and a life waiting for her on the west coast.

A damn good business that a lot of people were going to know about thanks to *Platinum Life*.

Plus, she didn't even really *like* him. He could be a real jackass.

Of course, she thought he was a jackass who seemed principled. Esteemed. Honest. And even though he wanted her chasing down one-hundred-year-old proof of innocence that probably didn't exist, she'd also throw in the trait of integrity. He was doing a lot to save his ancestral home and to protect its place in history.

So there. With those honorable qualities, she didn't have to worry about him even being interested in her under the circumstances. The boundary between them was safe.

And if she ever felt remotely attracted to him again, she could probably rely on him saying something offensive that would pull her head back to reality.

She tossed her phone on the bed and took in the ocean-front view from what must have been a little girl's room. It should have relaxed her. But the space smelled of paint, age, and stain. A dark feeling curled around her like wisps of smoke from an early fire. Something had gone on in here—something bad. As in, make-you-feel-ill kind of bad. She could sense tears and tragedy, disappointment and death.

The room stinks of death.

The shiver started subtly around the base of her spine and vibrated upward until both her shoulders quivered close to her ears. She thought she could do this, but she couldn't. So, no, she decided, she would not sleep in here. Or anywhere in the house. In fact, until a hotel room or rental opened up, she probably wouldn't sleep much at all. Which was fine. The golf tour wouldn't be in town forever. In the meantime, she could use this room and its adjoining bathroom for dressing and bathing. In the light of day.

After dinner with Henry, she would go to an all-night diner. There, she would sip tea, munch on a plate of hash browns, and work on her plans for the house until the sun came up. Then she'd cab it back to the manor and start work.

The twin-sized, faded cherry bed was covered in a rose-print quilt, and she tried without success to remember the last time she slept in a twin bed. A wide shelf extended around three of the four walls and was crowded with a collection of porcelain dolls. Each of them wore a unique and fancy costume, some featuring a lace-edged bonnet that tied beneath the chin. Others wore ribbons around low, curled ponytails or pigtails. A few leaned to the side, as though they slept. She frowned at several pairs of cloudy glass eyes that followed her around the room.

She opened her bag and removed a short pile of shirts. The chest of drawers had a fold-down flap, and she reached toward one of the antique pulls.

But chills crawled up her back as if she were no longer alone in the room, and she fought the temptation to turn around.

She didn't need to. She knew no one would be there when she did. At least no one that she could have seen.

Though she did work on her nerve to leave the room.

She didn't need to be consumed with crazy thoughts, either. Or rather, thoughts that would drive her crazy.

Did I sense something? Or was that my imagination?

Yes, she sensed something. Or someone. Maybe it was someone who lived here a long time ago and loved the house too much to leave. It didn't have to be Benjamin. It didn't even have to be a family member. It could have been someone who came to a party years ago and decided they didn't want to go home.

Couldn't?

She didn't know. But she did know that she would speak with Henry about this room. Some clearing needed to be done in here, and if she knew its history, her work would be more effective. Without it, her work might just not go deeply enough.

For now, she would find that all-night diner.

She'd make more calls tomorrow to find a room. Someone would have been a no-show and their room would be available. She dropped the stack of shirts and they thumped into the open suitcase.

The moonlit waves were barely visible thanks to the bright light which cast her reflection in the window. She lowered the too-bright flame on the kerosene banquet lamp that was patterned with pink dogwood blooms.

"This ought to have been converted to electric." Candles aside, she wasn't thrilled to have a flame in the room that wasn't associated with a fireplace. It wasn't a safe option.

Only a shadow of her image remained in the panes of the window. The bedside table lamp was low enough, and she stared at the illuminated movement of the ocean. She listened to the peaceful crashing of its waves against the sand and thought about what she would tell Henry as to why she would have to step out for the night. A cricket chirped from somewhere inside the room and she jumped.

Calm down, girl. Just gather your things and leave.

He'd guessed that she was uncomfortable with ghosts.

Who wasn't disturbed by them? She could just come clean with him about how she wasn't going to stay here at night. He would say something jackass-y, she would toss him a bullet-proof smile, and they'd move on. Being away from the manor at night wasn't going to ruin the job.

Something creaked behind her and her body twitched. This time, she did turn around, though only an empty room was laid out before her. She was alone, excepting the dolls, some of whom returned her stare. She laughed and rubbed her hand across her stomach. It had been a long time since she'd experienced the continual unquiet of an older home.

She returned her gaze to the ocean and found it fading in the dark, so she listened for the waves. She never tired of that sound. It could regulate her breathing and bring her to a sense of calm in no time.

She could clearly see her reflection in the window and her hair shone brightly, like fire around her pale face.

"Your great grandmother had red hair, just like you," her dad often said when she was little. She leaned closer to the window and tucked a piece of loose hair into her ponytail. And in that one unguarded moment, a tall man in a black suit passed behind her in the reflection.

Her hand flew to her throat and fear grabbed her heart in a tight fist that locked down hard.

The low flicker of the kerosene lamp cast itself against the empty, semi-dark room.

No one here. No one here. Just get your things and get out.

Only she knew someone was there. She could feel his chilled presence on every inch of her skin. And she had seen him.

They did that, damned ghosts. They would walk around you and just out of your sight until some reflective surface would pick up what you couldn't.

He won't want you here. Henry had said something like that.

She thought of the artist and the young girl who had died here. Yes, maybe Benjamin really was a murderer.

She forced her body to move, even though every part of her was cement block solid on the inside. One short stride to the left. Then another. She counted: one, two, three, four... like it was her job to do so.

Her feet blindly sidestepped their way toward the bed to recover her phone, the sill of the windowed wall pressed firmly against her lower back. Breath barely entered or left her lungs.

When her feet reached the bedside, she found something else to count: dolls, from right to left. One, two, three, four, five... While she counted, her fingers searched along the soft quilt where she'd tossed her phone. There was something odd about the texture of it—wet and sticky. She cringed and privately chastised herself for not noticing the mess before she threw her phone into it.

There it was. The hard-curved edge of the phone case. A small touch of comfort. A little bit of control.

Her eyes dropped to find her hand and phone enmeshed in a puddle of red. Blood red and sickly sweet. Her body drew even more rigid and her mouth opened in a scream too filled with terror to find its voice.

"Mama? Are you okay, Mama?" A tiny voice asked from across the room.

She gasped and couldn't help but look in the direction of the voice. A warbled doll's voice. A far away child's voice. Like someone had pulled the string on its back to make it open its foggy eyes and say, "Mama, you're bleeding!"

She raced across the room and twisted and yanked repeatedly on the brass doorknob that would only turn an inch to the left and an inch to the right.

I didn't lock the door. I didn't lock the door. I didn't lock the door.

The door wouldn't open.

She could feel the man in the black suit reaching for her. She all but felt his cold hand on her back, his chill shooting through her clothes and hitting her skin while his fingers curled around her shoulder. Working, for whatever reason, to keep her in this room. In this house. With him.

"Mama!" the child's voice cried.

She banged on the door and hoped that Henry, who would probably still be downstairs, would hear her and come running. "Henry!"

Surely, he would come running.

"Open the door. Damn it, open!" Her heart thumped so loudly in her chest she knew she was going to have a heart attack. Its rapid beat sent blood hurtling against her head, and she thought for a moment that everything might just burst beyond her skin in a fit of terror...her heart, her blood.

Mama, you're bleeding!

"Henry! Help!" She banged on the door with a closed fist. She didn't care now if he knew how scared she was, or that she really was afraid of ghosts. She just needed—

"Help!"

Her screams were louder than any noise she'd ever heard from her own mouth. And when the locked doorknob turned cold in her hand, the screams came faster, one after the other. The loudest one yet came when the door finally released, and she slammed into the solid chest of Henry Alcott.

CHAPTER 10

He grabbed her, both hands firmly on the sides of her arms. "Gemma!"

She wrestled free and dashed down the stairs two and three at a time. She clung tight to the railing with both hands but still lost her footing on the bottom few steps and hit the final floor on both hands and knees. She stumbled through the kitchen and out the back door and didn't stop until she reached the wide grassy lawn that stretched just beyond the back porch.

She inhaled the salty ocean mist that floated on the wisps of fog. To her, that scent had always been a magical elixir that simultaneously calmed and lifted her spirits, though tonight, it wasn't nearly enough.

Henry caught up with her. "Gemma—"

"I'm fine. I'm fine." Though everything inside of her shivered as if she'd just been taken from icy waters. Her breath showed on the air with each shaky exhale.

"Let's sit for a minute." The warmth of his hand on her back was calming and comforting, but when he turned her toward the house, she resisted.

"Just over here." He pointed to the open-air back porch where a candlelit dinner had been arranged on a table set for two.

"Tell me what happened." Missing from his voice was every trace of the attitude she'd witnessed earlier. All that was evident now was compassion and an interest to help her.

She tried to answer but honestly couldn't figure out where to start the story. When she was unable to stop shaking, he gathered her into his arms and they sat together on the deep wicker couch that, in daylight, would overlook the horizon.

When he drew her close, the fit and the comfort of their bodies came together easily. Ready-made. She'd not expected Henry to have this soft side to his personality—let alone one that offered her such a casual familiarity.

"He wore a black suit," she said and tried to summon the motivation to pull away. "And there was blood." She examined her hand though it remained as clean as it had since she'd left her room. She placed her palm on Henry's chest and she rubbed her thumb over a bit of fabric, silently counting each stroke.

One...two...three...

He held her closer and stroked her hair. She realized she couldn't remember walking to the porch.

Panic attack. She'd had them before. Always around something ghost related. After which, she could remember very little.

Engage every sense, the therapist had taught her long ago. *Ground yourself, get into your body by noticing what you hear, see, smell, and so on.*

Henry's soft touch stroked her hair again, and somewhere in the back of her mind was a warning that she was crossing a boundary with an important client. But she couldn't move away. Not yet.

She clung to him and focused on the sounds and scents

around her—the symphony of crickets and bullfrogs that filled the air between crashing waves, the sweet, earthy scent that rose from Henry's chest, the solid feel of his body against her palm.

Inside, she felt like she had when she was a child. Terrified, struggling for air, trying to figure out why someone wanted to hurt her when she'd done nothing to them.

Henry's strokes were soft and slow. He didn't encourage her to sit up or to calm down or to be brave. She'd expected him to do all of that. Because that's what people did when they were uncomfortable with emotions. But he didn't. He simply held her, and she thought he understood the quiet comfort she needed.

The slow rise and fall of his chest released an exhale that caressed her temple and drifted across her cheek. This was the most even, patient contentment she could remember in recent years. The gentleness of his whisper touch replaced her panic inch by inch, breath by breath. In their silence, she listened for the next wave to crash on the sand. And then the next one. And the next one, as well. Until, like the tender opening of a flower petal, she noticed kindness. Then trust. It wasn't long before she felt she was in the center of a steadiness of all that was good in the world.

She took it in, like a memory. Like a long-ago melody she'd known from her childhood—one she'd forgotten, one she'd ached to hear again. She let it play for as long as it would.

She wasn't sure at what point her trembling had stopped. She only noticed that it had. There was quiet, as much as nature afforded.

And in that quiet, as it often happened these days, a vision wormed its way into her heart. Its presence shifted from side to side until it forced its way past her defenses: Preston's ecstasy-filled face popped into her mind, the one from the night she'd surprised him at his office. She squeezed her eyes shut to push the mental photograph away.

She sat upright and brushed the hair from her face, then swallowed against an old, familiar pain in her throat.

"Here." Henry filled a glass with wine and placed it in her hands. She drank a long sip and inhaled apple, citrus, and melon that rose from the glass. The scent reminded her of summer afternoons and jumping through the lawn sprinkler with her brothers.

His hypnotic eyes—green and brown and green again—traveled across her face, and the comfort she'd felt from him earlier swirled around her again.

"Do you want to tell me what happened in there?" he asked.

She sipped her wine and dreaded reliving the events from the guest room.

He placed his hand on her leg, and a shock of attentiveness ignited in her like sparklers on the Fourth of July.

"Take your time. We're not in any hurry. We have all night."

All night. That was too long to be in such close proximity to him like this. With Henry in the room, she tilted too much toward instinct and not nearly enough toward critical thinking. At the same time, all night didn't seem nearly long enough to get over what had happened upstairs. And being near him was helping her to do just that.

She wasn't sure how much time she'd need before she felt comfortable enough to go into that house again, but a few hours wasn't going to cut it.

With the help of a little more wine, she finished telling him what happened. Seagulls squawked to each other from the beach as if they'd heard her tale and couldn't bear the details of it.

"I had hoped you might be able to finish the restoration

without this sort of interference." He ran his hand along his face with what looked like genuine concern.

"You'll have to hope harder next time."

His eyes scanned the exterior angles of his family's home. "The manor has always been more like a member of the family than just a house. She has a long memory. Forgets nothing. Very possessive."

Her. The house definitely had a feminine, protective vibe to it.

"She makes things happen." He shook his head as if he couldn't believe he had said it, and one dark curl fell over the corner of his forehead.

She makes things happen. When he'd said it, she'd felt the truth in it. The house was a force. Every home had its own personality, the result of its energetic imprints, the land, and definitely the people who had lived in it.

Like Benjamin.

But this one was so strong and determined. It was pure crazy to even think it, but the manor seemed to have some sort of agenda.

"Makes what things happen, exactly?" The artist and the young girl who had been killed flitted across her mind. She thought of her mother, too.

Henry's eyes fixed on her and an uneasiness flickered in the depths of them. "The manor has a difficult history and it's as if it can't move on from it. It relives the past, and bad things can happen when it does."

An uneasy breeze lashed over the lawn and twirled a pirouette around her, cold over warm as it had been for a while now. The wind danced past her, teasing her hair like child's play, then held, like a voiceless servant along the outer wall of the house.

With bits of leaves caught in the debris, she watched the evidence of the air current prod the outer wall, like a nudge to get the home's attention. Like a young girl who wanted her mother to see her dance or even a cat who wanted its owner to see the prize it dropped at their feet.

With her eyes open wide in the candlelit darkness, she thought *she* was the prize, the gift that had been delivered, the offering that had been made.

The house responded as the interior wall had earlier, with a gentle expansion and contraction. This time, it moved along with the subtle creaking of old wood, a noise that anyone else might have written off as one of the meaningless noises that older homes made.

But she knew differently. It was as Henry had said. This house made things happen.

CHAPTER 11

Henry knew the sun would be high in the morning sky long before Gemma would be willing to go inside the manor again. Plus, she wanted to know more about its history, and it wasn't wise to discuss too much of the home's past while within its walls. That tended to...wake things up. With the anniversary of Anna Alcott's death rapidly approaching, the estate's memories were provoked enough already.

He picked up the wine and a blanket and escorted her across the expanse of the green lawn, past the rose gardens, whose scent filled the darkness, to an area on the beach where they could be more comfortable—where they would be safer.

He spread the blanket wide and smooth on the sand, just to the side of a gathering of pine trees. Dead pine needles and holly berries scattered along the white sand edges like decoration. The glow from the half moon cast just enough light that they could see one another and their immediate surroundings. The tang of the green pine mixed with the salt in the ocean air.

She sat upright on the blanket and held the two wine glasses ready for him to pour.

Though he hadn't thought it possible, much less expected it, holding her close on the back porch made him feel things he couldn't have predicted. He had deliberately closed himself off to women and relationships for such a long time. He had no interest in repeating the pain and loss he'd experienced with his wife. But Gemma had a way of making his long-held rules unravel. And with them, his self-control.

She had laid in his arms for almost an hour. He didn't think she realized how much time was passing. And while he held her, he hoped she wouldn't.

The floral scent of her skin and hair seduced his senses and an ache spread through him. He envisioned them together, Gemma in front of him, offering herself to him without hesitation. He imagined her breasts in his hands, in his mouth, her body beneath him as he moved her slowly and powerfully until she cried out.

He fought the self-incriminating wave of selfish desire and rebutted it. He *had* tried to get her to leave, in every way he knew how. Infuriatingly, she wouldn't listen to him. She had a job to do, and nothing he did talked her off of it.

He knew she wouldn't be successful with this restoration. But there was no convincing her of that. Benjamin was a formidable opponent, and he'd tried to tell her that. And though he thought she was beginning to grasp the manor's *eccentricities*...tragically, he didn't think that deterred her, either.

She was the most frustrating mix of fire-edged beauty, natural intelligence, and bull-headed determination he'd ever met. Though if he were pressed to admit it, he did find the fact that she didn't *yes* him to death infuriatingly attractive. Refreshing.

No matter, because it was wrong to get involved with her.

Wrong to encourage her to mix business with pleasure and wrong to entwine her with this house in any way. It had taken too many lives already.

She's doing it for her father.

She was lost to reason, lost to rational thought. She'd made an emotional decision to work on this house in order to help her family. He could understand that. Hell, he had done that.

And so, in a twist of logic he refused to question because he knew it wouldn't stand up to reason, he made a decision. Since he couldn't get her to leave, he would protect her. In fact, that's just how he felt with her. Protective. Maybe even possessive. She had no idea what she had walked into here, and he was going to have to put up one hell of a fight to keep her safe.

He poured the wine and they held their glasses to one another. "To the restoration."

"To the *completed* restoration." She clinked her glass against his and nodded in a just-you-wait-I'll-show-you sort of way.

"I stand corrected." He bowed his head slightly, then sipped the wine. He felt like he'd just offered a toast to the launching of the *Titanic*. Waves tumbled over one another and crashed a few feet from them, sending sea foam dangerously close to their blanket. They both watched the bubbled edge of the cool water approach and retreat. "When did you decide to help out with your parents' business?"

"My dad asked me to help with some of the property's more unique needs. After the accident, he wasn't ready to work again. So, I'm here doing both sides of the job for him, and for everyone who works for us."

Unique needs.

He ran his hand along his jaw and wondered just how

much her parents knew about the manor. How much they might have told her.

"They must appreciate everything you're doing." He took a sip of wine and held her gaze over the rim of his glass. "What sort of unique needs does the property have?"

A few nerves limited her smile and she paused as though she reflected on something, then charged ahead. "I refer to them as *negative* energetic imprints," she said with deliberate boldness. "Every home, every place has them. Some more than others. They're caused by anything from excessive arguing to tragic events, and they tend to build on themselves. In my own design business, I clear them for my clients."

He understood now what she must have been weighing privately. Not everyone believed in energy work. Not everyone saw the effects of it. And, of course, not all practitioners were good at the craft. Both of the latter tended to sully the reputation of any who did it well. He'd seen his fair share of energy workers at the manor, some who were talented, many who were not. None of them had been effective. The manor was well beyond that kind of work.

"Before I spend any time redesigning their space, I'll find out what sort of challenges they're having, if any problems are repeating, or if the home has any negative history I need to know about. Then I go in and clean up those negative imprints. It's very effective for helping people to create a fresh start."

"And this is the sort of work you plan to do on Alcott Manor?" He thought this was a bad idea. An awfully bad idea. He didn't know if clearing imprints would eliminate the manor's current *eccentricities*. But he did know that the manor wouldn't be in favor of any process that limited its way of doing things.

"I promised my dad that I would, so, yes, I need to. From

what I've seen, it's...necessary. It's going to be the key that lets us finish the restoration." She nodded toward the house. "How much do you know about the history of the manor?"

"I've studied it for several years, so I would guess I'm the closest thing to a resident historian."

"Do you have any idea what happened in that guest room?"

Henry tilted his glass and stared into it. "Anna Alcott died there. At least, I think that's where she spent her final moments alive. She was shot over there." He pointed to an area on the green lawn.

"Oh." She stood and stared in the direction he pointed.

"Look, Ms. Stewart, the manor has a long and difficult history. It might be easier if you just focused on the restoration. The past is the past, and there's nothing that can be done about it now. Besides, if we have to go through every difficult experience that has happened on this property, we'll never make our deadline."

From the expression on her face, he could see that his attempt to protect her was going over like a lead balloon.

"Well, that's a matter of opinion, I guess. Seems to me the past is still quite alive in this place. To your point, though, I *am* focused on the restoration. I don't need to know *every* dark detail about the manor's difficult history. But if I can clear the major ones, the effects *will* help us get the overall job done more effectively. *Mr. Alcott.*" His name was beginning to sound like an epithet coming from her mouth.

Her fiery side was in full blaze now. And as much as it irritated him, he was not disappointed to see her strength. She'd come a long way in the last hour or so.

He sat up slowly and with a heavy sigh. "Henry. Please. Call me Henry. And with all due respect to your work, it's just that I don't think the manor's history is quite so easy to resolve."

Just over her head, Henry watched a lamplight come on in the guest room window. He nodded to it. Gemma followed his line of sight and gasped when she saw it.

"Benjamin?" Her eyes widened with fear, and Henry guessed that she was happy not to be in that room presently.

"Might be him. Hard to know."

"Well, who else would it be?"

"Gemma. Do you remember when I told you that we needed to finish the restoration before the anniversary of Anna's death?"

The light went out in the guest room window and she jerked back, surprised. "Yes. Because Benjamin is overactive on that night, I would guess. That light is an oil lamp. So, we can't say that it was an electrical short." She pointed her thumb in the direction of the guest room.

It was time to shoot straight with her. Despite her fear, she wasn't going to be discouraged or scared off. Trying to push her away just made her angry. "I know you realize by now that Alcott Manor is not your average historic home. That's not just because of Benjamin's presence and what we think is his undying need to prove his innocence. But also because of what you witnessed tonight in the guest room."

Henry glanced briefly toward the house, worried even at this distance from the manor that someone else might be listening to him. His voice was low and his tone was cautious. "The house has a spirit of its own, and it can't forget what happened on the night that Anna died."

"I'm not sure I know what you mean."

He studied her for a long moment. "Each year, on the anniversary of Anna's death, the house relives the entire night she died. Starting on the very next day and throughout the following year, the house begins to sputter forth a few memories now and then. There doesn't seem to be a particular order to them. Then they become more frequent throughout the year until eventually, they all play out, just as events happened that night."

"And what happens?"

"Everything. The entire night replays from beginning to end."

"I thought those stories were just fodder for paranormal websites." She closed her eyes and rubbed her hands over her arms. "So, Benjamin kills again? Is that why people have died here on the anniversary of Anna's death?"

"I honestly don't know," he said. "But my point is that the house, its memories...they're a link somehow to that night. They're living memories, and I think they're dangerous. I also think they are beyond imprints and clearings."

"I have to restore this house, Henry." Her voice was firm, and yet, he could hear the pleading behind it. She looked at her open palm and then again at the now-dark guest room. "Maybe the imprints have been around for so long that they have taken on some sort of real life appearance. I'll have to clear as much as I can as quickly as I can. Maybe that will keep Benjamin from killing again. And maybe he'll leave our work alone."

"I don't know if your clearing work will be enough to help. And I don't know what Benjamin is capable of. Especially when he's tearing apart this house. I don't even fully understand the manor, let alone its agenda, other than the fact that tragedy is somehow at the core of it. Because that's what repeats here.

"But with the anniversary of Anna's death approaching, the memories will play more frequently now. You need to be extremely careful not to interact with them."

CHAPTER 12

Ocean winds snaked through the gardens and coiled around Gemma's legs with the same quiet intensity of Henry's warning. The breezes remained cold air over warm, and she brought the corner of the blanket over her legs.

She didn't know what he meant by "careful not to interact with them." She thought of the blood—what she knew now was Anna's blood. She would never have intentionally stuck her hand into that mess if she had seen it ahead of time. She wasn't an idiot. Neither was she foolish or even all that curious about such paranormal happenings.

Mama, you're bleeding!

The doll's voice—the child's voice—echoed in her mind. Her heart skipped over its next beat as if someone squeezed it to a temporary stop.

"One of Anna's children must have watched her die. Aside from the event of Anna's violent death, that child's experience was a tragic enough event to leave a very black energetic mark on that space. Energy such as that would attract like energy in the form of experience, and the negativity would repeat. Frightening as they are, these are imprints. Energetic memories. A lot of them." She rubbed her palm against her chest.

"I think you're right in that tragedy is at the heart of this house. I'm not going to interact with any imprints. I don't know that they—" She had started to say that she didn't know that imprints would or could hurt her, not directly. Though these haunting scenes could frighten her and drive her temporarily from her mind. And she remembered Benjamin. He wasn't an imprint *per se*. He was tied to the house by them. "Anyway, I'm not going to interact with them. I'm going to remove them."

"I don't know, Gemma." He studied the rear facade of the house with concern and worry. "Whatever this house has, it may be too much for anyone to clear."

She glanced at the house and remembered how the wind had stroked the back wall like a cat, how it seemed to know the manor and how it knew her, too, for that matter. It wanted her here for a reason.

"I'll do my work during the day when the house is quiet and when its memories aren't active."

When she looked at Henry, she found him staring at her, his eyes shadowed with worry. She would have said that he was concerned for his project, as all clients were worried for their own projects. But she felt her heart soften, and she thought that maybe he felt concern for her, as well. So, she shared her new theory. One she wasn't entirely certain was true.

"For a while now, I've thought that doing this work on the manor was a detour in my life. But there have been a few signs lately that make me wonder if this is where I'm *supposed* to be—in a divine way, I mean. My mother used to tell me how important my work was, even if people couldn't understand what I was doing or why. They would still reap the benefits of it: less fear, more freedom, new beginnings that wouldn't have been possible before I helped.

"Maybe that's what's happening here to some degree. I do believe my work will finally clear this home's past, set Benjamin free, and put things right for your family's future. So, I'm going to do what I know how to do as a gift to you, my father, your home, and even Benjamin."

He blinked twice as if he couldn't quite believe what he'd heard. "Even Benjamin..."

"Ghosts are people, too." She pressed her lips together to restrain all the exceptions she felt in response to her mother's belief.

"I don't think I've ever heard anyone say that before."

"A relative of mine used to say that. She had a gift for seeing ghosts. And I guess it's very easy for me to sound gracious to Benjamin when I'm way out here, and he's stuck in there." She nodded toward the house. "By the way, I won't be working at night."

"Agreed," he said.

She couldn't tell if he just agreed that she ought not work in the manor at night, or if her role to play in this job was somehow divinely ordered. She decided not to ask for clarification—she might not like his answer. He'd already said he thought the house was beyond imprints and clearings.

"That must have been an interesting upbringing to have a relative who saw ghosts. What would she have said about Benjamin?"

"Mmmm. Probably that he's here because of unfinished business." She didn't want to get into a conversation about her mother's gifts, so she decided to cut the conversation short. "I guess I'd better go." She brushed the sand from the legs of her jeans.

"Go where?" He stood with her, as a gentleman would for a lady.

"I'm going to find an all-night diner, someplace I can sit and work. I'll go back inside to work tomorrow morning when the sun is up and everyone else is there. Tonight, I need to be on the outside of those four walls. I'm sure you understand."

They walked in quiet until they reached the porch area. The door to the house was still open, and she found the access unnerving.

His hands fidgeted. They rubbed together, then slid into his pockets, then out again to rest on his hips. "You need your rest. It's been a long day." His right hand brushed the side of her shoulder, a sweet sentiment of concern that bridged this moment to the time they had shared earlier on the porch. She remembered his earthy scent and the way she felt in his arms. Excitement stroked at the inside of her belly.

"I'll call around tomorrow for a new place to stay. I'll be fine for tonight as long as they serve lots of tea."

"I don't think I like the idea of you being by yourself all night in some restaurant." Henry stood at the open doorway and extended his hand to her. "Why don't we sit together in the living room tonight? It's just past the kitchen. I'll stay with you, and we'll talk about the restoration."

She bit her lip and hovered at the entryway to the kitchen. The idea of sitting with Henry for the rest of the night was a far more attractive option than lingering in an empty diner like a vagrant. A little more time with him was such a comforting thought. She could get to know him better, and, she rationalized, that would bode well for the job.

She studied the kitchen that was just beyond the doorway, and then the wide hallway in the distance. All seemed quiet and well-lit. With Henry nearby, she didn't think any ghost would make an appearance.

"Okay," she said. She lifted a foot to take a step inside the house, but it refused to move on her command. Fear gripped her insides with cold, oily fingers.

Come on, Gemma.

She wanted to be professional. Unafraid. Her hands gripped the doorway and she tried to swallow the strangling pressure on her throat. Waves hissed against the distant shore behind her.

All she could think about was how Benjamin had taken out a wall in the downstairs area. Could there really be a safe place in this house? Henry seemed to think there was.

She cursed the fact that she couldn't move, that her fear of some force, some monster in this house, kept her from doing what she needed to do.

She didn't want to need Henry. The last thing she wanted was to be dependent upon any man for anything, least of all for safety.

She looked at the black-and-white tiled kitchen floor and tried in vain to step in that direction. *Come on, Gemma. One. Damn it. One.*

"Stay with me and you'll be fine." Henry pushed his hand closer to her.

Like a little girl who'd just agreed to jump into the deep end because she knew someone was there waiting for her, she placed her hand in his.

He nodded. "It's okay." He held her fingers in his palm and guided her along as if he were escorting her onto the ballroom floor.

One, two, three, four, five... She silently counted every step she took to keep herself from giving in to the fear. The interior of the house was bright from the original kerosene table lamps that had been converted to electric and candle sconces, and it had generally taken on a different vibe. With the workers gone and the safety of Henry at her side, it felt like a

ALYSSA RICHARDS

house after a party. There were echoes of guests, their movement, and their laughter, but no one was around.

"This house never really feels empty, does it?"

"Not usually," he said. "You okay?" Henry placed a hand
on her shoulder. "I'm just going to run and get your bag. I'll
be right back."

"Oh. I didn't realize... Actually, I think I'll just wait
outside for you." She rubbed the front of her tightening
throat. She would not stand in this house alone at night. Not
even for a moment.

From the next room, violins played a soft strain of music
that peaked, then faded just as quickly as it started. Her
throat closed almost completely, and she ran toward the
outside door, forgetting to count any of her steps along
the way.

When she reached the outside, she dragged the night air
in through her throat that felt three sizes too small.

Henry sighed from somewhere behind her. "I'm sorry. I
didn't think that would happen again tonight."

"I'm okay," she said. "I appreciate the offer to sit together
in the house, but I'm going to head on to that diner." Her
tone was final. Completely final.

"I'm really sorry about that."

To her surprise, he disappeared around the far-right
corner of the porch. She thought that enforcing her choice to
stay out of the house was going to be more of a battle.
"Good. That's settled." Though her heart sank when he left.

She returned to the bench and tugged the light blanket
around her shoulders. The night was clear with just a little bit
of a chill. She wasn't cold. She wasn't comfortable, either.
She'd ask Henry to get her purse and phone, then she'd call
for that cab. She would survive the night and the next day,
too. This wouldn't be the first time that she had managed a
big job on no sleep.

She ran her hand along the cushion where Henry had held her. She wanted to say that he understood her, but she wasn't sure how that could be true. He hardly knew her, and there was no way he could know why, exactly, she felt so afraid.

"Gemma," he said from just a few steps away, making her jump. "Come with me."

"I'm not going inside, Hen—"

"No. I know. I have another idea."

She stared at him and exhaled hard. The debacle with Preston taught her to keep her distance. And now here was Henry, a man she didn't really know, but who was insistent on helping. She decided she would follow him and ask for his help to retrieve her things. She cast off the blanket and joined him. "Just so we're clear."

"Completely." He led her to the other side of the porch that wrapped around an all-glass room. The lower half of the room was boarded up, the upper half comprised of glass panels set in iron.

She paused cautiously at the threshold of this room that shared its existence with the outside world. The fact that it was attached to the manor kept her from going inside. But it also seemed to be its own world and separate somehow from the tragedy she'd seen earlier in the day. Her gaze climbed the arched iron beams that spread from the ceiling like spider legs, and it skated along the glass panes fitted between them.

"We closed this room off from the rest of the house once the restoration priorities were set. There had been some break-ins through the glass over there, so we boarded that up." He pointed to the far side of the room where thick wooden boards had been affixed to the lower half of the dome.

Shards of broken glass had been swept to the edges of the side wall among the vines of ivy that had begun to grow wild inside the room. Even still, she thought this may be the most magical room she'd ever seen. She found herself standing next to the warmth of the fire that Henry had built in the small fireplace, and feeling reasonably comfortable with it.

"This was Anna's winter garden, as she was known to call it. She disliked any sort of weather that resembled winter, so she had this room built just for her to enjoy during the colder, grayer months. The glass trapped the warmth of the sun and was her favorite room of the house. It was written in the local paper that she held bridge parties here for her lady friends, and spent a lot of time in here reading and knitting."

"Yes, I can see why she enjoyed the room. It's magnificent." It was like a playhouse but for a grown-up little girl, with an ornate mantel and exquisite views of the sky and the ocean. Gemma imagined that in its day, the furniture and the decorating must have been fit for a princess.

She noticed several throws and pillows on the floor in front of the fire, including an embroidered pillow with an A on it. She assumed Henry had put them there for her and she found her fears and thoughts too tangled to express. She quickly turned the conversation professional, to cover the personal.

"Does this have to be completed before the judge's deadline?"

"No, this represents a project for the second half of the job. You would technically be inside the house by spending the night in here. I don't think you'll be disturbed by anything." He waved his hand toward the rest of the house.

"With all due respect, how would you know?"

"Other than the broken glass, we haven't had any disturbances in this room. It may be, as you say, due to the energetic imprints. In here, they must be overwhelmingly positive."

Gemma teetered between wanting to snuggle next to Henry under the pile of blankets and saying "thanks but no thanks" with an abrupt exit. She thought about the chamber music she'd heard just a short while ago. If she had her sense of direction right, it would have come from the room on the other side of the old beige door. The one with the burnished knob that blocked access to the rest of the house.

Though the music had been lovely, there was no one around to play it. No one with an actual body, anyway. Whatever scene played along with the song was probably as macabre as what she had witnessed in the guest room upstairs.

"I don't know about staying in here." She ran her hand along the back of her neck.

Henry rearranged the pillows and folded an edge of the covers back as if he were turning down her bed. "You ought to get some rest." The light from the fire reflected on his face, and the cinnamon brown came alive in his eyes. Her thoughts were hung on the way she felt when he'd held her on the porch. She'd seen a side to him she hadn't thought existed, a side that had reached her, a side that had touched her.

"Well, if I do stay here, where will you be? Just so I know, in case I do need anything."

"I usually sleep in the master. But I can stay here with you if you like. I'll find some other blankets."

A hitch caught on her breath. "No, that's okay. I can manage."

"You're certain?" He stepped toward her and she desperately wanted to ask him to stay. Just to talk and to get to know him better. To revisit the connection they'd shared earlier.

"I'm sure I'll be fine." She dismissed him with a smile, her professional one that came with a nod. The one that said there was nothing left to be said.

"Okay, then." He reached into his pocket and dropped a

key that landed with a *clank* on the side table next to him.
"Lock yourself in after I leave." He closed the door
behind him.

She sat in the middle of the blankets and wrapped her
arms around her knees. "Damn it."

She flopped backward, closed her eyes, and counted her
breaths, one for the inhale, two for the exhale, and so on.
Deep belly breathing the therapists had taught her when
anxiety was a more regular visitor in her life. Control the
breath and you'll control the mind, they'd said. But tonight, it
wasn't working. She turned to her side and pressed a pillow
over her head.

She felt off-center and rattled. It was the house. Certainly.
But it was also—partly, at least—the accident and almost
losing her father so soon after her mother died. A monu-
mental change she still was not completely used to.

Her dad and Janey weren't here like they were supposed to
be, and her father's entire livelihood was on her shoulders
now. And, of course, she was stuck in this haunted house that
was forcing her to face her worst nightmare.

She didn't just feel lonely. She felt alone. Frightened.
Frankly, she didn't know if she could do this job, not under
these circumstances.

Henry's face drifted across her mind and she thought of
his lips. What would it be like to kiss them, to feel them on
her breasts, her stomach. Her lower abdomen tightened. She
groaned and rolled over, facing the fire this time. She didn't
need to complicate this mess she was in.

Violins played soft and slow, and she jerked upright. The
music passed through the walls and danced through the
room. The door on the other side of the room had several
boards crossing it. To keep anyone who broke in through here
out of the house, she guessed. But ghosts didn't need open

doorways to enter a room—they came and went as they pleased, did as they wanted to.

She pushed to her feet and backed to the door. Henry would be upstairs and she couldn't get to him there. Her purse and her phone were up there, too. She *wouldn't* go up there. All she could do was leave the house, get outside.

She kept her eyes glued to the boarded-up door across the room and felt for the doorknob behind her. The door was unlocked—she never locked it after Henry left. When she opened it partway, a cool breeze slid inside and she breathed a sigh of relief. Out. Free. Alive.

But not alone. From the shadowy end of the walkway, a tall figure moved toward her. Her hands flew to her mouth. Her memory of Benjamin in the guest room came back to her. He was a tall man like this one, moving slow and purposeful.

Rather than run through the dark screaming, she chose to take her chances with Anna's winter garden. Maybe the positive imprints there were strong enough to keep him at bay. When she was halfway across the room, the violin music surged from the next room, and her heart thrummed into a long snare drum roll.

The door creaked as it opened slowly, then bounced against the wall. The hand that opened it hung mid-air and the man's face appeared slowly after.

"God, Henry." She grabbed the front of her shirt in a fist full of fabric.

"I'm sorry, I didn't mean to startle you. I was on my way upstairs when I heard the music. I thought you might be able to hear it and— Gemma, are you okay?" His tone was low and gentle.

She sniffed and wiped her eyes. "I'm good. I'm fine."

"If I thought anything could get to you in this room, I wouldn't have brought you here."

She pulled a slow, deep breath through her lungs that were rigid with panic.

The door shut behind him with a *click*.

She spun around. "No, I—the music and the ghosts. I can't. I have to leave."

"Nothing bad ever happens in this room. I promise we'll be safe."

We.

"I'll stay with you. I don't want you to be frightened." He ran his hands along the outside of her arms, his touch soft with care.

This arrangement wasn't her first choice. But for the life of her, she couldn't find a better one. She drew in a deep breath and her inhale stuttered. If they were going to stay in this room together, they would have to set rules that kept the distance. "Henry—" She spun around to face him.

He left his hands in place such that she was now in his arms, and the warmth of his palm glided against her cheek. He was going to kiss her. She wanted him to kiss her. Maybe more than she wanted to breathe. She shouldn't. "Henry—"

He didn't let her finish. He crushed his lips against hers in the kind of kiss she'd only dreamed about. With his hand cupped against the back of her head, his tongue slid against hers and her body caught fire. She gave in to the heat that spread through her.

She tugged his white shirt free from the waistband of his pants and raked her fingers across the bare skin of his back. He lifted his head with a ragged moan and pulled the shirt over his head.

"We shouldn't," her voice rasped, and she hoped he wouldn't listen to her.

A smile curved his lips. He slid her jacket over her shoulders and let it fall to the floor. "I think we absolutely should."

He slipped his hands under her black T-shirt and dragged it over her head. It flew somewhere to the side of the room.

His lips and tongue feasted along the side of her neck, and she heard herself moan. He lowered them onto the twist of blankets, and his clever hands trailed over her curves, marking a path for his tongue to follow.

It was an irresistible heat she'd never known, each touch driving her need for more of him, each kiss promising fulfillment. He ignited a passion she'd always wanted to feel with someone but had decided that it only showed up on the screen or in the pages of a book. And there was an openness from him, a selfless giving she hadn't seen when they'd first met. But it was there now, loving and caring for her as if he knew her in a way no one else did.

His tongue caressed the valley between her breasts, and she ran her fingers through his dark hair. She hardly recognized herself. This was so unlike her to throw concerns overboard and allow someone she hardly knew so close to her. Some distant voice of responsibility cautioned her to stop, but when he filled his mouth with her breast, she dimmed that voice into the quiet of the room.

He hovered over her, worshipping subtle places on her body she didn't realize could appreciate such attention. Her hips arched and pressed against him, and he took the invitation and responded in kind. Their bodies moved together in a slow dance, his hands and mouth asking the question, her writhing beneath him, offering the answer. The pleasure of his touch left her intoxicated, but the tune of forever that surrounded her left her breathless. As if their connection opened a portal that offered them a future together. The feeling left her senseless and understanding, for the very first time, what *swept off her feet* really meant.

She blindly loosened his belt and trousers, and his

stomach tensed when her fingers fumbled past the silk of his boxers.

All night, she remembered him saying. That would not be nearly enough time. Not now that this new horizon was before them—a beginning she had always wanted, a relationship she didn't think she would ever have. He made an art of sliding her panties down her legs with his hands on either side of the elastic, his mouth leading the way before the panties followed. A kiss to the inside of her thigh, then his tongue drew a route. His teeth nipped and teased, followed by more kisses, until he eased the black silk over her toes.

He raised and parted her knees, glancing at her once before pressing his face between her thighs. He was one of *those* lovers, she decided. One of the mythical ones who knew exactly what you—

"Oh, God, yes." She buried her fingers in his hair, and her mouth fell open, though no more words would form. He was graciously unrelenting with that featherlike tongue of his, spinning her body and soul toward a slow-building peak she couldn't resist.

He somehow knew to stop just shy of her point of no return, reading her body as a musician would play a well-loved song. He caught her momentum before it retreated too far and drove the melody again with all the intensity she'd ever wanted. When he directed her into the final crescendo, the tension poured forth in a release of building waves that pounded her from the inside and left her senseless.

She shuddered under his touch, and a log shattered in the fireplace, sending sparks into the air and onto the hearth. *More* was all she could think. If it was at all physically possible, that's what she wanted from this man—more of what he could give, more of what he brought her into.

He was hard when he leaned against her, his eyes ablaze, his face fierce and demanding. She lifted her hips to him, needing to feel more of him, wanting him inside of her. This time, he was the answer, and he pressed himself into the depths of her, stretching her, filling her. He made a low groan, stilling himself and holding her tighter. "Gemma," he said on a harsh breath.

She rolled herself on top and rocked herself over the length of him, waves of pleasure riding over his face. He sat up to hold her close, their sweat-covered bodies moving together. His steadying hand spread wide across her back when he moved her. His other hand cupped her buttock, and he lifted her as she wanted it, as she needed it.

Her arms latched around him and her fingers tangled in his hair. This was it, she thought while she rocked with him, their slick movements measured in an intimate rhythm accented by her moans. This must be what it felt like when your soul met its mate. The slow build of sensation ultimately consumed her and left her clinging to Henry's trembling body, their twin cries blending with the violins that played down the hall.

EMBERS GLOWED where once the fire had raged, and Henry stared at the orange and yellow that shifted in the dying cinders. Dark skies sealed a layer of thickness over their winter garden, though the occasional chirps of birdsong signaled that daybreak was on its way.

He stroked Gemma's hair as she rested her cheek on his chest, the weight of her body on his was more comfort than he had hoped for in rather a long time. She was awake, he knew, and worrying. There was the mountain of work that needed to be finished in the short time that remained. And there was the added pressure of needing to accomplish it for the sake of her father and his business.

Though he didn't consider himself a compassionate man, he felt for her that she had been through so much lately. Her mother's death, the accident, and now she was saddled with completing the restoration of the manor—something no one had yet been able to accomplish. She still had no idea the real dangers she faced with this house—the few incidents she had seen so far barely scratched the surface. The temporary silence in the manor was not a sign of how cooperative the house and its chief resident would be with her restoration efforts.

He dragged his finger along the curves of her torso, enjoying every sensation brought on by the unique connection they shared. He didn't quite understand why he had pursued her. Why, specifically her, when he had not been the least bit tempted by so many others since his wife's death? It wasn't just primal, though that was part of it. That first touch they'd shared in a simple handshake on the porch had stirred something within him he hadn't expected.

She rested her chin on his chest. Her blue eyes filled with caution and worry, a restlessness that came with knowing, if only subconsciously, that not all was right in her immediate world. In a moment of uncharacteristic selflessness, he hoped she would return to her life on the west coast before things spun out of control—as they often did in this house.

"What sort of imprints would you say we left the house with last night?" He twisted her long hair around his fingers. Trying to memorize the way the strands looked against his skin, knowing that if she did leave, he'd never forget anything about her even if he wanted to.

"Oh. Quite positive ones, I would say. In fact, we may have just changed the entire energetic trajectory of Alcott Manor. From here on out, it's good times and easy sailing."

She dragged her fingers downward along his abs and pressed her hand against him. Her touch was gentle, and the look in her eyes was adoring. As if he were the perfect man. As if, in all this flawed reality, she had found something ideal.

He groaned and thrust his hips, grateful that their early morning after was without restraint. She was every bit the eager and giving lover he'd hoped she'd be. When she slid down his body and took him in her mouth, he slipped away from her. He wasn't through worshipping her.

The feel of her breasts on his tongue was flavored by his worries that prowled around the edge of their early morning. She didn't know all that she was up against. He'd tried to figure out how to tell her at least several hundred times since they'd met. It didn't matter how he would put it to her. She wouldn't believe him. Everything would sound so far-fetched that she'd probably stop talking to him, or at the very least, her opinion of him would suffer. Neither option was one he could tolerate.

That didn't change the fact that she was still in danger for being in the manor and for pursuing the restoration.

He sighed when he slipped inside of her, needing more of her and what they shared. It was then that he realized what he'd tried to figure out earlier. Her. Why her? It wasn't a specific or a tangible, it wasn't even something he could quantify. It was a knowing. A wisdom that couldn't be denied or even explained. She was just the one. The one he'd known was real, who existed, and who searched for him. Just as he had searched for her. Without names, without clues or directions. She had been more like a dream or a promise of that dream, and now she was finally here and in his arms. Making his world right for the first time in perhaps his entire life.

"Ah." Her mouth opened slightly. "Tell me we haven't complicated things too much—"

He pinned her arms over her head, and his breath stuttered in the cool air while he held himself still in this grace he'd waited too long for. "Perhaps we have simplified them," he whispered.

When he finally moved again, she clamped her legs tight around his waist, and rocked so sensuously that he lost sight of everything but her. The worries, the deadlines, the danger, they flitted away from the two of them—for only the time being, he knew—but he took that moment with force.

With every inch of her body wrapped around him, he lost himself with her and in a way he never thought he was capable. The apple blossom scent of her hair imprinted itself on his brain and absorbed his coherent thoughts. Her sweet gasps and groans, the ones he doubted she even heard, as well as the heavenly slick of her flesh, sucked him further into her world. He no longer noticed the manor or any of its problems that had haunted his life for so long.

When she cried out, she took him with her, his final movements raw and wild with need for her. He was possessed and obsessed with her in a way that left him falling and with no way to regain control.

CHAPTER 13

Sometime later, and over the early morning songs of robins and bluebirds, she gently ran her finger across the scar just under his eye. "Where did you get this?"

He touched his cheekbone as if he had forgotten what was there. "Oh," he chuckled. "It was a long time ago. I was helping my father with some woodworking, and a piece of wood chipped loose and caught me."

"You're lucky it didn't catch your eye." She kissed the scar, light and sweet, tasting the salt on his skin.

"Mmmm. I'm very lucky to have met you." He found her lips and kissed them.

She savored their feel and essence. They were even better than she had imagined they would be.

"Now, are you more of a coffee or a diet cola person in the morning?"

She rolled onto her back and stretched, toes and finger-tips reaching in opposite directions. "Actually, I'm more of an early-run-and-hot-tea person."

"Ah. Excellent. I believe we have tea." He rolled on top of her, his kisses traveling down her body. "I'll get your suitcase for you. You'll probably want that, won't you?" He licked a figure eight right below her bellybutton and sealed it with a kiss. Then he set about the room retrieving pieces of his clothing, and donning them one by one.

She leaned to her side to look at him, something she hadn't done much of the night before when she had been more obsessed with touching and having him. He was a stunning man, solid and athletic, with light golden skin and dark hair neatly scattered across his chest and abs in a sort of a V pattern.

He focused on buttoning his shirt until he caught her staring. A slow, beautiful smile broadened like the rising of the morning sun.

She returned the expression, though she cringed inwardly. She'd broken the number one rule in her own business, one that she'd learned the hard way: never get involved with a client. When things fell apart—and eventually, things always fell apart—it muddied the waters professionally and caused problems. She rubbed the back of her neck and hoped she hadn't complicated this job any more than it already was.

She could still feel the distant cadence of forever from the night before. Like a heartbeat, it pulsed from him, and though she wanted to trust it, she couldn't. She needed Henry's help to get this job done, and she had to know as much as possible about the history of the house and how its energetic imprints were created so she could clear them. He alone had that information.

Henry kneeled at her side. "Don't worry too much about the house, Gemma. It's less eventful during the day, but be careful. As you've seen, it can be a frightening place."

"How do you handle all the craziness in this house?"

He shrugged. "I guess I've learned what and who to avoid. Essentially, that's the trick around here."

She nodded and returned his goodbye kiss, melting into it

and wishing they could spend the day tangled in the blankets that swirled beneath her. His appeal hadn't faded for her in the light of day. She'd thought that maybe, when the sun was high and the house was slightly less haunted, her feelings for him would have dimmed, as well.

Unfortunately, that wasn't the case.

When he closed the door behind him, she lowered her head to her hand. Yes, she was definitely in a frightening place. She'd just made the biggest mistake of her life.

GEMMA'S FEET pounded the sand along the beach that stretched in front of Alcott Manor. She had foregone her usual seventies rock this time, choosing instead to run to the tempo of the crashing waves that carried out the tide.

She stopped and gazed at the sunrise that was lifting itself over the horizon. "What the hell have I done?" She breathed hard and pressed her fingers into the tense muscles on the back of her neck. Last night had been a complete aberration from her typical priorities. She'd need to make a clean break and hope that she didn't irritate the one client her father's future depended on.

In fact, this may just be all too soon to have anyone in her life. She probably needed time—time to heal from her divorce, to reinvent herself, to find her center. As her mother had told her not all that long ago, she needed to get back to trusting her instincts.

And she wanted to do that. She bent at the waist and leaned on her knees to catch her breath. Something was off, like her internal compass had lost its true north. She knew she had made the right choice by dropping everything with her business to help her father. Though, maybe the all of it, as she had suspected last night—her mother's passing, the divorce, the magazine press, the accident, her father's inability to work this job, the haunted manor—was too much. Then Henry showed up at her most vulnerable moment, and she'd reached for him. It didn't take a psychiatrist to see that hadn't been a well thought-out decision. Let alone one that had been well guided by her intuition.

Henry's face flashed through her mind, glistening in perfection and hovering over her as he had the night before. God help her if she had just repeated the mistakes she'd made with Preston.

She rolled her eyes and ran toward the house again, not quite at top speed this time, but close to it. When she finally stepped from the beach onto the spring green lawn, she decided it was this damned house that had her feeling so off her center. She needed to get to work on clearing as much of its negative history as she could. The sooner she got back to her own world, the better she would feel and the smarter her decisions would be.

She walked toward the rose gardens that were distantly surrounded by tall, green hedges with white blooms. A blanket of soft ferns grew in their shade. Geometrically designed beds of red tulips and other flowers were arranged along the sides of the grass to soak up the sun.

The centrally placed rose gardens were quite large, fragrant, and filled with pink and red buds. They were varieties she couldn't identify beyond the standard tea rose, but she knew her mother could have. Gardening had been one of her favorite hobbies.

She walked the dirt paths between the squares of roses that were organized by color, and she tried to organize her thoughts before she saw Henry again.

She dropped onto a cement bench, opened a bottle of water, and took a long drink. Unable to keep last night's memories at bay, she chose to indulge them one more time. It was, she knew, the first time that a man had given all of himself to her—unreservedly.

Not just physically, though he left no part of her unsung. It was more of an emotional yielding. He had been passionate, uncomplicated, loving. Giving.

The way her heart and soul had responded to his openness left her deeply changed. As though her world now tilted at a different angle, unsteady, yet with a renewed outlook. It was as if she had loved, been loved, and lost, all within the last twenty-four hours.

Ocean breezes twisted around her body and carried the roses' heavenly scent. The foretelling winds had been accurate from the first time they'd circled her just weeks before. She was being transformed, though the puzzle pieces of her life didn't yet fit together as neatly as they had a few weeks ago. In fact, they were a jumbled mess.

Her thoughts bounced around without the order she hoped her run would mandate. She wondered why her lawyer hadn't phoned to let her know that she had the executed divorce settlement. Maybe Preston hadn't really dropped the alimony issue. She hoped, seriously hoped, she hadn't just screwed up this job. And what was with this together-forever tune her heart kept dancing to?

She shook her head. Normally, she was someone her father could trust, someone who always had her act together. Always. The wind definitely had the upheaval part of her fortune right.

Okay, she needed to be practical. For whatever they had shared, she ought to remember that relationships today weren't like they were when her mother and father found each other. No one was interested in that sort of genuine, the kind of forever they had enjoyed. She'd kissed enough frogs to know that princes didn't exist anymore.

She and Henry had shared one magical night together. He

had been a gentleman who helped her find a safe and warm place to sleep and who comforted her on a frightening night. A night she wouldn't soon forget, and she would have to leave it at that.

She rose from the bench and headed toward Anna's winter garden. Henry had brought her suitcase down from the guest room earlier, and she needed to get ready for the day. Like an orchestrated crescendo, the sound of a woman crying echoed in the gardens. She turned around to find its source, though she was the only person in the expanse of the back lawn.

"Hello?" The sound seemed to originate from all around her. She backed away from the flowers. The cries faded.

"Did you know that Empress Josephine is credited with introducing the stand-alone rose garden?"

She spun to find Henry standing behind her with two mugs in his hands. One corner of his white shirt was untucked from his black pants, and his hair was slightly mussed from the morning. "Oh."

He offered her one of the mugs and a smile.

"Thank you. Did you hear that?"

Henry didn't answer but appeared to listen for whatever noise she had mentioned.

"Someone was crying. A woman. I— It sounded like she was right here."

"I don't doubt it," Henry said. "Anna Alcott spent a lot of time out here. That might have been a memory of her crying."

An imprint. She'd clear it this morning. She drank from the mug. "The roses are beautiful."

"They're also original to the house." He gestured to the gardens.

"Really?" Gemma turned to the roses as if she'd missed their ancient lineage the first time she'd seen them.

Henry sipped his coffee. "Anna Alcott planted them. I think only the Queen of England and I have the oldest rose gardens in the world."

"Anna planted them," she echoed. Her eyes stayed glued to the beauty of the roses, and she thought about the woman's fading cries. "She spent a lot of time in the garden?"

He nodded. "She was known to read out here when the weather wasn't too hot. She also painted. Flowers mostly, I believe."

"Is this where she liked to be alone?" she asked.

"Not sure. I guess those are fairly solitary hobbies, though. Painting, reading, gardening." He stopped next to a rose bush and pulled a curling petal from the bottom of one of the delicate blooms.

He studied the flowers one by one, and she thought he might know their needs just by looking at them, as if they spoke to him. Loved him. She wondered why this beautiful, sensitive, intelligent man wasn't married.

Of course, why she thought there was someone for everyone except her, she wasn't sure.

"Just before the accident, my dad and I saw a woman in a wide-brimmed straw hat in the side rose garden cutting them."

"Hmmm. That may have been one of the ladies from the auxiliary. They've helped us with various gardening projects over the years."

"She waved at us." Gemma remembered that strange moment of peace she'd felt before the truck hit them. She wondered if the woman had been one of the manor's memories cast up at an ill-timed moment. Then she wondered if it had been intentional.

This house made things happen. She shook off the thought. The idea was too mad.

Henry took a pair of cutters from his tool belt and cut a

long-stemmed, deep red rose and handed it to Gemma. Its fragrance seduced her senses, lifted her heart, and removed the concern that had made her frown.

"Thank you. My middle name is Rose."

"Gemma Rose. I like the sound of that."

His gaze went too deep for her comfort, and she cleared her throat. "Henry, about last night... I have a lot of people depending on me to get this restoration work completed before the judge's deadline, and I may have jumped the gun—"

"I hope this isn't where you tell me you have regrets." The gentleness of his Southern accent painted his words slow and certain. His measure of confidence breathed in perfect sync with the century-old property around them—strong, solid, seemingly indestructible. The touch of the back of his fingers down her cheek unraveled her heart into a soft, jangled mess where her rehearsed speech rested unspoken and with a forgotten need to be heard. "Because I surely don't."

He could not have said anything more perfect at precisely the right time. She found herself, uncharacteristically so, without an ounce of insight as to where he was going next.

He led them to the garden bench. The delicate scent of the roses swirled around her like a gentleman's gift, like an enchanted offering, like a gallant token designed to make her feel cherished. She could have sworn he guided her to experience that bouquet intentionally.

"Gemma." He held her hand in his. "I know things are uncertain. I know this job is important to you. It's important to me, too. We both have so very much riding on this restoration." He ran his thumb over the top of her hand with all the strength of the waves that crashed in the near distance. In the pause of his words, she heard the melody between them again. The one she'd heard yesterday in the most unexpected moment, and for the first time since she'd dreamed of it as a little girl.

"But I don't want to lose what we found with each other last night."

Her lips parted and words she didn't know she was going to say slipped out. "I don't, either."

His smile broadened with genuine, boyish happiness. "Good." He nodded. "Good."

"I just can't do anything here that messes up this job."

"I don't want you to do that, either."

One car door slammed, and then another. The workers were arriving. Henry kissed her knuckles and stood. "Are you ready?"

She felt like she ought to have something brilliant to say. But instead, all she did was nod.

"All right." He took several steps toward the manor. "Let's go, then."

CHAPTER 14

Gemma, Tom, and Henry stood among the broken planks of wood that surrounded the grand staircase. A makeshift table of plywood atop four metal chairs was set up with architectural plans, and several paper cups filled with coffee laid before them. The pungent scent of their brew drifted through the air and she inhaled it. She never drank it, but she did love the smell of coffee. Reminded her of home.

With two full crews on staff, Gemma had spent most of her morning refiguring the work plans and getting everyone appropriately task-centric. Henry was right about the house being less eventful during the day. It might have been the sheer number of workers inhabiting the house, but the darker energies that ran free the night before were now subdued—not gone, however. She could sense their undercurrent coursing through the house. She glanced toward the upstairs guest room. At least the crowds and the lighter vibe meant that she had more freedom to get her work done.

The three of them approached one of the largest repairs left on the list, the grand staircase.

"Considering the amount of time we have left, I want to

double-team the staircase job," she said to Tom. "I realize we already have two groups in place for the general work, but these stairs were specifically on the judge's list. I want it completely done well before the deadline."

Tom rested his chin in his hand and squinted at the plans.

"It's not really an additional expense if the time is cut in half. I think 'better safe than sorry' is the right direction with this one. And here's a little twist I'm thinking of, given Benjamin's penchant for destruction..."

Gemma walked over to the flat wall just under the decimated stairs. "We need to add a door. Here." She outlined a section on the wall. "So, if he or whoever, gets curious again as to what might lie in the unseen, maybe they'll just open the door instead of...doing all this." She waved her arm at the crumbled stairs. "Silly, I know. Maybe I'm catering a little to Benjamin, but we're down to the wire here, so we ought to go with whatever works."

Paisley walked by in the distance with an iPad and a phone in her hands. Before their meeting had begun, Gemma watched Tom give Paisley a long list of marching orders for the day. For the first time, Gemma was glad the young gal was there because whatever Paisley got done helped the project move forward more quickly.

"Excellent idea," Henry said with a grin that she thought held shades of the smile she'd seen him wear outside. The excited one that promised nothing but seemed to believe that they had discovered something worth seeing through. "We should probably install secret doors all over the house."

"By the way, were any handwritten notes found among the rubble?" She still doubted that the suicide note existed, but she thought she would check, just in case she was wrong.

Henry shook his head, disappointment shadowing his smile. "I searched. Nothing."

"Too bad." She knocked a few small pieces of broken

wood with the toe of her shoe and wondered where Benjamin went to during the day and if he was watching them from someplace just beyond their view.

Tom took a pencil from behind his ear and sketched a door onto the drawings.

"Just like my dad." She tightened her ponytail. "Typical army guy, processes everything internally." She ran her hand along the French-inspired iron railing that ran along the wide staircase and up to the second-story balcony. "Was this original to the house?"

Henry smiled like a proud father. "It is, and produced by an ironworks company over in Florence—South Carolina, that is. Not Italy."

"Extraordinary. Tom, I want these reinstalled. There's no damage in here, and, well, this is where they belong." She looked at Tom, who hand wrote notes in the margin of the drawings.

"All right, he's got this." A ray of early morning sun reflected on a glint of gold, like a signal that called her into the next room. "Look at the stenciling on the wall there. Is that—"

"Gold. Yes, 24 karat leaf. Anna Alcott did it all by hand in 1880."

She gazed at the beauty left by the woman whose unresolved death still marred the home. Intricate floral patterns climbed the wall and repeated every fourth flower, and she could still make out several gentle strokes of purple in the pansies. Gold leaf defined the edges of the petals, as well as certain leaves and vines that reached vertically. Drafts of soft pink graced the roses, and the outline of a tulip remained.

"There's script on here." She tried to make out the words, but several letters had faded completely and the thumbprint-smeared plexiglass that covered it made it difficult to read details.

"You'll have to pardon the plexiglass. Paisley almost had this painted over, so we put this up to keep that from happening," he said.

She squinted her eyes to stem the stress that bloomed in her chest. "And here I was thinking she was actually helpful today." She finally tugged her phone from her jeans pocket, snapped a photo, and enlarged it on the screen. "It says Henry, I think. Age 7. This is a growth chart, isn't it?" Once again, she found Henry closer to her than she realized. A flutter of unexpected excitement ran through her body. She tightened her stomach muscles as well as her focus.

"Yes." Henry examined the vine over her shoulder. "Each of their children is represented by a particular flower. You can see how the pattern repeats with each new measurement."

Gemma realized the reason the vine had stopped, and a wave of sadness rode through her. She placed her fingertips next to the final flowers, a white bloom entwined with a tulip with the scripted letters that spelled out *Liz* next to it.

"That's, um..." Gemma hoped for an interruption this time.

"The vine stopped when Anna died," he said.

She dropped her hand from the vine that was once filled with life and hope for the future. "What happened to the children after their parents...were gone?"

"Benjamin's parents moved back into the house. They tried to take care of the children, along with a couple of nannies. But they were fairly up in age for that time, so it wasn't easy. Ultimately, the children went in different directions for guardianship. The older two went to Benjamin's brother, the younger two went to Anna's sister. A few members of the community helped out, as well. If I'm remembering correctly, I think one of the local businessmen even offered to adopt the youngest daughter."

She marveled over this generosity. "It was certainly a different time."

Henry ran his hand over his chest absently and studied her. She thought she knew which question was coming next. "That it was," he said. "Do you have children?"

That question. Sadness ached in her chest. "Ah, no. Unfortunately, not. Or fortunately not, I guess, since my marriage didn't work out. I think he would have been a very difficult person to share a child with—while divorced, that is. Maybe while married, too, now that I know a different side of him."

Curiosity shadowed his expression for just a wink of a moment, and she wished she hadn't said so much about her newly minted ex. Now there would be questions.

Workers could be heard out front, talking, gathering their equipment, and making their way toward the house.

"Well, then. Sometimes things do work out for the best. How did you meet your former husband?" They walked across the room, and Henry's work boots made a muted clunking sound on the hardwood floors.

"Oh." She reached beneath her hair and pressed her fingers against the tension that gathered on the back of her neck. She peered out the front window to see what was taking the workers so long. "We um, it started as a business relationship."

"He was a client?"

With her back to Henry, she squeezed her eyes shut and winced. "Sort of. He was a partner in his dad's company, and his dad's hotels are clients of mine." She felt her skin warm. She dearly hoped he didn't think that she slept with all her clients.

"The two of you grew apart?"

She scoffed. "After I found out he was sleeping with one of his grad students, yes. We grew apart. I knew he shouldn't have taken that teaching job."

"Men like that usually find opportunity no matter where they work." His features hardened into a scowl, as though he had a bone to pick with her ex. His protectiveness warmed her inside and out, but it also made her realize he was right. Preston would have pounced on opportunity wherever it offered itself.

"I think what has had me really burned about the whole thing, aside from the obvious, was that I knew better—ahead of time, that is. I guess we all have decisions we wish we'd made differently. My mother said I needed to get back to trusting my instincts. Sometimes, I think I can still hear her voice reminding me. Anyway, she said if I did that then I would—" She gestured her hand forward, suddenly nervous that she was once again revealing too much too soon. It wasn't her style to share personal information with someone she didn't know all that well. "See the right one for me."

"Wise woman, your mother." Henry put his hands in his front pockets when he walked past her, and she thought she saw a cat-that-caught-the-canary grin on his face. "I always liked her."

She caught up to him, and they walked together for a few steps. "I was thinking. You don't suppose the manor had anything to do with her death, do you?"

"No," he said quickly. "If she had died on the anniversary of Anna's death, I would be suspicious. But as it was, no, I don't."

She nodded, and a bit of tension left her chest that she hadn't realized was tied to that worry. Her mother had died of a heart attack. Stress-related, she guessed. The house had probably contributed, but maybe not in the way it, or Benjamin, had to the other deaths.

He was probably right. "Well, anyway. With my ex, she knew I hadn't paid enough attention to those nit-picky doubts ahead of time. She turned out to be right about that."

"Ah, yes. Those little voices of wisdom that never seem to speak loud enough when we need them to."

"You're familiar with them, I see."

"My life would have turned out quite differently if I had listened to them. There was a feeling that I now know was more of a warning." He shook his head. "Well. It's all water over the dam, as they say."

His words held a shimmer of regret, and she recognized it from her own experience. "You were married?"

He nodded. "Yes, she's passed now."

"Oh, I'm sorry."

"It's okay." He sighed and ran his hand over his face as though the memory made him tired. "But I do understand about honoring that voice ahead of time. Just as in your situation, I did not. I should have."

She wanted to say something eloquent and compassionate. Her tongue was tangled in a knot full of conflict, and she couldn't find either of those things. Despite what they had shared, they really didn't know each other well enough for her to offer a friendly response. As usual, she felt herself shifting into a business gear for the comfort and the insulation it brought. She tried to relax that tendency in favor of what they might be building together.

"If I had a glass of wine"—she held her hand up in a pretend toast—"I'd toast to trusting our instincts."

He raised his mock glass and met her toast. "To trusting our instincts."

Their fingers held together for a moment longer than was necessary, and the tenderness they'd shared the night before threaded between them.

The contractors laid their materials on the front porch in a clatter. They would walk through the door at any moment. But Gemma couldn't take her eyes off Henry's. His index finger glided along hers, and work suddenly felt like an intrusion in her day. She would rather have spent the day with Henry, enjoying long walks on the beach, picnics, and learning everything there was to know about him.

The group of noisy contractors burst through the door, and she waved them into the house. "Come on in, guys. Let's get started." She glanced at Henry one last time. They held a gaze over the frenetic group, a look that said there was more to come.

CHAPTER 15

The next few weeks brought Gemma everything she had ever hoped for, as well as what she had never expected. Her days with Henry were filled with hard work and extraordinary progress. The restoration team was tireless and the results were exquisite. And thanks, she knew, to the endless clearing work she did when no one was around, Benjamin had not destroyed their work *en masse*.

Several mysterious destructions continued here and there, and Benjamin was still a very real threat, but, overall, they made headway. They were even a little ahead of schedule to meet the judge's fast-approaching deadline.

Her nights with Henry in the winter garden were another world entirely. That one room had become their candlelit sanctuary. It was a magical space that gave them time to get to know one another, time to enjoy what they shared, and time to build toward what she hoped might be a future together. He had been right when he said that nothing bad would happen to her in there.

During the day, Henry often went in his own direction, and she appreciated that he gave her the space to do her job.

Most homeowners, especially those with larger budgets, tended to hover and helicopter each stage of the process. But Henry didn't.

He reluctantly gave her bits of tragic history about the house when she asked for it so she could clear the negative imprints. He was simultaneously concerned that her work would stir up some negative consequence. And he didn't think the clearing would solve the manor's haunted problems anyway. Both opinions were okay. She knew it would work. Because it had to.

Though there was a seemingly endless amount of clearing to be done. She would have to find and clear more of the fundamental tragic imprints in the house. Hopefully, Henry would give her that specific information.

On this particular morning, the workers gathered into small, task-specific groups, she showed them some of her drawings and told them her ideas. They were a quiet bunch. Not much discussion, only some head-nodding while they stared at the things she pointed to.

When she felt confident that one group understood what to do with the next stage of the flooring and the staircase, she moved on to the next one, who would repair the walls. She flipped the pages on the legal pad and walked toward one worker—thin, balding, tall. He stood close to the stenciling that framed the doorway to the kitchen. She didn't waste any time on niceties.

"Hi, there. I'm Gemma with Stewart Restoration. See here with this vine? I'd like you to get as close to the original colorings on these as possible. That original blue, as you can see, should be vibrant, like a peacock feather."

The balding artist tilted his chin and focused through the bottom part of his glasses where Gemma pointed at the stenciling. He made a low *mmmmm* sound. Then he picked up his sketch pad and made some drawings of the stencil.

"And the gold, here, on the vine." She moved her portfolio over and pointed with her other hand. "Notice how that gold isn't yellow or opaque. It has texture and shading to it with bits of brown. Like real bark. Over on this side of the vine, it's much lighter. Because, see?" She pointed to the large antebellum windows that covered the back wall. "The artist knew that the sun would be rising over here. So, when the sunlight pours in, it's creating a shadow on this side, as if the vine were real. Got it?"

The artist was quiet, but he examined the vine closely and made notes on the different colors. Then he studied the morning light as it came in the windows. He made a deliberate shadow with his hand and played with the light as it shone against the wall.

"Interesting," he said. "Fascinating."

"Amazing, isn't it? Don't embellish; recreate exactly what's there. And I'm not positive about this, but Tom has quite a few thick folders on the desk in the study. One of them may have close-up shots of this work. Worth a try." Gemma patted him on the back and gave him a little shove in the right direction.

"If I can just have everyone's attention, please?" She clapped her hands and the noise echoed in the vaulted room. All the workers looked in her direction. "Keep track of your plans and progress, as well as any changes you recommend. I prefer paper, please. Old-fashioned, I know, but that's the way it is. At the end of the day, I want your documentation on the desk in the office so I can review everything. I'll make comments there. Please check your progress papers before work begins the following day, and pay special attention to my notes. If you have any questions, let me know. Otherwise, let's get back to work."

The artist stood next to the stenciling with the photographs in hand that she had mentioned to him. He tilted his head to see her through the bottom of his glasses, then went back to work. Everyone else focused on their jobs.

With no questions left to answer, Gemma went to find Henry and Tom.

"Get out of my house, Asher Cardill!" Henry's voice echoed through the halls. "You're violating a restraining order! You're not allowed within one hundred feet of this property!"

A dull *thud* sounded from the second floor, then heavy footsteps ran toward her. She backed out of the doorway and flattened herself against the other side of the wall, out of sight. The youngish man with thinning brown hair barreled through the kitchen. His faded jeans, plaid shirt, and lace-ups made him appear like any one of the other workers. His hand grabbed the doorjamb for balance when he swung around the corner and headed toward the outside.

She jogged behind him until she was sure he was a safe enough distance ahead not to hear her, then she took off in his direction. Maybe she could get his car tag number and report it.

When she turned the corner of the house, all she could hear was the quick pace of shoes pounding against the pebbled driveway in the distance. She slapped her hands to her sides.

Henry ran up to her, his face drawn tight. "Are you okay?"

"Yeah, I'm fine, but he got away."

"Doesn't matter." He put his arm around her back and guided her toward the house.

"You called him by name. Something Cardill?"

"Asher. Asher Cardill," he growled.

She remembered him from the cafe and from her first day at the manor. "I've heard that name. Who is he?"

"He's a developer in town. Should we lose the house to the other side of the family, his company would be a very interested buyer. Then they'd mow this place down and put up condos.

"He's nosed around the estate too many times while we've been trying to restore it. Tom took out a restraining order against him. He's not supposed to set foot near the property until after the judge's deadline has passed."

"I've seen him here before—when I first arrived. I only noticed him because his outfit was so unique—he wore this pink belt." She ran her hands along her waistline.

"Where did you see him?"

"Off to the side of the house. He was just standing there as the workers were coming in and out."

"Timing their shifts, most likely. Bastard." His eyes went cold, flat, and unfeeling.

"I also saw him at this breakfast place I visited on the morning of the accident." She stopped short at the double door entry to the study, where a hole had been smashed in the wood cornice work over the fireplace.

"Damn it!" She charged toward the damage. "This is going to be really expensive to repair."

Henry stared at the hole, his mouth slightly open. His eyes now brewed dark and angry like a storm that threatened to strike.

Tom appeared with Paisley and several other workers. He cursed and kicked the pieces of chipped wood against the wall. "This room was completely finished!"

Paisley ran her fingers through her dark hair and squeezed her head in frustration. "Must have happened last night."

Gemma thought about the violins and the hauntings that played throughout the house. This damage could have been more of Benjamin's work.

Deep lines undulated across Tom's forehead. "Well, I have a security consultant coming in later today—not that he can help us with this."

"Add this to the project list," Tom said to Paisley before he stormed out of the room.

Gemma's sixth sense kicked in. It was a farfetched idea that she would have discounted if someone else had suggested it. But she and Henry had agreed to trust their instincts. And so she would.

"Henry," she whispered. "I have an idea."

CHAPTER 16

"I'm wondering about the furniture." Gemma couldn't quite believe she was going to suggest this.

Henry looked about the study at the desk and other pieces. "This furniture?"

She pointed to the second level. "The original furniture that was inside the museum. The pieces that Paisley had installed in the upstairs bedrooms. Benjamin has ripped through this entire house and found nothing. But what if the suicide note was hidden inside a piece of that furniture somewhere? What if it exists, but it just hasn't been here in the house?"

He nodded slowly, thoughtfully. "I suppose that's possible. One of Benjamin's enemies may have wanted to see him implicated in Anna's death."

"I doubt anyone has searched the furniture. If we're really going to try to find this note, then I think we need to turn every stone." She nodded to the gaping hole above the fireplace. "Benjamin certainly is."

"I agree. Finding that note is the only way to...stop this from happening." He turned toward the hole in the wall.

"The anniversary of Anna Alcott's death is fast approaching, as is the judge's deadline. We need to get Benjamin out of here before he has a chance to wreck things for us."

"Before he kills again." She whispered the words in the same way her paternal grandmother whispered words like *cancer* and *divorce* because she didn't want them to be true. Sick dread wormed its way through her chest.

And with that thought, the full effect of her suggestion dropped to her stomach and churned with the idea of heading back to the upstairs. The master bedrooms weren't too far from the guest room she'd visited once before.

Henry glanced at his watch and then down the corridor that was busy with construction workers tromping in each direction. "I should go with you, but it's only three o'clock, so you ought to be safe up there at this time of day. And I need to join Tom in the meeting with that security consultant first. We have to agree on a plan that keeps Asher off the property until after the judge's deadline."

"Okay. Sure." Her voice pitched a little higher than was normal for her.

"Unless you want to take the meeting with Tom for the security plan, and I can go search?"

Part of her wished he'd cancel his participation in the meeting and escort her upstairs. Though the cinnamon in his eyes held her with his gaze and she felt the heat thread between them, distance was best, she decided.

What they shared at night was their business. She couldn't have Tom or anyone else figuring out what she and Henry had started. Besides, it would be good for her to be alone up there so she could do some more clearing.

She took in a deep breath. "You take the meeting. I'll go up now and have a look at the furniture in the two masters. I've been over most of the house today, and it's been completely normal. I won't go anywhere near the guest room with the dolls." She flashed him a smile and stepped away.

"Gemma—"

"Oh, just to be sure. You haven't read or heard of anything disastrous happening in those two rooms, have you?" She thought of her theory about how the house wanted her. For what, she hadn't yet figured out, but she didn't want any more surprises.

Henry shook his head. "No. Not that I've read. Though let's hold off on any energy work. I wouldn't want anything... stirred up."

Her eyes remained on him. "It usually only helps to alleviate—but, okay..." She nodded without agreeing. If she saw something negative that she knew she could fix, she would. He wouldn't have to know about it.

"Sun sets just after eight. The house will be quiet until then, or mostly so. Don't be long up there."

"I won't."

She glanced at the upstairs and stifled the chill that ran through her body. "I'll be right back."

THE UPSTAIRS AREA was mostly complete and quiet as a result. Hammering, saws, and men's voices drifted up from the downstairs. Thankfully, Tom had taken her suggestion and double-teamed the grand staircase. At least thirty men swarmed it when she'd last checked. They would be finished constructing the forty-two wide steps and two landings in no time.

In the quiet, and while the sun shone through the second story windows, she calmed her nerves by counting off the benefits of being upstairs alone. First, she might get more information on this house that felt more human to her than inanimate. There was something about it that rose to her touch, that resonated with some part of her. She was meant to be here—why, she didn't know. Maybe that would become clearer to her if she had some time to herself. She ran her hand along the chair rail that lined the hallway.

Second, she would also evaluate the design details for the upstairs. Everything needed to be perfect for the judge's walkthrough, and aesthetics went a long way to giving people a sense of confidence. After seeing Paisley's dubious wall design choice in the foyer, checking the bedrooms was a good idea. She might be able to improve upon what was there.

And third, bedrooms were typically a very personal and unguarded space. She might figure out some vital information there that she could heal. Though, hopefully, nothing like the guest room.

The job was going well, she reminded herself—aside from Benjamin's newest destruction. She'd have to start clearing those deeper imprints as soon as possible to put an end to that. Any restoration was fraught with hurdles. Typically, homeowners' pained expressions accompanied endless questions of why and how much.

The court-imposed deadline apparently eliminated those for Henry. They were down to do or die, and he didn't want to lose his ancestral home.

It was important to him to help Benjamin move on. She appreciated the kindness in that. "Ghosts are people, too," her mother had always said.

The anniversary of Anna Alcott's death loomed. They had to get Benjamin gone, one way or another, before that night.

Asher was the other hitch. She sneered when she thought of him. "Opportunistic bastard." His presence at the house was suspicious, and she was convinced he was trying to sabotage the job in some way. Tom would need to hire another security guard and that would help. Though he would also need to have some discussion with the workers, or at least the foremen. He could offer a reward for anyone who reported Asher's presence on the site.

"Ow!" Sharp pain shot through her index finger, and she jerked it away from the railing. A thin nail was jammed beneath her fingernail. She inhaled a hiss through bared teeth, ripped it out, and cupped her hand beneath the dripping blood.

She jogged to the master bedroom at the end of the hall. The tarnished doorknob was loose, and the nearly black wooden door was thick and heavy.

Benjamin Alcott's bedroom was fitting with a Napoleonic sleigh bed, a bureau, a wardrobe, and a chaise in red at the foot of the bed. There was a lot of red—there were deep red walls, red carpet, and a crown of red fabric behind the bed. All of it seemed to recognize her as a female, and it pulled at her, making her feel like she'd landed in Dracula's lair. The room pulsed and she swooned to its hypnotic heartbeat.

She wondered if Henry would let her repaint and re-fabric some of this bedroom. She made a note in her portfolio with her left hand: *change carpet and wall coverings to beige/taupe combo to lighten the room.* She found her way to the master bath.

She pushed the iron-colored knob on the sink with the back of her hand and rinsed her finger. An unsettling stream of blood ran into the sink, then ran clear under the running water. The cold felt good on her skin, and without soap at hand, she continued to rinse. She hadn't asked where they kept the first aid kit. The kitchen, she assumed. A Band-Aid and antibacterial cream were in order.

Red swirled thick and free across the bowl of the sink. She gasped and held up her finger, but the cut was not bleeding. There wasn't any blood on her hands.

The water ran clear from the spigot into the sink, but

once it hit the bowl, it turned into a gelatinous, red liquid. Cautiously, she put two fingers into the sickly sweet scented liquid and rubbed it between her fingers and thumb. It ran down her hand in streams.

Blood.

Benjamin.

Murderer.

Panic jolted through her nerves and she shoved her hands into the clear running water until they ran clean. She turned off the water and the blood disappeared down the drain, leaving the white bowl tinted with red.

Her insides shook until she thought she might rattle, and she pressed both of her hands tight against her chest.

Settle, Gem. It's just an imprint. Maybe a living memory as Henry said. Something happened here. That's all. You'll deal with it. You're strong now.

Her body only calmed slightly at her words. The terror continued inside, in part from memories it seemed she'd never forget.

You have a job to do.

Her breath was shaky and her finger throbbed. She pressed her thumb against the pad of her injured finger repeatedly, which brought about an ache, a hurt, but a slight release of stress.

She stepped slowly, *one, two, three.* A scent floated by— orange, lavender, and something spicy like clove. She glanced around the room for a candle or a bottle of cologne, but there was no obvious source.

She tried to pull in a deep breath, but her lungs ached and were so tight they would only take in a shallow breath. It scared her to move, as if it might draw too much attention to her presence in the room.

Inspect the furniture. Move on. You're okay, Gem.

She could almost feel her mother comforting her, encouraging her, just as she had for years after it happened. Sunlight streamed in through the red-framed windows. The house wouldn't be truly active for some time yet.

Pick a piece. Focus.

She counted her steps lengthwise across the room, to measure, she rationalized. When she tugged on the wardrobe door, it opened more easily than she'd expected and a black arm swooshed toward her.

"Oh!" The muscles in her chest gripped at one another.

The lone black tuxedo swung to and fro, the metal hook squeaking against the gray rod. The sight of its movement spooked her, and she steadied it. The room spun and tilted, and events sped by her too quickly to see clearly: music and laughter, screaming and crying, patches of silence, and above all, someone yelling, "Benjamin!"

The sleeve of the suit filled out under her hand. Warm, muscular movement surrounded by fine fabric. Gemma found herself on the opposite side of the room and touching the back side of the arm of a man who slid white dress gloves onto his hands.

She gasped and stumbled backward until she bumped into the footboard of the bed on the other side of the room. Lively notes from a string orchestra danced into the room from the downstairs, and she recognized it as the same violin melody she had heard before. She stared at the man's broad back. His tuxedo tails swished while he seemed to adjust his sleeves to fully cover his wrists. A black top hat rested on the table next to him.

"Benjamin," a soft voice said.

Gemma leaned to the side with exacting slowness until she saw a young woman with tired, sad eyes. Her soft brown hair lay tangled on her white, buttondown undergarments, and a toddler, maybe a year old, was attached to her leg.

"Da-da," the little girl said.

"Anna. Get dressed," the man said.

"Promise me that I can have the divorce, Benjamin, and I'll do what you want."

"Do not try to force my hand, Anna. You won't like what happens if you do. Put on the white dress. The President and his wife will be here soon. Tonight, of all nights, pull yourself together and try to think of someone besides yourself." He said it through his teeth, like a growl, like a warning, like a dog whose bite would hurt far worse than his bark.

The little girl crawled along the floor and tugged on Benjamin's pant leg. "Up, Da-da. Up."

He lifted her into his arms and kissed her. She patted his chest with her tiny hands as if to say, *Mine. All mine.*

"Tonight is an important night for me. For all of us. You would do well to remember that," he said to Anna.

She sighed and pushed away a long brown curl that dangled to the side of her cheek and it fell again.

A young woman in a white frilled cap and apron entered the room. "There you are, Lizzie Mae." She stood in front of Benjamin and took the baby from his arms, and Lizzie Mae promptly let out a wail. "Mr. Alcott, I'm sorry, sir. She crawls too fast these days. I must have left the nursery door open while I was changing the bedding."

"It's okay, Dorothy," Anna said.

Dorothy bounced and patted Lizzie Mae, but the baby only cried and reached for her father. Benjamin took the child, kissed her head, and stroked her round, baby-doll cheeks to calm her.

Anna put her head in her hands and leaned on her knees.

"Dorothy, the children *must* be settled and quiet while the guests are here. If you need to, you can take them to their grandparents' home for the evening," Benjamin said.

"I'm sorry, sir." Dorothy curtsied. "It's just that whenever Miss Lizzie Mae knows that you're here—"

"Maybe it's best if you take her and the other three children to Mrs. Alcott's parents' home and keep them there until the morning." He handed Lizzie Mae to the nanny and the baby cried.

Dorothy curtsied again. She cut a glance to Anna, then scurried out of the room.

"Da-daaaaa!" Lizzie Mae screamed down the hallway.

Benjamin pushed both hands against his temples. "Anna. Tonight is the most important night of my life. After everything I've done for you, you can put on the white dress I bought for you, fix your hair and makeup, and at least pretend to be a good wife and mother. Just for tonight."

Anna looked at him with a blank stare. "I can't, Benjamin. I can't do this anymore."

"One night. One night, Anna. That's all I ask. After that, we'll keep you in the background."

"And what about when you're elected? What then? I'll never get out!"

"Well, you can't get out, can you? Not now. I gave you your chance to walk away before you married me. What's done is done. You've made your bed." He grabbed her by the upper part of the arm.

"Stop it!" She slapped at Benjamin's arm.

"Get. Dressed." He deposited Anna into the hallway, slammed the bedroom door, and both figures disappeared into a wisp of gray shadows.

The only sound left in the room was Gemma's shaky breath. The room returned to how it was when she first arrived, though the sun was much lower in the sky now. The shadows in the room were dusky. Her eyes scanned the area in front of her and found a black marble clock on the center of the mantel. Bronze cherubs flanked the white face. Six o'clock.

Six o'clock. How was that possible?

It had only been fifteen minutes, at most, since she'd come into this room. With her portfolio clasped to her chest, her hands trembling, she thought to check the space behind her. But she wasn't sure what frightened her more: what might be hiding behind her, or what could be staring her in the face when she turned around. This house was not predictable.

The spiced scent of cologne that had hung in the room faded. She eyed the door that Benjamin had slammed. It was about seven or eight steps away. She rolled her shoulders back and tightened her insides. No one was going to come and rescue her from where she stood. She needed to move. She had to get out of the house before the sun slipped from the sky.

CHAPTER 17

Benjamin's bedroom door shut behind her, and she fought the panic that whirled through her chest. She had never seen such vivid images in a client's house before. There were often impressions, feelings, and ideas about the energy that was trapped within a house—all in a sort of generally intuitive way. That, combined with conversation from the owners, often led her to implement some transformative changes.

What she had just seen was not that.

Pop, Janey, and even Henry had said the house was haunted. But those weren't ghosts. They didn't see her. It was more like...the house was replaying the past and pulling her into it.

What had Henry said about the house? Something about how memories of the night Anna died replayed. First in snippets and then, eventually, all the way through.

Living memories.

That's what he said. He also said he thought they were dangerous.

Shock worked its way through her system. She didn't

shake on the outside, but everything inside quivered. She grasped the smooth wooden chair rail that lined the corridor, but the lingering pain in her finger reminded her not to slide her hand along it blindly. Rather, she chose to touch it periodically and lightly to keep her steady while she cast several glances behind her.

Possessed. Possessive. The manor was intent upon replaying its history. Telling its story. From imprints, maybe, but she'd never seen imprints like this before.

Like the manor had an agenda.

An intent.

To solve something? The suicide note. Or it could have been something more than that—the mystery of it all.

Was that why the manor wanted her here? Because it somehow knew that she could clear the negativity it had absorbed over the years? Maybe the manor overheard her parents talking about her and what she could do?

She couldn't believe what she was suggesting. That a house could have a spirit or a want—or, God forbid—a way of getting what it wanted.

She'd clear as much as she could as fast as she could. Though she didn't know how to clear what she had just seen. Henry had asked her not to, not today. And, most importantly, at least for right now, she needed to get downstairs and out of the house before the sun set.

The long hallway extended ahead of her, and an eerie sensation of being watched crawled down her back. She took the quickest peek behind her. The hallway was completely empty, though she felt the presence of others.

Many others.

Talking. Laughing. Keeping their identities a secret from her.

They were a quiet presence. But she could feel them. Sort of like when someone passed by her in a library, and the cool, air-conditioned breeze brushed silently against her skin.

Footsteps sounded in the direction she headed. Along with a *clank, clank, clank*. Metal against metal. Maybe a ladder that jostled with each step, or painting materials? The footsteps weren't Henry's, or even a man's step. They were quick and light. Paisley, maybe. For the second time today, Gemma would be happy to see her.

The female figure appeared in stages when she rose to the top of the stairs. First the white bonnet, then the round face, and finally, the dark uniform with the white apron. *Clank, clank, clank.* She carried a coal bucket and small shovel that made noise when they jostled against one another.

Gemma jumped at the sight. Her hand felt where the end of the chair rail opened onto a door. The maid nodded and sent her a look with curious eyes. Gemma fumbled with the doorknob until it opened and she darted through it. After shutting the door quickly behind her, she waited. Hoped. Prayed that the maid—

The ghost?

The memory?

—wouldn't find its way to her. The jangle of metal on metal hit an even rhythm, accenting every other beat. It struck its peak when the maid walked nearest to the door. When the clanking metal finally passed into the once again quiet, she felt her heart resume a steady beat.

Her vision settled on her immediate surroundings, the sizable room with floral carpet and wallpaper in earthy gold, blues, and browns. Where Benjamin's room had been seductively bold with rich color, this must have been Anna's room. It was more understated and feminine, with print and flowers and a thin gold rope painted as a border near the ceiling that was scalloped every foot or so.

She sat on the side of Anna's Louis XV bed and filled her

lungs with air, waiting, just to be certain, that the hallway was empty now. Her empathy for the woman she had seen in Benjamin's room overwhelmed her. Anna appeared tired and sad, worn out from Benjamin's temper, Gemma supposed. Her hand traced the gracefully carved walnut headboard decorated with embellishments at the top and sides, as well as a few additions she'd never seen on a piece like this.

A painted bouquet was centered on the headboard, the stems hidden in a white lace doily and tied together with a blue ribbon. On either side were white flowers mixed with red tulips and tied in white ribbon—white flowers that appeared to be the same fragrant ones that lined the back-yard of the estate.

Other odd-looking flowers in red and purple were painted to look as if someone had laid them beneath the arrange-ments. Some curled, brown leaves were scattered around the flowers.

Anna's room was plain and orderly in a Victorian way. Everything in its place, all at right angles and centered around the rectangular windows that stood on end on the far wall. From the second story, they offered Anna a view of another world, but not a way out of the one she was sentenced to.

The beauty was stunted by walls that were too firm and a floor that was too solid. Benjamin's room nearly throbbed with a pulse, it was so bold. Anna's was more of a decorated holding cell. It was thankfully quiet and keeping its secrets to itself. She would inspect the furniture another time with Henry. For now, she would go downstairs.

When she stood, a strong scent of perfume filled the room, and she turned to find a crackling fire in the fireplace that heated the too-flowery scent. For the second time in the past few minutes, her heart skipped double time on its regular job.

The same woman she'd seen next door sat at an ornate

walnut vanity with a white marble top, wearing knee-length, beige undergarments. Two silver candelabras were lit and placed on either side. Several medicine bottles crowded on the left-hand ledge, and a glass of wine rested on the other side. A young maid stood behind her and pinned and twisted her loose curls into an effortless pile at the top of her head.

"So real," Gemma whispered.

Memories.

Imprints?

Three dimensional.

So alive.

She stepped toward the woman she now knew was Anna and held her position just a few feet from her. Anna's lifeless expression stared at her, unseeing from the mirror. Her eyes and lips were swollen, and a blush of red from crying dotted the end of her nose. Gemma waved her hand in a slow half-circle, but no one noticed her.

When the maid finished Anna's hair, she went to the closet and retrieved a long white dress with a high lace collar and blue sash. She laid it on the bed and brushed the wrinkles from the fabric.

"No," Anna said flatly. "I want the red one with the rose." She waved the glass of wine carelessly when she spoke, and the liquid sloshed toward the rim.

"Oh, no, ma'am. The senator said you were to wear the white—"

"The senator isn't here." Anna took a sip of wine beneath her glare. "Get the red dress."

The young maid dropped her head and curtsied. "Yes, ma'am."

She returned the white dress to the closet and brought two new dresses: a red dress that was cut low in the front with a matching rose sewn into the deepest point of the V, and a long, purple sateen dress with a high neck.

"This one would be nice to wear to meet the President of the United States. Don't you think, Miss Anna? It's so lovely. I think it looks especially nice with your skin." The maid drew her short, thick hand down the dress to show it off.

Anna stumbled when she snatched the purple dress from the maid's hands. She threw it toward the closet. "Put it back."

"Yes, ma'am." The maid pressed her lips together and gathered the gown from the floor.

When the purple dress was out of sight, she helped Anna into the red dress and buttoned it up the back. Anna pressed the stiff red collar to ensure that it would stand up, then lifted her breasts inside the bodice so that they would lead the way. They would not be a sight unseen.

"Oh, but Miss Anna, the President will be downstairs, and this is a very important night for the senator."

"Yes, Della. It's always an important night for the senator. Now leave me alone."

The maid curtsied and hurried out of the room. Gemma moved aside when she passed, and she wondered what would have happened if she hadn't.

Anna threw her glass against the closed door, and it shattered with a high-pitched crash, the red wine bleeding onto the door and rug. She slumped into a chair with her head in her hands, her body shaking.

The gas lamps hissed and the fire's low flames crackled. Gemma wanted to tell Anna she was going to be okay, even though she knew this story didn't work out well for her. She walked slowly toward the vision of Anna, whose sadness touched Gemma's heart in a familiar ache. Unable to do nothing in the presence of her suffering, she placed her hand on Anna's shoulder. Anna shot up with a gasp. "Who's there?" She sniffed and wiped her nose with the back of her hand.

Gemma's hand flew to her mouth to cover the scream

that wanted to escape. She'd touched Anna, felt the coolness of her smooth shoulder. Somehow, she was here.

Or, Gemma wondered, was she within the house's memory somehow?

"I've lost my mind in this godforsaken house." Anna yanked on the right-hand drawer of her vanity and removed several paintbrushes and four glass jars, each nearly full of a different bright color. She spread a cloth on the bedside table and arranged the jars and brushes. Then she leaned across the edge of her bed and began to give life to the odd-looking flowers Gemma had seen on the bottom of the headboard just moments earlier.

She watched while Anna carefully colored a combination of light and dark purple hues on the petals and added rich black centers. Anna was calmer now, not scared or frustrated. The anger was gone. Even the earlier drunken imbalance was missing. It was just her and her flowers, her private world. She sketched the dry, dead, and crumpled leaves Gemma had seen just a moment ago. Anna's focus was unmovable.

Gemma stepped away, careful not to make any noise or knock anything over. Both because she didn't understand how she could create a disturbance in this 1880s world, and Henry had said he thought these live memories were dangerous somehow.

Too, she didn't want to disturb Anna's peace. Flowers and painting must have been her solace.

She felt safer in Anna's room than she had in Benjamin's. And though she couldn't believe that she was going to do this, she was. If this was the night when Anna died, and if there was a note, maybe it was nearby.

She tiptoed to the open secretary on the off chance that a suicide note would be there. On the desk were several balled up pieces of white paper, a black fountain pen, an open bottle of ink, and a skeleton key tied to a ribbon. A stack of white stationery with gold double-scripted As at the center top were housed next to matching envelopes. One letter was askew, and the words Dear Sam were written across the upper left-hand side of the paper.

No suicide note.

She checked on Anna, whose concentration remained fiercely devoted to her painting. Gemma swallowed hard. The delicate knob on the desk was smooth and the narrow drawer slid open easily, quietly, and she sighed. She knew Anna didn't see her when she touched her. She couldn't imagine the stress she would cause if Anna suddenly saw her desk drawers opening and closing.

Inside the first drawer were two fountain pens. The other narrow drawer was empty. There were four drawers on each side, and she opened them all with the same disappointing result.

Anna finished the painting and examined her work from three steps away. Seemingly satisfied enough, she sat at her vanity and applied too much red to her cheeks and lips in rote movement. "You ruined my life, Benjamin. With one callous shake of your head, you took away any chance of happiness I could have had in this life."

Gemma glanced at the clock on the mantel: nine thirty p.m. Adrenaline poured too freely through her heart. That had to be Anna's time, not her own.

A rapid *thump-thump-thump* sounded from the downstairs, and she spun toward the open door, half expecting to hear or see Benjamin. No one appeared. There was only the quiet.

She twisted to see if Anna had heard the noise, but found that she was in the room by herself. The warmth from the fire was missing, the perfumed scent was gone. A tiny wisp of smoke spiraled from one of the wicks, then disappeared into Gemma's memory.

She scanned the room, stunned by the drama that was

held hostage within these walls. The house was teeming with this story, and she tried to think how she would heal the imprints that were left here. Nothing she could do seemed like enough.

A visit from the President of the United States, his announcement of the senator's candidacy for the presidency, a slightly drunk wife who had lost hope and was bent on revenge—this sounded a lot more like Benjamin's motivation for murder than a case for Anna's suicide.

She crossed the room to a full-length portrait of Anna that hung on the side wall. She wore the lavender dress the maid had shown her, with a white lace collar and fabric-covered buttons down the bodice. She held a small bouquet of white flowers and red tulips wrapped in white lace—the same flowers painted on the growth chart and her head-board. A closed-lipped smile graced Anna's gentle face, but her eyes held hints of the watery sadness Gemma had seen tonight.

The wind whipped through the branches and rattled the shutters on either side of the bedroom windows. She checked the clock again, and her heart clenched with the pain that fear brought. Ten p.m.

Impossible that it was that late.

With one last look about the room, she decided she had to make a run for the downstairs. There was no other way out, and she sure as hell wasn't going to wait in this room until morning.

Her carpeted footsteps seemed loud in the hallway of this house that was so different at night. In fact, every noise held more strength in the manor after the sun set. She kept forging toward the stairwell, one foot in front of the other. Drafts meandered effortlessly around her like ghosts looking for someone to play with.

Another thump from downstairs stopped her. "Okay," she

whispered. "Just keep moving." Her steps came slower than she wanted them to.

One, two, three, four...

She knew if she ran her fear would quickly ramp into panic.

Five, six, seven eight...

She paused at the top of the back stairway and glanced at the light shining beneath a narrow door. A shadow passed from right to left under the doorway.

Thump.

God. Please. Please, please, please.

She squeezed her hands into fists and placed one shaky foot on the top step, then the next. Rapid *thump, thump, thumps* echoed from downstairs. All her stomach muscles tightened into concrete and stayed that way. She planned her escape to the outside. Two turns, then a straight shot to the door.

She was almost out. When her foot hit the last step, she blew her nerves out on a quiet breath.

Silence.

Keep moving forward, Gem.

The wind whistled alongside the house. She wondered for a moment if Asher or some member of his clan were at the house again and working to keep Henry from meeting his deadline.

She just had to get past the library and the study, then she'd make a dash to the kitchen door that led to the outside.

She listened at the threshold.

Quiet. Whatever it was it had stopped. Her eyes closed and relief poured through her.

Thump. Thump. Thump.

They were louder this time, and she crossed her hands over her heart that beat so hard and fast it threatened to break a rib.

Thump. Thump. Thump.

It sounded like cabinet doors slamming shut, but not quite. She drew in the deepest breath she could. Then she stepped lightly down the long hallway, her feet picking up the pace with each step.

The grunting noise surprised her most. A homeless person looking for shelter or something to eat? Her father had suggested that the homeless might have been on site at night and responsible for that girl's death.

When she reached the library, several hardback books were scattered in the hallway. The title on one of the covers was illuminated in gold. Distractedly, she picked it up, along with the other two that were near it, and clasped them to her chest. The noises were the books hitting the floor.

Thump. Thump. Thump.

She inhaled sharply and more audibly than she planned. She felt his presence, heard his wheezing.

Another memory from the house?

He grunted again, and two more books fell to the floor.

Thump. Thump.

It was a stupidly rational thought in light of the danger she was in, but she thought it anyway. About how Henry had been right about his prediction that the books would end up on the floor again. Her breath shook in small, captured fits at the idea of what she had to do.

She wasn't going back upstairs—the only way out from here was to pass the wide opening to the library. She wasn't going to take off running or tiptoeing until she knew where Benjamin was.

One, two, go.

She leaned to the right. A man in a long-tailed tuxedo—the same one she'd just seen—clawed at the bookcase and threw books to the floor one by one.

Thump.

Thump.

When the shelf was empty, he pounded his fist at the backboard of the bookshelf until a hole broke through. He grabbed the edge of it and ripped an entire length of board, then gave it a toss.

He peered inside the hole, then without warning, he faced her. He had been dead for some time. A noose of rope hung around his neck, the length of it dangling against his suit, the ends of it frayed. A red, angled furrow spread upward across the side of his neck. Half his face was missing, and blood ran down the front of his neck and suit. The damaged flesh and muscles moved when he spoke.

"*Get out,*" he growled and took a step toward her.

The scream she wanted to give, in warning and for help, never passed her lips. Instead, it fell backward and inward and somehow became a part of her and made her feel the victim all over again.

"*Get out!*" he roared. Heavy footsteps clomped, and she ran toward the kitchen at breakneck speed. When she finally reached it, she slammed the door behind her and kept running. She didn't stop until she reached the beach.

CHAPTER 18

In the full light of the bright moon, Gemma paced in front of the rising tide, the books still clasped tightly to her chest. As much as she tried to let the medicinal crash of the waves calm her, all she had seen stood firm and wouldn't allow it.

Why *had* she seen him?

She stopped, and the ocean spilled over the toes of her black boots.

She didn't see ghosts.

Never had.

Unlike the other people she'd met this haunted evening, he wasn't a memory that the house had cast forward.

He was a ghost, pure and simple.

How was this even possible?

She stared at the back of the historic home that she was charged with restoring. It challenged her with a menacing glare and shadows that morphed with unexpected life.

Trees blowing.

Shifting moonlight. Clouds. Ocean breeze.

A tall figure approached her from the side of the house.

She backed toward the waves and prepared to break into a run down the beach.

Shadows, she tried to rationalize. But she saw him more clearly this time. A man running at her. It was happening again.

She took off in a wild terror, certain she would outrun him. But she didn't get very far before he grabbed her.

He spun her around, and her scream that had lost its way earlier found its voice.

"*No!*" Her voice echoed over the waves, and she wrestled against his hold.

"Gemma!"

She stopped everything and realized that it was Henry who had run to her, not Benjamin. It was Henry who stood there and tried to keep her from getting away.

"Oh," she gasped.

He pulled her into his arms and held her close, and it didn't take long for his embrace to calm her. His soothing effect was almost immediate. He was her ally, her defending force, the one she could trust.

"Where have you been?" His hand stroked the back of her head. "I've been searching for you for hours."

"I was just upstairs to look at the furniture and— I'm not even sure how to describe what just happened."

He held her at half an arm's length to see her face. "You saw Benjamin?"

She nodded.

"Did he hurt you?" There was a protectiveness in the way that he said it. An urgency, a quickness to his phrase.

She exhaled and noticed her breath was shaky. It wasn't just Benjamin or the fear of him. Something about unexpected comfort, she thought. She felt a little weak-kneed in the presence of it. An unusual response for her. She typically preferred to take care of herself. Now all she wanted to do was fall into the safety of Henry's arms.

Maybe in light of the fact that she didn't know how to defend herself against someone as terrifying as Benjamin, his protection was more welcomed and appreciated. Or maybe it was because it came from Henry and in a way that said he cared.

The memory of the man who lacked most of his face and chased her from his home was bright in her mind. "I'm fine. I'm okay."

"Damn it, Benjamin." He held her close to him once again and guided her toward the side of the house. "Come on."

They were headed toward Anna's winter garden, she knew.

When they arrived, Gemma looked at the iron and glass ceiling of her sanctuary. She thought about how this same room had served as a refuge for a woman a hundred years ago and now, once again, for her. Ironically, they were both hiding from the same man.

She and Henry sat together on the pillows and blankets. The low fire crackled, and its shifting light painted itself across the concern on Henry's face.

"You didn't notice the time passing?"

"It didn't pass. I wasn't upstairs for more than a few minutes, an hour at most. Time was just on its own schedule." She held on to the books she'd picked up in the library.

"When you weren't down by the end of my meeting, I went upstairs to look for you. You weren't there."

"I was in the master bedrooms and the hallway."

Henry shook his head slowly as if he didn't want to upset her. "Tell me what happened."

She ran a hand through her hair and tried to explain the kidnapped memories she'd seen and how they had come to life in front of her. She described Benjamin and Anna, how she wanted the divorce, the dress. "I touched her, Henry. Anna. I touched her shoulder and she felt it. She reacted to my touch. This house holds some sort of cross between this world and that one. Whatever that one is."

Henry shut his eyes for an inhale. "You shouldn't be in that part of the house at night."

"I wasn't. I mean, I was, but... It was three o'clock in the afternoon when I went up there to inspect the furniture, then there was this tuxedo, and next thing I knew, it was six something. After a few more minutes, it was nine thirty. It was the strangest thing. When I came downstairs, it was dark and late, and for the life of me, I don't know how that happened. I don't know how any of that happened."

Worry clouded his eyes. "Just promise me that you'll stay out of that part of the house at night. It's dangerous."

She stifled a pang of terror before it ran away with itself.

"It's hard to predict what the house will do. Especially now that we're so close to the anniversary of Anna's death. Remember what I told you. The house makes things happen. It pulls people into its world. You mustn't interact with those memories," he said.

She thought of the connection she'd felt from the house on the first day she'd arrived when she'd touched the pillar. She also thought of how the house welcomed her, pulled her inside. She had originally taken this as a good sign. Now she wasn't so sure. "I thought perhaps my reason for being here had a higher purpose. Now I'm wondering if the house is playing me for a fool."

He brought his hand to her face and pressed his lips gently to hers.

"True confession?"

He nodded.

"I haven't felt this frightened in a very long time. How is

it possible that I could have touched Anna? Or that she could have known that I did?"

He shook his head and inhaled loudly and deeply enough that it took up a good two seconds. "There's something about this house that joins this world with the one that used to be. I don't know how, but there's a connection, almost like a portal. If you should ever see these memories again while you're here, you have to promise that you won't touch anything. Or anyone."

"What would happen?"

"You could end up lost forever in a world that isn't your own. A memory that should be lost to the past, but refuses to stay there."

Gemma felt her lips part in a slow opening. For the first time, she wondered if her clearing work would be enough to fix the problems of the manor. She watched the mental replay of how Anna jumped when she had touched her and felt herself fall down a descending spiral of doubt.

"How do you know this?"

He shook his head as if what he had to say was hard for even him to believe.

"I've seen it happen over the years. People are here one minute, but the next time I see them, they're trapped in one of the house's memories. The people—I've caught glimpses—they look paralyzed, out of place, usually in the background of a scene somewhere. I can't imagine what sort of hell that must be for them, to be trapped like that in such a traumatic event. Benjamin, Anna, all of them are trapped there until justice is found. Time moved ahead without them."

She pushed her fingers along the stress that held tight to her forehead. She gripped the three books more tightly in her other hand.

How in the hell was she supposed to clear this?

"This job isn't exactly turning out the way I thought it

would."

"I imagine not. I'm sure the sight of Benjamin didn't help that, either. How did you stumble upon him?"

"I was in Anna's room when I heard noises like something was hitting the floor. Sort of like a mix between a bang and a slap."

"The books." Henry glanced at the three slender books that were still in her hands.

"Yes." She placed them on the floor beside her, she'd forgotten she still had them.

Henry ran his fingers over the gold titling of the top book: *Floriography—Interpreting the Language of Flowers.* Gemma thought of all the flowers in Anna's life and how she was so passionate about them. "He ripped open a hole in the bookshelf." She couldn't believe that she was actually talking about a ghost's actions.

"Did he *attempt* to hurt you in any way?" Henry ran his hand along her face.

"No. Actually, I don't know, I— He charged me and I saw that...face, and how he physically ripped the back of that bookshelf. I ran—" She forced the panic from rising too far. "I don't even know why I saw him. I've never seen ghosts."

He stared at her with that not-quite-smile, a mix of kindness and concern. The one that said he didn't wish this Benjamin encounter on anyone. His silence was patient. "A lot has changed for you over the past few weeks."

She shrugged and listened to the distant waves that crashed just softly enough that she had to concentrate to hear them.

"Accidents can change things for people," Henry said. "Was there an impact to your head?"

She nodded slow and sure, and lightly touched the right side of her head.

"So, you didn't see ghosts before the accident, but after

the accident, you do."

"That must be it." Her voice caught unexpectedly. "I don't want to see ghosts."

Henry placed his hand on her back and slid it gently into her hand.

"Something happened, didn't it?"

She took a deep breath and enjoyed the sensation of his hand around hers, realizing just how long it had been since she had really relied on someone for support. She had been busy taking care of everyone else: parents, clients, and of course, the divorce. She hadn't been around anyone who could be strong for her. "Just a hard memory."

He tilted his head as if to suggest he knew there was more. The glide of his index finger over her knuckle ignited a connection between them that made her feel alive. Somewhere between free and vulnerable. But insulation had become her habit, and she wanted to hide how he affected her.

Safety first.

If only she could. He saw her, understood her, and she wasn't yet willing to let that go. She leaned into the stillness between them.

He was so giving of himself to her in a way that roused the essence of her soul, bringing her forward such that she felt whole and like herself again. From the moment they'd met, there had been something special between them, a connection that now seemed foolish to deny.

She worried about the conflict with work. They differed in terms of how to restore the manor. She didn't know that she would be able to find the mystery suicide note that he wanted. That conflict might find new life when she set about her clearing work tomorrow instead of searching for the note.

And if she were honest with herself, she'd admit that she was still a little concerned that Henry might be like Preston.

Perfect on the outside, but really not on the inside, where it counted.

She thought of the manor, and how it needed to move forward, how it needed to let go of the tragedies and mistakes of yesteryear. Just like the manor, she needed to know that tomorrow would be better than yesterday. She wondered if trust was the only step toward a cure.

"I'm not trying to pry." He leaned back on his elbows.

"I know." She looked down at her hands.

"I just want to help."

She lifted her gaze to his. "I appreciate that. I enjoy talking with you, I do." And she did. Even when their conversation had been mostly sparring with one another, she found their exchange dynamic, attractive, and exciting. "What do you want to know?"

"What happened that made you feel so afraid of ghosts? Not that any of us are comfortable with them."

She drew in a deep breath. She wouldn't have thought it was possible, but she now felt even more vulnerable, as if she didn't have skin or muscle to protect vital organs. "I, um. I've never told anyone that story before."

"I understand." One dark curl had fallen onto his forehead and nearly reached the edge of his eyebrow. His expression was dark and fierce. She could tell that he knew how ghosts could be, how they could destroy almost everything that you were.

"Gemma, if you want to talk with someone about what happened, I'm here for you."

For the first time in her life, she wanted to tell someone what happened on that terrifying night when she almost died. Someone who wouldn't make fun of her. Someone who would believe her. Someone who understood.

She wanted to tell Henry.

He held very still, his eyes deep with understanding, fierce with protectiveness and present with care.

She began to tell the story she hadn't talked about since it happened all those years ago. "We traveled as a family to a home that my parents were restoring. I was about ten, I guess. My mother wasn't wild about having us kids there since it was an old and haunted house.

"At night, we stayed in a hotel across town. But one evening it was late, and my parents needed to work. They couldn't leave us at the hotel alone, so they had my brothers and me sleep in the den. We were just going to rest for a few hours and then go back to the hotel as soon as my parents were finished.

"It was about three thirty when I woke up to the feel of something brushing along my back. I remember thinking that I must be swimming, floating on the water, the waves moving me.

"Then I couldn't breathe. I coughed to clear whatever it was, but it just got worse. When I opened my eyes, I was on the floor in the middle of the room. He must have dragged me there. I felt these hands around my neck, choking me. I couldn't scream, I couldn't breathe."

She ran her fingers along the front of her neck and swallowed against her tight throat. "It was only because I kicked the floor with both feet that my parents came running. I was unconscious by the time they got to me."

"Good God." He ran his hand over the top of his head.

"At the hospital, they diagnosed me with a fractured larynx. There were these large thumbprint-shaped bruises on the front of my neck." She drew the shapes on her skin. "They gave me a white board and asked me repeatedly to write down who had done this to me. I just kept writing 'no one' and 'I don't know'."

"Who was it?"

"My brothers recalled how strange it was to see me

writhing on the floor, gagging. They thought I was having some sort of fit. My mother was the only one to see the ghost who attacked me in my sleep. She said it was a young man in his twenties, sort of overweight, who wore a black vest and a gray button-down shirt.

"My parents did some research and discovered that a man who fit the description had lived in that house fifty years earlier. He caught his wife in bed with another man and he strangled her to death. Then he shot himself in the house."

A log shifted in the fireplace and she jumped.

Henry stroked her arm gently. "Anyone who had been through that would be afraid of ghosts."

"It was a long time before I spoke again. And an even longer time before I worked on a haunted property." She gestured to the room around her.

"That's understandable." He took her hand and gave it a gentle squeeze. "You're braver than most to take on this project."

His comment gave her spirits a lift. Most clients wouldn't have understood at all. Most wouldn't have wanted to hear it. "My mother always said that when a ghost roams the earth plane for that long, they forget all or most of reality. They just relive those one or two moments that condemn them to this life. Like Benjamin, I guess." She breathed in, tipped her chin, and tried to open her throat. "Like the manor." She hadn't meant to let it slip that it was her mother who saw the ghosts in her family. She hoped that didn't make a difference to Henry since he was still the client.

"Unfinished business. That's what I've always heard," he said.

She nodded. "Something didn't work out the way they wanted it to and they keep reliving it, trying to get it to work out differently. It's why I chose to incorporate this clearing work into my design business. Sometimes, when the clearing is deep enough, a ghost can move on. Which is best for everyone."

"That it is." He squeezed her hands again.

"We all need to move forward." She stopped talking for a moment and realized how much time she had spent reliving the horrors of her breakup with Preston.

"Is everything okay?" He tilted his head to catch her eye.

"Yes." She exhaled and suddenly felt better than she had in a while. Maybe because she had gotten an old nightmare off her chest. Or maybe it was her realization. "I was just thinking about where I've done that in my own life. Going over and over a scenario that didn't work out well."

"Your ex-husband." He said it in a been-there-done-that kind of way, and she knew he must have his own history that haunted him.

"Mm-hmmm." It hadn't occurred to her that she would ever have had anything in common with Benjamin—or any other ghost, for that matter.

"A hard thing to overcome. I do wish you hadn't had to go through all of that. Though I, for one, am glad that the two of you are finished business." He kissed her hand. "You're safe now. With me. We'll figure this out together." He gestured toward the rest of the house.

She wasn't sure if he meant that in a just-for-the-job sort of way, or an I'd-like-to-explore-what's-next type of meaning. But it had been too wild of a half-day to figure anything else out tonight. So, she exhaled slow and deep and tried to root herself in the now.

The violins sputtered into their full haunted glory on the other side of the wall. He pulled her close, and she admitted that she did feel safe with him. She laid her head on his chest and enjoyed how good it all felt: the way he held her firmly against him, the solidity of his chest beneath her, and most of all...the trust.

CHAPTER 19

G emma looked out at the ocean, sipped her morning tea, and reflected on everything she had witnessed the night before. There was Anna and Benjamin, how she wanted a divorce and how he needed her to be the perfect wife. And, of course, Benjamin after his death. She remembered the gaping hole in his face, and a shiver traveled up and down her entire body.

Henry approached with his coffee and ran his hand along her back. "Chilled?"

"No, I was just thinking about what I saw last night. *Who* I saw last night."

"Ah. Anna and Benjamin? Or—"

"Yes." She scrunched her nose. "And Benjamin's face. What happened to it?"

He gazed at the horizon as though he knew the question was coming, as though he wasn't excited to answer it. "As the story goes, they were escorting him to the gallows to be hung, and a man from the crowd shot his face clean off—or most of it."

"Shot him in the face." She scrunched her nose.

"No one knows who it was. Or if they did know, they didn't talk. The town believed that Benjamin had killed his wife. The shooter could have been anyone who wanted to punish him for that." His tone was weary, as though he had heard or told the story a hundred times.

"Shooting someone in the face, that kind of violence is personal, like an act of revenge. If it was just someone from the community who hated him for killing his wife, they probably would have been satisfied just to watch him hang. Whoever shot him wanted to kill him himself," she said.

"She had two younger sisters. Her father was known to be overprotective of her, even into her adult years," he said.

"Yes, a father would." She thought of her own father and how protective he had been of her as his only daughter. She searched the windows on the backside of the house for the face she never wanted to see again. He wasn't there, though she felt an awareness from the house, a connection with it she didn't want. "An open and shut case."

"The trial only took two days. They hung Benjamin on the third. Of course, he was shot on the third, as well. Only man in the history of South Carolina's justice system to be shot and hung on the same day."

"They hung him even after he'd been shot?" Gemma wasn't a fan of Benjamin's. He was a shallow, self-absorbed murderer who thought nothing of destroying another person's life if it served his own benefit. But even she thought this was harsh.

"To make an example of him," he said grimly.

"I guess so." She envisioned an angry crowd cheering when he was shot. And then cheering even louder when he was strung up without a face. She shivered again and turned her focus to the expanse of the summer green lawn. It was time for her to do a deeper clearing. One that would move Benjamin on. "Where was Anna shot again?"

"Down there. To the right and in front of the ocean, before the steps." He pointed to the end of the green.

"Would you mind showing me specifically?" Gemma pointed in that direction. "I'd like to clear those imprints."

He opened his mouth as if he was going to say something, then closed it. As if he realized an objection wouldn't do any good. "Be my guest." He accompanied her over meadowsweet grass that was too high to surround such a majestic property as Alcott Manor.

"We need to get someone out here to cut this now that the weather is getting warmer," she said. "Though I recommend leaving the larger landscaping projects until last because we want to start preparing for this to be the beautiful estate that it will be."

"It's just here." He stopped shy of a patchy place of small rocks and white sand. The area baked in full sun, but it didn't burst with green like the rest of the lawn.

"Just as I thought." She rubbed her hand along her jaw. "This land is damaged. Nothing will grow here."

"Nothing ever has."

She held her open palm over the land to feel what couldn't be seen. There was a heat in the land. "It's going to take several steps to heal this, so I'd like to start with—" A dark red liquid bubbled thick and slow. It spread over the marred land in a puddle that crept toward her feet. She curled her hand toward her body.

Had Anna's blood risen to her touch just like the rest of the house?

Henry followed her line of sight and pulled her away from the blood that seemed to reach for her. "The anniversary of Anna's death is soon, so the memories will come more frequently now."

She held her hand over her mouth while the thick red substance crawled along the ground. When she finally let herself breathe again, it came quickly. "History always repeats itself with a ghost," she said. "Benjamin will kill again. Just as he's done before."

Henry didn't say anything but he walked her away from the blood, trying to keep it from touching her, she knew.

"The scene I saw upstairs showed a man who had political aspirations and a wife who wasn't playing along. He might have killed her just for that. Politicians don't like to be publicly humiliated." With her just out of its reach, the blood receded.

She summoned her strength, surveyed the roses, then stepped cautiously and far around the immediate area where Anna had been killed. "I think we should plant a new rose garden there, exactly where it happened, as well as one on the other side. There." She pointed directly across the emerald lawn.

"If we do two large rectangles and fill them with roses, that would create symmetry. We can carve a path through the rectangles, maybe a winding one. It should be like a golden square, and we'll measure the winding path inside of the square according to the Fibonacci sequence."

She marked off the elongated shape with her steps. Benjamin would kill again, she knew it. She had lived through it with another ghost. That ghost had killed once—twice if you counted how he killed himself. Then he'd tried to kill her. He would have, too, if her parents hadn't intervened. It's just what ghosts did. She rubbed the front of her throat.

"The center should hold a plant from Anna's original garden and a new plant. A little of the old to honor Anna and the roses she loved so much, and some of the new to celebrate the healing that's taking place."

He laid his hand on hers with a touch so gentle she only felt the sparks. She glanced at Henry to see if he felt it as well.

"That's a very kind way to honor her while marking the

path forward." His thumb traveled over her skin and sent chills up and down her arm.

"We ought to put a couple of love seats along the path, so people will linger in the area. Maybe someone will propose to the love of their life here."

"And eventually the energy of the land will become transformed?"

"Well, I'll do a little work on the land first, to remove the negative imprints. Then, yes. Good experiences will build upon what I've done. It can take time, but it will happen."

"How much time?" His eyes squinted with doubt.

"Varies. You'll notice an immediate difference as soon as I remove the old energy. The full transformation takes as long as it takes. The land has to absorb newer, far more positive experiences. We want it to let go of the past completely and move forward. We need to get a few people out here once the gardens are set. Maybe a community event to encourage that positive transformation."

His wide-set eyes held steady on her. "I don't see how land can absorb or let go of anything. It doesn't feel or think."

"Well, the words 'let go' might not be right. But the phrase 'move forward' definitely is. The positive experiences are the fuel that's needed to do that. It builds upon itself and takes on its own momentum."

He took one final step and touched his lips to hers, gentle and sure. She thought she felt a shift beneath her feet. From the heavy, thick vibe she'd noticed when they first came outside to something lighter. It was...happiness. Yes, that was it. A moving forward. A letting go of what was. Perhaps those were the right words after all.

"Maybe I do get the value of this." He pulled her flush against him, and her arms wrapped around him to hold on, to move forward. His kiss was long and slow, the thrust of his tongue sweeping across her own, cherishing her, wanting her.

She no longer noticed her feet against the ground. There was only him, the way he touched her, and the way he made her feel.

Her long-held ideals about professionalism on the job nudged her. Last thing she wanted was for someone to see them together. "I should get on with my work," she said, and he finally let her go.

"Be careful." He raised a cautionary eyebrow.

"It will only help." This she could do. Easily. She was excited for him to experience the results.

When he headed toward the house, her heart fluttered and leaped at the way he carried himself, at the man she was discovering him to be. Her teeth dragged her bottom lip to meet her tongue, and she savored the last traces of his earthy flavor.

It was twelve more steps until he disappeared into the house. Roughly the same number of hours that stood between them, until she could be with him again, skin to skin, amidst the tangle of blankets and the warmth of the fire.

If Tom ever found out, he'd have a fit. Worse, he'd tell her father. That would leave a heavy black mark on their relationship. *Gad*. She'd have to be more careful in public.

When she was certain he was gone, she knelt beside the area where the blood had bubbled to the surface. A flutter of adrenaline traveled through her stomach. There was a lot riding on the effects of this clearing.

She checked the area to make sure no one was around. She wasn't fond of having to explain her actions. When she knew the coast was clear, she closed her eyes for a few deep breaths and centered her mind into a neutral space to do her work.

With open palms, she ran her hands just above the land until she had a bead on the thick and haunting memories, the tragic imprints of Anna's death lodged within the land.

She chanted low and soft. "Hey oh ah, hey oh ah, hey oh ah ay ah ha, hey oh ah, hey oh ah, hey oh ah ay ah ha." She continued the ancient call of purification until dense black threads lifted from the earth like spiraling smoke.

With her right hand, she twisted the slithering black cords around her hand, pulling them from the depths of their attachment.

Her left hand raised to the heavens and waved to the beat of her chant in a figure eight pattern, searching for the white energy she wanted. When she finally found it, she fisted it quickly as if it was her unwilling captive. It burned and crackled in her palm, stinging and burning her skin while it built in strength like flames from above.

When she couldn't hold it any longer, she threw it into the ground, and a white fire burned next to her. She watched it to make certain it would hold, her left hand remained steady in the air to guard it. The acrid scent of burning twigs and leaves spun on the ocean breeze.

"Hey oh ah," she chanted. The energy of the blackened imprints balled around her fist like a thick glove. She flung it into the white fire, and the flames raged when they devoured the energy that had been trapped in the land.

Her chant coaxed the angry scars from the land until none were left to rise to the call of her voice. When the last ones pulled free, she flung them into the hungry flames that leaped for the dark, wriggling mass. With a wave of her left hand, she sent the fire skyward. A flash of lightning covered the sky just before the thunder rolled.

She inhaled the clean electric scent left in the air, measured the energy of the land with both palms close to the ground, then smiled with satisfaction at what she found. "It's empty."

She exhaled the exhaustion she always felt after she cleared a particularly difficult dynamic and set her eyes on the ocean in front of her. There was harmony here now between the land and the sea, between land and man. What she had erased would help Henry and his ancestral home. Benjamin, too. Even if none of them knew it or understood why.

The energetic pattern marked into the land by Anna's death would no longer draw like experience. It would no longer pulse the song of tragedy like sirens who lured sailors to shipwreck. All that was left to do now was to seed the positive and let it take root.

She stood and stretched in the sea air that was calm now. It was time to find the landscapers who needed to rearrange the rose gardens as she wanted them. With a cautious eye toward the manor, she wondered if the house could sense what she'd just done. If it would mind if her work helped solve the mystery it held within. Or at the very least, if it helped the manor to let go and move forward.

A quick movement from the upstairs window on the right caught her attention. She didn't see the face of the man who stood there, but a long, black sleeve moved from her view, and a chill gripped her heart.

She spun away from the house. He had seen her and the work she had done. She hoped that whatever his thoughts and feelings on what she was doing, he simply allowed the positive transformation to take place. It needed to.

A sweet scent drifted up from the white flowers on the green bushes that lined the back of the estate. Its perfume calmed her obsessive need to count, her need to find order in the midst of fear and chaos.

It was a familiar flower, one she'd seen somewhere before and recently. She racked her brain to no avail—flowers weren't something she paid too much attention to. But this one was just so familiar. She scanned the back of the estate, looking for clues. Maybe she'd just seen it in a different area on the property. Her sight landed on red roses and purple flowers, and an awareness jolted through her. Every flower in the gardens was also painted by Anna on her headboard.

The green linen book she'd picked up from outside the library popped into her mind. *Floriography*. She quickly ran to the winter garden and retrieved it, then returned to the garden to research the flowers. Anna had been very deliberate about what she painted, and obviously, in what she planted here, as well. There had to be a reason for it.

She opened the front cover and pressed two fingers against the soft cream page to hold it down. The name Anna Alcott was handwritten in faded blue script on the upper right-hand side of the page.

The binding was mostly separated from the cover, and several of the fabric-soft pages were loose. The copyrighted date was 1837. The book was certainly old and held signs of being well-loved. Certain flower names had been underlined, and some had tiny dots placed next to them. A few others had checkmarks and drawings in the margins.

Throughout the book, there were flower names followed by colors and meanings, and there were hand-painted pictures of individual blooms as well as arrangements.

Each flower, when given as a gift, communicated a specific message. Colors affected the meaning—a yellow carnation meant rejection, whereas a white carnation meant pure love. Arrangements added to the meaning of the message, as baby's breath incorporated the meaning of innocence or pure of heart, while dill meant lust.

She took the book out back and examined the white flowers on the hedge, remembering how Anna had painted them prominently on her headboard, along with some red tulips. And where else had she seen these?

Right. The growth chart downstairs.

She flipped the pages on her notepad until she found the sketch she'd made of the growth chart Henry had shown her.

Then she peeked at the garden. All the same flowers from the chart were in the garden. The rest of the blooms in the garden were painted on Anna's headboard. This had to be meaningful somehow.

First the white flower. Carnation? No, she knew what that was. Camellia? Maybe... She remembered the painted one on the headboard. No, the camellia in the book had yellow in the middle. This one didn't.

Gardenia.

Finally. That was it.

Her finger trailed to the definition. Secret love or untold love.

Gemma lowered the book to her lap. The entire backyard was lined in gardenias and Anna had painted them on her headboard. A tingling sensation scattered across her back.

Secret love?

She scribbled the flower and its definition in her portfolio.

Next were the blood red tulips. She knew that flower at least, and flipped the pages in the Ts. Red tulip: declaration of love.

These were the same two flowers Anna had chosen for Liz, the youngest child.

Declaration of love, secret love. Maybe Liz—her only girl —was the favorite of all her children, and this was Anna's secret.

Parents weren't supposed to have favorites. But the fact that they did was a dark secret that both parents and children alike knew.

George was Gemma's dad's favorite. The two men were just so much alike, in personality, interests, and even physical stature. In family photos, one looked like an exact younger replica of the other.

The next few flowers she researched were determined to

be larkspur, which carried the message of beautiful spirit; ivy, which meant fidelity; iris was a friendship that meant so much, or alternate meanings of faith, hope, and wisdom.

These flowers were painted next to the eldest child on the growth chart. That made sense because, according to birth order wisdom, the eldest offered his friendship to the mother and was often a caretaker to her later in life.

The blue snowball-like flower was the hydrangea. It bloomed with the meaning of perseverance and also had a few trailing strands of ivy (fidelity).

This seemed typical for a middle child—the one who had to work harder than the rest, the one who was neither the precious first nor the cherished baby, and the one who languished with less attention and had to persevere to find his place in the world.

She remembered when Anna painted a few additions on her headboard the night she wore her red dress with the rose in the center. Gemma carefully turned the pages to the description of leaves: dead.

Death of a loved one, sadness.

She remembered Anna at her vanity, making up her swollen eyelids and puffy lips to hide the traces of her crying. Then she'd painted the leaves, the dead brown leaves.

She stiffened against the cool wind that whipped off the water and bathed her face and the warm currents that followed and twirled around her legs like a snake.

"She knew she was going to die."

CHAPTER 20

I t was late in the day before Gemma finished with Tom and the landscapers and, frankly, found enough nerve to enter the manor again.

The portico was shaded now that the sun highlighted the other side of the house. She paused there before entering and breathed deeply. Like the tremors of an earthquake, the work she had just performed on the land would spread throughout the property, destroy the negative effects of Anna's tragic death, and birth a significant lightness.

She waited to feel it, the lack of century-old dark roots, the open space, the readiness from the house to willingly accept the good and positive she would plant at every turn.

Robins sang their evening song from the majestic magnolias that had seen the rise and fall of this home, and the manor's energy dragged beneath her unexpectedly. The improvements were barely perceptible. She ran her fingertips across her forehead and fought the feeling that she had just flunked an important test.

Removing the mark of Anna's death from the land ought to

have lifted the energy significantly. Almost instantly. After all that work, she ought to have been able to walk into the manor and experience it differently. Maybe not completely as it would have been before Anna's death, but she ought to have been able to feel a river of light flowing through the foundation.

She lifted her feet one at a time, as though tar stretched beneath them, fastening misfortune to the house. She could feel it. The manor was still too anchored to the tragedy that lurked in the shadows.

"Damn it. Why?"

She sighed and paced back and forth, barely acknowledging the contractors who walked in and out. The screen door squeaked and slammed. She thought of her parents' home, of family and children. She remembered the growth chart she'd seen and the children who would have run in and out of this door.

She stopped and stared at it with its perfect coat of white paint. Perfection. Benjamin. Her heart curled in on itself. Maybe the darkness that remained here was the result of Benjamin's presence. Perhaps it wouldn't lift until he was gone.

She tried to breathe through the taut muscles of her chest. She needed to create a much more *positive* environment, one that would be ill-fitting to who he was, one that would release his attachment to the tragic memories trapped within the house.

That meant she would have to find more places in the house to clear. If removing the mark of Anna's death wasn't enough, then she would have to find out what was. Henry might know what that would be. She'd have to convince him to work with her on this. Surely, he would. With all the extra workers on staff, they were well ahead of schedule, almost finished with the restoration, and they couldn't run the risk that Benjamin would destroy something else so close to the judge's deadline.

Once inside the Victorian kitchen, she paced her steps to the tune of jostling equipment, the voices of several men, and the distant cacophony of hammers and electric saws.

She knew she would have to go to the library first to survey the damage Benjamin had left behind. She and Tom had discussed the repair plans earlier in the day. He would already be there, pushing the implementation they agreed upon.

Being in this part of the house rattled her. Her steps were measured through the main hallway, fifteen...sixteen...seventeen...and quiet on the carpet, so as not to disturb any memories that might pour forth. They shouldn't at this time of day. But that didn't mean anything.

Every contractor who rounded the corner was a relief, a little beat of normal that encouraged her further into the house. Just like the sun that shone through every window on the western-facing front, it gave her a sense of protection. A temporary one, she knew. But she'd let those signs keep the darkness at bay for as long as possible. She needed the time to figure out what to clear next.

When she arrived at the library, Henry stood next to Tom and several other men. They surveyed bookshelves that had been ripped from their home, splintered into pieces, and scattered on the ground. A gaping hole had been smashed into the wall. Last night's scene with Benjamin's bloodied half face flashed through her mind, and she stifled a shudder.

"He never stops searching." Tom gestured toward the bookshelf, his voice was even and his anger evident, but controlled.

"He would tear this house to shreds if we let him. We don't have time to replace this with custom work, not before the judge passes through." Her head throbbed and her mouth was dry. This destruction couldn't go on.

"We'll have to find some ready-made shelves and stain them to match. Or maybe we can find some lumber from the leftover pieces we have out back." Gemma looked over at Tom. "Do we have anything that might work here? We could go back after the deadline and install a more custom solution."

Tom and the other workers discussed the idea and walked toward the door. "All right, let's go out back and see what we have that will work."

"We can't pull anyone off the staircase to do this," she called after them. "We're too close on that. But we need at least six to eight working on this right away."

She wanted to tell Henry what she'd discovered out back, about the flowers and their meanings. But he was busy staring into the hole that Benjamin had punched into the bookcase.

Secret love. Death.

Anna had planted those flowers so deliberately out back, then painted many of them on her headboard. In an era when most women didn't have much of a voice, she was communicating something she felt passionately about. And she continued doing it right up until she died.

This had to have something to do with her death. Maybe something to do with what really needed to be cleared for the manor, so that Benjamin could go home. She wanted to tell Henry about that, too. She needed more information about the manor, and quickly.

"There's something back here." Henry's voice echoed in the space behind the wall.

She looked over Henry's shoulder into the darkness. A sensation of death and dying swamped her, and she held on to the counter-like surface below the bookshelf.

Henry leaned in. "Is there a flashlight out here?"

A subtle breeze drifted in from the hidden area, and she scrunched her nose. "Smells like...decay. Like something died back here." She quickly tried to account for all the workers she'd come to know at the manor. "No one was missing on the job today, were they?"

Slowly, his eyes scanned from left to right as if he checked off names on a list. "No."

They both turned toward the opening. Gemma shifted a flashlight from the corner of the bookshelf so that the beam shone into the darkness. "There's something dead back here, I could swear it."

Henry squeezed her shoulder before he released it to crawl through the opening, then offered his hand for her to follow him. "I don't think anything has been disturbed back here for quite some time. Maybe it's just the stillness, because this has been sealed off for a very long while."

"Maybe not, Henry. You don't know that. Somebody needs to investigate everything that's back here."

"You're right. Let me go get a team together. They can go in one direction, and we'll go in the other."

He hopped out of the dank corridor as lithely as a gymnast and set off to gather a group who would help them investigate.

She stared into the inkwell of darkness that festered behind the wall. The "off" feeling she'd had since she'd arrived at the house intensified. Something was wrong in all of this. She'd attributed it to her circumstance-related over-whelm, the insane ghost who roamed the estate, and the house that held on to its horrific memories and replayed them throughout the year—all of which would be enough to knock anyone's needle off their internal compass.

The stygian tides shifted in the passageway and tugged at her. It was the same pull she'd encountered when she'd arrived at the manor and touched the pillar. And then it happened just as it had on her first day, a low groan crawling out of the opening. The kind of moan a dying man would utter when he realized there was no hope to be had.

Henry jogged into the room. "They're on their way, as soon as they find some more lamps to work with." He climbed through the opening and offered her his hand. "What's wrong?"

"There's something in here, Henry." She touched her hand to a beam, then pulled it away. "I need to work on this."

"Do you know what it is?"

She stared at the hand-hewn beams. "It moaned when you went to get the others."

Henry's eyes fixed on her and narrowed for just a flash of a moment.

"It's not the first time I've heard that voice, either. On my first day, I touched a pillar on the front porch, and I heard it then, too. I think it must be Benjamin. He's done something back here to someone. Or this is where he spends his time. You've heard this moan?"

His cinnamon-green gaze stretched up and along the beams that divided them from the rest of the house. "I've heard it."

"You think it's Benjamin?"

He shook his head. "I don't know where it comes from."

"I have to clear whatever this is. It would be better if I knew what happened here."

"Let's go this way, see if we can figure it out." He gestured to the left with the flashlight.

A rat skittered across her feet and she jumped.

"Here, let me go in front." Henry guided her behind him.

Gemma held tight to the back of Henry's shirt with one hand and placed her other hand on his waist. "Do you have any idea what this is? A secret passageway?"

"Seems like I read somewhere about how the original

owner hid slaves in the house before he could get them safe passage to the north. Maybe this is a part of that."

The muscles in Gemma's chest tightened. "Could some of them be buried here?"

Their feet shuffled along the dusty floors, and the flashlight beam weakened and shone only a foot or so ahead of them. "I don't think so. I mean, I guess anything is possible, the house has a long history. But I don't remember a story like that."

The view ahead stayed the same and stagnant energy pooled around them. The heavier the darkness settled in, the stronger the sensations of invisible hands closing over her neck repeated in her mind.

"Watch your step." Henry took her hand from his shirt and held it as their boots clanked against steep metal steps of a narrow, spiral staircase. The flashlight struggled through the heaviness of the dark and offered very few clues as to what lay ahead. It blinked now and then, its feeble battery-powered strength no match for the almost two-hundred-year-old blackness that lived within these walls. Henry banged its plastic side against the metal railing as a reminder to the flashlight that they needed it.

She didn't know if it was how clearly her memories shined in the darkness or the tight twirl of the spiral without light, but her center of gravity turned counterclockwise.

Henry tightened his grip around her hand. "Do you want to rest?"

Her breathlessness made more noise in the passageway than she would have liked, and she wondered how she managed to feel terrified, embarrassed, and sick at the exact same time. "No. Let's keep going. I'm just out of shape from the accident. I'm okay."

Though she thought she might not be. She'd trained herself to always say that. That's what the responsible did, to make things easier on others. She peeked downward into the pitch they'd just come from, and sweat gathered between her palm and Henry's.

Just before they reached the top of the stairs, the flashlight sputtered into darkness.

"Of course." Gemma grasped Henry's bicep with her other hand and tugged it close to her body. They were attached to one another like a unit, and when he moved, she followed. Leaning into him, depending on him for a sense of safety and security wasn't something she had done with any man. At least not since she was about eight and wanted her eldest brother to turn the light on in their basement before she went down there on her own.

"I'm putting this flashlight down." He bent toward the floor, and her body leaned with his. "Useless as it is."

"Henry, what if this landing just breaks off into nothing? We'd fall a full story." She would have preferred to be strong, but she didn't feel it. Instead, she felt watched and small. She knew what animal this house held within it, and she knew what it was he wanted to do. He killed any time someone interfered with his home. She shuddered.

Henry, as if he had known her for years, as if he knew exactly what she needed to feel safe, adjusted his arm around her waist and brought her close. Her entire world centered around that point of contact.

"I thought I saw something over here," he said.

Both of them took small steps forward, unwilling to take any broad footsteps when they couldn't see where they were going. She didn't breathe well in the dark. Fear had a way of shrinking lung space.

"Here." He banged on something that sounded like a wall, solid and resolute, and then the banging sounded more hollow, like a door.

Like an offering of life support, two thin rectangles of

ALYSSA RICHARDS

light appeared on the floor. "There." She nodded and squeezed his arm and hand at the same time. "What's that?"

Henry's hand touched her collarbone and she jumped. He adjusted and patted her nearest shoulder.

"I'll find out." He gently slipped out of her grasp, and she placed her arms around his waist. "It's okay. Remember, even if this is a dead end, we still have the way we came in."

He was right. She relaxed her grip just a little—not enough to be carefree, but just slightly because she remembered now that they weren't trapped by anything except the darkness that she could have sworn touched the skin of her face.

The jiggling of a doorknob echoed in the silence, and Henry's body jerked against her when he tried to push the door open. She finally let go of him so he could use both hands to open the door, but she kept one hand clasped to the back of his white shirt so she would be moored in this sea of darkness. And, if Benjamin appeared and tried to shove her down the stairs, he might not succeed.

The wood of the door scraped against the doorway with Henry's effort. When it finally gave way, he stumbled forward into a time capsule of a room. The last of the daylight streamed in through a small rectangular window that she remembered seeing on the front of the house.

A tiled hearth lay at the foot of an ornately carved fireplace in the middle of the room. Larger tiles that depicted yellow lemons and bright green leaves on a sky blue background surrounded the opening to the fireplace. Two small lamps were perched atop the mantel, their lampshades threadbare. Much of the hardwood floors surrounding the fireplace had been eaten away. "Worm damage." Gemma scrunched her nose and pointed to the flooring. "And mold."

She and Henry stepped carefully into the room that hadn't

entertained visitors in at least a century. The masculine walnut bed was almost as wide as a queen and boasted the remnants of painted imagery that she recognized immediately.

"These are the same flowers Anna painted on her bed."

"Where?" Henry scanned the room.

"I probably wouldn't recognize them otherwise, except I've seen larger versions of them just recently." She tiptoed across the damaged hardwood to the bed and gestured to a small bouquet of gardenias that had been painted on the front of the footboard.

"Do you think this was her personal getaway?"

"No, this was a lovers' den." Gemma cast a raised eyebrow at Henry. "A secret passageway and a bedroom that no one would have access to except through said passageway. Whatever it had been used for originally, this is where lovers met, Henry. I would bet that secret passageway extends from some private entrance to the outside. The doorway has probably been built over by now."

She told him briefly the story of the flowers and their meanings in the book—especially the gardenia.

Secret love.

Henry gave one long nod as though it all made sense now. "In his own home."

Gemma thought she could almost see the pieces of logic assembling in order behind his eyes.

He paced in tight steps back and forth. "I had heard that she had a lover. But I never dreamed they met here, right under Benjamin's nose."

"There's nothing else in here, except what's left of that chair and the bed. Some Victorian homes included a room as a getaway for the wife of the house—a place where she could read or knit or rest. But none of them included a bed. A chaise, maybe. A seating group. Not a bed. And if my sense of

direction is back, I think Anna's bedroom is right next door."
She pointed to the right wall of the room.

"I also think Anna's paintings of flowers were her way of
communicating a message about this affair. I read through
that book of hers, *Floriography*. Every flower she painted on
the growth chart and her headboard is also in the backyard.
This flower here, the gardenia— I originally thought it meant
something else, but it obviously means what it says. She had a
secret love." She gestured to the bed. "That means there's at
least one more suspect in her death."

"Maybe." He frowned and focused on something just
beyond her. "What's this?"

He and Gemma exchanged a glance while they hovered
over the trunk that hadn't been opened in over a hundred
years. The burnished iron key was still in the lock. He
wiggled it gently until the chambers turned completely.

"Anna Alcott was probably the last person to see the
contents of this trunk." Gemma stopped her breath on the
inhale. If there was a suicide note, it could be in the trunk.

"Over a hundred years ago." He worked the domed top
until the lid finally released its seal to the base with a *crack*
and a *pop*. The inside was lined with a pale beige linen with
elongated diamonds stitched into the fabric with red thread,
and filled with a cache of letters, some of which were still in
their envelopes.

"Look at these." She picked up one of the crisp and delicate letters that was in surprisingly good condition. "My
Beloved," she read the script across the envelope and turned it
over. A red blotch of wax was attached to the upper flap of the
envelope. The letter C was impressed into the hardened seal.

She bit her lip while she wiggled the letter from the
envelope.

Anna, my love,

Do not give up our hopes of a life together.

I think that perhaps we can look on Benjamin's political aspirations as a positive. With so much at stake, there will be secrets he will do anything to keep.

I will meet you tonight at eleven. Please remember to leave the outside door unlocked for me.

With love,

Sam

"Do you remember a Sam from the Alcott history?" she asked.

Henry frowned. "Sam..."

Gemma flipped the envelope. "Whoever he was, his last name began with a C." She remembered seeing the letter that Anna left on her secretary desk. *Dear Sam*, the letter had begun.

They dug through the collection of letters and read aloud each of Anna's and Sam's messages to one another. They were filled with love, each other's desire for one another, and plans for the future.

After they'd read the last note, her fingers searched along the linen covering, hoping the suicide note had been hidden in the trunk. Perhaps by a maid or her lover, who would probably want to frame Benjamin for Anna's death. Her fingers traced over a bulge that had been sewn into the lining of the lid and she gasped. "Henry—" She dug her nails into the fabric until it ripped, and she retrieved a piece of paper folded in half.

She read the title across the top of the page. "Report of birth." Her voice was hollow with disappointment. "Not a suicide note."

"What does it say?" Henry slid closer to Gemma to read the paper.

"Baby girl, Elizabeth Mae. Mother: Anna Alcott. Father:

Samuel Cardill. Oh, my gosh, Henry. Sam's the father. They had a baby together."

"Lizzie Mae." Henry fell against the wall with a *thump*. "I never knew."

"Liz. The red tulip. Of course. Entwined with the gardenia, secret love." Gemma shook her head. "Cardill. Why does that name sound so familiar?"

"They built Alcott Manor. The Cardills started a real estate development company in the early 1800s. It's still alive and well, and Sam's descendent, Asher Cardill, runs it now."

Gemma remembered the waitress mentioning Asher Cardill at The Iron Skillet when she first arrived. Henry had mentioned him, too, when Asher had trespassed on the property twice. She grabbed the top of her head. "Holy—Asher Cardill is a descendant of Anna Alcott. Do you think he knows?"

"He may suspect, and that may be the real reason why he's been nosing around the house."

"If he had this, would he be entitled to ownership of the house?"

"Voting stock in the company is divided among the remaining family members. He's married to an Alcott descendent. So, if this birth certificate is valid, and he found it, then yes, he would be entitled to stock. He and his wife would have a lot of power in the family corporation. This would not bode well for the family members who want the property restored. If it came to that, his votes could sway a final decision in favor of destroying the manor and developing the land."

"Is the certificate valid?" The paper crackled when she opened it again and flipped it over.

"Hidden like this, it must be. It obviously wasn't filed. Many weren't back then, as there wasn't a standard registration system for birth certificates in the U.S. until almost 1920."

"We'll keep it hidden." She tucked the birth certificate into the lining of the trunk and patted it twice. Sometimes justice needs a helping hand."

"Thank you." His voice was soft with gratitude.

"Justice will be a little more blind than usual this time." Gemma touched the birth certificate in the lining. "If he knew about this when he was alive, he might have killed Anna to keep it quiet or maybe just out of sheer fury.

"When last I saw her, she didn't want to be a politician's wife, she wanted that divorce. I'd bet almost anything that she threatened him about Lizzie Mae. She painted dying leaves on her headboard on the night she died. They mean death. I think she knew she was going to die. I think she knew Benjamin had had enough."

Henry's features darkened like a gray shadow had descended over his face from top to bottom. "We'd better hope he didn't kill her. If he did, there won't be a way to get him to go home. He could still wreck this restoration before the deadline and ruin everything."

This was the first time she'd seen Henry even entertain the idea that Benjamin might be guilty of murder. She didn't like his agreement as much as she thought she would because he was right. That solution didn't bode well for them.

Now she hoped there was a suicide note.

She pointed out the window to the sun that had begun its descent. "Let's get this downstairs and out of sight. Since people know the passageway exists, they're bound to find this room."

Henry tucked the trunk under his arm and Gemma cast a final glance out of the room before they left. She'd thought she understood Anna Alcott, but now she realized she didn't know her at all.

Once in the hallway, they stopped at the other narrow rectangle of light, and Henry pushed on the door. "Something's blocking it."

Gemma got down on all fours and peeked beneath the doorway. "Henry," she whispered. "I was right. This is Anna's bedroom."

Tom and several contractors talked to one another at the other end of the passageway, their voices growing louder with each step.

Henry grabbed Gemma's hand and she held on tight. "We have to hurry. We don't want anyone to find this trunk, let alone what's in it."

CHAPTER 21

After most of the contractors had left the main area, they brought the trunk down to the winter garden and hid it well behind boxes in a darkened corner of the room.

"I'm going to hide that certificate in a different place from the trunk." Gemma looked around and finally picked up a small pillow. "I'll sew it in here. To be extra safe, since Asher is roaming around, maybe searching for that very piece of paper."

"Good idea." Henry gave the trunk another shove and put a cardboard box on top of it. "Benjamin's and Anna's marriage had more secrets than even I realized." Shades of anger crossed Henry's face while he adjusted a few of the boxes that served as camouflage. She recognized the shadows as the kind of old, rotting anger that lived in dark corners and didn't show itself all the time. The result of betrayal, she decided. Anna's story was bringing something up for him.

He positioned himself on the floor next to her, and she wondered what his history was. She knew how difficult it could be to get rid of those old wounds and find a way forward.

"Gemma?"

"Hmm?"

"Where did you go?"

"Oh. I was thinking." She wondered if he would open up to her after he had been fairly closed off about his past. She decided to open her proverbial kimono first. Maybe he would follow. "It's so hard to get to the place where emotional wounds are completely healed."

He brushed at a patch of dust that the trunk had stamped on the leg of his black pants. "I guess Benjamin is proof of that. Even after a hundred years' time, he's never found a way to move on from the betrayal and the injustice. Apparently, time does not heal all wounds."

"No. It really doesn't." She agreed with him in a tone of hard-earned confidence and remembered some advice she had received a while ago. Advice she had worked to implement but didn't always achieve successfully. "In my own case, it was quite a while after Preston left to be with his young mistress that my therapist finally said I needed to accept what happened if I really wanted to get over it."

"*Accept*." He said the word as if it were foreign, as if he questioned the therapist's wisdom, and as if he had another form of resolution in mind.

"Mmm." She knew how unappealing the idea sounded.

"Wouldn't be my first instinct. But how did that work for you?" His expression was a little wise, and she knew the advice was hollow to him.

"Well, it wasn't my first instinct, either. I'll put it that way. There were plenty of times when the idea of strangling him with my bare hands was a far more appealing option than accepting. Though I think I'm finally getting the value of it."

He pressed his lips to hers in a kiss, and, after a while, she caught herself in a momentary daydream, envisioning a life with Henry.

When they finally parted, he asked, "How would acceptance possibly help you? Seems more like giving up to me."

"Well. She said that we are never angrier with someone than when they aren't being who we want them to be. But people are who they are. Ultimately, they choose to be who they want to be, not who we want them to be. So, I may have wanted my ex to be a man of integrity. Ultimately, he just wasn't."

"I should think accepting that would leave you bitter."

"I've spent some time there, as well. I think her point was that acceptance leads to forgiveness and then letting go. In fact, I think the best definition of forgiveness I've heard is that it's the acceptance that a person or an event couldn't have been any other way."

He tipped his chin up, apparently chewing on the idea.

"I'm not completely there with it all the time, either. But it's true in the sense that they make choices and so do we, and it adds up to a tipping point at some stage that can't be stopped. Anyway, I think of it in terms of redecorating."

"Redecorating?"

"So, maybe I really wanted a straight-back chair for a particular spot in a room I'm working on, and instead, I mistakenly got an ottoman. I can rant and rage that the ottoman is a pathetic excuse for a chair—you know, no back support and not functional and so on. Or I can just accept that the ottoman isn't what I want and go get a good chair." She laughed and he joined her, apparently amused by her example.

It was a good release to laugh, especially around a topic that had been so painful.

In the quiet that followed, a tumbling of deadlines, obligations, and haunting hurdles weighed heavily on her heart. She closed her eyes for a long blink. He needed to know what she had discovered today. She had told him that lightening the land where Anna had died would be a huge clearing. And it was. Yet with Alcott Manor, that effort amounted to an eyedropper-sized bailing from this flooding ship.

"By the way, I cleared the area where Anna died."

"Oh? How did that go?"

"I expected it to have more of a significant effect on the house, but it didn't clear as much as I thought it would. I think Benjamin is still here." She flipped her hands so they were palms up and folded them into fists. "So, that means I've got to find something more substantial to clear. Something profound that will shift the energetic history of this house, and right now, I don't know what that is." She remembered the way the shadows shifted in the dark passageway and the moan that chilled her soul.

She would clear that if she knew what the hell it was. She could sense betrayal and suffering, the desire for retribution. A need for justice. It felt like a river of Benjamin's evil flowing through the veins of the house.

Henry's eyes focused on hers, his stare deep, intense, and brooding. "Gemma, the manor was built in 1832. It's lived several incarnations over the years, many of them tragic, and as I suggested when you arrived, may be beyond your clearing work." He let the last end of his sentence dangle out there as if he expected an objection, and Gemma met him head-on.

"Henry, I can clear the negative effects of anything. *Anything.* We can still search for the note, but if you would help me understand what has happened in the various rooms of the house, that may give us a more immediate result. I can turn this place into an environment where Benjamin won't want to be. He'll leave. I—"

"Gemma."

"I can do the guest room if you'll accompany me there in the morning. Beyond that, I need to know where else to go in the house—"

"Gemma." He said her name more softly this time, and rather than fueling her contention, it stopped her.

"The only way Benjamin will leave is if we find Anna's suicide note."

Her knee-jerk reaction was to think his proposed remedy was right up there with pigs flying, and she preferred her tried and true methods. Even though it might have been the best option, and the preferred one, the chances were still too slim for her to admit that he could be right.

"Maybe."

She had a verifiable gift that worked. It could change a home's identity. It would change lives. She couldn't give up.

She pushed her fingers along her forehead, dread and disappointment tangling with one another in her heart. "But these mysteries in the manor's story—" She thought of Anna's lover and Lizzie Mae, the daughter Benjamin thought was his. Once again, she thought of the secret passageway and the mysterious, grim energy that lived there. "They seem so extreme and far reaching. If we can decipher them, maybe I could strike at the heart of the problem. You know these stories, don't you?"

"There have been too many events in the manor." Henry grazed her arm with his hand, and she knew he wasn't onboard. "Too many. And apparently, I don't know all of them. Besides, that just isn't a good idea. The house, as you've seen, is unpredictable. Let's search the furniture tomorrow. Carefully. Early. We've never looked at those pieces for her suicide note. You may have landed on to something there."

"Henry, a clearing isn't going to upset anything. It's only going to lessen the negativity that's embedded—"

"You don't know that. This house claims people, Gemma. It sucks them into its world and they never leave. How do you know that your work wouldn't open up a connection that would draw you in?" He waved toward the main part of the house and his eyes flared with heat.

She offered a confident smile that ultimately melted into a doubtful one. The manor was a mystery to her, and the truth was that she didn't know how her clearing work would affect these trapped memories. Or her. She thought of the scores of spirits she could feel but not see, spirits who loomed in the walls, spirits who might want her to join their party.

Still, she wasn't willing to give up. She couldn't. "It hasn't hurt me so far."

"We're much closer to the anniversary of Anna's death now. The house is becoming a different animal altogether."

That was it. Her frustrations spilled over and ruined all her diplomacy. "Henry, you have *got* to agree to a plan B when it comes to getting rid of him, because the chances of finding that suicide note are nil!"

The muscles bulged on the sides of his jaw once and then again. He leaned forward with a stare so intense it might have etched glass. She expected him to say no and then up and leave the room. Or maybe fire her.

"I'm pushing back on your plan because I don't want anything to happen to you, Gemma." His words washed over her in tidal force, knocking her guard down with it.

Several moments passed, moments where the quiet in the room was like glue that held their gazes on one another, until she finally said, "Oh."

He paced back and forth several times. "So, whatever this alternate plan turns out to be, it will have to be a safe option for you."

She nodded, stunned, her spirits secretly flying higher than she was comfortable with. She hoped that this was the opening of another door between them and that they were moving toward the future with him she'd just been dreaming of. She hoped he felt the same way she did and that he wasn't just protective of her well-being because he was a good human.

"All right. Well. We'll find the right plan B." Her thoughts spun. The problem of getting Benjamin to go home remained.

"You said that the Cardills built the house—are there any stories about how that process went? Seems like the feud between the Cardills and the Alcotts goes back a long way."

"Nothing that I remember." He leaned back onto his hands, giving her time, giving her space, letting things settle.

She ran her thumb over her knuckles several times. "Are there any books in the manor on its history?"

"There used to be some scrapbooks and other books dedicated to the history of the manor, but they've long since disappeared."

She nodded, the wheels in her head still turning, working toward a solution. "Maybe they were kept with the furniture in that museum you mentioned?"

His pacing stuttered for a step, then he resumed. "No. I don't think so."

"I need some accounting of the bigger events that took place here. A diary would have been ideal."

"I don't think it would have made a difference. It's too much water under the bridge for this place."

She sincerely disagreed, and she was pretty sure the grimace that pulled her lips communicated that. "Well, then it's too bad Benjamin can't be subjected to therapy." Her sarcasm was breaking holes in her steady demeanor like water bursting through a dam.

"Acceptance being the key part of this healing process."

"Yeah." It had to be some sort of a cosmic joke that she, Henry, and Benjamin were stuck at this house together. They could start the Lack of Acceptance Club where the motto would be: *Fighting to Enforce a Better Reality*.

"I don't think it would do him any good."

"Of course not. You know, Henry, eventually, we all get there, and Benjamin will, too. Whether we find the note or I'm able to effectively clear enough negative imprints for his attachments to release, ultimately, acceptance is what will move him forward in life—or death, as his case may be."

His stare was hard, and she wondered if he questioned how emotional healing occurred or just if it could happen for Benjamin. "So, you think he will find some sort of peace?"

She nodded. "We need to figure out how to help that along sooner rather than later."

Henry's eyes scanned the walls of the room that used to be Anna's favorite. He nodded every now and then and seemed to entertain what she had just said. "This idea seems counterintuitive to me. When things go so terribly wrong and people you care about act so badly, acceptance seems weak. Like it might make you a doormat." His eyes took on a faraway look.

"I understand that." And she did. God, she did. "There were countless times when I wanted to show my ex-husband just how bad his choices were. But, that's rather an endless pursuit. The goal is to get beyond it. Start living again."

That teeny bit of information appeared to make sense to him, and she saw a light ignite behind his eyes. "My former wife had been struggling emotionally for some time. We'd been to doctors. None of them ever really figured out how to help her. The few that made progress with her eventually threw their hands in the air because she wouldn't follow their instructions.

"They'd tell her not to do something, or to absolutely do something, and she'd do the opposite. To this day, I don't know if that was more a result of her selfish nature or the effects of whatever illness it was that she battled.

"I turned my life inside out trying to help her. Literally, I gave up everything for her." Henry shook his head and stared at the floor. "Then I found out she had been having an affair with this man we both knew. I told her she was being a fool, that he was just using her to get close to my money."

His eyes shone with quiet rage. "As you might imagine, that went over like a lead balloon. She argued that he loved her in all the ways that I didn't. She was wrong, of course. He didn't love her, and that played out soon enough." Henry smiled, but the sadness was still evident in his eyes.

She placed her hand on his and understood now why the knowledge of Anna's affair tripped a hot wire with him. "I'm so sorry."

"Well, it's no worse than what you went through. It seems you may be right. Your ex-husband, my former wife—there was no changing them." He leaned back and chuckled. "Acceptance." His earlier intensity relaxed into a smile that said he finally saw something that had been hidden from him before. "I think I get it."

The token of insight dropped for her, too, and she could almost hear the copper of the coin drop into the bottom of her own personal well. For the first time, she was able to think of Preston without a jab to the soft places in her heart. "I think I'm getting it, also. It's very freeing."

He lifted her hand and kissed it. A slow, mischievous smile spread across his face as though they shared a secret. "Let's do something special tonight. To celebrate."

She bit her lip. "I try never to celebrate before the ball is across the finish line. Or, the touchdown line. Whatever it is. I'd rather have the judge's signature on the approval papers first."

"I feel better than I have in a long time. This acceptance thing has real merit. You're moving forward. I'm moving forward. Hell, I think Benjamin will, too. We're even going to make the deadline—I can feel it." Henry kissed her fully on the lips, the playful kind of kiss that said his lips were familiar with hers now.

A twinge in her stomach reminded her that, although he was perfect, she still didn't quite know him. Not really.

"I have to review some paperwork and inspect some final repairs in the library."

"Okay, take care of that. I'll meet you back here in twenty." He disappeared out the door.

CHAPTER 22

With Henry gone and the sun still fairly high in the sky, Gemma went to the library to inspect the bookshelf repairs. She also hoped he was wrong and that she might find some books on the history of Alcott Manor, specifically, about how the house was built.

She'd understood Henry's point about being cautious, but she believed in her abilities and what they could do. Since the Cardills had built the manor, she felt certain something would be amiss there. The apple never fell far from the tree, and Asher was rotten to the core.

She opened every drawer, lifted every cushion, and turned every chair in search of the note Anna may have written. She also examined all the titles on the shelves but didn't find any scrapbooks or historical works documenting the development of the manor.

Tom and the other workers had placed a makeshift back in the bookcase to cover the hole that Benjamin had ripped open. The new shelves were fashioned out of leftover wood that was slightly thinner than the rest. The edges weren't rounded as the others were, and the ebony stain they used scented the room. But these repairs would do for now.

Henry was right that she wouldn't find any reference materials that would help her understand the energy in the house. When she passed the office, she took a few minutes to review the paperwork on her desk, and she eyed the main staircase. At least the restoration was falling into place. She agreed with Henry. They just might make this deadline.

Her wow-I-did-it smile was beginning to flicker at the corners of her mouth. But she wouldn't let it beam just yet. Not until the job was done and the judge was satisfied. Then they would wrap up the remaining elements in stage two of the restoration.

On her way to the winter garden, she searched the furniture in several more rooms but found nothing of any value. When she returned to the winter garden, she found candlelight around the room, an antique white dress laid across an armless wicker chair, and shoes placed on the floor beneath it.

An envelope was left on the dress with her name on it, and a pair of jeweled hair combs had been placed beside it. She'd never seen her name written so elegantly before, at least on something that wasn't a wedding invitation. The capital G filled two-thirds of the length of the envelope, and the rest of her name flowed beyond it in an evenly mannered script.

Dearest Gemma,

It seemed only fitting that we dress in the presentation to which the house was originally accustomed since you are leading its restoration to success.

I shall be waiting for you in the main foyer at six.

Most truly yours,

Henry

. . .

"MOST TRULY YOURS," she repeated. In spite of her need to be cautious with him, she believed he meant it and that he was most truly hers. She pressed the beautifully scripted note to her chest, then picked up the dress. It looked as though it had jumped right from an 1880s photograph.

The gold details covered the bottom third, and its exquisite design flowed up and down and undulated around tiny stars that dotted the entire dress and the brocade that decorated the bodice.

She looked at the label inside the dress: Jeanne Hallée, Paris, France. Her eyebrows climbed to her hairline—he was a well-known French designer from the 1880s. This dress was vintage.

She wiggled into the gown and carefully fastened the row of cloth-covered buttons. The dress's train made the gown look like a wedding dress, something she'd never worn before. When she'd married the first time, it was barefoot on a California beach in jeans and a white top.

Though she didn't have any stockings, the shoes didn't require them. They fit like Cinderella's slippers.

A large sheet of reflective glass that leaned against the wall served as her mirror. She inspected her makeup and then retrieved the two hair combs that sparkled. The tortoise shell combs with garnet and diamond details were as gorgeous as any two pieces of jewelry. She lifted two sections of her long hair, one from each side, and slid them into place.

The clock on the other side of the house struck half past five, thirty minutes before the time Henry said they were to meet.

When she placed her hand on the doorknob, a shiver of excitement traveled through her. This living, breathing home that had been witness to so much and endured even more throughout the years was looking forward to something. A new life? A healing? The absence of Benjamin? She hoped.

She pushed away the thought that the manor would be excited for some other reason. Something that had to do with why it wanted her here. Something to do with making her a permanent resident.

She glanced at the trunk full of secrets that Henry had locked and tucked into the corner of the room. They'd discussed whether or not to tell Tom about the trunk because the letters were of local historical value and ought to go into a museum for safekeeping.

But since the contents of them lent further motive to Benjamin as the murderer, they decided to hang on to them for a little while longer. Regardless, the birth certificate would have a new hiding place that no one would find until Gemma and Henry were ready for them to.

She walked carefully along the wraparound porch, the beaded train of her dress trailing behind her, step by step. It was a royal moment, the only one she'd ever known.

Henry waited for her at the foot of the stairs. He was tuxedo-attired, with hair wet with a neatly combed side part, appearing every bit the Victorian era gentleman. He bowed slightly, his eyes glued to her every move.

"Mademoiselle." He held his hand out to her and when she accepted, he kissed her knuckles. The gentle warmth of his lips against her skin sent a wave of pure happiness rushing through her.

Her fingertips lightly skimmed the bodice of her dress. "Henry, everything—"

"Is beautiful." His gaze sailed over the dress and the fit, and he didn't give her a chance to say thank you. Instead, he pressed his lips lightly to hers—soft, wanting, loving. "Simply. Beautiful."

She felt her cheeks flush warm. She touched the jeweled combs in her hair and wondered if he chose the red garnet specifically to coordinate with her red hair. "I can't imagine where you found it all."

He said nothing, but his gentlemanly smile was accompanied by a gleam in his eye. "This way." He gestured to the dining room.

She'd never been one of those girls to put on a rhinestone crown and pretend to be a princess. Since she was five, all she'd ever wanted to do was run her own business. But at this moment, she did indeed feel like a princess, escorted across this majestic home by her very own prince.

The table was set with fine bone china, crystal goblets, and ivory candles in silver candelabras. Red roses from the garden were arranged in crystal vases. She touched one of the pink roses that made up the rim of the china pattern. Such a delicate design. Hand-painted.

An older man in a waiter's tuxedo quietly filled their champagne glasses, served oysters Rockefeller and warm bread from a silver tray, then promptly left.

"Where did you find a waiter in a tuxedo on short notice?"

"When it comes to the manor, there's always someone around who's willing to help." Henry raised his glass, the effervescence sparkling above the rim. "To the restoration of a landmark, the celebration of an era, and to moving forward."

"To moving forward," she said. Their glasses clinked against one another. She entertained a vision of them dining together more often, less formally, but together and frequently. She could see it for years to come. She could also imagine the screen door slamming and happy giggles bouncing off the walls, replacing her earlier impressions of the manor—the more frightening ones that she could barely remember now.

She sipped the sparkling wine, and the low fire crackled in

the otherwise quiet house. "So strange to hear the silence." She set her glass on the French walnut dining table. "It's beautiful."

"It is rather lovely, isn't it? Especially since it's not the sort of thick silence that comes from an abandoned home, but just from the absence of hammering."

She listened into the far corners of the home for violins or the sounds of Benjamin's destruction, footsteps, or other disembodied noises.

There were none.

The sense of comfort she hadn't expected embraced her, like a perfectly sized shoe, an afternoon nap on an overstuffed couch, or the warm fall sun on her beach. The manor, at least at this moment, was happy. She exhaled fully. "Maybe the house is finding some small sense of peace."

"I think it's well on its way." He touched his glass to hers again. "At the very least, I'm certain that it enjoys our celebrating it." Henry smiled with ease.

Given how alive the house had been, she wondered if she ought to be concerned at Henry's comment or even the pleasure she felt. Then she decided that all homes loved being celebrated. It increased their positive energy considerably. That's probably all she was feeling.

Tomorrow things might return to normal, and she would sense those dark roots that lurked. Tonight, she could see that the haunted manor was becoming a home. A lovely home. Once again.

She and Henry talked throughout dinner as if they'd known one another for years. He regaled her with more stories of the history of the Alcott family and the home they had passed down for generations. She asked about his work in London and was happy when he confirmed that he would be with the house until the final phase of the restoration was completed. She shared details about her own business—how

THE HAUNTING OF ALCOTT MANOR

it had been a lifelong dream, how her work was going to be featured in a prominent magazine, and how that would be a game changer for her.

It was easy, the two of them. It hadn't started out that way, and occasionally she thought he was too obsessive about how things needed to be done. But, for the most part, the two of them moved together like a dance or a song. They fit and flowed, and she couldn't stop herself from hoping.

She decided to wait until after the job was over before she pushed for a discussion on plans for the future. Then they would talk. Then she would know. Not because she was needy —she wasn't. She had a life and a business waiting for her. She just wanted to know what he was thinking about all of this.

He nodded to the waiter who entered the room.

"Everything to your liking, Miss?" The waiter spoke in a smooth voice when he removed their dessert dishes and placed them on a silver tray.

"Everything was amazing, thank you."

He nodded, obedient and gracious, and poured two glasses of port wine.

Oddly, it was her favorite digestif. How did they know? She racked her memory, wondering if she had mentioned it to Henry.

She remembered the excitement she felt from the door-knob this evening.

The house knew what she liked. What she wanted.

She wanted to worry about that, but the wine's essence of fresh flowers and dried fruit curled around her like a warm blanket, causing her to laze about into her polished surroundings.

Henry relaxed into his chair at the end of the table, cross-legged and confident, as though this were their normal end-of-the-day routine. All that was missing from the picture was a cigar between his fingers and a hunting dog at his feet.

ALYSSA RICHARDS

"It's easy to see how this was once a family home."

"Always has been." He sighed long and deep and cast a familiar glance around the room. It was the kind of pride she'd seen owners show when certain stages of the restoration were near the finish line.

The concerns they'd held earlier about Benjamin and deadlines drifted out to sea as if she couldn't hold on to them. She thought it strange, given how afraid she'd felt since she arrived. Now what seemed most important was being here for the manor.

It's what it wants.

The thought drifted across her mind. Some part of her felt uncertain about her sudden comfort here, but the wine and the port made her head swim. Something else, too, but she couldn't put her finger on it.

Something that wound through the house. A current. A slither. Through the manor, in its deepest insides, like blood flowed through a vein.

"All the historical pictures of Alcott Manor include one or a few of the family members. I don't think the house would have been satisfied without a crowd of Alcotts wandering its halls." Henry rubbed his hand along the table.

Wasn't that what was already happening to some degree?
Benjamin, Anna, other Alcotts... They were here.
Or was it looking for a new generation of inhabitants?

The manor didn't move, necessarily, but she felt its energy give her the slightest squeeze, like a hug, a gesture of warmth or assurance.

Strangely, she enjoyed being here. It felt like home. As though she could be happy here. As though brighter, contented times lay just ahead.

Maybe the work she did at Anna's death site was beginning to take effect finally. Maybe, because the dark roots were

210

so old, it took some time for them to finally lift. Perhaps tonight was a celebration after all.

She admired the coffered ceiling that boasted a regal teal color inside the gold clover design. The entire room was celebratory now, a far cry from the darkened room it had been when she first arrived.

"The dining room really turned out beautifully, didn't it? These moldings are exactly as the originals were. And the wall that Benjamin destroyed is now open to the porch so you can see straight through to the ocean. This room will be magical in the morning light," she said.

Henry traced just one finger along a line of wood grain on the table. "It is...altogether perfect. I do think, Gemma, that without you, Benjamin would have destroyed even more than he did. I think you've calmed him." He gestured toward the library.

She turned toward him, surprised. "Do you think so?"

"The damage he did this time was minor. We survived it. Thus far, anyway. It hasn't always been that way. I think you might have brought him some peace."

"I was just thinking that the manor felt different to me tonight."

"I think it's quite happy to have you here." Henry's gaze quietly roamed the walls, as if he were being watched.

Alarm bells sounded in some distant hallway of her mind that she wasn't paying attention to at the moment. When he returned his attention to her, she was confident that it was more than attraction between them. She had decided to postpone a "what's next" discussion, but there was something she wanted to share with him. Something she wanted him to know.

They walked together to the porch window, where the last streams of afternoon light could be seen in sparkles on the ocean water.

"It's funny how things can change in such a short period of time. When I first got here, I wanted to restore this home for my father and his business and then jet back to my own life. I feel differently about the manor now. There's more work to be done, and I have a lot going on at home, but I want to see this through. Beyond the judge's approval. All the way through to the end. I think that done correctly, the manor could have a second life. A full life."

"Did you say you were feeling differently about the manor now?" He appeared concerned when he took her hand.

"I'm just saying that I'm glad I'm here. I'm glad we met." She licked her lips slowly and plunged ahead. "It's taken me a long time to let go of Preston's betrayal. When I first arrived here, I had no idea how much longer that process was going to take. But meeting you has taught me how to trust again."

"Gemma—"

"I'm not— I don't have any expectations of what's next." Happy family scenes played again like a movie in her mind. She heard the manor's back screen door slam and then slam again. As clearly as she heard her own voice, she heard that door. Then tiny thunderous feet and giggles owned the space.

Her thoughts? House memories? House plans?

"I just...wanted to tell you that. And also to say—because of you, because of what we've shared, I understand this house now. Better than I did. I understand Benjamin better, too. Moving forward is never easy when you've been wronged. But it's worth it. Really worth it. Maybe now I can affect the kind of deeper healing the manor needs. I think I can figure it out now."

I want to bring up these images. I want to ask Henry about them. Everything is so happy now. And it hasn't been happy for such a long time...

"Gemma. If anything good has happened here, it's because of you. You are the one who has been a genuine gift to the manor. And to me. You just don't know." He shook his head and glanced toward the shore as if he couldn't possibly find the words for what he wanted to say.

"You waltzed through my front door that day, took control, and changed my life. For the better. If the restoration meets its deadline, and if Benjamin has found any amount of peace, it's because of you and your work." He kissed her with a slow gentleness that brought meaning to his words.

When their lips finally parted, idyllic happiness swirled around her with a dizzying force. "Thank you, Henry."

"I tried to get you to leave, for your own good, to avoid the risks in this place. Honestly? Selfishly? I'm glad I failed." He inched closer to her, his eyes intent, steady, and focused. "I don't know what your plans are after the house is finished, but I want more of what we've begun here. I don't want to let you go. I love you, Gemma."

His words swept her up in a flurry of emotion, and in his kiss, she could feel the threads of their love weaving their way into tomorrow and beyond.

"Oh, I love you, too, Henry," she said with his lips so very close to hers. "I want this, too. I want us. And a future."

What a risky thing to say. But I said it. I went for it. I leaped.

Intermittent chatter mumbled from the next room, and she caught her breath. It stopped and started like a radio with a loose connection. She spun toward the wide porch window that faced the ocean and was startled to see how dark it was outside. It had been much lighter only a moment ago.

Only a moment!

Time didn't adhere to its regular schedule in Alcott Manor. "Henry!" she whispered.

"Time to go." He grabbed her hand, and her wine glass fell to the floor in a crash. They ran until they reached the foyer, where they both stopped abruptly. Gemma gasped and Henry squeezed her hand. He shook his head and placed a finger over his lips.

Several women in formal, floor-length dresses chatted in a circle and sipped glasses of white wine at the end of the great hall.

"The president," one said before they flickered out.

"Senator Alcott will get the nod," another one said when the image reappeared. Two other women leaned toward one another, and a whispered secret was shared only between them. When the image of them finally held firm, a small chamber orchestra appeared and played just loudly enough that the women's conversation was no longer audible.

"This way." Henry kept her hand in his and led the two of them past the circle of women, keeping as much distance from them as possible. They were just a few feet from the kitchen when the swinging door moved a little.

"Watch out." Henry moved them to the side of the room just before a young, dark-haired waiter pushed through carrying a silver tray of champagne glasses.

When the door swung wide, they made a run for it.

CHAPTER 23

Gemma kicked her antique shoes onto the back patio, lifted the hem of her dress, and ran like hell across the forest green lawn with Henry at her side. When they reached the sandy shore, they stopped, breathless, and turned toward the house.

The lower floor was bright with lights, music, and guests while the manor's memory fought to find its way to full life.

The warmth and encouragement she'd felt from the house began to unexpectedly dissipate. Like it had found another potential lover to court, another dream to weave, another guest to welcome.

"Are you okay?" he asked.

She rubbed her hand across her forehead. "Yes. Fine. Although I do feel differently now that I'm...not inside the house." The party sounded like fun and a part of her wished to be back inside where she had been one of the guests of honor.

"Let's stay outside for a while. Let your head clear." Henry patted her hand and threaded it around his arm. "Might be wise."

He guided her along the beach in the direction she'd not yet explored. From the caring firmness of his grip, she knew they wouldn't go back to the house, or maybe even the winter garden, anytime soon.

The mid-August full moon cast a sultry reddish glow across the sand and sea and eliminated any reflection. Henry pointed to the occasional leap of a dolphin and brought her attention to the call of a hawk. She knew he was trying to distract her enough that the effects of the manor would dissipate.

He stopped and faced her. His expression was serious, her hands in his. "Gemma. If you're no longer sure how you feel —now that we're outside the manor—please, there isn't any pressure to continue to agree with those statements."

"Henry. No." She shook her head, her gaze fixed on his. "I don't disagree with what I said at all." She cast a glance toward the house that was both empty and full of life at the same time. "Somehow, the manor made it look as though all my long-held dreams could all come true. At the manor."

"Your dreams regarding your business?"

"No." She exhaled a short laugh. "I realized those on my own. These were...other dreams." She shook her head because she wouldn't be describing them in any detail.

"The house wants you." He raised an arched eyebrow, a silent warning, reminiscent of the earlier, more verbal ones.

"I know." She felt like the biggest stuffed teddy bear on the carnival game shelf. She was the brass ring. The prize.

But why?

"I can't believe the manor would trap me just to make me a member of its ongoing party. I thought maybe I had a job to do, that it wanted me to clear the way for Benjamin to go home. But I'm no closer to that than when I arrived."

She felt the old, familiar anxiety rear up inside of her. Benjamin may not have destroyed anything recently, or at least nothing that they couldn't fix, but that wasn't a guarantee that he wouldn't strike hard before the judge's visit—and in a way that they couldn't recover. Hope was not her favorite strategy.

"I don't know. I can't explain the manor. Not entirely, anyway. But we're going to keep our distance from its influence for a good while."

They walked a good bit further until they reached a spot where the sand ran up into a small forest of pine trees. It was private. Peaceful. The scent of pine was one of her favorites, and she began to feel like herself again. Less of a prize.

Henry laid his jacket on the sand and offered his hand to her. Once they were both seated, he said, "Oh. You're not afraid of alligators, are you?"

"Uh, generally speaking, yes. Why?"

"There are some nights when they crawl from the swamp on the south end of the property and rinse off in the surf."

"Seriously?" Gemma's eyes darted around the area she'd just thought peaceful and safe.

"I am serious. Sometimes I see them make a midnight run." He gently lifted her hand and brushed a kiss against the inside of her wrist. "They sit very still where the sand meets the sea, never blinking, even when the water washes over their eyes."

She watched while he dragged his lips upward along the tender light of her skin, his kisses as gentle as a breeze or a precious thought. "Now I don't know who to be more afraid of...sea bathing alligators, miscreant ghosts, or overly possessive houses."

"Probably the latter. Or both of the latter. But, as your loyal knight, I shall protect you from all of them." His gaze lifted to hers between his kisses, and his lips parted into a momentary impish grin.

"Even the alligators?"

"Particularly the alligators."

Her giggle was quiet.

Maybe they were safe.

He relocated his kisses to the side of her neck, and her mind followed the slow purse of his lips and the measure of his movements. His rhythm nearly matched the slow slosh of the waves. The tide felt lazy and hypnotic under the moon's red cover.

She felt affected herself.

"Do you think that's how the house draws people in— makes them think the manor is where their dreams could come true?"

He marked her neck with two more kisses before he answered. "Maybe. I should think it would have to make itself appear like an attractive option."

"Well, it did at that. I'm not sure I've completely shaken that feeling that I've finally reached the pot of gold at the end of the rainbow."

He extended his arm and rested it on his bent knee, his eyes locked with hers in a gaze so deep she felt under a spell. "Well. If that feeling hasn't yet abated, Ms. Stewart, then maybe you have found gold. Maybe what we have here...is perfect."

Perfect.

"Not perfect."

"No?"

"Nothing is perfect." Her conviction was firm.

His eyes scanned her face, reading her, seemingly understanding her. He glanced toward the ocean for a brief moment. An inhale. As though he pondered how to get through to her.

"True. Perfection is probably overrated. Though I think what we have found here is perfect for us."

A softening washed over her, taking with it her former

convictions about ideals. The force moved through her from tip to toe, knocking over old walls and fences she'd erected for safe boundaries. Though now she felt stronger in the absence of them.

"Henry." She pressed her hand on his and drifted somewhere between worlds of gratitude and unbelieving. "The way I feel about you, I've never felt like this about anyone before."

"Neither have I."

"It's overwhelming."

"In the best of ways, I hope."

"In the very best of ways. I just... I mean, where are we heading with all of this? You work in London. You're here only until the house is finished. My life is established on the other side of the country." She hadn't wanted to ask, not tonight. Suddenly, she simply had to have answers. She needed to know what he was thinking. She didn't want this to disappear.

Henry fiddled with the jacket beneath him and positioned himself in front of her.

On one knee.

With her hands in his, he said, "We're heading into forever. Together. If you'll have me."

She felt her lips separate into an O. "Forever," she finally said. "Together."

"I know this must seem sudden. I've known for some time, Gemma. Almost from the beginning. And even before then."

He caressed the side of her face. Gently. "You see, I've known since I was a young boy that there was someone out there just for me. Someone who searched for me the way that I searched for her. I'd given up hope until you finally arrived."

Like a magician, he produced a ring with graduating gold

steps of diamond-laden squares, culminating in a large, step-cut emerald centered in the middle.

He slipped the ring on her finger. "I've loved you all of my life. Now that you're finally here, I want us to be together."

"Forever," she said again. Her entire life seemed to speed before her. From the time when she was a little girl, and she first heard the ideal melody that made her dream of the man she thought could be, on through the course of her life to this moment. When he was finally here. "You know, I think I've searched for you, too. I just didn't realize it until now."

"Marry me, Gemma. I'll spend the rest of my days making you happier than you've ever dreamed."

Giddiness spread through her in a chill, and at once her world righted itself. Her life made sense in a way she'd never expected it to. The scenes from her ideal life at the manor revisited her. Though she was clear enough now to know that she wouldn't live at the manor, maybe Henry was right. Maybe they *had* found gold. Apparently, with the right man, it could be that simple. "Yes, Henry. Yes, I'll marry you."

He kissed her, his breath warm and sugared such that her mouth opened to taste it. She heard the melody again. They created it together, she realized. Its lilt, its symphonic perfection, promising and delivering the sublime on the same structured beat.

"You're safe with me, Gemma. I want you to know that. I'll never make a promise to you that I can't keep."

"I do feel safe with you." She inched the hem of her dress upward until she could easily straddle his hips. She needed to be close to him, she needed to be heart to heart with this man she loved.

"I guess you must, to allow yourself quite so close to me in this way." His mouth widened into a generous grin. His hands explored beneath her dress, up her bare thighs and over her hips.

Her laugh originated from some magical place within that only Henry could share with her. Her happiness was more complete than she had ever known.

His eyes widened with apparent appetite. "Ms. Stewart. May I ask where you left your undergarments?"

She giggled. She'd forgotten. "They didn't work with the outfit. Panty lines are unseemly."

"I am glad that you are aware of these things." The smile on his face made her think he must be at least as happy as she was. The care in the depths of his eyes showed her that he remembered how broken she'd once been—how shattered they'd both been—maybe not that long ago.

The slowness of his tender strokes, albeit deliberate, offered a way forward, a path they would travel together. His manner was a steady force, like the strength of the tide, one she willingly joined and pushed the pace of now and then.

His gentling touch made her head and body spin in increasingly tight turns. Emotions switched effortlessly between ecstasy and doubts that called to her with tiny voices. Only the doubts were weak and withered now and touted the same warnings that she'd heard before. Warnings that she decided didn't suit what she and Henry shared and where they were headed.

No, she didn't know everything about him. But she knew enough to know she'd made a good decision this time.

She held on to his broad shoulders and gasped when she lowered herself onto the force of his flesh. A wave crashed hard behind her and his breath trembled against her mouth.

"Forever, you say?" she whispered against his ear.

"That was my hope. My prayer."

The visions she'd seen tonight danced in colored memory through her mind. "I can see forever from here." And she could. It required no effort to do so.

Maybe the manor had just relocated those scenes, she

decided. Maybe it stole a piece of real and threaded it against itself as the backdrop. It didn't matter. These dreams were her future now, she was sure of it.

Henry tugged her hips against him more quickly, and her body answered to the new rhythm in a shudder. He stiffened beneath her, pulling her flush against him until they were an extension of one another. She gasped and moaned against the damp of his skin. The wind spun around them, in warning or in celebration, she could no longer tell. So, she ignored the dance and the call of the wind patterns—and was unable to stop herself from melting into Henry and the future they would share.

CHAPTER 24

Gemma and Henry snuggled together on the back porch swing that overlooked the ocean. The deepest shades of the night had passed, and several birds announced the coming of the new day, though it was still too early for the sun to rise.

With a goose track quilt draped over them, she listened to Henry tell stories of the Alcott children who used to run through the hallways of Alcott Manor. He was a gifted story-teller, and in the way that natural gifts always were, it suited him. He could have been reading a recipe aloud, and she would have wanted to hear him tell it from start to finish. It was regal almost, the way he swept her into the story.

"When do you have to be back in London?" Her thumb caressed the band of her engagement ring. She couldn't stop looking at it.

"I'll be here until the project is finished. We've come this far. I'm going to see it all the way through." He lifted her hand so that the ring was between them now. "Do you like it?"

"I *adore* it. I've never seen anything like it."

"It was my mother's. My father gave it to her. No one has ever worn it but her."

She breathed a sigh of unexpected relief. "I can't imagine anything more perfect." She rested her head on his shoulder. "London doesn't need you back anytime soon?"

"Right now, this is my work. It takes priority." He ran the back of his fingers against her cheek. "Plus, I've waited for you for too many years to spend any time away from you."

She met his lips in a slow kiss. "How do you feel about Northern California?" She lobbed the question gently and hoped he might say his company had an office there that he'd always wanted to see.

"Let's talk about that—"

The clang of an old-fashioned bell rang through the house, and Gemma and Henry sat up with a start.

"What was that?" she asked.

They dashed inside, Gemma following Henry toward the front of the house. When an image of Anna nearly ran them over, Henry pulled Gemma out of the path. They stood together and watched while Anna opened the front door.

A tall, slender man with thick, dark hair greeted Anna cordially. Henry and Gemma followed Anna as she escorted the stranger to the music room. They slipped in behind the couple before she closed the double doors, and the man swept Anna into his arms.

She cradled his face in her hands, and they kissed and hugged as if they'd just been reunited after a long absence.

"What did he say?" He held her hands in his.

She sighed. "He won't give me the divorce."

The man's entire stature slumped two inches. "How is that possible? Did you tell him?"

"I told him about you. About us. I was absolutely clear that I didn't love him, that I would never love him, so he would let me go. He said he wouldn't divorce me because you were a dangerous, selfish man. He said that you were going to marry Sarah Baker, now that she's returned with her parents from Europe, because she's wealthy and you have her fooled. He said you only want me for access to his money and if you can't have me, then you'll marry her. He's absurd."

Sam walked to the empty fireplace and leaned against the mantel.

"Sam?"

"He'll give you the divorce, won't he, Anna?" He didn't look at her when he said it. And it wasn't a question, but a declaration with the most desperate tone. "You'll show him the birth notice, he'll see who Lizzie Mae's father is, and he'll give you the divorce then."

Anna placed her hand on her stomach in an effort, it seemed, to steady it. She didn't rush to Sam. Instead, she stepped away. It was that formal walk Gemma knew too well. It was the same circle step she'd taken after she found a voicemail on her home phone from an unknown female who asked for her husband to return the call. Gemma knew that Anna was hoping beyond reason that what she felt in her gut wasn't true.

"We've been over this, Sam. If we make Lizzie Mae's parentage known publicly, neither she nor I will have a future. At least not in this town. They'll shun us both."

Sam rushed to her and braced her shoulders with his palms. "Then we'll move. We'll leave here, the town can think what they want, and our beautiful Lizzie Mae will never be the wiser."

"How, Sam? Do you think Benjamin will pay for our new life together? Do you think that once he's told that Lizzie isn't his that he'll pay for her dresses and dolls and for us to set up our new family across the country?" Panic seeped into her voice and pushed it higher.

Sam dropped his arms from Anna.

"Your business is in trouble, isn't it? Benjamin was telling me the truth."

"I love you, Anna. This nonsense with my business isn't anything I can't handle." He gave her a little shake and her head bobbled.

"Have you overextended yourself in the business? Have your deals gone under?"

Sam laughed. There was a glow of sweat on his face and his eyes were a tad too wide. "I can handle my business. I always have. I don't think you're looking at this situation with Benjamin clearly. He wants to be President of the United States. He'll pay you to stay quiet about our affair and Lizzie Mae."

"I don't think he will."

"Then you'll ask your father. You'll tell him that Benjamin has threatened your life and that you need money to leave him."

"My father would have paid Benjamin to marry me. He won't do anything to separate me from him." Anna lowered herself into a chair and placed her fingertips over her lips. "I have no way out, and you're going to leave me, aren't you?"

The door to the library opened, and a young maid with blonde hair and blue eyes entered the room with a feather duster. "Oh, I'm sorry, ma'am."

Gemma frowned at the sight of the young girl, who looked oddly familiar. She leaned toward her and wondered if she'd seen a picture of her somewhere recently. Or had she seen her in some apparition that the house cast forth?

She walked several cautious steps toward her before the girl could leave the room. Henry grabbed Gemma's arm to keep her from getting too close to the memory.

When the girl spun around to close the double doors, Gemma saw her face full on. At once, her Alice-in-Wonderland features rang a bell. The blue grosgrain headband had been replaced with a frilly cotton hat, and only a wisp of her blonde hair was visible.

"It can't be," she whispered.

Sam and Anna faded until they disappeared into the past that was never resolved.

"That maid, it's the young girl who died in the house. She's trapped in these memories now."

"She must have interacted with them somehow." His words were an explanation, but even more so a warning. Henry's eyes were fixed in a stare, a wide and steady one. It was the kind that had seen too much, maybe even how the manor could retain a new guest.

"She was here on the anniversary of Anna's death. The memory would have played from start to finish while she was here."

"She belongs to the house now."

THEY SEARCHED every nook of the furniture in the music room, cautiously. They glanced up every now and then, in case they needed to avoid another impromptu memory that wanted to speak and relive its misery.

Regrettably, their search didn't bring any fruitful discoveries. Gemma sighed. Yes, it was possible that Benjamin would leave his home alone for another day and night. So, if they didn't find the note, and if she didn't clear imprints in the house, maybe it would be okay. Although, it made her feel stupid to trust a ghost.

The sun was just beginning to peek over the horizon, and workers would file through the front door soon. They headed toward the winter garden.

"That was Sam, apparently." She glanced at her hand in Henry's. Such a simple gesture. Innocent. Heartwarming. She wanted to do this for the next fifty years or so—stroll with him, hand in hand, near an ocean.

He nodded. "Yes. The father of Anna's baby, Lizzie Mae."

It was a shock. For some reason, Gemma didn't think of Victorian age dwellers as those who had illicit affairs. They wore dresses with high frilly necks and seemed so proper.

"So, I guess Anna never told Benjamin about Lizzie Mae," she said.

"So it would appear."

"Do you think Sam loved Anna at all?"

He sighed. "Didn't appear to me that he was a man capable of caring about anyone but himself. I think if she hadn't been a wealthy woman, he wouldn't have given her a second glance." He ran the side of his thumb along the top of her hand in slow and subtle strokes.

Maybe he enjoyed holding her hand, too.

"I can't decide if this new information gives more motive to Benjamin, or if Sam's deceit prompted Anna to lose hope." Gemma desperately wanted to clear the energetic effects of what they had just seen. She knew if she could, it would lighten the manor's emotional load, and therefore, Benjamin's. But she thought of the young maid, the teenager who was sentenced to another time. Henry's warnings about doing energetic work in the house now seemed more valid. Frustratingly so.

"I was just wondering that myself." Henry opened the door to the winter garden and immediately situated himself on the pillows and blankets in front of the fireplace. "Doesn't look to me like Sam shared Anna's reservations about telling Benjamin the truth. He might have told him without her knowing. Maybe he told Benjamin who Lizzie Mae's father was and demanded payment to keep quiet. Benjamin said no and Sam left Anna. Anna killed herself because she realized that Sam never really loved her and then he was gone."

"Or, Sam told Benjamin and made his demand. Then Benjamin might have confronted Anna and killed her in a fit of rage." Gemma slipped out of her dress, laid the gown gently over a nearby chair, and snuggled next to Henry. They had a little time left before they had to get to work. She was in no hurry to inspect the house for damages—too afraid of potentially bad news.

"I guess we still don't know." He held her close and kissed her head.

She worked two buttons open on his shirt and wriggled her hand onto his bare chest.

The chest of this man she would marry.

Marry.

Glee swirled in her stomach and climbed to her heart on the arc of a dream fulfilled.

In the quiet of the early morning, in the new light of the day, she wondered if regret would make an appearance. Her rational mind reminded her that this had all happened very quickly.

She waited.

The only thing she felt was blessed.

Blessed and happy.

As if destiny had caught her just in time.

"What was the name of that museum where you said the Alcott furniture was kept during the renovation?"

Alcott.

Her last name would be Alcott soon. Gemma Stewart Alcott. Yes. She liked the sound of that.

She thought she felt Henry's chest stiffen under her hand. "Henry?"

"Hmm?"

"Is everything okay?"

"Yeah," he sighed. "Just thinking of everything we have to do today. Judge comes tomorrow. We're out of time."

"Well, assuming there's no damage—"

"There won't be." He hugged her close. "There can't be." He placed his hand on hers and pressed it close to his heart.

"I hope you're right. If there isn't any, then we don't have much left to do."

"I'd still like to search the furniture in the upstairs bedrooms for the note. Probably best to do that this morning."

Now Gemma stiffened. "I'll go with you to help. But I'm not going up there on my own. Not this close to the anniversary date."

"No, I don't blame you. I'll take care of it." He hugged her twice when he said it, and she thought it strange to have someone just take something off her plate like that. She had been the one to face every challenge, slay every dragon, and put out every fire that had come her way over the past ten years. Part of the joy of owning her own business. But if she were honest, she didn't mind the assist. Not in this situation. Not in the least.

"What was the name of that museum you mentioned? The one that kept the furniture until the manor was fully restored?"

"Ah, I know the one you're talking about, but I don't remember their name at the moment. Why do you ask?"

"I was just thinking they might have some history books or scrapbooks there that I could use. Maybe they held on to an old diary. I'd like to do some additional clearing today if I can. You know, insurance."

"I'll tell Paisley to take care of that." With one deft heave, he slipped her beneath him.

"Henry!"

"I have to say, I'm not that interested in hearing about the history of the house, its memories, or what they might mean. Right now, my only focus is you. And us."

"We have to work." She pushed hard to lift him off of her to no avail.

"I am working," he mumbled against her neck.

"Oh, wow. You're a bad influence. I'll just get the name of the museum from Tom."

"Don't go anywhere today, Gemma. Stay here and stand guard with me."

Henry was intent. Possessive. Commanding.

So much so that it took her by surprise.

"I won't be gone long. If I go to the museum, I'll be right back."

His lips pressed together in a tight seal, and she knew he wouldn't tell her what was really bothering him. She assumed it was final stage jitters. The judge came tomorrow, and he was probably afraid that Benjamin was going to screw things up.

Frankly, she was, too. That was why she wanted to go to the museum to find some clearing opportunities. Not for inside the house, necessarily. She'd been pretty well scared off of that. Maybe another outside opportunity. She didn't know. But she couldn't sit around the house and do nothing.

He rolled off of her and sat up, head in his hands.

"What's going on?" Her voice was soft and curious, wanting to help.

"I'm going to take a walk. Clear my mind." He popped up and headed for the door.

"Henry—"

"I'm fine, Gemma. I'm okay. I'll be back." He turned around and kissed her, more than a quick peck, but brief enough to show that he was distracted about something.

After he left, she felt more alone than she had in a long while. She drew her knees up and wrapped her arms around them. Something was wrong.

Something was terribly wrong.

CHAPTER 25

Rather than searching for Henry, Gemma forced herself to take a short run on the beach. He obviously wanted space for some reason. She thought it wise to give it to him.

When she returned to the manor, she changed and decided on a lower level walkthrough to take her mind off worrying. Though inspecting the manor after a night where Benjamin had the run of the place did not do much for her stress level.

She passed through the swinging door that led from the kitchen to the more public areas and eyed the entryways to the rooms that surrounded her: the dining room, the library, the foyer, the sitting room, and the music room.

"It's going to be okay. Everything is going to be just as we left it yesterday."

She walked through the dining room. The slow beat of her boots clicked against the hardwood floors and echoed throughout the cathedral ceiling. No damage. No change. She breathed a gentle exhale, not wanting to disturb anything. Or anyone.

Her eyes searched critically for smaller flaws, and she made notes in her portfolio of any item that had not been done according to her direction. She'd let Tom know about them, but honestly, she wasn't that upset about the minor things at this point in the process. That Benjamin hadn't damaged anything last night was gift enough.

The library was next, and she paused outside the wide doorway when she arrived.

Please, please, please.

With eyes closed, she forced herself into the library and held her breath as though she jumped into the deep end of the pool. She opened her eyes when she thought she finally had enough courage to face whatever was there.

No damage. She exhaled hard. One lone worker who was touching up the stain on the shelves looked in her direction.

"Carry on." She waved.

The rest of the downstairs was also in good condition. No visible damage. Benjamin had taken another night off. Or maybe he was gone. That was possible. The clearing she had performed on the land had been substantial. Maybe that had turned into enough.

ALL THE MAJOR dangers and threats to human safety had been repaired, and considerable progress had been made with the aesthetic work. As testament to that fact, she glided step by step down the completed main staircase, feeling a bit like Scarlett O'Hara.

It wasn't a moment that competed with the royal appearance she made last night in her vintage dress, but she took pride in the fact that the staircase had been fully restored.

Next was the front porch. The cool ocean breeze whipped

from around the back of the house and brought its damp, salty scent with it. The rocking chairs and planters had been placed just as she had directed. She inspected every pillar and floorboard, and each step brought with it a memory of Henry that rested close to her heart.

There was a gentleness to Henry she hadn't expected to find. Not a lack of competitiveness—she had seen his fierce side when Asher came on the property. He was also determined. She had been witness to that quality with the restoration of his house.

There was no wimp factor, no shying away from what he wanted. He was the most tireless, giving lover she'd known. Her face flushed warm at the memories of their nights together, and she brought her hand to her cheek.

It was more of a wisdom, she thought, rather than a gentleness. A hard-earned wisdom, deeply ingrained. Timeworn. The sort that knew kindness was better than selfishness. It knew that self-definition brought more peace than trying to fit within someone else's ideals. There was no ceremony, no formality, but rather, a dedication to what he knew was right and best.

With previous relationships, she'd spent too much time navigating their differences, like a part-time job. Too few were well practiced in the art of accountability, so she constantly skated around the sharp angles of disappointment.

That's what made Henry a most pleasant surprise.

She rounded her way to the rear of the house and sat on the porch swing where she'd begun her morning and pushed off for a respite. The chains squeaked with each back-and-forth.

Where could he be?

She gazed at the sunlight playing on the waves. A lone figure stood on the lawn where the new rose gardens had been planted. Though she couldn't quite tell who he was, his tall figure resembled Henry's.

The screen door slammed. Gemma looked up to find Tom and two construction workers staring at her. She doubted they'd ever seen her sitting down, much less relaxing for a minute. She had a habit of working all the time.

"I'll be right back. I know we have a meeting in ten." She left the swing and tried not to walk too quickly toward the man. It was a long distance across the wide summer lawn to where Henry stood, and she was worried about him. He'd had some space, and now she wanted to know what was going on with him.

Henry turned when Gemma approached. "You okay?" she asked.

He nodded and turned toward the ocean again. "I'm fine."

"You don't seem fine." She tried to cast her worries onto the vastness of the sea.

"I was just thinking about the restoration. We've gotten close before. It's never worked out. He won't let it."

"We're going to do it this time." She looked up and found him intensely focused on something that wasn't in front of him.

He sighed, long and deep. "I've been working on this house for so many years with no success. Just one problem after another. I didn't think— I can't help thinking that I'm going to lose everything."

"Let's sit." She led them to a love seat in the middle of one of the new rose gardens and felt the beginning of it. Her happily-ever-after buzz always began on the last day or two of a job. This one, however, had new meaning for her.

The house was showing serious signs of picture-perfect. Like magic, this stage of the job would give her the kind of happy she'd begun to know as a child when she ran around the houses her parents worked on. She would walk from

ALYSSA RICHARDS

room to room and pretend to be in charge. She'd make notes of things that needed to be done. Then she'd show her mother.

That's what she always strove to create for her clients. The happily-ever-after. She knew it was only the illusion of a happy ending. Sometimes, though, in those surroundings, especially after the land and the homes had been healed, people could find new life, new beginnings, and happiness.

Gemma and Henry sat in the reed-like loveseat that matched the furniture in the other rose gardens. The workers had anchored the feet to cement footings, just as she'd told them to. "Furniture that blows out to sea on a gust of wind won't help us much," she'd told them.

"I have a good feeling about this. I'm not counting chickens before they're hatched, but I think we're going to be okay." She brushed the dark curl that blew onto his forehead, only to watch it fall there again. "What has you bothered?"

"Benjamin," he said flatly.

"We haven't heard from him in the last few days. It's possible he may have made peace with his past and with Anna."

Henry flashed her a look that said she couldn't possibly be serious. "After all this time?"

"He might finally understand that the note is gone, that the past is the past, and that the only thing he can do now is move on." Gemma shrugged.

"I just don't know if he's the type to give up on something that's been so important to him for such a long time."

"People change. They deal with their loss. They figure out how to get through it. That's the whole point of my work, to help people let go. Maybe that's happened for Benjamin. Maybe he's happy."

"Maybe." Henry's tone was disbelieving and his stare settled on the horizon.

"My mother had a saying about doubts like these. Whenever I'd worry that something might not work out, she'd say, 'Don't go borrowing trouble.' So, I'm going to say the same thing to you now. It's natural to be this close to the finish line and to want things to go well so badly that you worry they won't. But, don't go borrowing trouble."

His eyes left the horizon and he placed his hand on Gemma's. "You're probably right."

"I know I'm right. We all need this project to end well. For my dad and his company. For you and your relatives. For Charleston and its history. We're at the finish line, Henry. This could all work out just the way we need it to."

She ran her fingers through the back of his hair. It was soft and full with a luscious bit of wave to it. Henry closed his eyes when she did it. His long, dark lashes curled beyond his profile, and the angles of his face set his features into perfect balance.

He squeezed her hand, and the wind danced around him and blew through his hair.

She kissed him, their lips pressed together as they had so many times before, with unexplainable love. She knew it this time, with eyes and heart wide open, she'd finally found the right one for her. "Have you thought any more about California?"

"You love your work and you're quite good at it. I respect both of those qualities about you and the fact that they're important to you. We'll work this out. We have time on our side."

His words were pure magic. Except for the part about time being on their side, which she didn't believe. Since her mother's death and the car accident, she was more of the belief that time was a luxury that many weren't afforded.

There was just a little something she picked up on. Maybe it was the momentary twitch around the corner of his eye. Or it could have been a feeling. She couldn't hang her concern on anything specific. However, there was an elephant in the room. There was something unsaid.

She decided to give him some more space, but soon enough, she would need to know what that something was.

CHAPTER 26

Tom finger-combed the puffy curve of blond hair at the top of his head while he, Gemma, two architects, and Paisley gathered in front of a boarded-up entryway just beyond the music room.

Henry was upstairs searching the bedroom furniture that had been relocated to the manor.

Tom cleared his throat. "Thanks for agreeing to meet this morning, everyone. We're feeling pretty confident that Judge Wertheimer is going to like what he sees tomorrow on his tour through the property. So, we wanted to start some brief discussions on one of the larger projects that is slated for the second half of the restoration."

Tom knocked on one of the wooden boards. "This is the entryway to what used to be a two-story solarium." He swiped his iPad screen repeatedly. "There was a water feature, something of a one-story waterfall, if I'm remembering it right. Lots of green plants and a fish pond along the wall. Anna Alcott wrote in her diary that this was her favorite reading spot."

Gemma seriously hoped he wasn't about to open the

boarded door and expose the hideout she'd shared with Henry. That would be incredibly hard to explain.

"I don't believe it. It's not here." Tom finished flipping through his research file. He tilted his head toward the ceiling, then snapped his fingers. "Oh. I remember where I've seen it. It's at the Charleston Museum of History downtown. They have that exhibit dedicated to the house, the family, and such. Paisley, would you head down there and get copies of the solarium photos for us?"

"They have an exhibit? I'll go and get them." Gemma packed her iPad into her portfolio. "That has to be where they have all the history and scrapbooks on the house."

CHAPTER 27

G emma hopped out of the taxi when it stopped in front of the museum. The inside was dark, but when she pushed the door, she was granted easy access.

"Not crowded this time of day. That's good." She considered navigating crowds akin to waiting in line at the Department of Motor Vehicles.

"Hello?" she called.

No answer was returned. She took a few steps forward and called into the quiet again. "Hello?"

Nothing.

She searched the area for a *Be Right Back* or *Gone Fishing* sign, but found nothing of the sort.

"All right, I'll just help myself, then." She strolled around the small front office and quickly figured out that the exhibits Tom had mentioned were in the middle part of the building.

She meandered through Charleston's early history then advanced toward a gleaming black and white poster-sized picture of Alcott Manor. They posted two pictures: one from 1880 and another more recent one to show its dilapidation.

She read the placard aloud. "The community is debating

between preserving its history with Alcott Manor and tearing it down to allow for new growth. Lamentably, the house is rumored to be haunted by Senator Benjamin Alcott, and restoration efforts to date have yielded very little progress."

"Well," Gemma said into the quiet. "We'll see about that. Might want to make room for the next poster, my historical society friends. It's going to look very much like the original over there."

She examined the original photo and scrunched in close to see the family who gathered in front of the mansion they called home. Now that she had seen Anna and part of Benjamin Alcott with her own eyes, she wanted to see original photos of them from their time. Validation of sorts, she guessed. However, the photo had been blown up so large that the quality was too grainy.

The exhibit featured numerous pictures of the house and its early role in Charleston. Many of them she had already found on the internet. Some she hadn't seen before. She examined one of the pictures taken of Alcott Manor in its heyday and noticed that it featured an exterior shot of the solarium during a July 4th picnic celebration.

She found another of the room itself, lush with wide-leafed green plants and the waterfall, just as Tom had described. With no one around to help her with copies, she took her phone from her pocket and snapped several photos, then emailed them to Tom.

She lingered over an original guest book from the manor that held signatures from dignitaries who had visited the house. Many of them presidents of the United States and their wives.

The next group in the exhibit—the Alcott Family Tree— made her heart jump. She loved genealogy and had spent months documenting her own family tree with her mother years before. It was always fascinating for her to see who her ancestors were.

Small oval pictures of the members of the Alcott family sat at each relevant position on the tree. Someone painted an actual tree, and it was so beautiful.

A different artist had painted another family tree on a separate canvas. But that one was new-ish and held color photos of current-day people who were Alcott family members. She didn't care much about that.

At the top of the original family tree, there was Benjamin Henry Andrews Alcott and his wife, Bertha Mae Alcott nee' Roberts. Benjamin looked just like the picture she had seen of him on the internet. Gray hair, wide handlebar mustache, highly starched cravat, asymmetric horizontal bow, conservative black suit.

She noticed Henry as his middle name. Her Henry had told her that his name was a family name.

Her Henry.

She wondered about that connection and if that was a good idea for his parents to give him the same family name as a potential murderer.

Her mother told Gemma she gave her an original name so she could start fresh in life. She didn't want the energy of another relative to be linked to her given name.

Gemma had always been an independent thinker and her own person. No one ever said, "Why, you're just like your mother/brother/father/cousin." Never. She often attributed that to her mother's forethought.

She redirected her attention to the Alcott family tree. Benjamin and Bertha Mae had five children.

Wait.

Stop.

Bertha Mae? Benjamin was married to *Anna*. They had four children, not five.

Gemma's eyes scanned the photos of the five children.

The first born was a daughter with long, curled pigtails, who had drowned at age seven.

Their second child, a son—Gemma's breathing stopped.

"This can't be right."

She stared at the face in front of her, the one that looked at her with all the frank pleasantness, mystery, and charisma that had entranced her from the moment they'd met.

She read the details beneath the photo:

Benjamin Henry Alcott, son of Benjamin Henry Andrews Alcott and Bertha Mae Alcott nee' Roberts, born July 5, 1850, died August 16, 1883, married Anna Frances nee' Hall, born October 20, 1852, died August 13, 1883.

Her heart tap-danced against the wall of her chest and her head twitched involuntarily.

"That's not possible."

Her fingers felt fat and not quite her own when she snapped a photo of the face that was Henry's doppelganger. She enlarged the photo on her screen. The photo was black and white, but his eyes were obviously light in color, his eyebrows were perfectly symmetrical, and his jawline was squared off at the edges. All perfectly explainable genetic details.

Except that he had a tiny scar just below his right eye. Just like her Henry.

Her Henry.

The phone slipped from her grasp and clattered on the tile floor. She noticed the next display case, which held several yellowed newspaper articles about Senator Benjamin Henry Alcott, Jr. and how he was convicted and hung for murdering his wife. She lifted the plastic cube that rested on top of the white base and set it on the floor.

Gemma leaned close to the yellowed newspaper article and stared at the photograph that held the clear, light-colored, wide-set eyes she'd looked at every day for the past few weeks. This was Henry. Henry Alcott. The same Henry Alcott who was paying her and her family's business a significant amount of money to restore Alcott Manor.

The same one she'd fallen in love with.

The one she agreed to marry when he proposed to her just last night.

This article said his father was the original owner of the home. Father and son were both South Carolina senators who fought hard for justice in the South. The son, however, was accused, convicted, and hung for killing his wife.

She took the ancient article in her hands and examined the date. It was printed one hundred and thirty-one years ago, almost to the day, in fact.

Tomorrow was the anniversary of Anna's death and Henry's arrest.

CHAPTER 28

The right side of the room tipped up and then up again, and Gemma leaned against the opened display. The article floated to the floor. She breathed in and out through her nose as slowly as she could. That's the way they taught her a long time ago when she was recovering from her first encounter with a ghost.

Her mind ran at top speed, reaching for some sort of logical understanding. If Henry and Benjamin were the same person...if Henry was a ghost...how was it possible that she could experience him as a real person? Someone who was solid enough to kiss and hug, hold hands and fall in love with?

No.

She laughed—actually laughed—though she felt more like running from the room screaming.

"This is a joke. That's what this is. A stupid joke."

She grabbed the top of her head hard where the pounding culminated in a pain that hurt more than she thought she could stand.

"One, two, three." Careful steps to the family tree exhibit.

She searched the updated family tree painting and traced

the branches with her shaking finger until she found the most current-day Alcott family members. Henry's face would be there. She knew it. Then she would put her sanity back in its rightful home.

Obviously, she wasn't managing her stress level as well as she thought she was.

Henry had had his freak out this morning. She was having hers now. That's all this was. She was overreacting to something that wasn't even possible. Stress could do that to you.

She scanned all the pictures of current descendants. Each person was positioned in front of a formal, gathered rose-colored curtain, the kind you might find in a church parlor. When she didn't find Henry, she decided she'd overlooked him.

She searched names this time and near the end of the line was Henry Alcott.

Who looked nothing like her Henry.

This man had straight brown hair with a side part, and he was pudgy.

On the other side of the cubed family tree exhibit was a larger photo of this same man with a brief typed summary beneath: *Henry Alcott is a hotelier who spends most of his time in London, England. He has most recently donated the largest share of funds required for the current restoration of the Alcott Manor.*

"No." She backed away from the exhibit. "This is not happening." This must be the house, she decided. The house manipulated the way she saw things last night. Maybe it had been doing that for longer than she realized.

And the house did have some kind of portal connection with the past. Maybe Henry—Benjamin? Maybe he was somehow able to interact with her because—

"No. This is ridiculous. I don't believe this."

He was Henry. He was perfect. Almost perfect. Perfect for her.

She'd finally found the great love of her life.

And he was a ghost.

No.

Whatever he was, the bright future she'd had the courage to dream of was now a total impossibility. She pressed her hand to her forehead and noticed a clammy sweat there.

"You don't believe what? Or do I need to ask?" Henry leaned against the wide doorway of the room, hands in his pockets.

"Henry." For a moment, she thought when she said his name that all would go back to normal. Back to when she knew that he was everything she'd ever dreamed of. Back to when she was happy.

The newspaper article on the floor between them caught her eye.

"How?" She picked up the article and waved it. "How is any of this possible?"

"You mean, how are *we* possible?" His voice was as deep and calm as she'd always known it to be.

"Among other things, yes." Her engagement ring reflected the light and she clasped her hand to her chest. The paper floated to the floor.

Henry watched it land, picked it up, and walked to her.

"All I know is that you're the first person to see me and to interact with me as a real person in over a hundred and thirty years. I didn't want to question it too much in case the magic all went away. You're the first good thing to happen to me in a long time." He reached to caress her face and she moved away.

"You're Benjamin." She said it, though she didn't want to. "Benjamin. Alcott."

A flicker of sadness softened his face for a flash of a moment, and she knew he didn't want to admit it. "I am."

"Who lived and died in the 1800s and who killed his wife."

"I did not kill my wife."

She didn't believe him. She had never believed that Anna had committed suicide. Now it was clear to her why he had been so desperate to prove Benjamin's innocence.

His innocence.

"Oh, God." The dizziness flipped the room on its head again, and she lowered herself to the floor. The cool tile felt good to her open palms, and she tried to focus on that alone.

Henry squatted next to her and placed his hand on her back. "I'm sorry, Gemma. I know this is a shock."

"Why didn't you tell me the truth? You let me believe— God, I must have looked like an idiot this entire time. And you—you proposed to me! What the hell, Henry! How was that supposed to work? How—" The words were large in her mouth, and they lost their footing on her rapid breath.

"I'm sorry. I'm sorry. I wanted to tell you. So many times. But if I *had* told you the truth, what would you have been able to do with that?"

"What do you mean?" Gemma placed her hands on her forehead.

"If I had told you the truth about me—who I was, who I am. You wouldn't have believed me. Would you? One of the first things you said to me when we met was that you didn't see ghosts."

All she could think about was how she had lost the one she loved. She had lost Henry. Every inch of her body ached. "No. I wouldn't have believed you."

"You would have thought I was crazy. You would have written me off as some nutcase. You wouldn't have wanted anything to do with me." Henry dipped his head and raised his eyebrows. "Am I right?" He reached for her hand and held it in his.

She slowly licked her dry lips and looked away. "You're right."

A loud truck engine rumbled past the building.

"You're Benjamin. Not Henry." Betrayal and hurt widened the distance between them.

"I'm Benjamin, yes."

"The same Benjamin who killed several others over the years at the manor."

"I've never killed *anyone*." He pulled his hand away, and a fiery defensiveness lit behind his eyes. She wondered if half of his face would disappear into rotting flesh and if a rope would appear around his neck.

She squinted to focus hard while details from their time together played through her mind. Henry's insistence about the note. Benjamin's searching. The destruction. "You don't know if you killed Anna or not, do you? That's why you want that suicide note so badly. You're trying to prove to yourself that you didn't do this awful thing. That's why you're still here."

"Honestly?"

"Yes. Honestly—for a change."

The pace of his breathing quickened and his nostrils flared. "I don't know."

"You don't know what?"

His body was still, his eyes focused on her. "I don't know if I killed Anna or not."

She sat down all the way now.

He did the same.

They stared at one another.

She kept looking for a loophole in this experience—a way to hit the rewind button and to go back to the Henry she fell in love with. She wanted a way to erase everything else. "How is it that you don't know?"

He looked around the room with his fists flexed. Probably

searching for something to hit, she figured.

"I don't remember entirely. It was a long time ago. I have *always* had a strong conviction that she killed herself, even when I was alive. I can't have been wrong for all this time."

"Ghosts are often wrong," she said flatly. "Over time, a ghost's memory is boiled down to a few moments that may or may not be accurate, and they sure as hell don't allow any room for insight." She thought it especially cruel that he was only an arm's length away, and yet the man she loved wasn't anywhere anymore.

"I've had the benefit of quite a bit of insight over the last few weeks. Thanks to you." He reached for her hand and she moved it just out of his reach.

"What happens when you—when you're Benjamin?" She hoped he didn't show her. She hoped he wouldn't turn into the half-faced man she never wanted to see again.

"I don't intentionally change. It just happens. The memories of the house play: the injustice of my trial, the way I was murdered, Anna's death, the missing suicide note. The change happens, and I'm just searching for that damned note. The next morning the house is wrecked, but I don't remember destroying anything. That hasn't happened for a while, though."

Henry rubbed his hands against one another. He was real to her. Not a ghost, but real.

"Wait." Something he said hit her funny. "What did you say?"

"I don't remember anything when I turn—"

"No. You said 'the *missing* suicide note.' Why do you say that?"

"Because I think I remember seeing it. Before I died."

"You saw Anna's suicide note?"

"Maybe in her room. On her secretary desk."

Unexpected hope deflated in her chest. "I searched that

desk on the night I saw the memory of her. It's not there. Are you sure you're not lying?"

He ran his hand over his face, though seemingly more in disappointment than frustration. "I'm not lying."

She couldn't decide whether she wanted to throw herself into his arms or beat him senseless.

"Why did you go to such lengths to have a relationship with me? Were you bored, or did you just want to see how far this would go?"

He leaned forward and took both of her hands in his. His hazel eyes narrowed and focused. "Gemma. I did not tell you the truth about who I was. That was selfish, and I'm sorry. But I never played any games with you. These last few weeks with you have been the happiest times of my"—he let out a sigh—"my very long, very tortured life."

He wiped the tears from her cheeks and paused as if he searched within for the right thing to say.

"I don't think I'd ever get over losing you." Henry took Gemma's face in his hands and kissed her lips.

She closed her eyes to the warmth and the softness of his kiss until she cringed and dropped her head.

"Oh, Gemma." Henry pulled her close, and the betrayal in her heart hurt beyond her ability to bear it.

"I can't do this. I have a life back in San Francisco. A career. I don't have room for people who can't be honest with me." *Ghosts.*

"I didn't tell you because I didn't want to scare you. I didn't expect you to see me, much less something to develop between us. From the first day we met, I knew how afraid you were of ghosts. I also knew how important it was for you to finish the restoration so your father's company would get paid.

"I haven't been able to leave the manor for any real length of time in over a hundred years, and I couldn't just leave while you did your work. I thought that maybe I could help you. That we could help each other. You needed to know more about the manor's history so you could clear the imprints of the past. I'm the only one who has that information."

"You could have sent me here." She waved to the exhibit. "I would have done all the right research."

"I lied to you about where this information was. I admit that. But even if I had sent you here, you wouldn't have known where Anna died or what happened in that guest room. You wouldn't have known what to do with the memories that flash through the house throughout the night. Hell, you could have been sucked into that world!"

She glanced down and then away. Her line of sight landed on the large photo of the house. Henry was probably one of those grainy, shadowy figures in front. This was a living nightmare. "You're right. I thank you for that."

"What we have is real. This could work," he said. "People have private relationships all the time. They keep them out of public view to protect them. I think if you just give this a chance, you'll discover it can work quite well. It already has."

She laughed through the pain. "Think about it. We couldn't even go to dinner together. We couldn't go to the movies or have vacations. We couldn't take a walk on the beach while holding hands. I couldn't introduce you to my father, my brothers, or my friends. The most important part of my life would always be in hiding—invisible to everyone I care about." She glanced at the Alcott family tree.

He ran his hands across the sides of his head. "Gemma, we'll work this out. We have each other."

"You're a ghost, Henry! There's no working it out! And what about—there would never be children. There would never be a family." She thought of the slamming screen door and the sandy feet and the sweet giggles that once again eluded her.

He leaned against the wall, defeated. His eyes had lost their sparkle. "No. You're right about that. We could never have children together."

"Our lives would never work as a couple. Not to mention that I'd be written off as a nutcase at some point. I'd be the crazy lady who constantly talked to someone who wasn't there."

"A love like ours doesn't come around very often. I'm proof of that," he said. "Please, let's just give this some time. We can figure this out."

"Time is on our side. That's what you said." She scoffed. "Because time doesn't pass for you anymore, does it?"

Tears glistened in his eyes. "I think because of you, for the first time in what for most people would be two lifetimes, I have hope that time will finally move forward for me again. With your help, I think I could finally leave this house and start a new life. One that has nothing to do with my old life. That tragic end will finally find the healing it needs and that house will let go of me forever."

She shook her head. "So, that's why you did it. You helped me work on the house because it would help you. *Benjamin*. It would finally free you from your suffering. That's the real reason."

He closed his eyes and sighed. "Do you have any idea how many people I have seen come through the manor over the past century? How many people have claimed to remove Benjamin from the house? I had long given up on anyone being able to help me. When I said I could begin a new life, I meant a new life with you.

"Your work, Gemma, on the land, it did shift things. Maybe not as much as you wanted. But I can feel the beginning of it. And you. Your care, your love. It changed me." He caressed her face. "I know you were happy, too."

"I was happy. Truly happy. There was a big part of who

you are that I didn't know about, though. That changes everything, obviously." She moved his hand from her face. "I know what I want. What I need. I want us—I wanted us with a future and a family. I wanted to live a full life with you."

"We could have a good life together. It might not be exactly as you planned. Nothing ever is."

She rubbed the back of her neck. "You are not capable of a future, Henry. You are the past. Besides, what would happen to me in the middle of the night when you turn into Benjamin? What would I do then? Hand you a towel so you don't drip blood on the carpet? Or would I need to run for my life?"

"Nothing bad happened to you when we were together at the manor." His tone was soft, apologetic.

A shiver ran across her skin. "I had no idea I was taking my life in my hands by being with you."

"You were safe with me," he said.

She turned away. "No one is ever truly safe with a ghost."

She felt oddly stupid. Fooled. She should have stayed loyal to her work, focused on the job. Henry was as she had originally thought, too perfect for paper, too good to be true.

"Where was the real Henry Alcott my father worked with? The one he wanted me to meet?"

"He lives in London most of the time but was on site when your parents were here. He left before you arrived."

"So, when I met you and called you Henry, you just didn't correct me, did you?"

"I was stunned that you saw me. When we shook hands, I felt your touch. I felt something between us. That hadn't happened in a long time. So, no, I didn't correct you."

"I can't do this." She spun away from him.

"Gemma."

"No! Just. Leave."

CHAPTER 29

Gemma sat in the corner of the Historical Society's Alcott Manor exhibit area. There was no noise, just the heavy quiet of her disappointment that weighed on her like a lead blanket.

Realizing that someone you loved isn't who you thought they were was a death. The one you trusted, the one you gave your heart to, was gone. No notice, no reasonable explanation. Their deceit just ripped them from you while you were left to figure out how to stitch yourself back together and move on.

He was a ghost. The walking dead. Even her mother would have advised her against this one, and she tended to have a special compassion for ghosts. "Most of them don't even know they're dead, honey," her mother had often told her. "How can you not have compassion for someone like that?"

She shook her head. Henry knew he was dead. He'd known all along, and he hadn't told her. The real Henry Alcott who worked in London wasn't even on site anymore.

She and Tom and miserable little Paisley were the only ones in charge.

What an idiot she was not to be able to tell the difference. Her mother occasionally mistook a ghost for real now and then. She told Gemma a story of how they entered a house they were working on in Minnesota one summer. The owner had just passed away, and the daughter wanted the home, which was also her childhood home, restored. Gemma's mother was the first one to arrive. She met a lovely woman who said she was the previous owner's sister. She showed Gemma's mother around the home and described exactly what she wanted to be done. She also told her about a secret hiding place where the owner's private papers were held.

When the daughter showed up, Gemma's mother told her about the lovely conversation she had with the woman. The daughter said that sounded exactly like her great aunt but that she had been dead for ten years.

A heavy door slammed at the back of the Historical Society. She didn't move. Under normal circumstances, she would have hopped up and introduced herself to whoever was on their way in. As it was, she just sat there. She couldn't bring herself to be sociable. She felt sort of invisible to life, anyway. Maybe they wouldn't notice her.

An older woman with short, white-gray hair tottered in low, fat heels across the room, never the wiser that Gemma was seated in the corner. A large ring of keys jingled like muted bells.

When she reached the front door, she flipped all the locks and turned the open sign to closed. A short while later, Gemma heard the back door slam shut. All was silent again.

She decided that either the lady had been hard of hearing and hadn't heard Gemma come in, or maybe she had left the building for a few minutes. That was the way it often went with smaller town businesses. If they wanted to step out for coffee or a sandwich, they just did. Being gone for fifteen minutes here or there didn't usually make a difference. Though she might have wanted to lock the door before she left.

She inhaled a deep breath. At least they had done well with the manor. The deadline was tomorrow, and Asher would not get his way with the property. Tom would take Judge Wertheimer and his committee through the house and show him all the marvelous progress on the restoration. That would give the judge a strong sense of confidence that a full restoration was not only possible, but imminent, and that would move them on to the next phase of the job.

She realized she would have to find someone to take her place for the final stage of the work. She couldn't work there with Henry, and he couldn't leave.

The anniversary of Anna's death was tomorrow, as well. Whatever happened as a result of that wouldn't occur until after the judge's tour, late into the evening. By then, they'd be home free.

Her dad's company would get paid, his financial problems would be over, and she would go back to life as it had been before Alcott Manor.

She rose out of her corner and strolled through the exhibit. Henry mentioned that this is where they kept the Alcott's furniture until recently when Paisley had it brought back to the house for the inspection. And didn't he say that they had most everything stored here for a while?

There was a room dedicated to every major era in Charleston's history. She wandered through most of them until she found what she needed: a door marked Employees Only.

Immediately inside was an employee break room, sparsely decorated with a round table and plastic chairs, a microwave, and a fridge. An industrial-looking door opened into a small, disorganized room with brown boxes of files that smelled damp. The wooden door marked PRIVATE led to a narrow but packed library. Six shelves lined every wall, chock-full with books of all shapes and a few antiques, including old box cameras.

"Banzai," she whispered.

She started on the left, just behind the door where materials beginning with the letter A were located. Alcott Manor took up five of the six shelves in that section. Figuring that no one would be back in the museum until morning, she helped herself to every book and scrapbook on the manor and piled them on the rectangular table in the middle of the room.

The seams of the first scrapbook crackled when she opened it. In the dust that rose from the center pages, she heard violins, laughter, and tears, and she saw a billowing of dreams birthed and lost. As was the standard cycle with the manor.

Inside the album were interior photos of the Alcott home that highlighted endless decorating and design details. She'd make sure these were referenced in the final stages of the restoration. Red was a common theme throughout the manor, as was often customary in many Victorian-era homes. Every two pages displayed a new room of black and white photos, but red was an easy color to decipher—red couches in the library, red curtains in the dining room, red everything in Benjamin's room.

She turned another crisp page. Only Anna's room held minimal touches of red. In the deep crevice of the two pages devoted to Anna's boudoir was a frayed and faded ribbon, lavender in color, with a tiny skeleton key tied to the end. The kind that might fit into a diary lock, she wondered? Or some keepsake box of Anna's? She slipped the key into her pocket. Whatever it fit into might be around the museum somewhere. Maybe it held some valuable piece of information she could use.

She finished that scrapbook and moved on to the next volume of Alcott history. She no longer trusted Henry to be her source of information on the house. Neither should she. He was most likely keeping something else from her. Something that probably made him look bad.

The next book was a collection of yellowed newspaper clippings. Tiny bits of peace and hope fluttered under the tips of her fingers. Now that she had these books, she'd figure out what gave the house its tragic aura and its scent of death that literally moaned from its timber.

CHAPTER 30

Henry stood in the empty winter garden that had been his hideaway with Gemma. He kicked the blankets, and they folded over on one another. She had every reason to be upset with him. He had gone to great lengths to make sure she wouldn't find out his true identity. For his own sake, he would admit that. His existence here over the last century had been solitary, lonely, and sad. Aside from a few psychics who could confirm his existence, no one saw him. No one interacted with him—certainly not the way that Gemma did.

But he had also kept his secret for her. He knew she needed to finish the work her parents had started.

She had respected him, enjoyed his company, and he knew she had fallen in love with him. At least, she used to feel that way.

His eyes scanned the glass walls that surrounded what used to be Anna's favorite room. When she was alive, he gave up almost everything to help Anna, only to discover that she had betrayed him in every way. The news of Lizzie Mae's parentage stuck in his heart—he had loved that beautiful girl as his own.

Once again, he had helped someone who needed it, a woman who he thought might appreciate his kindness, who he hoped to spend a lifetime with.

Once again, he was wrong.

His future stretched out ahead of him like his past, full of broken dreams and lost hope. The old rage bubbled inside of him, and he let it rise, let it change him into someone he should never have become. Someone he would never escape.

With one hand, he held on to the edge of the white marble fireplace and pulled. It split from the wall with a terrifying rip and burst into shards when it hit the floor. Before he left the room, he turned his hardened stare to the wall to see if a handwritten note had been hidden there.

There was nothing.

He disappeared through the wall and into the main living areas of Alcott Manor to do the only thing he could do, continue his search for that damned suicide note.

CHAPTER 31

The courthouse was smothering with its inadequate air conditioning and too-large crowds of disgruntled citizens who would rather have been anywhere but there. Gemma pushed her way through the front revolving doors with scores of other people, then waited in the security line.

She'd arrived early at the manor only to find Tom, Paisley, and their attorney, Morris "Mo" Pate jumping into their cars. Tom wanted to meet with Judge Wertheimer before they commenced with the tour, which Gemma agreed to, as long as the tour didn't extend into the evening. The manor couldn't be trusted at night. Especially not this night.

Several police cars were also parked in the driveway. Gemma assumed Tom brought them in to protect the house and their work. *Smart.*

Once on the other side of the security sensors, she found a portable marquis that listed the names of all the cases to be heard that day. Fortunately, it wasn't a large courthouse, and their courtroom was easy to find.

It was fairly empty, and a few men in business suits were on the opposite side. Others, she didn't recognize, and she thought were probably Alcott family members. She identified Asher Cardill, who sat on the front row on the opposite side, looking smug and whispering to the men in suits. Someone sat next to him who looked familiar to her, but she couldn't quite place her.

She found an available seat on a bench halfway to the front and squeezed in. When the woman who sat next to Asher turned all the way around to speak with someone behind her, Gemma recognized her. It was Layla Alcott. Her father's nurse. Asher put his arm around her and Gemma frowned. Layla was far too genuine of a person to be hanging around someone like him.

She hated to think it, but she wondered if he married her for her last name and the stock she held because of it. She remembered Layla saying that she wanted the property restored. But if Asher had any idea that he was due Alcott stock, as well, the two of them together would wield a lot of voting power. His company might even be the one to develop the land. The promise of cash might persuade Layla to vote for financial comfort instead of her conscience.

The clerk brought the court to order, and everyone stood noisily when the judge walked in.

"Mr. Pate, your client was given the final chance to make significant progress with the restoration of Alcott Manor. Did they accomplish this, and do you have proof of the results before we take our tour?"

"They did, your honor." Morris Pate, attorney for the side of the Alcott Family who wanted the restoration, stood and handed a stack of photos to the bailiff, who delivered them to the judge. "We have video, as well, your honor."

The judge flipped through photos. "This will do." He dropped the photos on his desk and picked up a stack of papers and began to sign. "We'll meet at the manor at twelve thirty then."

One of the suited men near Asher stood and raised his hand. His dark hair was slicked straight back, and Gemma thought she caught a whiff of his perfumey cologne. "Your honor, if I may?"

"What do you want?"

"I'm Tim Jessup, an attorney representing the other half of the Alcott family."

"I know who you are," the judge said. "What do you want?"

"Your honor, I would hazard a guess that those photos you're looking at there do not reflect the most recent state of Alcott Manor. Otherwise, I don't think they would show them to you."

The judge stared over his half glasses at Morris Pate in such a way that demanded an answer.

"Your honor. The fact that he knows this suggests foul play," Morris said.

"What are you talking about Mr. Pate?"

"Your honor, last night, between the hours of ten p.m. and six o'clock this morning, a crime was committed. Alcott Manor was vandalized. That Mr. Jessup knows about this shows not only that he had immediate knowledge of the incident, but that he or someone from his organization was involved."

Gemma shook her head. "Oh, no, Henry," she whispered. Her heart dove headfirst and landed hard. He destroyed the house after she broke it off with him.

The judge banged his gavel. "When were you going to tell me this, and where in the hell was your security?"

"I was about to tell you, but I wanted it established first that my client satisfied their obligation prior to the deadline. We had security. He was killed last night by whoever destroyed several key elements of our restoration." Morris Pate handed the judge several additional pieces of paper, along with photos attached. "Officer Dobbs with the Charleston Police Department is here if you have any questions." He waved to the officer who sat two rows behind Gemma.

"Another death? Murdered?" The judge's baritone voice pitched high. The lines on his forehead deepened and lifted and showed no patience. "Jesus, Morris."

The judge crumpled up the piece of paper in front of him and tossed it to the side. He picked up another pack of stapled papers and started signing. "I've given your client plenty of time to get this deathtrap into shape, Mr. Pate. There won't be any more chances."

"Your honor. My client did the work and met the deadlines. Vandalism and murder could not have been predicted and should not count against him. If you look at the time stamp on the photos, you'll see that as of yesterday, the work they agreed to finish according to your last order had, indeed, been completed."

The courtroom was thick with quiet when the judge picked up the photos again. He held them at arm's length and frowned when he focused on them. He finally dropped his arm to his desk, and the face of his gold watch banged against the dark wood surface.

"Approach the bench, counselor," the judge said. "You say this is vandalism?"

"Yes, sir," Morris answered.

"Do you have photos or video of an intruder?" the judge asked.

Morris cleared his throat. "The cameras were knocked out."

"Then do you know what the community and the other family members are going to say about your vandalism?"

"Yes, sir, I do."

"Let me just say it so that we're both clear. They're going

to say that the damage is the result of some sort of supernatural interference. They'll say that Benjamin Alcott did it, and you don't have any proof that they're wrong. Then do you know what they're going to do if I give you yet another chance? They're going to rally together as a community and demand that the house and whatever evil within it is burned to the ground." The judge pounded his fist on his raised desk to meet his final word, and everyone jumped.

"It is just time to put this whole damn thing to rest. Restoration has been attempted too many times, and each time, it's failed. Hell, most of its owners are even too afraid to step foot into it. With good damn reason, it appears." The judge waved to the police at the back of the room. "No, I'm siding with the prosecution, condemning it, and signing the order to require its immediate sale."

He banged his gavel.

Asher and his attorneys grinned and back-slapped.

Gemma had kept her father in the dark about all the happenings at the manor. She hadn't wanted him to worry. But now she felt everything she'd done for her father gather momentum in a downward swirl and slip from her grasp.

CHAPTER 32

G emma spent the next hour outside the manor, sitting in one of the two reed-like gliding chairs and watching the ocean's waves rise up to the cloud-framed sun.

She glided back and forth while she glared at the light that played on the waves. The gentle rocking motion of the chair made it feel as though she were riding on the waves. She'd planned it that way.

Though no one would enjoy it now. Alcott Manor would be leveled and the grounds destroyed, all in favor of tacky condos that would suit nothing and no one but Asher Cardill.

She'd not yet called her father to give him the news that she'd failed. There would have to be a plan. First, she would have to help him shut down his business, then she would have to convince him to move near her so he could work with her. Then there would be a call to get them both enrolled in therapy.

Any respect she had left for Henry was gone. Just like Preston, he had turned out to be overwhelmingly selfish. He destroyed lives in exchange for temporary satisfaction—in his case, the short-lived joy of victim-ish anger.

She finally found the strength to inspect the damage and made her way inside. She passed the flower pots she'd had placed around the screened porch and the outer edges of the steps, the ones she'd had filled with hydrangeas just to make the judge feel a little more welcome. One of them had been smashed, the flowers ripped out and crushed to bits. "Thanks, Henry."

Slices and shards of wooden walls laid on the floor of Benjamin's study. She stared at the fragments of the master craftsmen's handiwork. She squatted to the floor and nudged the bird and branch motif. The short stack of wood tumbled and echoed through the empty house.

She remembered how she and Henry had spoken to the contractors in harmonic counterpoint about how the walls and the carvings should look, their coloring, and the positioning of them. Of course, now that she thought about it, apparently, it was only she who spoke to them about it. The workers wouldn't have been able to hear him. At least not consciously.

She tried to find the words to break the news to her father, whose financial health had been solely dependent upon this project reaching a successful completion. A full year's worth of pent-up anger bubbled just beneath the surface. She kicked a plank of wood and it flew across the room.

Henry simply wanted what he wanted. When he couldn't get it, he lied, he manipulated, and he murdered. She thought of poor Everett, the security guard that Henry had killed to ruin the job.

He did kill.

She was certain.

She was right when she suggested that this house and Benjamin repeated the same behaviors every year on the anniversary of Anna's death: the house relived the story, and

Benjamin murdered. She'd bet he even killed that teenaged girl and the artist her dad had hired. He was every bit the monster she had seen that night.

They had been right to hang him.

She stood in the great hall and surveyed the damage. The right half of the staircase was missing, the railing and most of the posts were gone, as well. The left side of the stairway hung together precariously. Floorboards had been ripped up to reveal giant holes, their remnants left in such a way that someone could be impaled.

Had the judge walked in on this, he probably would have assessed fines or filed claims against them on top of siding with the prosecution. The stress and the fury burned in her heart. Every piece of this destruction was in direct opposition to the judge's punch list. In fact, it looked as though Henry had used it as a checklist.

A floorboard creaked and she turned to find Henry standing in the doorway.

The blood in her veins turned into fiery lava, and her hands curled into fists. "You bastard."

CHAPTER 33

H er entire body tensed, rigid and solid.

"Gemma," Henry said.

She advanced toward him, her steps calculated and swift as though the wind was at her back. She paused in front of him, her right hand opened, and for the first time since they'd met, he looked uncertain.

She slapped him. Hard. His face moved to the side from the force, his expression remained unemotional.

"It's bad enough that you did this, you selfish bastard, but do you realize what you did to my father? You've destroyed him! You've ruined his company and harmed everyone who worked for him. Without his company, he has nothing left!"

She slapped the other side of his face, harder this time, and he flinched.

"Gemma—"

"No! *You* do not speak to me." She slammed her palms into his chest. The tears she couldn't manage to cry the day before welled up in her eyes. "You were so filled with perfect perspective when it came to my ex or Sam. You're no different than they are!" She waved her arm in the direction of the library where she'd met Anna's lover.

"You present yourself as one person, but you're someone else entirely. You lied to me to get what you wanted. When things didn't go exactly as you wanted them to, you did this!" She waved to the destruction of the house. She reared back and aimed her open palm at him once again.

Henry grabbed her wrist before it could land on his face. "I didn't do this."

"Oh," she said and laughed. "I know who you really are. *Benjamin.*" She spat his name like poison. "I know what you do."

"I didn't...*do* this." His words were slow and his voice was calm.

She stared at his face, her breath ragged and quick. The rage she expected to be returned to her wasn't there. The argument she wanted wasn't happening, and his touch on her arm steadied her unexpectedly.

An insight she didn't ask for settled over her like a light, like a warmth, like a guide. "Trust your instincts," she heard her mother say.

She looked at the destruction that surrounded her. Really looked at it. She'd seen Benjamin's handiwork before—the wall in the dining room, the staircase, the bookshelf. Each time, he was searching.

Yes, he could have destroyed the house out of sheer anger. He was capable of that, she had no doubt. But this damage wasn't his trademark work, and it just didn't *feel* like his doing.

Something had indeed changed about Benjamin in those last few days before she found out who he really was. There was love, the promise of a future, acceptance, and maybe even forgiveness. Even if he were angry that their plans had been wrecked, the other intangibles would have had their effect. They would have changed him.

She studied his eyes, which were clear of guilt. At least, where the house was concerned. "Then who did?"

"I don't know." The green in his brown eyes was lit and focused like a laser, his jaw set, and his dark hair tossed about.

"Well, weren't you here last night?"

"I stayed on the beach side of the property, where I proposed to you." He flexed his hands in front of him and stared at his empty palms. "After we spoke at the museum, I spent a little time in the winter garden, then I was going to search the house for Anna's letter. But I decided I just couldn't wander these halls for another night, not after losing you. It would have made my already miserable existence unbearable."

The normally strong and beautiful features of Henry's face had lost their vigor. She didn't know if ghosts could cry, or even if Henry was the type of man who would, but he was clearly distraught. They had both lost a dream.

"I guess that was the second critical mistake I've made lately. If I had been here, I might have been able to save Everett's life and protect the manor." This was not a man who had a future to look forward to, and neither his past nor the manor would let him go. "I love you, Gemma."

She crossed her arms in front of her and stepped away. "When were you going to tell me who you really were?" The tone of her voice was strong with anger.

"I was trying to find the right time, even though I couldn't imagine a scenario where you thought my condition would be a tolerable one. Each time I played the discussion in my head, no matter how I said it, it ended with you leaving." He took another step forward. "I know you're hurt, and I handled this in a terribly selfish manner. For that, I am sorry." He brushed his hands along the outsides of her arms.

She didn't step away this time. As much as she never wanted to see him again, his touch calmed her. Her heart reached to him, for the love they still shared.

"I've thought of nothing else all night, and I can't see a way where I could have handled this differently. No matter when the truth came out, it ran the risk of devastating. I can only hope that you'll remember the beauty of the love we shared and that it will be worth enduring the uniqueness of our situation," he said.

He tried to close his embrace around her, and she resisted it. He leaned away and wiped a tear from her cheek. When he slid his arms around her a second time, she allowed herself to rest her head against the firmness of his chest, needing to feel close to him just one more time.

When she did, amidst all the destruction and the broken dreams that surrounded them, she found the love they had once shared, and it softened the hard edges of the hurt.

It was illogical, it was unreasonable, and as far as she could figure, it wasn't even possible. And yet, here it was, the thing she wanted more than anything else in the world. The love of what must be an almost two-hundred-year-old ghost.

"I should have guessed who you were."

"How is that?"

"Because men these days don't refer to their behavior with phrases like 'terribly selfish manner.' Tragically so."

His chest bounced in time with two short and quiet chuckles.

She leaned away and ran her hand along his jaw. "Why are you so real to me? Instead of being, I don't know, transparent or something? Why do I see you when others don't?"

He placed his hand on hers. "I couldn't say. I've not experienced this with any other person since my death...one hundred and thirty-one years ago." He sounded statesmanlike, even when he discussed his death. His own murder. Of course, he was a senator. He made more sense to her now.

"Almost to the day. This is why you wouldn't discuss moving to California. Because you can't leave?"

"The house has had a hold on me that I haven't been able to break. Traveling to the museum yesterday to find you was the farthest I've been from the house since my death day. I would guess that's because of the energetic clearing you've done on the land. My hope was that one of us would find the note and that would set me free forever." He gently brushed a strand of her hair away from her face.

"What will happen to you now that Asher will buy the property and tear down the house?"

"I suppose I'll stay with the land until I can be set free. Whatever that will require."

She imagined him standing lonely at the corner of the estate while bulldozers and cement mixers groaned and beeped where the manor once was. "No. We can't let that happen." She reached into her portfolio. "Henry, last night at the museum—"

"First, we have to figure out who did this," he said. "Tom and Mr. Pate came by earlier today, and I heard them say they want to try to appeal the judge's decision. Mr. Pate doesn't think they have a chance, but they're going to try. I thought if I could find out who the responsible party was—"

"Asher," she said.

He stroked his throat with a grimace. "Asher," he confirmed. He kicked an angled piece of floorboard and it flew down the hallway. "They complain that *I* have haunted these premises when the Cardill family has haunted my family and its home for generations."

"I think he's the only reasonable option if it wasn't Benjamin." She still wasn't entirely accustomed to thinking of Henry and Benjamin as the same person. "Then Asher is the only one with motive." She thought of the startling similarities between Sam and Asher. Both were users who were willing to deceive to get what they wanted. Apparently, weak character could be hereditary.

"I'm going to take care of this." His voice was as low and slow as a growl.

"What do you mean you'll 'take care' of it?"

"I paid a visit to Asher earlier today. I'm going to make a follow-up call."

Gemma's stomach lurched with the now-familiar fear that Henry had killed someone.

"When I'm done torturing him, he's going to run naked through the streets confessing to anyone and everyone what he did."

She let out a slow breath of relief. "I see. And how did he react to our friend Benjamin?"

"Not well, fortunately." Henry winked at her. "I'm about to head over there again. I'll fix this, Gemma."

"I need you to. For my father's sake. He doesn't deserve this." She gestured to the mess around them.

"No, he doesn't," he said.

The faint strains of a small chamber orchestra tuning their instruments sounded through the house and the lighting flickered to a more dimly lit room.

"It's starting," Henry said. "You need to leave the house until tomorrow when it's all over."

"Why?"

He placed his hands on her shoulders. "Nearly every corner of the house will be flooded with memories of that night. If it kidnaps you into its story, I have no idea how to break you free from its memories."

She remembered touching Anna's shoulder and how Anna had known that someone was there. These memories were alive.

Unresolved.

Always unresolved.

"I think the house wants the mystery of Anna's death solved, Henry. And it wants me here to do just that. That has to be it. If it's not the parentage of Lizzie Mae and if the suicide note can't be found, then the house must be spitting out these memories so that this can be resolved once and for all. Every memory I've seen, they're all on a theme of some unfairness. I think healing this house requires settling an injustice."

She paced in a circle and pressed her hand across her stomach. "What happens to you when the night replays?"

"I relive the story, the entire night."

"As Benjamin..."

"As myself, yes."

"So, you never see how she died?"

"I don't remember what happened to Anna on the night she died. There was a gun involved, and I thought I saw the suicide note in her bedroom."

Her chin quivered. "If you could know how she died, Henry..." Her voice caught. "Once you know for sure, you'll be able to move on and you'll cross over." She grabbed the fabric of her shirt at her midsection and pressed against the nerves in her stomach. "You have to find out."

"I can't. My only perspective is my own. No matter the one hundred and thirty times I've lived that night, I never see what actually happened to her."

"I'll be your eyes and your ears tonight. I'll help you resolve this so you can finally go home."

"Gemma, no." He held her hands and squeezed them. "It's too dangerous. And I was different then— Plus, what if I'm wrong and I did kill her?"

"Then you'll have to deal with that. The point is that we have to solve the mystery, and in order to do that, you need someone to help you. You deserve to be set free from all of this."

Violins played down the hall. Gemma closed her eyes and braced herself for the dangers she was about to face. She didn't want to become a part of the Alcott story.

"If being set free means being without you, I don't want it. I won't leave without you." His voice pitched with panic and he hugged her close with more love than Gemma thought she'd ever known before.

She clung tightly to him in return, and to all that she knew would soon be a memory. "After everything you've been through in your life, you deserve a peaceful existence." She let go and pushed until there was distance between them. "Go ahead and do what you need to do at Asher's. I'll be fine. I'll see you soon."

His lips drew tight. "I'll return before the evening goes into full swing. Don't touch anything. Or anyone. You don't want to engage with the past on this night."

Her inhale was shaky and she nodded in agreement. He swept her into his arms and kissed her. It wasn't the goodbye kiss that she feared—it was an I'll-love-you-forever-kiss that made it next to impossible for her to let go of him.

When he finally did leave, heartache gripped her with such heaviness that she sank to the floor and cried quiet sobs that shook her from the inside out. This was the beginning of goodbye.

Once she helped Henry and the manor resolve the mystery of Anna's death tonight, Henry would be a free man.

He would cross over to the Other Side and she would be parted from him forever.

CHAPTER 34

Gemma pressed her portfolio to her chest and walked slow, heavy steps to the library. In the past twenty-four hours, she had lost Henry and regained him, and before they could work everything out, she knew she would lose him again—this time, forever.

Her parents had always told her that there was someone for everyone. Just when she was confident that they were wrong, Henry had happened. In a few hours, he'd be gone, and she knew there would never be another man for her. Tears burned her eyes and blurred her vision.

She didn't think he realized that he was going to have to leave. Maybe he thought it was a choice to go or an option to stay. That wasn't what her mother had told her. Once a ghost's reasons for staying here were resolved, they left. They just moved on.

When she reached the library bookshelf, she searched for a suitable hiding place for her portfolio. She didn't know if any of the memories would touch the library, but she needed to be careful. She needed a way to keep this safe until Henry could see what was inside. It was important for him to understand.

Afterward, she headed down the wide hallway until she passed Henry's office. She stopped short. Something made her turn around and want to go inside. She was just about to ignore that invisible nudge when she remembered her conversation with Henry about honoring instincts.

They had each retold their own horror stories about how their lives went to hell when they didn't listen to that little voiceless voice. Then they agreed to honor their instincts from that point forward. On that note, she stepped inside.

The room was trashed as she'd seen before. The desk was a mess with papers scattered, which wasn't unusual. Tom and Paisley shared this desk with her, and neither one of them were all that organized with paper.

Trying to create a bit of order, she started organizing the chaos by putting invoices in one stack, unopened mail in another, pens and pencils in the drawer, and so on. She had the strangest sense that she'd left something here, something she needed to find.

At the very least, organizing, counting, creating order out of mayhem, always helped to calm her. She hadn't always had that habit. It had started later, after she'd been attacked by the ghost.

Obsessive Compulsive Disorder, the doctors called it. "Self-calming behaviors," her mother called it. "It won't last forever," she'd said. She even encouraged it. "When your life is a mess, organize some small area of it. Like your wallet or your purse. You'll feel better."

Tonight, it was this desk.

It took some time, but when Gemma saw it, she knew she'd been right to follow her instincts. This was something she had needed to see. She quickly took a post-it note from the drawer and wrote a note to Tom. Then she anchored it with a coffee-stained mug in a prominent position where he wouldn't miss it. Just to be safe, she also fired up the laptop and sent Tom an email.

"Gemma!" Henry called from the hallway.

"Henry—" She dashed into his arms, grateful that he had made it back before the anniversary night began to replay in full. She was more grateful that she got to hold him again. She inhaled the spiced scent of his skin, wishing she could bottle it in her heart and save it for another time. A time when she would need to taste these memories with him, relive them, and let them warm the soon-to-be-empty place in her chest.

"Gemma." He stroked her hair from the top of her head to the nape of her neck and held her against him.

She ignored his calling her. She didn't want this to end.

She also tried, though less successfully, to ignore the slow crawl of fear that worked its way through her. When the manor's remembrance kicked into high gear, she would have to face the threat of that time portal alone.

She was still the prize that the house wanted, the one who could solve the mystery of Anna's death, the one who could set Henry free, the one who could put a stop to a long-held miscarriage of truth and fairness. She had to do it without becoming a part of the house. Because the manor didn't know its boundaries. It was greedy and possessive in the most seductive way.

No matter what it made her feel tonight, no matter what it showed her, she would have to resist the temptation to stay here. She would have to fight what would surely appear to be an ideal life.

Henry pulled away. "It's Asher. I overheard him talking with someone. He knows and he's looking for proof. Is the birth certificate hidden?"

"How could he know?"

"Is it hidden?" His hands clasped her upper arms tightly.

"Yes, yes. It's hidden, I sewed it into the pillow. But how—"

"He has Sam Cardill's journal and there was a mention of Lizzie Mae. If he finds that birth certificate, even if the judge grants an appeal—Asher and his wife will have so much stock, they can swing the family vote to destroy the manor and develop the land."

She saw Alcott Manor through Benjamin's eyes now. How he saw the suicide note that tragic night. How much he needed it now. How much the house needed it, too, to set things right.

The walls creaked when they shifted. Warmth from the house pressed against her and stroked her back in gratitude and encouragement.

She startled more upright, shoulders back, and breathed in with a gasp. "Henry. The suicide note. If it existed that night, I ought to be able to find it for you. Tonight. I could get it for you."

"You can't touch it, Gemma. You can't touch anything from that night." His voice was stern and senatorial, and it struck fear inside of her as well as respect.

"But if it's what you need to find peace... I think the manor wants me to get it. It could be what changes everything for everyone."

"Don't, Gemma. It's too big of a risk. Do you think he'll find the birth certificate?"

"He won't find it, Henry. I'll burn it. There's no sense in keeping it." She knew her father's business wouldn't have a chance at redoing the restoration if Asher was able to swing the vote to build condos. It was a long shot that they would win the appeal to redo the restoration anyway. But she sure as hell wasn't going to give Asher the final nail to put in their coffin.

He nodded in agreement. "I only have a few moments left." He jumped back and pushed her away.

"Henry—" She reached for him.

"Don't touch me!" He looked at his fading midsection.

She pulled her hands to her chest and stared at him.

"It's happening." His eyes, wide and frightened, locked with hers and he began to fade. "Gemma," his voice called like an echo on the wind. "I love you."

He was gone.

She stood quietly in the house that hadn't been empty since she arrived, and she felt alone.

CHAPTER 35

The murmurings of the crowd on the main floor grew louder. Light laughter sprinkled through the rumblings of discussion, and kitchen noises were probably more audible than Benjamin would have wanted them to be on that night.

She stood at the top of the front stairwell and peeked around the corner in amazement of the crowd below. Women and men dressed in their party finery, and a small chamber orchestra positioned at the ocean side of the long hall played soft classical music. The house was remembering the anniversary of Anna's death with full clarity.

Gemma pressed against the handrail and descended the left side of the stairs with great care. It was hard not to be mesmerized with the living memory. But in current day reality, the staircase was not stable. Asher, she thought, had wrecked it. If she mistakenly balanced on a step that wasn't there, she would fall. Probably to her death.

Everything was just as Henry had said it was. This was the reason for his vibrant, detail-oriented storytelling. It wasn't from all the research and reading he'd done over the years, as he had claimed. He had been here when it all happened for the first time. Now, he relived it every year in agonizing detail. As she would if she weren't careful tonight.

Ladies with hair piled and twisted wore long, button-front dresses and talked about Senator Alcott and how the president was visiting tonight. Most wore classic and simple jewelry, like pearl stud earrings. The woman standing next to her wore diamond drop earrings in the shape of *fleur de lis*, and Gemma quickly became entranced. Engaged. She belonged to this group.

She belonged to Henry. To Benjamin.

She held the *fleur de lis* earrings on the tips of her fingers and heard herself say, "Nellie, where did you get these, they are divine!" She released them and watched the earrings dangle back and forth. Back and forth. The tips of her fingers tingled with a strange energy.

"Oh, do you like them?" Her southern accent drawled a long *I* and made everything sound like a poem. "Ray bought them for me on his last trip to Paris. I'll tell you what I really love is this dress you're wearing. It's *got* to be from a European designer. I can tell."

Gemma ran her hand along the brocade of her long white dress. She'd worn this dress before. With Henry.

Who was Henry?

Benjamin.

Men in long-tailed tuxedos talked business while waiters weaved throughout the crowd with silver trays of champagne or appetizers. The small orchestra played just loud enough to keep the guests entertained, but not so loud that people couldn't hear each other talk. It was a very civilized gathering.

The distant echo of a child crying rang from the upstairs.

"Da-daaa!"

Gemma returned into her own body with a start, into her own life, into the mission she was here to complete. "Lizzie

Mae." She ran up the stairs just in time to see the nanny take the baby out of the master bedroom.

She snuck into Benjamin's bedroom and watched him with Anna, just as she'd seen before. Only this time, she stepped cautiously to the side of the room so that she could see his face, not just the back of him.

Benjamin. Henry. *Her Henry*. She understood now why he was so angry. His wife had cheated. She'd cheated and she wanted to leave him.

He shoved Anna into the hallway. "Get. Dressed!"

Gemma stayed with him. She would have to shadow him all night to get at the truth of this story.

After Anna had left the room, Henry slid his arm across his dresser and sent three large glass decanters crashing to the floor. "Damn it!" His curse was so loud Gemma startled and bumped into the side of the mantelpiece.

Somewhere within that angry 1883 Benjamin was the man she loved, held captive by the memory that wouldn't let go.

Henry answered a knock at the door.

A young man with dark hair and the air of ambition stood in the hallway. "The president has arrived, Senator."

"I'm on my way. Find my wife," he said. "Make sure she's... ready." He waved the young man off.

His pace was brisk down the long hallway. Gemma followed, quick on his heels, and nearly stumbled when he chose the servant's stairwell instead of the majestic front stairs that led into the crowd.

"Good evening." Henry inserted himself into a small circle of guests that gathered at the far end of the formal hall. He took a glass of champagne from the tray of a passing waiter, then moved toward the foyer to greet the president and his wife.

He rehearsed potential excuses for his wife's absence in a whisper, until finally he declared, "I'll just use the usual one."

When the president arrived, he shook Henry's hand in vigor and leaned close to his ear. "So pleased to receive your telegram, Benjamin. This is a good decision for our country. A smart decision. We'll announce it tonight."

"Thank you, Mr. President. This is a real honor."

The president's wife touched her husband's arm. "Where is that lovely wife of yours, Benjamin?"

"Tragically, she isn't feeling well, and I don't think she'll be able to join us this evening." The president's dubious expression seemed to catch Henry by surprise. His effortless smile slipped for a glimmer of a moment. Maybe he'd used that excuse once too often.

"Nothing serious, I hope," the president said while the three of them walked into Henry's home. "The job of being the first lady is an arduous one. I hope she's up to the task."

"I have no doubts, sir." When he said it, Gemma knew that Anna was not up to the task. She realized that Henry knew it, as well, and she hoped that when he was Benjamin he hadn't remedied that problem with his own hands.

When they entered Henry's home, guests crowded the president. They reached to shake his hand and asked about the big announcement that they'd been promised. There were no security guards or secret servicemen. It was a very different time.

"All right, all right," the president said. He climbed to the fourth step of the grand staircase. "I can see that there is not a drop of patience among you."

Everyone laughed as if each was an insider at the president's private gathering.

"As you all know, my term is coming to an end—"

Disappointed groans rumbled through the crowd. "Run again!" someone yelled.

"Yes, well... I've decided that it's time for a younger man to take the helm. A man not as experienced as I am, perhaps, but someone who has accomplished a lot in just a few short terms. A man who has done more good for the great state of South Carolina than any politician in the last one hundred years."

A cheer went up from the guests.

Henry searched the room and raised his glass to an older couple who stood near the fireplace, smiles of pride spread across their faces. They raised their champagne flutes to him.

His parents, Gemma guessed. She looked around for Anna but didn't see her. She was missing one of Henry's finest moments. He might have been happy about that given her current emotional state.

She debated as to whether she ought to find Anna and stick near her. It was possible that she was writing her suicide note right now. But what if she couldn't find her?

It was Henry's innocence that she needed to prove. If she stayed with him, she would certainly see if he killed Anna.

"I've asked Senator Benjamin Alcott to run on behalf of our great party for the office of the President of the United States of America. And I hope he'll have your support!" The president raised his glass to the crowd and lifted Henry's hand in victory. The guests applauded and cheered.

Then, like storm clouds rolling in, a strange murmur spread over the crowd. The president's wife gasped at something behind them.

The president and Henry glanced at the stairway in time to see Anna sauntering down the steps with a glass of wine in her hand. Each step seemed to arrive under her foot more quickly than she anticipated, and her movements were inelegant and ill-timed.

She hadn't chosen the white dress that Henry had purchased specifically for her to wear this special evening. Instead, she donned the deep red dress with a far more revealing décolleté than was fashionable—or sensible for an important political gathering.

"Benjamin, darling," Anna said when she reached him. She kissed him on the cheek, then surveyed the crowd.

Henry glanced over the crowd, as well, taking in the mostly shocked expressions and secretive whispers. One man, however, was smiling.

Sam Cardill leaned against a dark-stained pillar. A cigar was stuck in the corner of his smile. He uncrossed his arms from his chest, laughed loudly, and clapped. "Bravo!"

A few other men in the audience clapped until their wives elbowed them in their sides.

"Anna, you always did know how to make an impression." The president lifted her hand and kissed it.

"Everyone! A drink to celebrate. Maestro!" The president waved his arms at the director of the orchestra, who took the cue and struck up a lively victory march. The president took Henry by the arm and pulled him aside. "Get that under control, or you're dead in the water before you start," he said as he gestured to Anna.

Henry nodded short and quick. Fury tinged his cheeks a light shade of red, and he turned and extended his hand to Anna. She had remained on one of the steps, slightly drunk and swaying in the attention from the crowd.

Her breasts nearly leaped from the too-tight dress, and a rose was perched at the deepest point of the V. Her makeup was artfully applied, though there was too much of it, and she appeared more like a prostitute than the wife of a presidential candidate.

Her smile was sloppy and loose, her eyes glassy. She held tight to the railing with one hand, and her black velvet evening purse was tucked beneath her arm. Gemma wondered if Anna might add a magnificent fall to top off the evening's performance.

"Enough is enough. Mrs. Alcott," Henry said to Anna. "Won't you join me for a walk in the garden?"

"Like my dress, Benjamin?" Anna placed her hand in his, which was fortunate because she stumbled on the hem of her dress when she took her last step off the staircase.

Henry caught her and held onto her arm while he escorted her from the crowd. Anna tried to pry herself from his grasp.

"It's a little revealing, don't you think?" Henry smiled at guests while he navigated his wife through the crowd.

"I picked it out just for you," she said, slurring her words. "You think I'm a whore, so I might as well look the part."

When they entered the kitchen, Henry dropped the crowd-pleasing pretense. "The President of the United States is in our home. As well as the governor and a room full of people who are important to my career, and therefore, our family. For once in your godforsaken life, why don't you think of someone other than yourself?" His tone was sharp enough to cut a razor-thin slice of marble, and he jerked her arm twice for emphasis.

An older gentleman with wavy white hair burst into the kitchen and stormed toward Anna. "You've been drinking?" His accusation boomed to all edges of the vacuous kitchen, and yet, the kitchen staff ignored him. It appeared they had seen and heard Anna in trouble before.

She wriggled her arm away from Henry only to have her father grab her by the other arm. "This doesn't concern you, Daddy."

"The doctor warned you not to drink when you take the medication he gave you. Have you even been taking your pills?" Her father spoke to her as though he scolded an errant teenager.

Anna broke free from her father's grasp and stormed out

the screen door that led to the rose garden. The door squeaked and closed with a slam.

"Having trouble, Senator Alcott?"

Both men turned around to find Sam Cardill standing in the doorway to the kitchen.

"Or shall I say *Senators* Alcott?"

"This doesn't concern you, Sam. In fact, I don't remember your name being on the invitation list. Why don't you make it an early evening and head home?" Henry said.

The closer Henry moved to Sam's face, the wider Sam's smile spread. He took the cigar from his mouth and flicked the ashes on the kitchen floor.

"Anna invited me. She thought I might enjoy one of these political pep rallies. Can't say I'm disappointed." He propped the cigar in the corner of his mouth and searched the kitchen. "Didn't I see Anna come this way? I thought I might have a word with her. That dress is magnificent."

"Stay away from her, Sam. You've done enough damage." Henry blocked Sam's path with his body. "There won't be another warning."

Sam crossed his arms and puffed twice on the cigar. "Set Anna free, Benjamin, and your life will get a whole lot easier. You don't want her, and I could make her happy. Plus, it doesn't look like she's made for political life."

The kitchen staff cut glances at Sam when he said it.

"You mean you think my money could make you happy. Get out of my house, Sam. Come here again, and I'll kill you."

Sam pushed close to Henry. "I'd like to see you try."

"Gentlemen. Tonight is not the night for this." Anna's father grabbed each man by a shoulder and tried to separate them but didn't manage to move them an inch.

Henry balled his hand into a fist. "Get out, Sam."

Gemma fought the urge to grab Anna's father by the arm and move him out of the way. Fists were about to fly. She pressed her hands against her chest, in part to keep herself from touching anything, but also because her heart thrummed against her chest like an endless roll of thunder.

Warm, salty air seeped in through the screen door. Anna was outside on her own.

Henry, go get Anna.

She wondered if she spoke loudly and directly enough to him if he would hear her. Or would that create a connection to the past, as well? She wondered if, for the first time in over a century, the past could play differently and set Henry on a different course. One where he didn't have to suffer alone for a hundred years.

But the needle of the past was in full play, running along the well-worn grooves of the only story it knew. She didn't see a way to change what was. At least, not yet. She backed away from the men, who circled each other like wolves, and she bumped into a man in white kitchen garb.

She scuttled away quickly, scrambling to find a safe space not to interact, at least, not carelessly. He lifted a basket of potatoes onto the wooden table in the middle of the room. His white hat masked his hair, just as it had for the young teenager who had fallen into this world a year ago. But the shape of his face and something about his hands gave him away.

His hands.

She looked closely at them while he peeled the potatoes.

Swipe, swipe, swipe.

The metal peeler clinked in his hand and brown, flimsy potato peels flew onto the light wooden surface.

His hands. There was paint on his hands. Smudges of blue, purple, brown, and yellow. An artist's hands. He was the artist her father had hired to restore the frescoes on the ceiling of the music room. He had been killed a year ago.

By Benjamin?

By something or someone, and he had been taken into the history of the manor.

Excitement rolled through her and she'd felt this kind before. Enticement. The fine brocade in the bodice of her dress sparkled and she felt the manor's promise. She could be the lady of the house. A special honor. A cherished position.

The manor wanted her.

Just when she was about to give up her resistance, and only because she couldn't remember *why* she was resisting, the sound of footsteps bounding up the back stairway shook her into her original focus.

She stood in the kitchen with the uniformed staff, Sam Cardill, who pressed a white rag against his bloody mouth, and Anna's father, who yelled at Sam.

"Stay out of her life! You don't know what you're getting into here."

Henry was gone.

She dashed up the back stairs and poked her head into open doors until she found him in Anna's bedroom, retrieving a wrap from her closet. To cover the most revealing aspects of Anna's dress, she suspected.

Two envelopes were laid out on her secretary desk. One addressed to Benjamin, the other addressed to Sam.

Henry growled and snatched the letters, quickly scanning through the one addressed to him. "No, no, no...damn it, Anna!" He dropped the letter on the secretary where he had found it and ran downstairs at top speed.

Anna's father and Sam stood face-to-face in a heated conversation when Henry ran through the kitchen.

"Anna!" Henry yelled when he was outside. "Anna!"

By the light of the moon, Gemma saw Anna several feet from the sandy edge, right where Gemma had performed the healing ceremony. Anna held her purse in front and close to her chest.

The screen door slammed and Gemma turned to see Sam Cardill walking toward them. Hesitant. Curious.

"Anna, don't do this." Henry ran his hand over his face and sighed. "Come inside."

"No, Henry. I'm not going inside."

"I'll take you up the servants' stairs and you can spend the evening in your room. Would you like to paint? I'll tell the president and the other guests that you aren't feeling well." He was weary of her antics and was probably expecting her to take off running into the ocean.

"I won't ever go inside that house again." She stared at the house as Gemma often had. As though it had a spirit and an agenda of its own—one that didn't agree with hers.

Henry's head tipped to the side in a what-is-she-going-to-do-now kind of way. "Then what will you do, Anna? Live on the beach? Go ahead then. Go to the beach. Wander through the night. See how well you do without my protection."

He pressed his fingertip and thumb against his forehead, and it wasn't hard to see that he had lost his patience. Maybe some part of him even wished for Anna to wander off into the night and not return.

The affair, her mental illness, four children to care for. The world was watching. All of this poorly timed with a career dream coming true, and it was too much for any one person.

Now Gemma would see how Henry handled it.

Maybe he would walk away and she'd pull a trigger. Or maybe he would strangle her. Or maybe she would walk off into the night and someone else would finish the job.

With Henry trying to calm himself, his head lowered and his eyes closed, he didn't see that Anna had opened her bag and removed a gun.

"Henry. Henry!" Gemma couldn't help herself. She yelled and shouted to get his attention. "Benjamin!"

Henry's head lifted with a jerk. "Anna. What are you doing with that?

His hands were raised in front of him for protection. In surrender.

"It's better this way." Her voice was strangely calm. The tone was lower and more settled than Gemma had ever heard it.

"No, Anna. Stop. You have children, think of them."

"I'm not a good mother." She laughed a little as if Henry's food for thought was absurd. "They'll be better off with someone else. You'll be better off, too, Benjamin." She waved the gun, and his palms followed her aim in case he needed to stop a bullet.

Henry stepped forward. "Do you want a divorce? You can have it. If that's what you want."

She stepped backward in counterpoint to Henry's attempt to reach her. "It wouldn't matter. I don't need a divorce anymore." She pointed the gun at the side of her head.

"Oh, God, Anna, Don't. Please don't do this."

"I'm tired, Benjamin. I'm sick and so tired of not being able to make anything work. I keep messing everything up." Her hand shook.

"No, no, no!" Henry's arms stretched toward his wife, his fingers splayed and rigid, his feet rooted where they stood. "What about Sam? Don't you want to be with him?"

"Sam doesn't want to be with me." Her head shook slowly and slightly from being drunk, making her appear as if she'd reverted to being a little girl. "You were right about him."

"Then, whatever you want, sweetheart. You can have it. Just tell me what you want."

"Anna?" Sam called. "Anna, what are you doing?"

Henry lunged toward her.

The sound of the gunshot blasted loud enough to rise above the noise of the chatter of the crowd and the music of the chamber orchestra. Two by two, guests poured onto the back lawn and found Benjamin Alcott standing over his dead wife's body with a gun in his hands.

Sam Cardill stood a few feet away. "You killed her."

Gemma stood by in horror, unable to move.

"You killed her!" Sam yelled. "You killed her, you son of a bitch!"

❧

HENRY RUSHED ANNA'S LIMP, bloodied body upstairs to the first room on the right and laid her on the bed. He knelt at her side and held her hand between his. "I'm sorry, Anna. I'm so sorry. I failed you."

Several staff elbowed one another at Henry's apology. "He's confessing," they whispered.

The overly warm room spun and events sped by in a blur. Gemma shook her head and held onto the wall. "No. No." Dolls were lined along the shelves, blood spread along the mattress, and she held her stomach, tracing the raised, stiff brocade of the white dress Henry had given her.

She released the wall as if it were hot, as if it were poison, as if it stuck thorns into her flesh. "Leave me alone," she scream-whispered. "I am trying to help you!"

She said it to the house and to whoever haunted it. It must have known she told the truth because it did leave her alone. The white dress Henry had given her melted away in favor of the black T-shirt and jacket she usually wore.

A young girl ran into the room and stopped short with a full-on scream when she saw her mother lying there. "Mama, you're bleeding!"

A moment later, the nanny rushed in and ushered her out of the room. The nanny stared at the scene before she left, her eyes stretched wide in horror.

Anna's father rushed in and cried over his daughter's body. "Oh, Anna!" he wailed.

Sam stopped at the doorway, and his eyes fell on Anna's lifeless body.

"You." Henry stepped toward Sam. "You did this." His face, hands, and white shirt were smeared with Anna's blood.

Sam backed into the hallway and sweat glued thick strands of his dark hair to his forehead.

"You might as well have been the one to pull the trigger, you weak son of a bitch. Why couldn't you just leave her alone?" Henry said.

"She wasn't happy with you. She asked you for the divorce, but you wouldn't give it to her, you selfish ass. You killed her because you just couldn't stand to see her happy."

"When you knew you weren't going to get my money, you made other arrangements, didn't you? You've been working behind the scenes to find some other well-to-do lonely woman. Someone who would trade her bank account for some company." Henry slammed his fist on the side of Sam's jaw and a *crack* filled the air.

Sam fell to the ground and Henry shook his fist with a sense of satisfaction.

"Did you know she was sick, Sam? No? I guess she didn't tell you that, did she? And you were too self-obsessed to figure it out. She's been seeing doctors since she was a teenager. Her own father put her in a sanitarium. That's why she wasn't happy. She had problems. I tried to help her."

Sam crawled backward like a wounded crab until he ran into the wall. He scrambled upward and away from Henry, who stalked him like his next meal.

"The stable life I gave her helped her. But then you—" Henry laughed through a sneer and shook his head. "You set your hooks into her and ruined everything. By morning, the whole town is going to know exactly what kind of a dead-weight you are. How you target women for their money because you can't keep your business afloat."

Sam threw a punch, but Benjamin blocked it and sank his fist into Sam's stomach. "If I ever see you again, I'll kill you. Now get out of here!"

Henry returned to the little girl's room and stared at Anna's lifeless body. Sam leaned against the wall, bent over, and staggered down the hallway until he paused at the open door to Anna's bedroom.

Gemma watched him carefully, shifting her glance between him and the doorway to the guest room. Sam didn't seem like a man willing to go down the way Henry threatened. He made his way to the edge of her bed and cried, only for a moment, as if he were trying the emotion on for size but didn't like it.

Gemma decided he cried more for himself out of panic than from grief.

He spotted Anna's painting on her headboard and sniffed and wiped his face. "You might change your mind, Senator, when you realize you have a secret of your own to keep quiet. Maybe tomorrow the papers will share a little something about Lizzie Mae that you didn't know. I'm pretty sure they will call it motivation for murder."

Sam glanced toward the secretary, where two pieces of paper were laid out in plain view. Gemma quickly followed. He picked up the letter addressed to him and read it, then read the letter that was addressed to Benjamin.

The suicide note.

It was real.

Henry *had* seen it.

Police sirens screamed into the night. Sam parted the curtain then looked around the room briefly, she assumed for someplace to hide the letters. He folded them and stuffed them into his jacket pocket and headed toward the door.

He was framing Henry.

"No!" Gemma fought the urge to tackle Sam and retrieve the letters.

Henry's warning came back to her: *Don't touch anything.*

She reached for an armless chair to throw in his path to stop him. She pulled her hands back at the last second. There had already had been several close encounters with the house tonight.

"Find him!" Benjamin yelled from down the hall.

Sam stopped short of the doorway.

Gemma released the breath she'd been holding.

His hand rested over the letters in his pocket. He dashed to the secretary and began opening drawers. A herd of footsteps sounded in the hallway.

Gemma kept an eye on Sam while she stepped to the doorway. Five or so policemen bounded up the stairs. Their rounded hats and single-breasted, gold-buttoned jackets reminded her of keystone cops. She hoped that wasn't the case, but given the known outcome, it had to have played a role. She doubted any of them had had to solve a murder before, and they probably didn't have a clue when it came to forensic practices.

She gasped when an unwelcome but familiar face followed close behind the police, an architectural drawing rolled and kept under his arm.

Asher.

She searched for a hiding place.

Sam brushed the wrinkles from his yellow suit, composed himself with a heavy exhale, and met the police in the hallway. "I saw the whole thing, officer. I can tell you what happened."

One of the policemen listened intently as Sam recounted a creative interpretation of what had happened between Benjamin and Anna. "He told her he'd make it look like a suicide and that everyone would believe him. He said he'd be free of her at last and finally able to pursue his dream of being president. Then he aimed the gun at her head and shot her."

Asher lurked along the side of the hallway with wide eyes and a half smile. "Sam Cardill. My God. He really was the hero in this story."

Gemma tucked behind Anna's bed again. Arrogance was hereditary. She'd have to wait until Asher left the hallway before she could leave.

"I'll prove it to you," Henry growled from the hallway.

She leaned around the doorway and jumped back just in time to avoid Henry when he stormed into the room.

He moved things around on the secretary and searched the area under it. "The notes were here, I saw them."

Sam Cardill and the policeman stood at the doorway with arms crossed.

"You sure about that?" Sam pasted mock concern on his face.

"What did you do with them?" Benjamin's eyes focused with fury. "Search him!"

"Senator—" the policeman began.

"Search him!" Henry pointed at Sam.

Asher appeared in the doorway and Gemma ducked behind the bed to avoid being seen.

The policeman opened his mouth to say something to Henry.

"It's okay, officer. I'm happy to comply." Sam raised his arms in mock surrender. He handed his jacket to the policeman who searched the pockets. When nothing turned up, he patted Sam down.

"There's nothing here, Senator."

"Make him take off his clothes. He probably shoved them into his pants."

The policeman turned to Sam, who was already unbuckling his belt. He stared at Henry with the same cockiness Gemma had seen on Asher's face in the courtroom. He finally stood in Anna's bedroom in boxers and socks only. Gemma thought it probably hadn't been the first time.

"There's nothing here," the policeman said.

"Unless you'd like to search further, Senator?" Sam said.

Asher laughed.

"Don't let him out of your sight," Henry said to the policeman.

Henry rifled through drawers, searched under the bed, shook sheets, blankets, and curtains. The suicide notes were nowhere to be found.

The police gathered in Anna's room. Everyone searched except for Sam, who stared at Henry with one corner of his mouth tipped in a satisfied smile.

With the room torn apart, the police officers finally gathered in the hallway to discuss next steps.

"What do you want, Sam? Money? Is that it? What do you want in exchange for the notes?" Henry asked.

"Oh, I have money. Sarah Baker is waiting for me. In fact, it all worked out pretty well, thanks to you. My affair with Anna will remain a lifelong secret. If you tell anyone about it, it will just give you motive for killing your wife. Yes, I have everything I want. And you will be too busy swinging from the end of a rope to get in my way."

Asher leaned against the wall with his arms crossed, a Cheshire cat smile broad on his lips. "Well played, Sam."

Anger singed the surface of Gemma's skin. It was all she could do not to lunge at him from her hiding place behind the bed. But he was bigger and stronger than she was, and she was certain he did not want to be found in this house. She needed to get down to the winter garden to retrieve the birth certificate she'd re-hidden. It needed to be burned.

The police took Henry and Sam into the hallway, and she

overheard their heated discussion. Both of them would be taken to the police station. Asher stood in the doorway watching the action, blocking her exit.

She had an idea for getting out, one she prayed would work. She crawled along the floor to Anna's closet, only looking back once she thought she could stand up without being seen. Asher was just as she'd left him, with his eyes glued to the argument in the hallway.

Anna's closet was packed with full-length dresses, gorgeous hats, and shoes. She stood where she thought she needed to be and parted the sea of fabric. "Thank God."

The slender doorway did not have a knob. There was just a thin mark that outlined the door. She pushed on one side of it, and it opened into the darkened passageway. With the light from the closet, she saw the spiral staircase. Carefully, she felt her way along the railing and down the stairs, then all the way to where the hole had been in the bookcase.

She pushed against it until the makeshift back and shelves fell, and she climbed through to the library. The celebration had ended, and everyone had gone home.

All that was left was an eerie quiet.

CHAPTER 36

She turned to replace the shelves she'd knocked down only to see that everything was in perfect order. She frowned and shook her head. There wasn't time to figure that out. She raced in the direction of the winter garden on the other side of the house, tripping several times and falling once. "What the hell?" She focused on the path she'd just traveled but didn't see how she could have stumbled.

She froze when she saw it. The internal door that led to the winter garden, the one that had been boarded up when last she'd seen it, had been replaced with a decorative stained glass door.

Her brows drew together. "That's not possible. Tom wouldn't have put that in, not after we lost the case." She touched her fingertips to the colored glass, just briefly, expecting to feel a cool, smooth surface. Instead, she felt solid wood. She scratched her nails over the exterior, and they caught in the ridges of the unfinished wood.

Then it clicked. "The glass isn't real. It's just a memory. The image of how it used to be on this night." She knew she'd have to walk carefully the rest of the way or she could end up really hurting herself.

She walked as if she'd lost her sight, hands and feet feeling their way before she put her foot down. The winter garden appeared as it had on this night in 1883, with its two-story waterfall and lavish cushioned seating. She traveled slowly to the far right corner, losing her balance several times along the way due to the unseen hurdles.

She knelt on the floor and searched until she finally found the small rectangular pillow. She popped the stitches she'd carefully sewn and retrieved the birth certificate from the center of the pillow mold. She didn't think Asher would ever have found it there, but since he was in the house, she felt better for it being on her person. She slid the paper into the side of her pants until it caught in the snug fabric against her hips.

Footsteps and voices echoed through the house, Henry's voice being the loudest of them all. Gemma scrambled her way toward them to see what was happening.

When she reached the great hall, she hid behind a pillar and scanned the area for Asher. She found him leaning against the top of the staircase near the far wall, watching the parade of disorganized policemen and other uniformed bedlam.

Henry, still covered in Anna's blood, was escorted down the stairs by two policemen. Her heart tripped and locked tight at the sight of him. Tonight was supposed to be the night when he launched his campaign for the presidency. Instead, he ended up accused of his wife's murder. Early this morning, the man had had a bright future. In three days' time, he'd be dead.

Sam trailed behind, giving further details to one of the policemen, who scribbled notes on a tiny notepad. "I think he planned this for some time. He just picked tonight so he could win the sympathy vote."

The ceremony proceeded out the front door. Gemma stayed behind her pillar. Henry would be back by daybreak, and the nightmare would be over soon, and another one would begin—the nightmare of losing Henry.

She thought of the winds that had blown around her just a few weeks ago: chaos riding on the appearance of calm. Her mother was rarely wrong. *All truth can be found in nature.*

The last people out were two men in long, dark coats, black pants, and hats with short, shiny brims. They had wrapped Anna's body in a white sheet, which already had a large red splotch of blood at the top, and carried her down the stairs on a narrow, brown stretcher. Her lifeless arm dangled out from under the sheet and swayed with their steps.

Asher slow clapped and laughed aloud. He whistled and yelled, "Bravo!"

She didn't think she could possibly hate him any more than she did right now. The man lacked a soul.

"That was amazing. I'm glad I finally got to see that," he said. "Heard about it all my life, never saw it all the way through like that. Now I can cross that off my bucket list." He picked something out of his teeth, examined it, and flicked it away.

He unrolled the plans and rested them on the top railing. "Now. That secret room has got to be here somewhere. I've busted a hole in just about every room in this house, and I can't find the damn thing. It's here, though, and I'm going to claim my birthright. Right? Great-great-great-grandmama?" He waved in the direction they'd just carried Anna's body.

Gemma really hadn't remembered how destroyed the grand staircase was. Not after watching everyone descend it just moments ago. Neither did Asher, apparently, which was funny, in a way, since he was the one who had wiped out most of it.

But when she saw him take his first step on the right side of the stairway, it all came back in an instant. His arms flew into the air and he screamed on the way down. It was a genuine scream of high-pitched terror that was quieted by one of the many wooden boards he had left angled and upright in the destruction. He fell facedown when he missed that step, and a jagged board impaled his stomach and exited the other side of him. Blood poured from Asher's dead body and pooled onto the floor.

Gemma stood with her hands pressed against her open mouth, her insides shaking with horror.

Asher's spirit stumbled from his dead body. He examined his chest and midsection, then laughed. "Thank the—Ha! I thought I'd—" He turned and saw his dead body. His body was limp and arched and still.

Anna's father and one last policeman came from the bedroom wing. The policeman patted her father on the back.

He wiped his eyes with a linen handkerchief. "I can't believe he'd hurt her. He's always taken such good care of her. She was a handful, you know, especially when she was young. We had to put her in a sanitarium once, when it all got to be too much. I actually asked Benjamin to marry her. I've never told anyone that. But she needed stability, someone strong and levelheaded to care for her. She always had such terrible taste in men on her own." Her father blew his nose. "Benjamin grew up with her, and he cared about her. He just took her in. Did us all a favor."

Asher watched them carefully. When they reached the bottom step, he approached them. "Excuse me. I've just had an accident and I need your help." He grabbed them both by the arm held on to them tightly, refusing to let go. The minute he touched them, he seemed to regret it, as if something passed through him.

Currents of dark energy poured from the walls, humming with fury like angry bees. They circled him as though they answered an alarm, surrounding a trespasser who would now pay the price.

They held his arms and legs and lifted him into the air with ease despite his struggle. They tugged at him like strands of tar he couldn't escape, and he screamed, in pain or panic, she couldn't tell. But, inch by inch, he disappeared into the walls that surrounded him. Writhing slowly, like a second death, or maybe a second life, he became one with the house he had long felt entitled to.

CHAPTER 37

She had no interest in sitting in the house with Asher's dead body, so she waited for Henry where the grass met the sand.

When he returned, she knew it. Even with her eyes closed, she felt it in the same way she did when the sun broke through the clouds. A warmth, a shift in energy, a smile she felt inside and out.

He swept her into his arms and swung her in a circle. For a moment, she thought she might actually be flying. "You're back. You're my Henry again."

"From here on out, I always shall be."

She quickly looked around to see if anyone saw her pretending to hug and kiss someone who wasn't there. Policemen, detectives, and the coroner had been coming and going for several hours.

"Henry." She needed to give him the news. Right away. He'd waited more than a lifetime to know. "You didn't kill Anna. She killed herself. You did everything anyone could do to talk her out of it. But she was just...lost. Determined. I don't think anyone could have stopped her."

He stepped away and exhaled a century's worth of guilt. "Are you positive?"

"I saw the whole thing from start to finish."

He strode several steps toward the water and pushed his hands into his hair. His smile broadened inch by inch revealing his first sense of freedom. He had just been pronounced innocent, he had finally received the proof of his blamelessness, and he now had the fresh start he'd more than earned.

"Thank you, Gemma. You have no idea how much this means to me." He kissed her.

She choked down the painful lump in her throat and hoped he wouldn't disappear right in front of her. At least, not yet. She wasn't ready.

She'd never be ready.

The back door opened and two men wheeled a covered body on a stretcher.

"I guess you saw or maybe heard?" She nodded toward the house.

"Yeah," he scoffed. "I saw it on my way through. They left the body where it fell. The detectives have been inside making sure there wasn't any foul play. Or that the evil Benjamin Alcott didn't kill him. You'll pardon me if I can't shed a tear for Asher."

"No pardon needed." She desperately wanted to put her arms around him. "I'm so glad you're okay."

"I always come out alive." He patted his own chest twice with his fist. "So to speak, anyway." His eyes twinkled, and just for a moment, she felt the possibility of their life together again. It was a broken dream that forgot to let go, which, she decided, was the cruelest type of joy.

She took him by the hand and headed toward the manor. "Come on, there's something I want to show you."

❧

ANNA'S BEDROOM was not as chaotic as it had been the night before when the house relived 1883. It was peaceful now, with ambient light drifting through the windows.

She sat at Anna's secretary, opened the main compartment, and ran her hand along the writing surface. "The notes were left here." She patted the finely crafted, gilded wood. "There were two. One to you and one to Sam."

Henry lowered himself to the edge of the bed, his eyes wide and intent and cautiously optimistic.

"You first saw them when you came up here to get Anna's wrap. One she could wear to cover up a bit, I think." Gemma waved her hand over her chest. "Sam discovered them after Anna shot herself and after your argument with him. When he found them, it didn't take him long to put his plan together. He knew that without the proof of the suicide notes, how Anna died would be your word against his. So he hid them. In here." She patted the desk again.

Henry nodded slowly as if this was finally making sense for him.

"I saw him come over here and put them in a drawer. But I had to hide from Asher about then, so I missed their exact location. I also saw when you and the policemen searched these drawers for them and they weren't there. So, I have a theory."

"I'm all ears." He shrugged as if he didn't have anything left to lose. But she knew what was at stake—his peace and his ability to move on from this life. There was a lot left to lose.

She sighed through her heartache and kept going. "When my parents restored a home, it wasn't unusual for there to be period furniture in the house." She ran both hands over the open secretary. "Sometimes my dad and I would restore a desk or two while we were there. It's therapeutic to give something a second chance at life—" When she looked at Henry, he raised one eyebrow.

"Well. Anyway. This secretary reminds me of a few I've seen before."

She opened all the drawers, and all were empty. She gestured to them like an illusionist.

See? No rabbit in the hat and nothing up my sleeve.

"That's what we all saw when you checked the drawers," she said. "But let's see what happens if I do this." She opened several doors. "Yep, they have all these secret compartments, see? There are four on each side and then four more behind them." She opened all the little drawers.

"I never knew the secretary could do this," Henry said. "Anna always had her secrets."

"The internal mechanisms are very delicate. Heat and humidity can affect them, and they may have gotten stuck over the years from not being used. I did see one of the movers bump the secretary when they were leaving the moving truck. They might have knocked something loose, which may be why these drawers are opening now."

"None of these drawers are large enough to hold a letter. Unless it was folded several times over, I guess."

"You're right." She took an antique key from her front pocket that was tied to a faded lavender ribbon and held it up. "I found this in one of the books at the museum. It was a scrapbook of sorts, and it was tucked into a section that was dedicated to Anna's rooms. That got me thinking." She moved the two front panels aside and a long drawer slid out.

"When the note wasn't on Sam, and it wasn't visible in the room, I knew it had to be hidden because I had seen it." She pulled the drawer just a fraction of an inch. It popped out all the way and then swung outward on a hinge. Then she went to the other side and did the same thing. Behind one of those open drawers was a box.

She gently took the first one from its home, used the skeleton key to open it, and lifted the lid.

"What is this?" Henry asked.

"I think this was Anna's hiding place. Sam must have known about it."

At the bottom of the box were two delicate handwritten notes on yellowed Dempsey and Carroll stationery. Henry accepted the first one from her as if she had just handed him a delicate baby bird.

Dear Benjamin,

Though I know I have no right to ask you to forgive me, I hope that someday you will. I'm doing this for you and the children as much as I am for me.

You were kind to marry me, Benjamin. I know you tried to help me. You've done nothing wrong. Please know that.

I am broken, I know this. The doctors have not been able to fix my head, and I cannot continue to be a problem to my family. I won't go into a facility again. Never again. I barely survived it the first time my father put me there.

You can't have me at your side at the White House. This is the easiest way. The voters will feel sorry for you and cast their votes in your direction. The brilliant man with the demented wife. You will find another wife. Women will flock to your side when they know I'm gone, and especially how I left.

Take care of the children.

Love,

Anna

. . .

TEARS glistened in Henry's eyes. His countenance was as soft as a down pillow and just as vulnerable.

"There's another one." She handed him the second note.

MY DEAR SAM,

I've often wondered what would have happened if I had been able to marry you instead of Benjamin as my father insisted. What could it have been like when we were young and we still had a very real chance at happiness? I like to think that we would have had our beautiful Lizzie Mae all to ourselves, and we would have been a happy family together.

But I can't help but think that maybe you would have been the one to deal with my many emotional problems instead of Benjamin. Perhaps you ought to be relieved that my father chose Benjamin to care for me and not you.

I know you told me I should leave with you because you believed you could make me happy. But I think Benjamin may have been right when he said that you wanted my money more than you wanted me. I wouldn't have agreed with him, but now that I know about Sarah Baker...well, maybe you'll be happy with her.

Please tell Lizzie Mae how much I loved her, even though my sickness prevented me from showing it as I wanted to. Maybe now that I'm gone, she will find real love with another mother.

Love,
Anna

HENRY HELD both notes in front of him in slightly quivering hands. They were the keys to his happiness, his passes to freedom, his reward for a long-fought battle.

"Thank you." Tears rolled down his face. "Thank you."

Her throat was too tight to speak, and she knew if she said anything she would completely fall apart. So she let

Henry have this moment that he'd waited more than a lifetime for, crossed her arms tightly around herself, and held on.

❦

AFTER HENRY READ the notes several times, he handed them
to Gemma, who returned everything to the strong box. On
their way to take in the early morning over-the-ocean sunrise,
they stopped in the study. She lifted the coffee-stained mug
she'd used as a paperweight and put the box prominently next
to it, along with the skeleton key attached to the lavender
ribbon.

"Henry." She took the birth certificate from the inside of
her waistband. "Asher's wife. I think she ought to have this."

"You've met her?"

"Her name is Layla, she's this lovely nurse who took care
of my dad when he was in the hospital. She wants to see the
manor restored, and I think this would help her. It would
help us. She would get whatever stock and voting rights
Asher would have been entitled to."

"Okay. If you think it's the right thing." His face was
nearly serene now. All traces of his last life were slowly being
erased. The note had given him every bit of the vindication
he'd searched for over the years.

She slid the folded birth certificate into the handle of the
box and tied the ribbon of the skeleton key there, as well.
"There's just one more thing I need to show you."

"Something else?"

She nodded, slow and sure. This was most certainly something he needed to know.

He bowed and gestured like the 1880s gentleman that he
was. "Then lead the way."

CHAPTER 38

Gemma drew in a deep breath and fished her portfolio from the bookshelf. "That night at the museum, after you left, I found all of the scrapbooks and history books on the manor. I was searching for something that might give me some insight into the structure and why it held on to such a dark vibe. I found this."

She laid a yellowed 1830 newspaper article on the counter of the bookshelf for Henry to read. "Cardill Builders' Business Practices Called Into Question. Why am I not surprised at this?" he said.

"This was a series that played out in the paper for a number of weeks." She placed several more articles on the counter for Henry. "Apparently, Sam Cardill's father had already begun building Alcott Manor, as well as a few other majestic homes. He overextended himself in the process and had a hard time getting the lumber he needed to finish the jobs."

She pointed to one paragraph on the top page. "When he was unable to pay his vendors, he decided to harvest the lumber himself. From several of the barrier islands, more specifically, Bloody Coast."

Henry's mouth dropped open, and Gemma could almost feel a part of him drop to the floor. A disbelieving part, that someone could possibly screw up so badly. "The site of that Native American massacre?"

"The one. So many of the Yemassee tribe were killed in that battle with the English that the sand and the marshes ran red."

"Don't tell me," Henry said.

"He cut down the trees that had not only soaked up the blood from that battle, but also trees from their nearby sacred burial grounds. At the time, there weren't any laws protecting the land or preventing him from harvesting those trees, so nothing ever happened to him for doing that—other than being publicly bashed in the papers.

"But that tragedy, the injustice of those Native Americans' deaths, is imprinted into the very fibers of this home." She gestured toward the hidden passageway and felt the insides of the house—the Yemassee Indian spirits—lean toward her touch. "When he took down those trees, he brought their spirits and their suffering into this house. Both are literally attached to the wooden framework of the manor."

"Those imprints have continued to attract like experience for almost two hundred years. That's the original reason why we've had such a history of injustice in this house, isn't it?"

She nodded. "Once I clear the imprints of that injustice and the adversity that's trapped in the wood, the house should finally have a clean slate." What she almost said, but couldn't, was that he would finally be free. With all mysteries solved and his innocence proven, he would move on.

At that very thought, her heart wailed and reached for him, wanted him more than she'd ever wanted anyone.

Just like Lizzie Mae had.

Henry walked a wide circle around the library and pushed his hands through the length of his hair as if there were no words. Just no words for what the Cardills had done and how they had cursed the Alcott family for generations.

Henry was beyond smashing walls and destroying things. He was beyond the anger. He was enjoying all sorts of new freedoms now. As soon as she finished this clearing work, she knew he would enjoy even more.

§.

A WHILE LATER, Gemma curled into Henry on the gliding love seat she'd had placed among the roses. It was the call of the spirits of the Native Americans that she had first heard, and it was their dark and tortured reach she had felt through the walls. Their suffering and their need had appealed to the Native American heritage she had inherited from her mother.

They knew her ability to clear their tragic imprints would set them free—Henry, too—and bring justice to the land and the Alcott family.

The wind knew that, too, and foretold it.

All truth can be found in nature.

Their spirits had left with an upsurge. The house released them when she sang the ancient chant that freed Native American spirits from an earthbound attachment. This time, it was her intent that ruled the house and dictated what would happen.

She'd never used this particular chant before. Any spirit she'd previously encountered usually just moved on when she cleared the land or the building she was working on. This situation was different.

The chant had worked like a spiritual waterspout, lifting the Yemassee Indian spirits out of the depths of the manor and sending them into the sky and beyond. Where they ought to have gone over a century ago. When it was finally over, the house was quiet—truly quiet—as though everyone had finally left the party and gone home.

A little spent from the final clearings on the house, she rested heavily against Henry's shoulder and enjoyed the beginning of the sun that rose in front of them.

"I don't think I got that young girl and the artist to cross over," she said.

"They wouldn't go?"

She clicked her tongue. "Well, my process was to free Native American spirits. Besides, I don't think those two are here. I think they're more there, in 1885. I'm not sure how to reach them—or for that matter, how to close whatever portal this house has in it."

Henry glanced at the house behind them. "I don't know, either."

Gemma decided she'd work on that. Another time, though. For now, she tried to memorize everything she could about Henry—the spiced scent of his skin, the deep, rich timbre of his voice, and the slow, poetic cadence of his words. Soon enough, the memories would be all she had.

Henry caressed her cheek and kissed her. "You've changed my life in ways that no one else could. I shall always love you."

"I guess I could say the same about you. I will spend the rest of my life loving you. And missing you." She wondered if this was it. If he would simply fade from her view, slip from her arms, cease to exist. She thought her own heart might stop when he did, and she quickly understood how people could die of a broken heart.

Car doors slammed and they turned around in time to see Tom, Paisley, and their attorney, Morris Pate, walk inside through the back door. Gemma didn't hurry to run inside. Her final moments with Henry were ticking away.

"I guess they'll find the notes we left for them. As well as the birth certificate," Henry said.

"Not to mention one other thing." She decided he ought to know about this last thing.

"What one other thing?"

"Let's just say that there are benefits for all when you choose to honor your instincts."

When they finally went inside, Henry and Gemma found them in the study. She stayed close to Henry and hung with him in the background. She guessed that she only had a few minutes left with Henry, and she didn't want to use that time on work. Plus, she knew they'd find what she left on the desk for Tom, and the ball would start rolling toward final justice.

Morris Pate ran around the lower floor of the house with his cell phone to his ear. Tom and Paisley shook their heads in quiet, wide-eyed amazement while they read Anna's suicide letters.

Gemma nudged Henry. "I guess we've given them a lot to think about."

"He's got it." Morris lifted the phone away from his mouth and whispered to Tom and Paisley. "The security company says there is clear footage of Asher killing the security guard and entering the house. We've got enough to win the appeal."

"How did they— I thought the cameras were destroyed?" Henry asked.

She smiled with the satisfaction of a war finally won. "The original ones, yes. But the workplace security cameras that my dad ordered were so small that Asher apparently never saw them. Private Eyes? Remember them?"

His eyes glazed over as if he searched his memory banks. "They were here on the day you arrived at the manor."

"I felt guided to organize the desk, and I found a past due invoice from them. I moved it into plain sight and emailed

Tom about it so they would check it out. From what Morris is saying, it sounds like the company has recorded proof, and we'll win the appeal."

She did a weak fist pump. She was excited that her father's financial future had been saved, but she was also filled with dread at the prospect of redoing this house without Henry. She wouldn't be able to touch an inch of this place without thinking of him.

"The newspapers are going to want this," Tom said and waved the suicide letters. "We are going to turn public opinion to our side with this story."

Gemma glanced toward the library. She would also give Tom the articles she found in the museum so he could pass copies of that on to the newspaper. The background about Sam Cardill's father raiding the Bloody Coast and sacred burial grounds to build Alcott Manor would make for award-winning reporting.

And Tom was right. It would also turn the tide of public opinion in their favor. They wouldn't have any trouble finishing the restoration now.

Right on cue, the morning newspapers hit the front porch with a *thud*. Paisley retrieved them and immediately unfolded the front page of the first paper.

She showed something to Tom, who waved it off.

"I'm not even going to read that. Get that reporter's name, though, and set up a meeting. ASAP." Tom waved the birth certificate toward her.

Paisley parked the unfolded newspaper on a round side table in the corner of the office and pulled out her phone. "Do you want me to tell him the reason for the meeting? Or just ask him if he can meet?"

"Just tell him we uncovered..." He finger-combed the puffiest part of his hair and whispered, "Or *someone* uncovered..." He cleared his throat. "Tell him Anna Alcott's suicide note was found and ask him if he wants to see it. That'll get him over here. I'll be out back with Morris."

Paisley stepped onto the front porch with her phone to make the call.

Henry wandered over to see what Tom hadn't wanted to read, then he called Gemma over. "You ought to see this, Gemma." His tone was serious, and she knew it was bad press.

It was a full-page spread entitled The Alcott Manor Curse Claims Another Life. It was a feature on Asher's death and the destruction of the latest restoration.

On the top left-hand side of the page were photos of Henry's father and mother, along with a short paragraph about them. There were photos of Henry—*Benjamin*—and Anna, and their children. The history of their lives was written in condensed paragraphs so that even the shortest attention spans could take in all the pertinent details.

Gemma scanned the story, then her eyes jumped to the top of the right-hand side of the page. Pictures of her, her father, and her cousin were spread under the smaller headline: Stewart Family Members Also Fall Under Alcott Manor Curse.

"What sort of nonsense is that—fall under Alcott Manor curse? No one called me to vet this article. That's inaccurate and bad PR. We're overcoming everything that's happened here." She noted that the paper must have taken the photos from her father's and her respective websites. "I need to update that photo."

"Read the article," Henry said.

She sighed. "The four primary members of Stewart Restoration were among the latest, but not the last, to fall under the Alcott Manor Curse. Asher Cardill was found in Alcott Manor yesterday, impaled on a broken piece of wood after a likely fall from the second-story balcony. After winning the bid to restore the home, Glenn Stewart and his wife Rose worked on the home for over a year before she had a heart attack and died suddenly.

"After burying his wife, Glenn brought his daughter and niece to join the job. The threesome were blindsided by a truck in front of Alcott Manor before they could begin work. The three family members were taken to Mercy Hospital, where the two women died from injuries within the week. Glenn Stewart died two weeks later. Funerals were held in their hometown of Moorestown."

Gemma's mouth fell open. "Is this a joke?"

Henry's stare was the kind of serious compassion she'd seen several times before. It was the this-is-going-to-hurt-and-I'm-really-sorry-about-that look. Her father had this expression on his face when she saw him for the first time after her mother died.

"It's not a joke, my love. I've just been waiting for the right time to tell you."

"Tell me what? Henry, this is not funny." Chills spread over her body from the inside out, like she'd swallowed a bucket of ice.

"It's okay." Henry ran his fingers along her arm. "Just stop and think about it. When was the last time you drove a car or brushed your teeth or ate something?"

"I ate a bagel this morning. I eat a bagel or a muffin almost every morning when I drink my hot tea."

He nodded patiently. "Are you sure? I used to think I had coffee every morning until I realized it was just a habit I was attached to. It wasn't real."

"I think I know when I'm eating and drinking, Henry."

"When is the last time you remember brushing your teeth?" he asked.

She ran her tongue across her teeth. "My teeth are clean, I —" She tried to remember brushing her teeth that morning—

or any morning since she'd been at Alcott Manor, but she couldn't come up with a specific memory of the simple twice-daily task.

Panic shimmied through the cold in her body at the thought that maybe she'd lost her mind. It was a feeling that she wasn't really living the reality she thought she was, and that scared her. A rude awakening. Like the one when she thought she was happily—or mostly happily—married and then she learned that her husband was carrying on with one of his grad students.

She really couldn't remember the last time she'd brushed her teeth. "Teeth brushing is one of those rote habits that you do every day, but you don't necessarily remember doing it every day." She said it to console herself, then walked away from Henry. She looked out the grand window at the ocean. The rose gardens she'd designed to celebrate Anna's life were in full bloom.

"If I'm dead, how was I able to restore this house?" She said it as the perfect retort. The one statement that would prove to herself that everything was fine. She was alive and well, on the job, and saving her father's business.

"When was the last time you had a conversation with someone who wasn't me? I don't just mean someone who listens to you, but a person with whom you've had an actual conversation."

"This is so ridiculous. I've had plenty of conversations." Her hands flew to her hips and she sent him a glare that would make him regret this foolishness.

"Name the last thing that Paisley or Tom said to you. Or any of the workers." He leaned against the wall with his arms crossed, as if he had all the time in the world, as if he were just waiting on her.

"That's—" She tried to remember an actual conversation, but mostly, she'd told people what to do. "That doesn't

ALYSSA RICHARDS

prove anything. I'm in charge around here, so I tell people what to do all day." Her words had taken on a sharp edge, a toothy bite, and the flavor of feminine fume—as they should. This was some fine way to spend their last few moments together.

"At some point, you would have had a two-way conversation, right?" He offered the suggestion delicately. Reasonably. As if he tried to tell her that she had spinach in her front teeth, ice cream on the seat of her pants, or toilet paper stuck to the bottom of her shoe.

This only pissed her off more and she paced the floor, stuttering over half words that made no sense. This was the most ridiculous argument she'd ever had in her life. "Fine. How did I die?"

"The car accident." He pointed to the newspaper. His tone was final, and relief drifted over his face, as though he had wanted to tell her that piece of information for a long time.

"I— My dad— If I'm dead, then what in the hell am I doing *here*?"

Henry shrugged and gestured to the house around them. "Unfinished business?"

Gemma gasped and put her hand to her forehead. It rested there while something sunk in. Something horrifying. "This isn't possible. If I were dead, I would simply know it. I'm not one of those—unconscious types."

Her mother's words about ghosts came back to her. About how most of them didn't know they were dead. They relived their lives or parts of them, over and over. The few that did know they were dead, didn't know how to move forward or cross over. It just wasn't automatic for everyone as many often thought. It all came down to what their attachments were.

"No, no, no, no, no, no, no." She repeated the word over

and over as if she could prove this idea wrong. Make it untrue. "Dear God. Please. No."

Her first thought was of her father, and how she couldn't leave him. If she were dead, he'd be devastated. Then she thought of the newspaper article. Good God, was he gone, too?

She thought of her childhood home, the warm, happy place where her father still lived. She wanted to see if he was there. As quickly as she thought of his house, there was a rushing, a whooshing of colors and sounds that flew by her and sucked her forward. There was no inertia, just a tugging forward, and then she was there.

The house was empty of his things, and he was nowhere to be found. Some other family occupied her childhood home. It was a young family with crayons and Play-Doh scattered on the dining room table. People she didn't know. A dining table she didn't recognize.

Then she thought of her own home on Stinson Beach, and with a surrounding muddle of colors and noises, she was there. She landed in her kitchen, only to find a too-thin woman with long blonde hair who argued with a man whose Popeyed biceps boasted large, dark blue tattoos, one per arm.

Gemma circled the couple and listened to the man growl that the woman had spent too much money on clothes the week before. The woman popped her right hip out, grunted, and left her mouth open an inch.

She went to her foyer and found that her grandmother's mirror was gone. In its place was a coatrack, a stone side table, and a half-mirror hanging above it. She drifted through the house searching for the familiar, but nothing was, other than the layout of the house.

The colors the couple had chosen to use for decorating were awful. "No one should use this light maroon color on a wall, especially in a beach house." She pressed close to the wall to examine the color and scrunched her face as if the paint smelled like garbage. "Actually, this is puce. You don't put puce on any wall. Ever."

When she passed through the kitchen again, the couple was still arguing. Gemma stood next to the island in the middle of the kitchen. She put her hand on the side of a white plate that held a hot bowl of sauce-covered pasta and shoved it hard enough that it crashed on the floor.

The husband stopped mid-bitch. "Did you see that? It just flew through the air!"

The wife looked at the plate of pasta on the floor in amazement. "Do you think we have a ghost? Do you think it's the last owner of the house? She could still be here."

Both the husband and wife searched the upper half of the room in awe.

Gemma shook her head and walked out. "Morons."

She stood on the back porch and watched the two striped cats that she used to feed run up to the house that was situated beside hers.

She followed them and found Cameron, her neighbor with the angular glasses, whose attention she did her best to ignore. He put two white bowls of fresh meaty cat food on his back stoop for the cats.

When the cats ran up, they stopped and gazed at Gemma. She knelt next to them and they purred and circled her.

"What are you doing there, kids?" Cameron asked. "Don't you want your dinner?"

"Be good to him," Gemma said to the two cats. "He's your meal ticket now."

The cats meowed and pranced to their bowls.

"Did they finally show up?" A dark-haired woman exited Cameron's house, sidled up to him, and threaded her arm around his waist. She wore teal-colored scrubs and a large laminated name tag around her neck that read: Cynthia Harris, Nurse.

Gemma laughed. She smiled at Cameron and crossed her arms. He wasn't a bad guy. He just wasn't her guy.

Her mind shot to Henry. Beautiful, complicated Henry. He had spent his short life trying to do the right thing by others, only to be blindsided in the end. Then he spent his afterlife angry over the injustice of it all, trying to right the wrongs that had been done to him. In the process, he lost his way forward.

Anger could do that to a person. Anger could turn into a crutch that you used as an excuse to keep from moving forward.

Though sometimes, with the right person at your side, you could come back to yourself and find the most fitting path onward.

❧

WITH THE SIMPLE thought of him she was back in his arms.

"Are you all right?" His soft touch caressed her cheek, his sweet earthy scent surrounded her.

She stared at him for a long moment, still stunned, but feeling oddly grateful. She finally nodded, slowly. "I thought dead would be different. Empty somehow. And yet, here I am. Still alive."

"Come on," he said and led them outside.

A yellowish glow came over the rose garden, just as it had on her first day at Alcott Manor when she saw the flowers with her father.

"Why didn't you tell me? Right from the beginning, you must have known...what I was." A sick feeling washed over her stomach for saying it. And though she knew she wasn't actually sweating—ghosts didn't sweat—she could feel a cool, sticky damp cover the back of her neck. "A ghost."

"You didn't know you were dead, you were on a mission, you were insistent on helping the property. I tried to discourage you, but you wouldn't hear it. What could I have said to you about your current state that wouldn't have scared you off or made you think I was a lunatic?"

She thought about what he said. Ultimately, she decided he wasn't wrong. If he had told her early on that she was a ghost, she would have thought him a nut. She would have gone on about her business at the manor, trying to restore it for her father—who wasn't even here any longer.

Ghost stories didn't get any more classic than hers. That thought made her feel a little ill. She had always prided herself on how independent she was. Accomplished. Smart.

That she could miss something so obvious humbled her.

Though not as much as Henry's love. "You stayed with me all this time just to help me?"

He nodded. "It started out that way. I couldn't let you be damned to the kind of life I'd had to live for the last hundred-plus years. So I thought we might work together to help with the restoration and, hopefully, find the note." He pulled her a little closer, his smile soft with love, forever love. "Then I fell in love with you."

She didn't think ghosts cried. But she did. Her mother was right yet again.

Ghosts are people, too.

"Thank you, Henry." She ran her hand along his chest, which was still solid to her touch. "I think you saved my life."

His eyes, the most mesmerizing form of hazel she'd ever seen, like a tempest in the sea, seemed to warm and respond to her. "I think you may have saved me right back." His South Carolinian accent charmed and claimed her, setting her world to right.

The warm ocean winds drifted calm and gentle around her now. Several months ago, they had foretold her future, and they had been accurate. Her life as she knew it had exploded in tumultuous change, and all the while, she moved ahead on the appearance of calm.

"The good news is that we're together and we don't have to be apart from one another." His kiss caused her to melt into him as if he were a dream come true, as if he were tailor-made for her, as if he were the only one who could be.

When she finally pulled away, she wondered. Who's to say that he wasn't? If silver linings existed, and she was inclined to think now that they did, who's to say that wasn't a part of what the manor wanted for her all along?

"Would we stay here?" She looked at the back of Alcott Manor and wasn't at all excited about the idea. Thanks to Asher, the inside of the house was in far worse shape then when she'd arrived. It was completely untenable.

At least the soul of the home had been restored. Refreshed. Perhaps even completely reborn. She had been able to accomplish that for Henry, for the Alcott family, and for future generations.

"No, I'm ready to move on." He kissed her left hand and gave her engagement ring a nudge. "With you."

She had no idea how it was that that ring could sit on her finger in her current condition, but she was pretty happy that it did. "Where shall we go? Would you like to see the world?"

Henry shook his head and clasped her hand to his chest. "This way." He guided them toward the rose garden.

For the first time in a very long time, Gemma wasn't thinking about clients, her career, or fixing someone else's problems. She was thinking about something far more important.

There was a warm yellow glow around the rose garden. More of a golden glow, actually, and a pull to it that tugged at her midsection. They glided forward together, into the light. In the distance, she thought she saw her parents, arm in arm, smiling. Waving.

"This way?" She pointed toward the endless light that appeared to surround her and love her from all directions.

"Gemma. When I said I wanted to spend forever with you, I really meant forever."

When he kissed her, she heard the melody again, the one she'd always known but had forgotten about until Henry held her one night.

When she was a child and heard it the first time, she knew it was a sign—the promise of the perfect man.

Now that she heard it again, she knew Henry was the fulfillment of that promise—the man who was perfect for her.

CHAPTER 39

Layla Alcott's two young girls pressed against the window, hands over their mouths, laughing while they overlooked the rose garden closest to the back of Alcott Manor.

"Girls! What are y'all giggling about?" Layla called to her daughters. She had never stepped foot inside the manor before today because she never felt comfortable with the energy of it. It had always felt too dark to her.

Unexpectedly, Tom with the Historic District Commission called and invited her in. She'd met Tom when his friend Mr. Stewart had landed on her hospital floor after a terrible car accident.

She wasn't going to accept Tom's invitation. But he said he had news. Big news.

"They're kissing!" Emma Catherine, Layla's youngest daughter, could not contain her laughter. Her long dark ponytail swished against her back.

Tom had explained that there was a strange turn of events —a birth certificate, of all things, had been uncovered in the restoration. Anna Alcott had had an affair with Sam Cardill, who was one of her newly deceased husband's relatives. The affair resulted in a child, a little girl they called Lizzie Mae. That made Asher a verified Alcott descendent. Which, in turn, made Layla the largest stockholder in the Alcott family organization.

Layla's work clogs *ka-thunked* against barren floors that were in the process of being cleared of ripped-up pinewood and other dangerous items. She leaned to the girls' height and peered out the window. "Who's kissing?"

Tom explained that they would win the appeal in the courts, thanks to the video proof they'd found of Asher destroying the property. And, also, that there would probably be another vote among members of the Alcott family. Since she was the leading stockholder, he encouraged her to take a position as the family representative and to oversee the manor's—hopefully final—restoration.

She wanted to turn him down. After all, she was a trained nurse. She didn't know anything about restorations or historic properties. She also tended toward the shy side, and if there were a family battle, she didn't know how she felt about that.

But Tom reminded her that she tipped the scales in their favor, and she could be a positive influence if she wanted the restoration. And she did. That she knew. She believed in second chances.

The property was different now, Tom had told her. He admitted that it did have rather a creepy past, but something had changed for the better. He couldn't describe why or how the manor changed, he just insisted that it had. "Something has lifted," he'd said. He wanted her to come to the house to see it for herself. To feel it for herself.

So she did.

It only took a few steps onto the land for her to recognize that change. She and the girls usually stopped on the beach and didn't go any farther, because that's when she got that tight feeling around her head and heart. Like she was suffocating.

Today she could breathe, and she decided Tom's description was right. Something had lifted. Something was gone. Something had left. It was enough of a change to motivate her to walk right inside and look around.

Emma Catherine made a goofy face and pointed her thumb in the direction of the garden. Anna Kate, her eldest and most blonde, faced the other way, wrapped her arms around herself in a mock-make-out session. Both girls squealed with laughter and ran off.

"Y'all be careful! Take it outside!" Layla's smile was an honest grin that bloomed from her heart whenever her girls were in sight. She shook her head while she watched the girls chase each other through the kitchen, and she heard the screen door squeak and slam.

Such a nice sound.

With Asher gone, she and her daughters would live a very different life now. A better one, she hoped. A new beginning, she decided. Maybe she'd finally lose the rest of the weight she wanted to.

She pressed toward the window and searched the outside. She didn't see anyone out there, much less a couple kissing.

But she did notice a beautiful yellow glow around Anna Alcott's rose garden.

Keep reading for an excerpt from A MURDER AT ALCOTT MANOR
by Alyssa Richards

A NOTE FROM THE AUTHOR

AUTHOR'S NOTE

I've often heard that a story can choose its author. Such was the case with THE HAUNTING OF ALCOTT MANOR. As I finished LOST IN TIME, my intent was to write more in THE FINE ART OF DECEPTION SERIES. But the story you've just read dropped in on me. Like a butterfly it landed gently on the forefront of my mind and refused to leave.

I tried to argue with this creative nudge—I had plans for a different book, a different series. But for nearly a week I felt Henry's presence while he retold his story, it was as if he was in the room with me. I was so touched by the ending, I finally decided to put down my own plans and write his tale.

If you enjoyed THE HAUNTING OF ALCOTT MANOR, there are two more stories in this series: A MURDER AT ALCOTT MANOR and A STRANGER AT ALCOTT MANOR.

You can learn more about them on my website www.AlyssaRichards.com

Or if you've already read them, you might enjoy THE FINE ART OF DECEPTION Series. These books focus on Addie and her touch that reveals secrets. And Blake whose secrets might be more than she can handle. If you like paranormal suspense, past life love and a touch of time travel, then you'll love this series!

I love to hear from my readers. You're welcome to get in touch with me at alyssa@paranormalromancebooks.com or via my website. While you're there, sign up for my mailing list so I can let you know when I have a new title.

I hope you enjoy your visit to Alcott Manor!

Alyssa Richards

A MURDER AT ALCOTT MANOR

Don't miss the next story in Alyssa Richards' ALCOTT MANOR Series—**A MURDER AT ALCOTT MANOR**!

Mason and Layla have waited a long time to be together, but her ex-husband could ruin everything from the grave.

Layla is down to her last cent. Her late, abusive husband left her homeless, in debt, and with two young girls to care for. When she's offered the position of caretaker at her old manor home, she chooses to overlook the hauntings... and the spot where her husband was murdered.

Mason left the stressful stockbroker business for a simpler life in construction. He's hoping the seasonal renovation job will lead to something greater and give him the chance to reconnect with his childhood friend Layla. But a series of strange happenings may force Mason and Layla to reveal dangerous secrets they've never shared with a soul...

When Layla realizes she'll need to tap into her otherworldly abilities to protect the manor, Mason is more than skeptical. But she'll need both her supernatural strengths and his support to solve the deadly force that threatens her family...

A MURDER AT ALCOTT MANOR is the standalone second book in a series of gripping paranormal romance novels. If you like contemporary gothic settings, mystical dreams, and danger-defying romance, then you'll love Alyssa Richards' haunting tale.

Read on for a sneak peek!

CHAPTER 1 - A MURDER AT
ALCOTT MANOR

"I know this must be hard for you," Layla's attorney said.

Billy Langmire sat composed, his tanned skin as smooth and flawless as his expensive navy blue suit. He would never understand just how hard this was for her.

She knew this from the polished and perfect gold band on his well-manicured ring finger. And she knew this from the silver framed photos of his beautiful blond wife and little boy, on the dunes at the white sand beach. And she knew this from the trophy fish that was hung on the wall behind his desk. She often wondered if someone like him ever had real problems, or did he only have difficult choices.

She pinched the soft skin of her thigh beneath the teal green of her scrubs. Numbness was covering her inch by inch like a thick blanket and she hoped the sharp nip from her nails would snap her out of it. Guilt was swallowing her whole, as if a giant whale engulfed her into its dark, watery belly, and she descended into nothingness.

She hadn't felt this lost since the end of high school, when she had been accused of killing Brooke Williams—an event that caused Layla's life to jump its rails. It simultaneously destroyed her future with Mason, the man she thought she would marry. And it landed her in a marriage with Asher Cardill—her newly deceased husband who continued to ruin her life, even from the grave.

Back then, an entire summer of official charges and public humiliation had taken place before the police had ultimately proven her innocent. "There just isn't enough evidence to support the claims," the detectives had finally said.

But what the police and everyone else had never managed to figure out was that she had done it. She had killed Brooke Williams.

"Isn't there anything I can—" Emotion caught in her throat now. "There has to be something I can do to stop the bank from taking our house."

"I'm afraid not." His lips nearly disappeared into a sad smile he must have conjured for the most pathetic of situations. No lips, no teeth, no compassion. Just...unconcerned.

"There *has* to be something. We have nowhere to go. I have children—two girls who have lived in that home all their life." The hatred she had for that house bubbled up in sour grape flavor and swirled around her mouth. The bedrooms were too small, the kitchen too dated, the yard didn't have enough trees.

The small, two bedroom ranch-style house had been Asher's house before they married, never hers. Apparently, it was still his house because he never added her to the deed. That's what they sprung on her today.

She'd wanted to leave Asher's bachelor-era house so many times over the last ten years. Now she would. Not in the way she had wanted or expected, but she would go. She and her girls were all flying the coop, with no place to land.

"The bank cannot leave us homeless." Her voice sounded as though it came from someone else, from somewhere else in the room. She was disassociating. A psychologist described that reaction to her years ago and she knew the signs. Numbing out was one of them.

Billy pushed a letter toward her that was littered with numbers and harsh language. She'd seen the letter before, read it several times; she didn't need to see it again. So she ignored it and kept her eyes on his.

"Your husband's business owed the bank $552,000 on a line of credit. Since his company didn't have any revenue, they're entitled to seize his assets to settle his debt. He signed a personal guarantee with them." His pencil tapped a sentence at the bottom of the paper. She ignored that too, and maintained eye contact. She was determined that he see her as a human being, that he help her with this.

"Your house is worth roughly $245,000. I've spoken with the bank and they're willing to give you a discount of seven thousand dollars. But they're going to hold you to the remaining $300,000."

"How kind." She tried to tamp down her anger that was developing its own momentum, like a gallop that sped toward a cliff.

She was acutely aware of how anger could ruin your life. It could make you do things you later wished you hadn't. But the emotion she felt today was the special kind of anger that made her sprout fangs and claws, and forced grown men to cower in her path. It grew its substantial roots on the day her first child was born and its protective nature was bigger than she was. She called it her mama bear side, since it only reared itself when someone threatened the wellbeing of her children.

Right now, someone was taking away her children's home. When she tapped her fingers on the table she fully expected to hear claws on polished wood.

. . .

CONTINUE the adventure with A MURDER AT ALCOTT MANOR *today!*

ALSO BY ALYSSA RICHARDS

THE FINE ART OF DECEPTION SERIES

THE FINE ART OF DECEPTION, UNDOING TIME

SOMEWHERE IN TIME

LOST IN TIME

THE FINE ART OF DECEPTION, BOXED SET

THE ALCOTT MANOR SERIES

THE HAUNTING AT ALCOTT MANOR

A MURDER AT ALCOTT MANOR

A STRANGER AT ALCOTT MANOR

THE CHASING SECRETS SERIES

CHASING SECRETS

CHASING SECRETS BOOK 2 (coming soon!)

Be the first to know about Alyssa Richards' next novel, sign up here: www.AlyssaRichards.com

and follow her on Amazon or BookBub to receive a new release alert!

ABOUT THE AUTHOR

ALYSSA RICHARDS is the USA TODAY BESTSELLING AUTHOR of romantic suspense and mystery thriller novels. She loves living in the South with her husband and two children. She also loves good espresso, her rescue dogs, magnolias and gardenias, and, of course, reading a great book. She grew up running barefoot in the Blue Ridge Mountains of North Carolina, where her favorite weekly adventure was a trip to the library with her mom.

Sign up for Alyssa's newsletter at www.alyssarichards.com to receive special offers, and news about her latest releases.

For More information
www.Alyssa Richards.com
alyssa@paranormalromancebooks.com

facebook.com/alyssa.richards.942

twitter.com/1alyssarichards

instagram.com/alyssaauthor

bookbub.com/authors/alyssa-richards

Made in the USA
Middletown, DE
23 May 2020